Praise for Caleb Fox and *Zadayi Red*

"Caleb Fox has written a magical novel that is deeply rooted in the oldest storytelling traditions of North America. His skillful reworking of mythic themes and archetypes rings true on many different levels. I highly recommend *Zadayi Red* to all who love mythic fiction and fine fantasy."

—Terry Windling, editor of
The Year's Best Fantasy and Horror

"Fox possesses a rare skill in masterfully telling a story. He is a true storyteller in the tradition of Native people."
—Lee Francis, associate professor of
Native American Studies at the
University of New Mexico

"[*Zadayi Red* is] an epic interpretation and retelling of ancient Native American myth and legend by a masterful author."

—Clyde Hall, Shoshone/Metis Tribe
author and historian

"*Zadayi Red* is a brilliantly woven tapestry. This fantastical epic adventure set in the traditional Cherokee homeland takes us from the depths of the Emerald Cavern to the highest mountaintop roost of eagles to beyond, to the realm of the Immortals. Caleb Fox depicts a pre-Cherokee world peopled with richly developed characters caught in an intriguing plot. From love to war, this novel has it all."

—Dr. Kimberly Roppolo,
national director of Worldcraft Circle of
Native Writers and Storytellers

ZADAYI
RED

Caleb Fox

A Tom Doherty Associates Book *New York*

This is a work of fiction. All of the characters, organizations, and events portrayed in this novel are either products of the author's imagination or are used fictitiously.

ZADAYI RED

Copyright © 2009 by Winifred Blevins and Meredith Blevins

All rights reserved.

A Tor Book
Published by Tom Doherty Associates, LLC
175 Fifth Avenue
New York, NY 10010

www.tor-forge.com

Tor® is a registered trademark of Tom Doherty Associates, LLC.

ISBN 978-0-7653-5959-9

First Edition: July 2009
First Mass Market Edition: July 2011

Printed in the United States of America

0 9 8 7 6 5 4 3 2 1

❖ *M, let's dance!* ❖

ACKNOWLEDGMENTS

Thank you, wife, for being my partner, my muse, and my gang foreman.

Thanks to my mentors, John G. Neihardt, Clyde Hall, Dale Wasserman, and Larsen Medicine House.

The first distinction we need to make here is between prehistoric and historic. . . . "Prehistoric" has to the average ear a misleading ring of the primitive, the savage, even the prehuman, whereas all it really means is preliterate. Life without pencils is still life, and stories need not be written down to be remembered.

—Robert Emmet Meagher and
Elizabeth Parker Neave

ONE

A Time of Turmoil

"Sunoya, isn't it time?"

She couldn't tell him. Couldn't tell him about the dream, couldn't tell him what was basically wrong.

Sunoya looked into the warm, acorn-colored eyes of her Uncle Kanu. The two of them sat across the center fire of the home they shared with the rest of their family. She knew he loved her. She loved him. But he didn't understand. She'd been hiding the dream from him, uncertain of its meaning— terrified of its meaning. And she'd been dishonest with him. No doubt about that, and no choice.

Now he thought it was time to honor her, to lift her up to replace himself as the village's Medicine Chief.

Impossible.

She puffed breath out. She had to say something. "Uncle . . . ?

"Sunoya?"

For weeks she'd been seeing something. It came to her at night, when she was sleeping. It came to her in the mornings, when she woke up early and lay in her elk blankets, looking at the small disc of sky through the smoke hole in the hut. It came to her in the afternoon, when she bent down to the river to fill her gourd with water for the family. She couldn't stop seeing it. Dream, vision, it didn't matter what she called it. She'd seen the Cape of Eagle Feathers bloodied, corrupted, fouled, stinking. It haunted her.

She had to do something. Except that she was flawed. *Might* be flawed.

For now all the tribe praised her. They pointed to the webbed fourth and fifth fingers of her left hand, an omen that came among women of her family every few generations and always marked a shaman. She had gone to the Emerald Cavern and been initiated in the tradition of the most powerful tribal shamans. Kanu said she had prodigious gifts, and told everyone that even at such a young age—she was barely beyond twenty winters—she should be Medicine Chief. The entire village was ready to honor her with position and power.

"Sunoya, is something wrong?"

Suddenly the hut felt oppressive. The faint light from the smoke hole at the top. The strong smells of burned wood and tobacco, the scents of the herbs hung over the door to keep out disease, odors of a dozen human beings living in close quarters. "Let's go for a walk."

At least she had gotten some words out.

She gave the old man a helping hand up and led him, ducking, through the door flap.

She looked around at this village of the Galayi people as they strolled. Though their name meant People of the Caves, they now lived in dome-shaped, wattle and daub huts circled around a village green. On the east side of the circle stood an opening, and the two largest huts in the village faced each other across the space. On the north side mounded the hut of the White Chief, whose door was outlined in a geometric design painted in white, symbolizing peace. On the other side was the hut of the Red Chief, with a door outlined in a red design, symbolizing war. The Medicine Chief, Kanu, and his family lived in an ordinary hut in the circle of ordinary villagers. Medicine power, in the common view, didn't rank with politics or war.

Smoke wafted out of the holes in the tops of all of the huts. Inside some women were cooking evening meals, and the fires warmed the huts against the night. Outside other women were grinding corn from the harvest. Still others were making moccasins for their men for the coming fall hunt, which would supply meat for the winter. Men were flaking points for the spears, or lashing points to shafts with buffalo sinew. A few skilled men were making darts for their *atlatls,* long rods that acted as levers to hurl spears with great speed.

Several families lived in each hut, grandparents, two or three daughters with their husbands, and a pack of children. She watched some boys throwing balls for their dogs in the middle of the green.

These were her people, and this was their life, ordinary human lives painted in red and blue, the tribal colors representing success and failure. The men wore palm-sized discs of rawhide inside their shirts indicating the state of their endeavors, red paint for victory on one side, blue on the other side for loss. These emblems were called *zadayis.* When a war party defeated the enemy, it came back wearing the red sides outward. If it lost, the men wore the blue sides showing. The same held for hunting parties. All the tribe's life was written in red and blue.

Any Medicine Chief's duty was to help these people lead red lives. Sunoya especially was bound by that calling. She knew that she could justify her existence only by taking care of the people. Otherwise, by the augury of her birth, she should have been killed at first breath.

Her people were good at making physical lives—corn crops along the river, berries, acorns, chestnuts, and seeds, meat from the deer, elk, and sometimes buffalo. Clothes cut from tanned deer skins, blankets of elk robes with the hair left on, and every sort of implement that could be made from wood, stone, and the bones, hoofs, horns, and even stomachs of animals. In practical matters the tribe was strong. Their weakness was that they did not realize, not fully, that these blessings were gifts of the Immortals, earned by walking the red path of goodness and not the blue path of ignorance.

Did she have the courage to act? Did she have the right to act? She was lost, and no one knew it.

She had to tell her uncle. She turned to face him. "First I want to go to the Emerald Cavern again."

There, it was said.

Kanu waited. It was the way of the Galayi people to be patient, let others speak their minds fully, and only then reply or ask a question. They had met other peoples who talked in a criss-cross way, comments and challenges flying like dogs barked, and they thought this behavior very rude.

Sunoya couldn't tell Kanu her vision of the Cape. If it was real, it was given as a responsibility to her, not to him.

"I know you think I'm stalling. I know you want me to be elected and given your duties."

She also knew why. Since his wife died, he felt older than his sixty winters. He was afraid he couldn't keep up with what the people asked of him. A few wanted spiritual counsel, or healing of illnesses of the spirit. Parents wanted a name for a newborn child. Barren women wanted charms that would give them babies. Would-be lovers wanted songs to mesmerize the girls they pined for. Elderly people, as they approached the time of crossing to the Darkening Lands, wanted interpretations of their dreams. And much more.

"You are right," she admitted. "I came here to do what you're asking." She fingered the webbed fourth and fifth fingers of her left hand. Her mind drifted back over the seven winters she'd been here, ever since her mother died. She'd been sent to this village precisely to learn from Kanu. She thought with pleasure of her own growing mastery, and his delight in her flair for learning. He had no doubt she was a true shaman.

She looked into her uncle's eyes and felt awful for not being able to tell him everything he wanted to hear. So simple to say, 'I accept this responsibility now. It is my path in life.' But if she was a true shaman, and her birth had not corrupted her spiritual eyes, then what she had seen was true. That meant she was obligated first to do something about her dream.

She twisted her mouth. All she could do was repeat lamely, "Right now I have to go to the Emerald Cavern again."

Kanu wondered what the devil was bothering his niece. Did she doubt herself? With her preparation and talent? Madness. Or was it something else?

Galayi manners didn't let him pry into her mind. When she wanted to tell him, she would. *If* she wanted to tell him.

She said, "Maybe you will get your sons to take me."

"Of course," Kanu said. He pivoted away and looked at the setting sun. That was that. His family's effort would be considerable. She'd have to be escorted, even though all the territory was Galayi. His two sons-in-law (Galayi men always married into the woman's family, not the other way) would have to pack food, moccasins, blankets, and winter coats on the dogs, take their wives, and walk with Sunoya for five days across several mountain ridges to the Soco River, up the river to the Cheowa village, and up Emerald Creek to the Cavern. Then they would visit relatives in the village and wait while Sunoya did something he didn't understand.

He turned to her and caught a flicker of fear on her face. She controlled it instantly.

"Do you want to leave tomorrow morning?" Kanu asked. *You who frighten yourself. You who hold yourself to standards no one else meets.*

"Yes."

"I'll speak to my daughters' husbands now." He walked away, his step uncertain.

As Sunoya followed him, she shivered again. *If I am flawed, how can I help anyone?*

By birth she had been bounteously blessed or hideously cursed, she didn't know which. It was a secret she had to keep. If the people knew how she was born, they would kill her.

2
_____

When Sunoya was thirteen, her mother Lyna knew she was dying. "Come sit close to me," she told her daughter, her only child. Sunoya snuggled up against her mother and leaned down close to her lips. Since her mother believed the old story about skunk smell keeping sickness away, the last person in the village to credit it, the creature's stink glands hung above the door. Sunoya wondered whether, except for that, she would be able to smell her mother's death. She could see it in the jaundiced face.

"This story, it's your story," Lyna said, "you deserve to know. But if you tell anyone, the villagers will kill you."

Sunoya flinched. Her mother clutched her hand, as though to keep Sunoya from running away. She wanted to run, from her mother's death, and from her dangerous knowledge. Lyna had been a difficult mother. She insisted on living alone, just the two of them, in a hut outside the village circle. Sunoya never had many friends, never got comfortable being around most people. She and her mother were misfits, loners.

Lyna said, "Before your birth I had terrible fears." She'd often told this part. She had a husband for ten winters. She yearned for a daughter or son, and she and her husband did what makes babies, laid for hours in each others' arms exchanging breaths. Yet no children came. When she got a baby in her belly, she spent every day fantasizing about holding it, rocking it, tending to it. Then her husband, Sunoya's father, was trampled by a buffalo and killed.

But now Lyna went into a new part of the story.

"I started having foul dreams where I gave birth to something unnatural, something horrible. I could never quite see what it was.

"When my time came and at last I felt the big pain and the big letting go, I heard the midwife gasp. Fear grabbed me. I looked and saw her staring at your right hand.

"I shrieked—I guessed it."

Sunoya could barely hear the whisper as Lyna spoke.

"The fourth and fifth fingers were webbed. Both hands."

Sunoya felt dizzy, like she'd fallen and hit her head on a rock. The webbing of the left-hand fingers was the best of omens, of the right-hand the worst.

"For a long time afterwards I wondered what I did, how I offended the Immortals like that.

" 'A girl,' the midwife told me. Luckily it was my aunt Oyu." Lyna's voice was graveled thick with emotion. " 'Both hands are webbed,' said Oyu. It is true.

"I couldn't get air. When I did get it, I couldn't let it out again. Finally I made wheezing words. 'So long, so long'—I gasped for breath—'Want child.'

"Oyu raised her belt knife. Then I saw she was only going to cut the cord.

" 'Girl . . .' I coughed and threw words like rocks. 'Cannot lose my baby. Cannot stand it.'

"I watched Oyu tie the cord off. Her face was set hard.

" 'Both hands webbed,' I said. I was afraid she wouldn't

understand me. 'Maybe the double sign, it's new, it's a good sign?'

"Oyu set you down with her back to me and examined the hands.

"I hissed out, 'Let me see my daughter's face!'

"Oyu's lips trembled and then began to move in a silent prayer. I thought, It must be the prayer that cleanses her from the taking of a life.

"'Be like the warrior's *zadayĭ*?' I wailed. 'Fail or succeed, could be either?'

"I kept babbling, like my words could grab Oyu's hands and keep her from wringing your neck. 'Maybe this is a gift, a great gift, twice a gift. Both hands webbed, never happen before.'

"Oyu looked at your fingers with a sour expression.

"'Blessing *and* curse. Can't we *make* it what we want?' Hard time saying so many words in a row.

"Oyu made a grunting sound, sliced the web of your right fingers, and stitched the skin with sinew. She was good with a needle. Then she laid you on my breast and hurried out.

"A mother, me! Then I had a panic. Was my aunt hurrying to give out the good news or fleeing from a shameful act? Or both?

"I decided that, whatever the medicine man named you, I would call you Sunoya. Do you know why? You were born under a bright, full Grandfather Moon, a huge *sunoya*. I kissed your forehead, wrapped you in a hide blanket, and tucked your right hand out of sight."

Lyna smiled and squeezed Sunoya's left hand.

"The family was so happy. About you, and even more about your left hand. In return for the loss of my husband, another medicine bearer born, a gift.

"We fooled them, Oyu and me. I have never known if it was right thing to do. I will never know. At the end of your life you will know. Are you a gift of red? Or blue?"

Lyna's face rolled away, toward the flickering fire.

Sunoya could hardly believe that her mother was suggesting that . . . *Maybe they should have killed me.* She thought of her name. It meant "moon," or what her people called "sun living in the night." Was she a sun? Or was her life enveloped in darkness?

Lyna turned her face back to her daughter's. "Oyu is dead now. Soon I am dead. You bite your tongue. If you tell, they kill you."

In two days her mother was gone to the Darkening Lands, and after another week the family sent Sunoya to the Tusca village to live with Uncle Kanu. On the way she had her first moon time. That meant that when she got to her new village, she was immediately given a becoming-a-woman ceremony. At that ceremony she revealed the name given her by the medicine man, and from then on she was called by that.

Her medicine name was Ay-Li, meaning middle, or half.

She never told anyone, but she thought it had a bitter perfection. Her mother called her Sunoya—moon—so her proper adult name was Half. Half Moon.

But was the moon waxing toward bright fullness, or waning toward darkness? Was her life painted red or blue?

Sometimes at night, when she thought about that, her fear gave her a wrenching pain from neck to crotch.

She would stick to the name Sunoya. She would *make* her life red. The first step was to go back to the Emerald Cavern to ask for a blessing for the people.

The panther Klandagi led Sunoya through the dark stone passages toward the room where Tsola, the Seer and Wounded Healer of the Galayi people, made her home. Blind, Sunoya kept her hand on the rising and falling shoulder blades of the black cat. Even when they walked in the cool water of the small stream that followed the tunnel, or got down on their hands and knees to crawl, Sunoya had complete confidence in Klandagi—he saw perfectly in the dark.

She remembered the legend about how at the beginning of this life on Earth, all the animals had been challenged to stay awake for seven nights. Only Panther and Owl managed not to fall asleep, and their reward was good night vision. Though Klandagi was also Tsola's son, few people had ever seen him in human form. His role was to guard the Cavern and its mistress, and no man could match a panther at that.

Sunoya saw the low fire that was Tsola's hearth, and made out the dark shape of her mentor next to it.

"Welcome, Sunoya Ay-Li," came the voice, Half Sun Living in the Night. Tsola was always formal.

"It is good of you to see me, Grandmother." Among the Galayi any respected older person was called "grandmother" or "grandfather." Tsola was said to be over a hundred winters old. In the firelight she looked about fifty, slender, still beautiful. She wore a dress woven of the inner bark of the mulberry tree and dyed in colors Sunoya couldn't make out in the dark. Mulberry weave was the rarest cloth the Galayi had. Tsola also wore a necklace of discs of gleaming mother-of-pearl, cut from sea shells and very valuable. Sunoya admired this woman who lived deep in a cave and received very few visitors, aside from her family, yet dressed like the wife of the richest man. After all, she was the Medicine Chief. For her own part Sunoya dressed plainly.

Tsola could barely leave the Emerald Cavern. Decades of living in its miles of corridors had sharpened her sight in the darkness and made her blind in the sunlight. Usually her family, who lived in a hut beside the pond just outside the entrance of the Cavern, came to visit her. If she went to see them, it was at darkest midnight.

Tsola poured tea for the two of them and offered Sunoya cakes made of grass seeds and honey. She sipped the tea and declined the food. Klandagi crouched off to one side, curling his tail up and down on the cave floor. Except when he transformed himself into a human being, he ate only meat, and not flesh cooked over any fire.

When courtesy allowed, Sunoya said, "I have come to speak of troubles."

"Yes." Tsola knew that. Why else would Sunoya be back so soon? Often she saw her initiates only once in their lives.

"Grandmother, I have seen. . . ."

She waited. Torment shuddered through her body. She leaned on Tsola's confidence in her.

"I have seen the Cape of Eagle Feathers desecrated. Spotted with blood. Smeared with dirt. Ruffled. Ruined."

All three of them froze. Even Klandagi's tail was rigid.

"You saw this after you drank the tea of the *u-tsa-le-ta?*" It was a hallucinogen known only to shamans.

"Yes, then. Also in my dreams. Also when I am wide awake and alone, looking at the sky or into the river water. I see it over and over. It will not let me alone. I see it every day."

Tsola considered. In her long career as Seer and Wounded Healer, in entire her life, she never expected to hear such terrible news. The Cape was made of eagle feathers because eagles carried messages from the Galayi to the Immortals, and more important, from the Immortals to the Galayi. Only she could listen to the Cape, or put it on, or even look upon it. Once a year she did this, deep in the Cavern, while the tribe was beginning the Planting Moon Ceremony. She sent whatever guidance she received to the people. This had been the chief responsibility of all the Galayi Seers and Wounded Healers for a thousand winters.

"Granddaughter," said Tsola, "I will have to ask you to leave the Cavern for a while. Go with Klandagi to visit my family for a few days. I must look at the Cape. I must put it on and listen to it."

Sunoya stood up and put her hand on the panther's shoulders. Tsola was doing what had to be done, but Sunoya could hardly bear the thought of several days on tenterhooks.

❖

A small stream flowed out of the Cavern entrance and formed a pond a short distance below. Tsola's two daughters lived in a hut just above the pond. These waters were known as the Healing Pool, and they were a place of curing for all Galayi. Aches, fevers, stomach and bowel troubles, all could be improved if a pilgrim drank from the waters, or immersed himself in them. Tsola's daughters helped the pilgrims and taught them songs for healing.

Sunoya drank from the stream just above the hut. She sat in the waters for as long as she could bear the cold. She chatted with the family. Eventually Klandagi came and led her back to Tsola's home in the Cavern.

Tsola said, "We have to talk." Her face was grave, stricken.

So what I saw is true, thought Sunoya. Her chest quivered like a plucked string.

Tsola had mounted her teapot, which was a buffalo stomach, on a tripod over her fire. Sunoya saw her crumble in the *u-tsa-le-ta,* a lichen. That meant Sunoya would make the longest journey any human being could make, except for going to the Darkening Land.

She sat cross-legged, as close to the fire as she could, taking comfort in its warmth.

Tsola said, "I have looked at the Cape. It is fine, at the moment. But I, too, saw the coming desecration." Her voice was rough, like limbs grating against each other. The firelight showed the trickle of a single tear down her cheek. "This means great suffering for our people."

Tsola pursed her lips and hesitated. "Someone has to go see the Immortals and ask what can be done. They have called to you. You are their choice for this journey."

"I know," Sunoya said. Every step of the way here, this was the moment she had feared.

"I am surprised. I would have thought . . ."

Sunoya thought so, too. *Why me? I am too young, too inexperienced. I am corrupted.*

She tried to console herself. *If the Immortals have chosen me, I can do it.*

And if she didn't, the Galayi would be shut off from all guidance from the Immortals, the wisdom their entire culture was founded on.

Tsola grasped both her hands and looked at her directly. "Are you sure you're willing to do this?"

Sunoya told the truth. "Since I decided to come here and tell you my story, I have dreaded it." She didn't know how to go on. "But to do it, maybe this is my destiny." *Maybe it will redeem my life.* "Sometimes I am afraid. Sometimes my heart pounds with desire for it."

"Now?"

"Now."

"Then prepare yourself."

Sunoya closed her eyes and shut out Tsola, Klandagi, everything but the world she was going to.

This time the journey to the Land beyond the Sky Arch would be easier than the previous time. Every shaman had to make the first trip by swimming with Tsola a long way underground to the Emerald Dome, performing certain rituals, and then swimming again, alone. The experience was terrifying, but you only had to go through the Cavern once.

After that first journey, most shamans used the *u-tsa-le-ta* to make the trip. At the least the experience reminded them of which world was real and which a shadow. Sometimes they also got wisdom they could use for the people.

On this trip Sunoya would have Tsola's help again. She was grateful that her teacher would go with her, not physically but in her mind. When the Seer and Wounded Healer sent you across the boundary to the Immortal world, she traveled inside you.

The Wounded Healer handed Sunoya a buffalo horn cup of the hot tea. In one gulp Sunoya drank it all. Tsola gave her a kiss and sat beside her. To Tsola, Sunoya was a girl called on to bear far too much responsibility. She was afraid for her protégé, and aghast at the possible consequences for her people.

She wrapped one arm around Sunoya—the old could help the young only so much—and waited until her body went limp. Then she laid Sunoya down and covered her with an elk blanket. Last, Tsola focused her mind on that other world, where she would fly inside Sunoya.

4

Sunoya woke up lying on a bed of soft grasses. She smiled at them because they were pink. Turquoise sedges lined the creek. Rhododendrons clumped out in spurts of wild hues, scarlet, cobalt, and canary yellow. The rocks of the hills glittered like gem stones. Above them the sky glowed a gentle salmon and gold that never changed, and the soft air was warm, always warm.

She stepped over to a stream, bent down, and took a drink of cool, orange water. In the Land beyond the Sky Arch no creatures ate—Immortals could not die, and they did not eat other beings—but everyone drank.

She wondered why she had dreaded this trip. She loved this world. She wished her people had never left here. A long time ago, before they came to Earth and the big expanse of land called Turtle Island, the Galayi and all other animals and plants lived in this country beyond the Sky Arch. They were the children of the Immortals, progeny of the models all creatures sprang from, shadows of the great Bear who was primogenitor of all other bears, offspring of the Raven who was the archetype of all ravens, and so on. At that time archetypes and descendants alike were immortal.

But they were crowded, bumping elbows and knees in a country that was too small. Looking down from on high, they saw a planet that seemed to be nothing but water and wondered whether they could find a place there to make lives. Several animals tried to find land, but only little Water Beetle succeeded. He dived to the bottom of that strange world and brought up dirt, and more dirt, and finally all the dirt that made Turtle Island. So the people migrated onto that muddy ground. They didn't know the troubles they were in for. In Sunoya's opinion you could sum up all of Earth's problems in a single word: *mortality*.

Sunoya spoke to Tsola in her mind. *Are you with me?*

Yes, said Tsola, but she volunteered nothing more.

If I call them, they'll come, right?

Sunoya, you know that. Be your full self.

So she walked up the creek lazily. She could simply think of any particular being, or say his name, and he would appear.

Or wouldn't. Immortals were whimsical and not particularly interested in the doings on Earth. Occasionally, they went to Turtle Island, looking after their offspring planet. Sunoya thought of those she'd met before and wanted to see again, and those she hadn't gotten to meet. Very carefully, she did not think of the very last thing that happened here beyond the Sky Arch—the way Thunderbird had said good-bye to her.

Sunoya, you have nothing to be afraid of.

She knew that meant, 'As far as I know, you'll be all right.'

She walked along and said from time to time, "Little Deer, come. Bear, come. Bluebird, come." She mentioned a lot of creatures, and left out only Thunderbird, deliberately. He did what he wanted to do anyway. "Spider," she said, "come to me. I have made a long journey to get here. I want to ask for your wisdom."

As she walked, she looked around at this eternal world. Here the sun appeared to be rising perpetually, no stem of grass ever turned brown, and no leaf ever changed color or fell. Here time did not exist. Mortality itself did not exist, except for visitors from Earth like herself.

It was Little Deer who appeared first. She hadn't met him the first time, and he was a delight to see. He was a glistening, snowy white, and only the size of an ordinary dog. He ran toward her in bounds, and his grace was a marvel. They introduced themselves.

"Thunderbird is waiting for you over by that huge chestnut tree," he said.

Thunderbird . . . Oh, well.

Just be yourself, said Tsola.

But which one of me?

She walked alongside Little Deer. She was tempted to reach down and pet him, but knew better. Little Deer was the king of the Deer People, and the hero of a great story. When the deer got angry at human beings for shooting so many of them, taking more than they needed for food, Little Deer persuaded his people to put aches into the joints of any person who killed a deer. Not that the deer really died anyway. As everyone knew, the lives of the creatures that human beings hunted on Turtle Island were set when they were born, and couldn't be altered. If a hunter slew a deer, the deer waited until the hunter was gone, gathered himself from his blood scattered on the ground, and went on about his ruminant life.

When the human beings got tired of their joints hurting, Little Deer struck a bargain with them. He taught them a song to sing over the body of any deer they killed. If the hunter sang the song, honoring the deer and apologizing for taking his life, he would go home healthy. If not, within a few weeks he would be crippled.

The chestnut tree was truly enormous. Tales had it that Turtle Island had a similar tree, known as the Tree of Life. It had been difficult for Sunoya to learn that on Earth *life* was a word of double meaning, because it implied death, which didn't apply here.

Thunderbird stood at the foot of the tree next to a giant wooden vat. The vat was very beautiful, knee deep and wide as a man's reach, carved with a skill beyond the capacity of any human being, and oiled and polished to a gleam. It was filled with water that sparkled with small bubbles.

"Taste it, my dear." Thunderbird was in one of his strange forms. He looked like a shadow, not a real bird. Of course, he could take any shape he wanted. As a shadow, he was still the size of a buffalo, and somewhere in his feathers he still carried thunderbolts.

Sunoya sipped the water. It was fizzy. It tickled her nose and made her smile. She liked it.

Thunderbird laughed, a sound like boulders bouncing down mountains.

Others emerged out of the trees, and every one was an

Immortal Sunoya had not met on her first trip here. There was Wolf, a friend to human beings, for Wolf had been the hunter and watchdog for First Man. Owl fluttered down, known for his understanding of death. Rabbit darted across the rosy grass to join them, the master of pranks. Rattlesnake crawled to a place in the circle, and Sunoya wondered why he was called. Last, Buzzard floated down and joined the others, with an air of reluctance.

See how they honor you by coming, Tsola said in Sunoya's mind.

Every one of the animals was the most magnificent specimen of its kind Sunoya had ever seen, and all except for Little Deer was enormous, as a tree is to a bush. Each sipped ceremonially from Thunderbird's vat and thanked the king of eagles for his hospitality.

The one that surprised Sunoya was Buzzard. Instead of having mottled red skin, his face was fully feathered. From his crown sprang a handsome topknot of bright feathers of every color, and these plumes curled forward until they nearly touched his beak, making a rainbow.

"Why have you come to see us, Granddaughter?"

Thunderbird was in his come-on-and-spit-it-out mode, and there was nothing Sunoya could do about that. "Grandfather, I have seen the Cape of Eagle Feathers bloodied and fouled." She could be as direct as he.

"Yes." Thunderbird was not in the least surprised. "Why do you think that will happen?"

"I don't know, Grandfather." It wouldn't do to try and seem smart in front of Thunderbird. *Tsola, are you there?*

You're doing fine.

"Do you remember how death came into the world?" said Thunderbird. "Your world?"

This was going to be an inquisition. "Yes, Grandfather. A very long time ago, near the beginning, a man and a woman had a large family, and they never had any trouble providing food for all their children. One day the children got curious about how they got the food so easily, so they followed their parents. The father went up to the mountain to where a large stone covered the entrance to a cave. He rolled the stone aside and called to a deer who stood behind some other animals. The deer came forward and gave itself to him.

"When his sons saw how easy it was to get meat, they waited until their father was out of sight, went to the stone, pushed with all their might, and rolled it away. But instead of coming to the boys, the animals burst out through the entrance, scattered in all directions, and disappeared into the forest. Every kind of animal escaped—buffalo, elk, deer, panthers, raccoons, squirrels, wolves, foxes, and lots of others. The boys were alarmed at what they'd done.

"At the same time other children followed their mother to a hut they had never seen before. There she stood over a basket and shook herself like a wild woman. Suddenly, ears of corn began falling from under her skirt into the basket. Soon it was full, and she came out and prepared their breakfast as usual."

The shadowy Thunderbird threw Sunoya an imperious look. *Go on!*

"After breakfast," she said, "the father said he knew the boys had let all the animals escape. Now, he said, he had to die, and from then on they would have to hunt to provide for themselves. He told them how to make weapons.

"Then the mother said that, since they knew her secret of planting and harvesting, she couldn't do anything more for them, but would die. They must drag her body over the ground, and she told them exactly where. In those places corn would grow. She told them how to grind it and make bread from it, and reminded them always to save some seeds to plant next year."

Thunderbird nodded curtly and finished the story himself. "Yes. Thus you brought death into your world. And since it was there, nothing to be done about that, we Immortals gave the Galayi people the Cape of Eagle Feathers. In such a world you needed more wisdom. Now Granddaughter, you remember that with the Cape we gave you one central command about how to live, a number one *thou-shalt-not?*"

Sunoya needed no further prompting. "It was that we should never kill each other." She didn't mention the single exception, ending the lives of girl children born with the fourth and fifth fingers of the right hand webbed. Such creatures were not considered Galayis but evil spirits.

"Exactly. I will spare you from wondering. Your people have obeyed that commandment so far."

"So far." She didn't want to go on. "So it seems we will soon . . ."

"And that is why the Cape will be ruined, and its power destroyed." Thunderbird's tone was like a father saying, *You deserve this.*

"Who will do this, Grandfather?"

Within her mind Sunoya heard Tsola start to speak, but the Wounded Healer stopped.

Thunderbird looked around the circle. "Among us, there is one with a particular gift of prophecy. Will anyone tell our granddaughter who will commit this violation?"

Silence.

"Is there no help you can give this young woman? She possesses the eye of the spirit."

Sunoya quivered to hear such words from the master of birds.

Silence.

Shrugging, Thunderbird turned back to Sunoya. "Granddaughter, you have done very well. You saw with the eye of the spirit. You paid attention. You came here and asked for

Zadayi Red ❖ 33

help. Partly because of you, I am inclined to make your people a gift."

Sunoya could hardly believe what she was hearing.

"You would do well to have a spirit guide."

Sunoya gasped, and she heard Tsola do the same. No Galayi had been blessed with an Immortal helper in generations. They remembered only tatters of rumors about them and . . . The old tales said this gift was a mixed blessing.

"Grandfather, I . . ."

His shadowy eyebrows bristled as she hovered in indecision.

"You hesitate because your old stories say that there is a price to be paid for such a gift."

"Yes, Grandfather."

"That is correct. I want you to understand precisely what the price is. Because of your devotion to your spirit guide, you will be permitted no personal life. No husband, no children. You will not accept the position of Medicine Chief or any other position of honor. Do you understand?"

Sunoya felt herself quail.

"Child, are you a virgin?"

She was ashamed. No man had courted her. She was an old maid. No other woman in her village over eighteen years old was unmarried.

"Speak up. I know the answer anyway."

"Yes, Grandfather, I am."

"You will remain one. This is a strict condition of the gift. If you have carnal knowledge of any man, even against your will, you will die at the end of the next day. Upon your death the guide will be released from the world of mortality and return to our circle here."

In Sunoya's mind Tsola said, *Be careful. Look into yourself. If you can't accept the conditions, don't accept the gift.*

"Granddaughter, do you understand?"

Be sure, said Tsola.

She shivered. "Yes, Grandfather. I am honored, and I accept."

"Then you will devote your life to this guide and to following the wisdom he gives you. You will live apart from your family, alone with your spirit companion. You will learn from him, give your people the wisdom you get from him, and use his counsel wisely."

"Yes."

"Very well. There are certain other guidelines. Your guide will have some ability to see the future, but he is not permitted to tell you what will happen. He can tell you what to do, but not what will happen according to whatever choice you make."

Sunoya looked down.

"I see you don't understand. Suppose your guide knows that an enemy waits along the left-hand path and says, 'Take the right-hand path.' Do as he says, but don't ask him why, or what would happen if you went the other way. He is not allowed to disclose the future to you."

"I understand, Grandfather."

Thunderbird's eyes gleamed at everyone in the circle. "Then what remains to us? To choose this young woman's guide. Who wants to go with her? Who wants to live on Turtle Island for the rest of her life and help her people?"

No one answered.

Sunoya felt something crumple inside her. *It is all going to be taken from me.*

Thunderbird said firmly, "I want every one of my guests to tell me, and this young woman, why he should not go to Earth and spend time as her guide. After all, time means nothing here."

Rabbit spoke up immediately. "The world is tricky. Everybody says I'm a trickster, and I guess I am, but the world is much trickier than me." His split nose twitched, and his whiskers bristled. "Also, they say the way I run is crazy, wild with changes of directions. But life is the same. And human beings . . . ? Well, no one would let a trickster be your trusted guide."

Wolf growled at Rabbit, and they both chuckled. Then Wolf turned seriously to Sunoya. "The world is not what it appears to be, Granddaughter. For instance, in this land Rabbit and I are friends. There is no hunting here.

"I have a reputation for being fierce, and your people have an expression, 'the lone wolf.' But I am the opposite of a loner. As much as any animal that exists, I am bound tightly to my family. Our pack is the hand, the individuals merely fingers. And fierce? Yes, we are fierce together, and for each other. We hunt as one, and survive as one.

"Guide you? I cannot live in a human family. They seem so alien."

Little Deer said simply, "The anger of the Deer People has not disappeared entirely, so your guide won't be me. I can only say that I'm not surprised that your people are about to get themselves into trouble by killing."

Owl hooted his words. "You human beings don't understand me. Though I do have wisdom, it is about the realm of death. In your world I am the most silent and deadly of killers. Of all the animals, only I hunt, kill, and eat my own kind. You don't want me for a guide to put a stop to killing."

Rattlesnake said, "Everyone knows that my people are the great friends of mankind. Long ago, when Grandmother Sun was angry and determined to burn up all the human beings, various animals went against Sun to stop her. After all others had failed, I succeeded. I bit and killed Sun's daughter, and Sun was so grieved that she cried and cried, and on many days did not shine.

"We rattlesnakes are your great benefactors in other ways.

With our fangs your healers make cuts to apply medicines. Your warriors wear our rattles on their heads. You rub the oil from our bodies on your joints to take the soreness away. When great sicknesses sweep the land, you eat our flesh to ward them off.

"You pray to us, and well you should. I think we have done enough for human beings."

Only Buzzard was left. His words were, "I have nothing to say."

"Very well," Thunderbird said. "I gather that Buzzard has guessed the truth. Buzzard, I appoint you to be the partner to our granddaughter Sunoya."

They glared at each other.

"Now say the words," Thunderbird instructed. "As nicely as you can." Thunderbird *was* in a kindly mood.

Buzzard fixed Sunoya with his red-gold eye. She trembled a little at the oddity of having him turn his head sideways to her. Then she realized that was the only way he could see her.

"Sunoya," he said, "you are a young woman of great courage. I would be pleased to go to Earth with you and help your people."

Sunoya was stunned.

Say 'Thank you,' said Tsola.

"Thank you, Buzzard."

5

Sunoya strolled through the pink grass, knee high in places. She kept glancing sideways at Buzzard on her shoulder, thrilled and shy at once. She could hardly believe what she'd done. Her blood fizzed.

Tsola's drum sounded faintly in her mind, the first warning.

"Are we going to be friends?" she said.

To her relief, Buzzard nodded. When she got to the orange creek, she sat on a knee-high, ruby-colored boulder. "Would you like me to stroke your feathers?" Buzzard hopped onto her knee, and she did.

Tsola's drum flicked an occasional accent into the rhythm, beginning to call her away from this mystic world, back to her home, Turtle Island. Listening, she calculated that she had a little time left here.

"You didn't want to come with me." She figured that if she was going to brave, she might as well be foolhardy.

Thunderbird was having some fun at my expense.

She flinched—Buzzard was speaking inside her head.

I will tell you the story. A long time ago, Thunderbird, Osprey, Hawk, some others, and I were visiting Turtle Island. When we're there, we eat, like all animals. The others found the carcass of a buffalo calf and fed on it. I sat on a snag nearby and watched. They invited me to join them. I told them carrion was disgusting.

Thunderbird was amused, in his superior way. "Fastidious, are we?" *he said.*

He gave one of those gigantic laughs of his and flew straight into the air, facing me. You know he carries thunderbolts in his wings. Or maybe you don't. Anyway, he picked out the smallest one he had and shot it just past my head into a branch.

It burned this beautiful head plume right off. It scorched my face. That's why, when you see a buzzard on Earth, the face has no feathers. He seemed to shudder. *Instead there's that ugly, mottled red skin. And no rainbow.*

Now Tsola's drum, so far away, began to insist.

"I didn't hit you," *Thunderbird always says. But he's never quite forgiven me for my so-called fastidiousness.*

Since Buzzard didn't go on, Sunoya slipped off her moccasins and dipped her bare feet in the cool water. Now Tsola's drum was throbbing. They didn't have long.

You and I will do fine, he said. *But this is Thunderbird's little punishment. While I'm on Turtle Island, all the years of your life, I'll wear that ugly red face and I'll have to eat carrion.*

She couldn't help smiling. Then she said, "Let me see your full beauty now."

He took a couple of flaps into the air, faced her, and hovered. His rainbow plume was very pretty, but the underside of his dark wings was magnificent, black on the body and the leading edge of his wings, silver on the flying feathers and tail. These colors were a high honor among the Immortals.

"You're magnificent," she said.

He turned his head the other way, spearing her with his other bright eye.

She held out her arm, and he settled back onto it.

"Here's a gift for you," she said. "A name—Su-Li." It was the word for *buzzard* in her language. "I think it is a beautiful name." Among her people, the Galayi, Buzzard was honored as the animal that shaped their world into mountains and valleys.

A flutter in the drumbeat reminded her that her time was running out.

She looked around at this eternal land. Su-Li was more beautiful here than he would be on Turtle Island. All the inhabitants here were immortal. When she was lucky enough to make return visits, she herself would always be young here.

At that moment the drum shifted its rhythm. From a slow, easy heartbeat it accelerated to a hint of anxiety, then of urgency. It rapped harder and faster, thrumming like a pounding rain, hints of thunder flickering along its edges. Then it surged into a tremendous crescendo and ended with a ferocious bang.

Sunoya jerked. Her body stiffened. The final whack of the

drum froze her heartbeat in the Land beyond the Sky Arch, and that world eye-winked away.

❖

She rubbed her eyes and let ordinary reality come back into being, the realm they called Turtle Island, her home. She felt Su-Li shift his weight from claw to claw on her shoulder. Glowing embers came into focus, and she raised her eyes into the face of the drummer, her mentor and friend, Tsola.

"Look around," Sunoya said to Su-Li. "This is your new home."

They sat in deep shadows just inside the Emerald Cavern. Immediately the buzzard hopped to where he could see outside, uneasy with the confinement of the cave.

To calm him, Tsola said, "Isn't this world beautiful?" Before him glistened Emerald Pool, and at the far end its creek trickled away. The trees gushed with leaves of every autumn color. The mountain ridges cut jagged edges against a sky of puffy white clouds.

Su-Li cocked his head this way and that, one eye outward to the bright world, one inward to the dark cave. But he said nothing.

Uneasy, Sunoya said to him, "What do you think of all this?"

No answer.

Sunoya felt a sharp pang of sadness, like a string in her heart had been plucked, resonating all through her body.

She shook her head and gave her attention back to Su-Li. "Do you like our world?"

She felt swept away by grief, tumbled off her feet by feelings rampaging like a river in spring flood.

When the river let her go, she understood. She traded a glance of understanding with Tsola and looked back into Su-Li's red-gold eye. "So you also talk to me through emotions."

She heard his answer inside her head. *Feelings are so much stronger than words.*

Sunoya nodded to herself, grasping to understand more about her spirit guide. Then she took thought and asked what she wanted to know. "You're sad? Why?"

Everything here is in the death-grip of Time. What could be more terrible?

6

Time meant tribulations. Sunoya didn't mind the journey from the Cavern to her home village. She took advantage of the walk to get to know her new spirit guide, and got a very good idea from him.

She didn't hesitate when she got to the village. She walked directly through the village green, where everyone would see Su-Li. He seemed to make himself larger and take on a glow. She saw the gawks and heard the whisperings. She wished someone would shout, "Hooray! Unbelievable! We got a spirit guide." But few human beings were that comfortable around magic, or around Sunoya.

She went directly to Kanu's hut. The old man came out blinking, his eyes unprepared for the noonday sun. They changed when he took in Sunoya and—*incredible*—Su-Li sitting on her shoulder.

"My child!"

Sunoya grinned at him. The older generation wasn't given to big exclamations.

She broke the news to him right away—she would not be able to take over as Medicine Chief, so he would have to stay in the job. Maybe an apprentice could be brought over from another village.

Kanu barely heard her. "A spirit guide!" he said. "And a buzzard!"

He held out his arm to Su-Li, but the buzzard turned away. "I don't think he'll attach himself to anyone but me."

One of Kanu's dogs jumped up at Su-Li, and the bird fluttered up to the smoke hole of the hut. He said something crabby in Sunoya's head.

"Excuse me," said her uncle. "Do you want to eat?"

Kanu was a little late. Courtesy demanded that those be the first words to welcome a traveler.

Sunoya called Su-Li from the top of the hut. As she stooped through the doorway, she felt his claws clutching and releasing her shoulders. The bird would never be comfortable cut off from the sky.

As she munched cornbread, she and her uncle talked about necessities. She needed a hut to live in privately with Su-Li. Kanu said, now that they were back, he would ask his sons-in-law to make her a brush hut covered with hides today, and tomorrow start building a hut of mud and sticks.

When she finished eating and accepted tea, Kanu could wait no longer. "What did you do, what did you say to the Immortals that made them . . . ?"

She told him what she had hidden from him earlier, that she had seen, repeatedly, the Cape of Eagle Feathers bloodied and soiled. Kanu dropped his head into his hands. When he finally looked up, he said, "What are we to do?"

She didn't answer his question as he meant it. "Change the future." She was riding high on the confidence that the Immortals had shown in her. "Not even a seer's visions always come true. They can be prevented. You know that."

Kanu's right hand trembled. "Just the two of us? What . . . ?"

"The two of us and a spirit guide," Sunoya reminded him. Then she told him what Su-Li had suggested on the walk home, and how she and the buzzard had turned it into a plan.

Kanu chewed on it. "All right," he said. "The next meeting of the chiefs is in three days." They met on every new moon and every full moon. "We'll stick our necks out."

❖

The White Chief Yano, the Red Chief Inaj, and her uncle Kanu took their seats at the sacred fire in the council lodge. Sunoya thought for the hundredth time that she wished the White Chief of peace didn't look so pitiful next to the Red Chief of war. Yano was a thin wisp of an old man, doddering, barely a physical presence. Inaj was as fine a specimen of physical manhood as she'd ever seen, magnificently muscled.

She waited until she was invited to sit with them. Every eye was on Su-Li.

Since the village was at war with the Lena people who lived along the coast, the Red Chief, Inaj, was the head man. As a sign of their high purpose, Inaj lit the sacred pipe and smoked it ceremonially, adding tobacco to the aroma-thick room. It was a beautiful pipe, long-stemmed and with a bowl of polished black stone. Eagle feathers dangled from the stem.

Sunoya rubbed the flesh that webbed the fourth and fifth fingers of her left hand. She smiled to herself. The real manifestation of her power perched on her shoulder, appraising the three chiefs with his brilliant eye. She knew their feelings. Though they told themselves they should be honored by the presence of the spirit guide, they were in fact intimidated.

Su-Li said, *Men of power don't like to share it.*

Sunoya looked at her buzzard friend and thought of what a gift he was. She also knew the obligations he brought, and the challenges they faced right now. *We must change a people's direction. We must prevent unspeakable suffering.*

You must, said Su-Li.

Kanu handed her the pipe. She puffed on it and watched

the smoke rise toward the hole in the roof. She thought, *Carry this smoke, my breath, my prayers to the ears of the Immortals, and help me do what must be done.* As she sent her hopes to the sky, she felt Su-Li echoing them.

When she handed the pipe back to Inaj, he took a moment to consider his ceremonial address. To speak first was his right. He was astonished to see Kanu lift a hand to stop him.

"My niece and I apologize to the Red and White Chiefs," he said. "I know that you think I have brought her here today to be elected the new Medicine Chief of the Tusca village. But, because of surprising circumstances"—he nodded toward Su-Li—"I will remain as Medicine Chief for the time being." His ancient voice sounded like sliding stones. The job would be hard on him. She looked at her uncle with pride.

"Then why did you bring her?" Inaj's tone was peremptory.

"First, to present her to you as one of the two Medicine Chiefs of all the Galayi people. You can see she has ascended to that station." He indicated Su-Li with a hand. "Second, to present to you formally a great gift the Immortals have made to us," Kanu said. He spoke as though he didn't know that these chiefs, practical, earth-bound men, didn't have much patience for magic. "This is Su-Li, one of the Immortals, the Buzzard of the ancient legends, the one who shaped the land of the Galayi into high mountains and deep valleys. He has come to help Sunoya and all of us. As you know, this is a very great honor."

Neither of the chiefs spoke.

Su-Li said, *It seems your rules of etiquette don't cover accepting an introduction to a spirit creature.*

She looked into the bird's face for an ironic smile, but it was unreadable, as always.

"Additionally," Kanu said—council speech was always formal—"we have a proposal to present to you."

"Our Medicine Chief offers us a plan?" Inaj's eyes flashed from Sunoya to Su-Li, showing what he meant: "Our Medicine Chief, who is a mere advisor, not a real chief, plus a young woman who is not even married, and her bird—and you dare to instruct us?"

Sunoya leapt straight in. "Chiefs, I know I have no standing here. I come only to bear the physical body of an Immortal, and to give us all a chance to hear his wisdom."

"Wisdom he will impart to you alone," said the Red Chief.

Now Yano, the White Chief, spoke. "Let's hear them, Inaj."

Sunoya thought maybe Yano was frustrated. *He's been second in command for nearly ten winters, and maybe he suspects we could change that.* Which was exactly what she wanted to do.

She plunged in. "I have seen things." This was the crucial part. This was what they had to believe. "I saw—foresaw—great troubles for the people. It would grieve me even to speak the words that tell those troubles. That's why I went again to the Land beyond the Sky Arch."

She took a deep breath and let a long breath out. "Since Su-Li and I came back to Turtle Island, he and I have talked about the troubles." She paused. "You remember that Buzzard has the gift of prophecy."

She studied the faces of the two men who held the power. Fortunately, they weren't the only voters. "Kanu and I talked things over, and we have made a decision."

She heard Inaj sniff. He preferred women and Medicine Chiefs who stayed in their subordinate places.

"At the dance for Grandmother Sun"—which meant the ceremony for the Galayi people that took place on the shortest days of the year—"we will meet with the other Medicine Chiefs and ask them to come to all the White Chiefs and all the Red Chiefs with a suggestion."

'*Suggestion,*' said Su-Li. *Your Red Chief doesn't look eased by that word.*

"Our people have been at war with the Lena tribe and the Thano tribe for nearly ten winters." The enemies on the coast to the east and the ones on the prairies west of the mountains. "Blood smears the grass of our land, and theirs. Every year the creeks run darker with crimson."

She made herself ready. "Three of our four villages are now governed by war chiefs." The fourth village was a sanctuary, a peace village that never entered fighting. "Su-Li and I believe that bloodletting is leading us toward something terrible."

She could see that Inaj was now having difficulty observing Galayi custom, waiting until the other person was truly finished speaking. This was her one opportunity.

"We are going to suggest that we go to the Lena and Thano people—the Medicine Chiefs only—and make a treaty of peace with them."

Inaj could wait no longer. "You are too young to understand. Tribes are not weakened by war—they are strengthened. Men are forged in the fires of battle." He rushed on, caring nothing about his rudeness. "For several years now the band has grown stronger through tests of blood, the only way boys can become warriors. It is the hope of the White Chief and me that our strength will soon be so great that our enemies will be afraid and let us alone."

Everyone around the fire breathed, waited, breathed.

Sunoya now went beyond the words she and Su-Li had planned out. "I have a question. How long do you think we'll stay at war?"

Something feral flickered in Inaj's eyes.

It was an unfair question. Since the Red Chief governed during times of war, she was really asking, "How long do you plan to be governor? When do you plan to turn leadership back over to the White Chief?"

She told Su-Li, *Give him your I-can-see-right-through-you look*.

Inaj stood up, abruptly signaling that the meeting was over.

"You have the wisdom of experience," she said anyway, "and of a War Chief." She let that sink in. "Kanu and I have the knowledge of Medicine Chiefs, and the guidance of an Immortal. At Grandmother Sun's Dance we will approach the other Medicine Chiefs with our proposal."

Stare him down, Sunoya told Su-Li.

Inaj didn't flinch. His face was full of rage, not just at her but at Kanu for his part in the scheme. He was breathing like an enraged buffalo bull. Except for the decorum required by the council, she thought he would have erupted.

"My advice to such a young woman, such a beautiful woman," Inaj said, "is to leave the responsibilities of governing to those who are trained for them, and elected to them."

Then he changed to a gentler tone. "Tomorrow is the first day of the Hunting Moon, so my men and I leave on our hunt." Every autumn they took enough meat—deer, elk, buffalo—to get the band through the winter. "We'll leave behind enough warriors to defend the village. Then we will take all the villagers to Grandmother Sun's ceremony. This is the work of men."

Sunoya inclined her head to him. In her opinion Inaj used the hunt mainly as a training ground for war. He reveled in war. He was like a boy killing bugs with gleeful cries. He undid the spiritual work of the Medicine Chief.

Inaj turned his back on everyone and walked out.

In her mind Sunoya asked her spirit guide, *What's in his heart right now?*

Lust, said Su-Li.

She squelched her fear. If any young woman stood up to Inaj, he wanted to mount and tame her. Sunoya couldn't run that risk.

The White Chief took his leave politely. She hoped he would wish her well in her mission, but he didn't.

Outside, Sunoya said aloud, "Su-Li, am I beautiful?" Hearing that from Inaj had felt strange.

No, said her spirit guide. *To their way of thinking your face is diamond-shaped when it should be round, and your eyes are too dark.*

Sunoya walked along, picturing her face as it looked in a still pool.

But you're sexy—men are attracted to you.

"How do you know?"

The way they look at you when they think you don't notice. The way they breathe when they stand next to you.

Sunoya considered this. She liked it.

Don't be a fool, said Su-Li. *Better if you were an ugly hag.*

Her neck stiffened.

Let me assure you. They remember the old stories about spirit guides. I've listened to them. They recall what will happen if any man knows you carnally. Never forget. Inaj would gladly rape you.

She thought of her death, and then looked into Su-Li's eyes. She hid her thoughts from him. *Would you be glad to leave?*

7

During this Hunting Moon, with no Inaj to battle, Sunoya used her time to get to know her spirit guide better and learn remedies for ailments from Iwa, Inaj's wife. Since Sunoya was not to be Medicine Chief, she could do something else to help the people. She told Su-Li, "I have no family of my own. I want to feel useful."

You are a good person.

Her time with Iwa brought her a special and unexpected gift. Noney, Iwa's elder daughter and Sunoya's cousin, started coming over to talk. The two of them sat in the sun on a log on the south side of Kanu's house, doing small tasks like punching awl holes in deer hide or grinding seeds. What

Noney wanted was a confidante. She had a child in her belly and no husband. At last year's Planting Moon Ceremony, she had gotten together with a young man, Tensa, the son of the Red Chief of the Soco band.

Her stories about Tensa were what any young girl's would be.

"Does Tensa know you're carrying his baby?"

Noney shook her head no. Sunoya put her arms around the girl. Though she was only five years older than Noney, Sunoya felt like her mother. And pregnancy without a husband was common enough. You got pregnant, everyone knew, by embracing a man for hours and exchanging your breath with his. Young people were going to do that, and usually they got married. The custom was to marry someone of another band, and you ended up with family in every village.

The difficulty was that Inaj resented the Socos. The big council had chosen their Chief Ninyu over Inaj as the head of all Red Chiefs.

"Father will never let me marry Tensa," Noney wailed. She shook with sobs now.

She was right about that. Marriage would have invited a Soco to father his grandchildren, even to move into Inaj's own house.

"I don't know what he'll do when he finds out I'm . . ."

"He doesn't know?"

Noney's mother certainly knew—every woman in the village did, despite the shapeless deer hide dress she wore every day. Sunoya chuckled to herself. *He can track a deer, and even tell by the pee whether it's a buck or a doe, but he doesn't notice his own daughter.*

"I'm scared of him."

"You should be." Everyone in the village had heard Inaj raging at his wife, and how she wailed when he beat her.

"There's something else . . ."

Tears spilled out with the stories. Noney was having terrible dreams about the infant within her. When the child came forth, lightning burst out of her, killing mother or child. Ahs-ginah, the Evil One, rose out of the smoke.

These dreams gave Sunoya a shiver, but she said nothing.

Su-Li said, *Take care of the child.*

Sunoya asked him what he meant, but he said nothing more, and Sunoya gave her attention back to Noney. As soon as her cousin went home for supper, Sunoya asked, "Why is this child so important?"

I'm can't tell you the future. Only what is important for you to do in the present.

"You're a nuisance sometimes."

She had the impression that he would have chuckled if he could.

Soon Noney was spending every afternoon with Sunoya, sitting in the sun and doing a little sewing or other domestic chores. Mostly they didn't talk, because they had no need. Sunoya wondered what story was being written in her belly.

❖

Two young women squatted in front of Sunoya, sisters, one sweet-faced, Pica, one blocky of body, Toka. Though they'd known Sunoya half their lives, they were a little uneasy about looking into the red-gold eye of that buzzard, who seldom left Sunoya's shoulder. Toka was in the style of a woman eligible for courting. Her black hair was brushed to a high gloss and pulled up into rolls the thickness of three fingers. On a thong around her neck she wore a disc of mother-of-pearl, a very dressy accessory, and expensive. She was round and chatty as an autumn squirrel.

Pica wore the plain hairstyle of a married woman, straight and chopped off at the shoulders. She was long-faced and had cause enough to come to Sunoya. She'd been married for two years and was childless.

Sunoya showed her how to begin. She cut a hank of hair

longer than a finger from Pica's hair. Then, carefully, she trimmed a tobacco leaf into slender strands of the same length. She gathered hair and tobacco into finger-thick bunches, three each, and braided them together. "Now," she said, "cut a hank of your husband's hair the same size. Braid it into each of these. You'll end up with a circle of his hair, your hair, and tobacco, about the size of two cupped hands. When you're done, bring it to me and I'll show you the rest." It was a charm every medicine person knew.

"*Hai! Hai! Hai! Hai!*" Shouts coursed and echoed from the upriver end of the village. People thronged in that direction, and Sunoya recognized Inaj's bull voice proclaiming a triumphant return—"*Hai! Hai! Hai! Hai!*" He and his cadre of warriors were back from the fall hunt, apparently bringing lots of meat, for they wore their rawhide discs outside their shirts, the red sides showing victory.

Though only men wore the discs, and only on hunting or fighting expeditions, Sunoya had quietly made one for herself. She wore it all the time, hidden in her bosom, and with the red or blue side out, according to how she felt, a confession of her emotions. Even having Su-Li didn't always lift her up. Sometimes she suspected she was destined to rise high, then fall low. The curse.

The men's families crowded around them, children shouting for the attention of their fathers and women making the trilling noise that praised the deeds of heroes. Tonight these families would put away their cornbread and seed cakes and feast on meat.

Inaj strode past Sunoya's small hut without acknowledging her. Kanu came out of his own hut and hailed the Red Chief as he went by, Medicine Chief to War Chief.

Sunoya's guests grinned at each other. "I think he'll figure a certain something out pretty fast now," Toka said. A lot of women were tickled at the prospect of the proud chief being shamed by his daughter.

He walked with the cockiness of a herd bull. A dozen warriors, young men who wanted to become the lead bull, trailed after him, carrying hide bags of dried meat. Aside from getting food for their families, they'd probably spent the Moon boasting about the bloody deeds they would rain on the heads of their enemies when spring arrived.

"Do you think there'll be trouble?" asked Pica.

"Let's hope for the best," Sunoya said. She told Su-Li, *I can smell the trouble already.*

Me, too.

Inaj's wife Iwa embraced him and then lavished her attentions on their two sons, carrying the family's winter meat. Inaj's small daughter Igalu clung to her father's hand. Her name meant "red leaf."

"Noney hasn't come out of the house," Sunoya said to Pica and Toka. "She's hoping the shadows inside will help hide her condition."

With only the small hole for light, a Tusca village house was shadowy on the brightest day.

She raised a quizzical eyebrow at Su-Li. Sometimes the buzzard at least hinted at the future. He said, *Times like this make me sorry to live among you human beings.*

Pica looked at Sunoya peculiarly. She couldn't figure out quite what was going on with this young medicine woman, and besides, she had what she came for. "Let's go find Mom," she said to Toka, and off they trotted.

Iwa scurried across the village circle with a big sack and handed it to Sunoya with a merry smile. Since Sunoya had no father or husband to provide for her, it was Inaj's duty to give her some meat. Iwa skipped and pranced back toward her husband, young and silly enough to be eager to see him.

Kanu walked up. "She likes him in the blankets, I guess," said Sunoya.

"A lot of village women like him in the blankets," said Kanu, "or in the bushes." It was a compliment.

"Let's eat," Sunoya said. The pack dog Kanu gave her, Dak, was sniffing at the meat bag. Sunoya stooped low and ducked into her house, Su-Li on her shoulder. He didn't like to hop around on the ground, partly because he hated the earth compared to the sky, and partly because he never quite trusted any dog.

❖

That night the Red Chief gorged himself on hot food and hot flesh. Then, even satiated, Inaj awoke at first light as usual. He watched from his hide blankets as Noney got up and went out, carrying the pot she would use to get water. Through the shadows, Inaj studied her carefully. He took a moment to sort through his mental pictures of his daughter for the past day, especially the clumsy way she walked. As Iwa started to get up, he grabbed her by the hand. Finally he said, "What's going on with Noney?"

No answer.

Now he demanded, "Is she carrying a baby?"

Iwa still didn't answer.

Inaj slapped Iwa so hard she tumbled sideways onto Igalu. Startled awake, the child bawled out.

Inaj towered over his wife. "Iwa, is Noney pregnant?"

Iwa hesitated.

Enraged, Inaj shoved her with both hands. As she fell backward, one bare foot landed on the warm stones encircling the center fire and the other jammed straight into the coals. She screamed, jumped, and collapsed to the ground.

At that moment Noney slipped back into the hut. Inaj whirled and fixed her with a withering look. A little water sloshed out of her clay pot. Inaj stepped forward and put a hand on her belly. He felt her roundness and the tight stretch of her skin. He glared at her and said in a low growl, "Who's the father?"

She looked daggers at him, walked past, stooped, and checked Iwa's burned foot. She poured some water on it and said, "Let's go get some ice from the river."

Inaj grabbed Noney's arm and jerked her up. The water pot dropped and smashed. The rest of the water soaked Noney's legs and moccasins. It splashed Igalu in the face, and the child cried louder.

Inaj barked, "Who is the father?"

She shoved his hand off her arm and glared.

Inaj could see fear in Noney's eyes. He loved weakness. "You'll tell me," he said, "or I'll beat it out of you."

He raised his arm, but Iwa spoke up in a quaver. "It's Tensa."

"Mother!" snapped Noney. She never kowtowed to her father.

"Tensa?!" shouted Inaj.

He cocked his arm high. Iwa grabbed it and held on.

"Yes, it's Tensa," said Noney, her voice hard as a spear tip. "I love him."

His face changed from amazement to rage. "You slut!" he shouted. "You bitch! That bastard Soco boy—he won't be the father of any of my grandchildren."

Abruptly, he launched himself at Noney, but Iwa grabbed one of his legs and threw him off balance. In horror she watched him topple toward the fire face down. At the last instant he rammed a hand hard onto one of the stones and flipped himself away. Her husband was amazing and scary.

Noney ran.

Inaj grabbed her hard by an ankle.

She tumbled and landed on her butt.

Inaj scrambled to his knees and pummeled Noney's belly. Iwa threw herself on her enraged husband. He hit and kicked blindly. He bit an ear and came away with blood on his tongue. When he had his wife reduced to whimpers, he thought to wonder where Noney was. He realized that she'd scurried out.

He bolted out of the hut and looked up and down the river, up and down the mountains. He saw nothing of his daughter. He stared for a couple of minutes in every direction, then looked up at the sky. Dark clouds crowded down from the peaks. Rain, not snow—the day was unseasonably warm. He smiled and went back into his house.

"She's gone into the woods," he told Iwa. He chuckled. "But where's she going to go? She has no food. She doesn't even have a robe to keep warm. Looks like it's going to rain today," he said. "She'll be back."

Iwa said nothing. Igalu whimpered in her pallet of blankets and robes.

"Let's send Zanda out to find her," whined Iwa. Her lips were swollen, her tongue cut, and she could barely speak the name of Noney's older brother.

"No need. Noney will be back. Give me something to eat."

8
_____

From outside the hut, Su-Li a-a-arked. Sunoya stayed half asleep as she let him in. Part of her mind wondered what was wrong. The buzzard loved the sky and hated to be cooped up in the house. Why would he come back in the morning, when he loved to ride the warming currents of air?

He let her hear his thought. *Noney is running away, up Willow Creek. She has no food and nothing to wrap herself in.*

The medicine woman shook her head and woke up. "Up Willow Creek?"

Yes, too fast and hard for a woman carrying a baby. Maybe hysterical.

Sunoya murmured, "Toward the Soco village."

A storm is coming, Su-Li told her. *Take care of the unborn child.*

"Yes." She considered. "Yes, all right." She'd have to move fast.

She trotted to her uncle's hut and gave him the news. "Can you go find out what people know?"

"Yes, but old bones are slow in the morning."

Sunoya rushed back to her hut and started packing.

In a few minutes Kanu came to the door and confirmed it. People had heard Inaj's family have another fight this morning, a big one. Some saw Noney run out of the hut bare-headed and bare-handed.

"He doesn't care," Sunoya said, "he lets her go, dares her to go. Inaj doesn't know his daughter."

The girl was running blind to nowhere.

Rolling dried meat into an elk hide, Sunoya told Kanu, "Don't tell anyone what I'm doing. Let's not stir Inaj up."

She told Su-Li, *Go watch Noney. When I'm packed, I'll start up Willow Creek. Come back and lead me to her.*

Su-Li showed Sunoya his fear.

She was scared, too. Two lone women trying to walk all the way to the Soco village in the winter? With a thunderstorm gathering? And rain that would turn to snow tonight?

"You got any other ideas?" she asked the buzzard.

Kanu spoke first. "Catch up with her and stay in a cave during the storm."

Yes, said Su-Li.

"All right then," Sunoya said. "Go!"

Su-Li did.

Kanu wrapped another elk hide full of dried meat. Together they lashed the rolls on each side of Dak's back. "Praise the spirits, the dog is big and he's tough," Sunoya said.

Kanu threw a buffalo robe around her shoulders and plopped a rabbit skin hat on her head. Sunoya tucked an extra pair of moccasins down her dress, between her breasts. She couldn't risk ending up barefooted, not in the winter.

She could hear the rain on her roof. "Everyone's inside," she said. "I'll sneak out of the village, no one will see." She gave Kanu a peck on the cheek. "Don't tell anyone."

"Surely the spirits will be with you and Noney," said Kanu.

"And with the child," said Sunoya.

"You're sure Su-Li thinks the child is important?"

"More than important."

Just as Sunoya lifted her door flap, the entire sky flashed white. She felt like her eyes were seared. Almost instantly, thunder banged her ears.

"Ahsginah, the evil one, is afoot," Kanu said in a quaver.

Sunoya sucked breath in, held it, let it out. "I've got to go!" They held each other's eyes. Each sensed the end of something.

Kanu shook his head sadly.

"You're right," said Sunoya, "I have no eyes, no ears, no brains—I just go!"

Sunoya pushed Dak out and stepped into raindrops hitting her face like pebbles. "Move!" she said to the dog. He padded forward. She smiled to herself and took heart in her dog's loyalty. She put one foot in front of the other and spoke to Dak in the rhythm of her steps, "Willow Creek, Willow Creek, Willow Creek."

She kept her face down, out of the pelting drops. The dirt path got muddy, and she moved onto the grass. Dak led the way. The mountains that were her homeland stood in her way now. She loved the smell of the pines on hot summer days, the muggy evenings, the sparkling fireflies, the swift relief of sudden rain. She loved the great crags, and liked to clamber in them. Now all of those turned into enemies.

Sunoya's arms yearned to embrace Noney. What young girl could stand being beaten by her father? What young girl wouldn't flee to the father of her unborn baby?

Sunoya quailed, though, when she pictured in her mind what Noney was trying to do. Their own village poised on the eastern edge of the huge sprawl of mountains that made up Galayi territory. It took a family about ten days to walk across these mountains east to west, and twelve from north to south. In the middle of the sprawl, several high ridges away from them, the Soco River drained most the mountains to the south and then southwest. If you went north on the Soco for two days, you came to the Cheowa village, where the big ceremonies took place. If you went south, you came to the Soco Village, and then far on to the southwest the last Galayi village, Cusa, the village of sanctuary.

In good weather a family needed five days to walk through the mountains to the Soco River and two more days downstream to the Soco village. For two women and a dog in the winter? Longer. For a lone, pregnant woman without food? Never.

This rain was nasty. With the part of her brain that could still think, Sunoya asked herself, *What does it mean?* Rain was a supreme gift brought by the messenger of the South Wind, who was called the Light Magician. Lightning was the greatest of dangers, brought by the messenger of the West Wind, the Dark Magician. Ahsginah, the Evil One of the Immortals, tried to kill First Man by throwing lightning at him.

Why do they come together at us? What does it mean?

A medicine person was one who asked such questions, and somehow found wisdom.

She put the hand with the webbed fingers on her *zadayi*, red on one side for victory, blue on the other for defeat, both part of the same disc, the same life. She thought again, *Is my life blessed or cursed?*

Su-Li appeared suddenly in the whirl of raindrops and landed on her shoulder. Sunoya looked at him fearfully.

You've got to hurry, Su-Li told her.

Medicine woman, buzzard, and dog forged their way into the storm.

❖

Midmorning, noon—Sunoya lost track of the time of day. She slogged up the path, wondering if Dak felt as wet and cold as she did. Though she was scared for Noney, Sunoya felt alive. She was doing something that mattered.

The rain was easing up. Sunoya could see the winding creek ahead, the path as it left the stream and angled toward the ridge line. Above that she could make out the dark humps of the treeless summits on either side—the "balds," as people called them. The track to the Soco River crossed mountain ridge after mountain ridge. She caught no glimpse of Noney.

She glanced at Su-Li on her shoulder. The bird lifted off and wing-flapped up the mountain. If he couldn't see the girl in the rain, he'd be able to smell her. Though he had the eyesight of an eagle, a buzzard's real power lived in his nose. He could smell flesh at the level of a mountaintop, and decaying flesh at twice that height. This was Thunderbird's joke on Su-Li—during his time on Turtle Island he *wanted* to eat carrion.

In another hundred steps the rain lightened to a drizzle. Dark clouds bunched up near the top of the balds. Sunoya spotted Su-Li circling near the saddle, the low point of the ridges, where the path aimed. The buzzard slid down the winds toward Sunoya again.

She held an arm out straight and Su-Li lit on it. *She's angling up to the saddle now. She's struggling. Something's wrong. Maybe Inaj injured her.*

"Bastard," said Sunoya, peering up. "Wait, I see something." She couldn't see Noney, not really, but she glimpsed movement, and who else could it be?

She's almost to the ridge, Su-Li said.

Helpless, Sunoya yelled, "Crawl into a cave and get warm and dry!"

KA-BOOM!

A blinding flash, then a mind-numbing bang.

"Ahsginah is attacking her!"

Dak barked fiercely at the storm.

"Immortals, help us!"

Su-Li didn't let Sunoya see into his mind.

The young medicine woman pumped her legs as fast as they would go. She panted, "The Evil One is upon us."

❖

Noney was spread-eagled, limp, and unconscious. Her hair was scorched, her ear and neck burned, and her dress torn open on the upper left side. Sunoya pulled the burned edges back but saw no bleeding. Her breast showed an angry red burn, forked like lightning.

"Ahsginah!"

Sunoya felt her neck—no sign of a beating heart.

She shook her cousin. "Noney! Noney!"

She's dying, said Su-Li.

"Noney, come back to us!"

You've done all you can. Save the baby.

Sunoya felt frozen in place. "Noney! Noney!"

She's gone, Su-Li told Sunoya. *Get the baby out before he dies, too!*

Eyes wild, Sunoya stared into Noney's face.

Now!

Frenzy seized Sunoya. She slipped her knife out of its belt sheath. She lifted Noney's dress, then hesitated. She breathed deep and made a firm, vertical cut from belly button to pubic bone.

In brutal haste she sliced until she could grab the baby with both hands and wrestle it free. The child wailed. A boy. A lot of hair. Ten fingers and . . .

The fourth and fifth fingers of the left hand were webbed. Her breath caught. *The child of prophecy, the one of legend.*

Before she could hold the fingers out for Su-Li to see, the buzzard said, *Yes.*

Sunoya's thoughts clicked into place. This was why Su-Li urged her. She shivered. *The child of prophecy.*

Su-Li told her, *Hurry up!*

"Find us a cave," Sunoya said out loud.

Straight over there!

Sunoya cut the cord. Dak tried to lick up the blood, but Sunoya shooed him away.

9
———

Sunoya was drowning in troubles. Yes, she was grateful for the shelter and for the warmth of the little fire. But she had a bawling child in her arms—a hungry child born before its time—and not a drop of milk. The body of her cousin lay in the open on the rough mountainside, open to the ravages of rain, snow, insects, worms, ravens, wolves. . . . Worst of all, she had no way to give Noney a proper burial.

The child comes first, said Su-Li.

Sunoya pursed her mouth. Su-Li hated mortality, and had no patience with ceremonies for the dead.

But what about the baby? They couldn't go back to their own village, that was for sure. Even if Inaj wasn't enraged enough to kill his own grandson, he might kill Sunoya, and would certainly take the boy away from her. *This medicine child the Immortals gave me.*

Yet the infant wouldn't last until they got to the Soco village—not without milk. His screaming was about to drive her crazy. *The child of prophecy,* she thought, *is noisy.* Since before the memories of the grandfathers of the oldest men, the tribe's legends told of a boy child who would be born with the last two fingers of his left hand webbed. That had been a good omen for generations, but it happened only among girl children. When this boy was born, said the tale, he would save the people.

Sunoya had a sudden impulse, pulled her dress off one shoulder, and put her dry nipple in the boy's mouth. *The only child I'll ever suckle,* she thought. *The child all our people have waited for, and I have no milk.*

I have an idea, Su-Li said.

She raised an eyebrow at him.

I'll go to the village. He shielded the rest of his thought from her. *For this I have to change shape.*

Su-Li hopped to the mouth of the cave and looked back at her with a gleam in his eye. He backed up and started to transform himself. It was a work of imagination, visualizing himself in detail as a different creature. A new form took a little time. His feathers darkened. His wings lengthened. His head turned from red to orange. Backing up again, he spread his wings and extended them hugely—each wing as long as a man was tall. His body swelled, like an arm becoming a leg.

Sunoya had never seen such a creature.

Condor, Su-Li told her.

She had the impression that her spirit companion was tickled at himself, but with him she could never be sure.

With a whoosh of wings, he lifted off.

❖

Cautiously, in the recess of the cave, Sunoya inspected the infant boy's left hand. *Webbed, truly.* She kept rubbing the skin between his fingers, lost in thought, tumbled by conflicting currents, the confusion and guilt of her own life and the promise of the fulfillment of prophecy.

Clarity, she told herself. Her mind tonight was on the miracle in her lap. She fingered the webbing. *A boy,* she told herself for the thousandth time in joy and trepidation, *and the left hand*.

Flashes of fear jolted through her arms and legs, glimmers of terror she hadn't felt in years. Not since she'd accepted, genuinely, that the two people who knew her secret were dead and no one could expose her.

Now, if the old tales were true, Sunoya had arrived at her moment of truth. *Am I a half moon waning or a half moon waxing?* Her spirit rebelled. *I am too young for everything to be decided now.*

She looked into the eyes of the boy, which looked back at her, imponderable. *It all depends on whether I save the life of this new being who bears strong medicine into the world.*

She looked down to make sure her *zadayi* was red side forward. At that moment the boy tugged hard on her nipple. "Well," she said to him, "the least I can do is give you a name, the one you've earned, Dahzi." In the Galayi language it meant "hungry."

❖

Su-Li hovered in the air just outside the cave, wings flapping hard and loud. Gently, he set down a dog. A bitch, Sunoya saw—a bitch with swollen tits. He covered the animal with his huge wings, and she was too scared to run off.

Sunoya said to the Immortal, "Su-Li, you're smart." She said to the child, "You want some of that?" She went on, talking to Su-Li, "I gave him a name, Dahzi." She pulled hard to get him off her nipple. "Later I hope he craves something more spiritual."

She set the child down, grabbed the dog, flopped it into position inside the cave, and put Dahzi to the tits. "Come now, suck a dog's milk. She's an animal, just like you and me."

If the dog will let the boy feed, said Su-Li. After he spoke, he pulled himself back into buzzard shape. Sunoya let out the breath she didn't know she'd been holding.

Dak padded forward and sniffed the new dog. The bitch suddenly realized where she was and started to get to her feet. Sunoya put a stop to that and shoved Dak away. She set Dahzi back in the right position and pushed his head forward. When he tried to grip her nipple in his lips, the mother dog growled at him.

"It's all right," Sunoya told the dog, stroking her head. Then she took thought. "We're going to call you Mother. That's your calling, to mother."

Sunoya got out some dried meat and gave Mother some. The dog chewed on it nervously. "You're scared, poor thing," Sunoya said. She rubbed the dog's ears gently. "Who wouldn't be scared, kidnapped by a bird monster?"

The young woman also gave pieces to Su-Li, Dak, and herself. "Everybody has to eat." She gave Mother some more. "You, soon your tits hurt. You're too full. Then Dahzi gets all he wants."

And he did.

❖

Sunoya wept. She wept as hugely as the skies wept yesterday. On this beautiful, sunny day she laid her hands on Noney's cold body, raised her face to Grandmother Sun, and sang.

Nothing lives long
Not on this Earth

Nothing lives long
Nothing but the Earth
Nothing lives long
lives long
lives long

When her voice disappeared on the wind, she was left with only wishes. She wished that she could hold her cousin and trade the warmth of her own body for Noney's cold one—it was the young mother who should live, who should raise this child. Sunoya wished she could sing with a more beautiful voice. She wished she had her drum, to give her song a heart-beat. And she wished most of all that she could bury Noney properly.

Tradition called for a mound of stones on the side of the mountain that faced east, the direction all good things come from. Tradition asked Noney's women relatives to wrap her in a winding cloth they had woven themselves from the inner bark of the mulberry tree. It required them to send her favorite possessions along with her, and a little food.

Except for the food, Sunoya could do none of this. She and Su-Li had tried to move the body, but it was too heavy, even with Su-Li at condor strength. They had no winding cloth and little meat to spare. Noney had fled from the village with no possessions but the clothes she wore.

Since Su-Li was checking their back trail, Sunoya started gathering enough stones to give the body a light covering. She picked up rocks as big as she could manage with both hands and started making a mound on top of Noney. It was a terrible job, laying stones directly on her cousin's body—Sunoya started with the feet and didn't think about covering her face.

In a few minutes she sat down to rest beside the sleeping child. Dahzi, the Hungry One, whimpered, and she held and rocked him. She looked across the rocky mountainside and faced her own situation glumly. She wasn't strong enough to build a mound high enough to protect Noney properly, and she didn't have time. Inaj would come soon and find his daughter. He would be furious about her death, incensed at the desecration of her body. She looked at her cousin's body and felt a shiver of helplessness.

So she wrapped Dahzi tightly, set him in tall grasses, and went back to carrying what stones she could. As she worked, she got her mind clear about what she truly had to accomplish, only one task, a great one. Save the life of the boy child.

To get it done, she, Su-Li, Dak, and Mother had to walk to the village of the Soco people and present Dahzi to his father.

She looked up at the ridge top. They had to cross that ridge and several more ridges on a trail that was steep but easy to see. Then cross the Soco River and walk downstream to the village. Difficult, but she would do it. And receive a small additional blessing—she had spent her girlhood in the Soco village.

She covered Noney's bloody belly, glad to get it out of sight. She set stones on her breasts, and another one just below her neck.

She stood up, panting, partly to get her eyes away from Noney, partly to catch her breath. She saw Su-Li gliding down toward her. She waited for him, arm extended.

The instant he landed on Sunoya's shoulder, Su-Li said, *Time to get out of here. Inaj and four other men are coming up the trail.*

Sunoya packed Dak, lifted Dahzi into her arms, told Mother to come, and barked at Su-Li, "Do something."

He winged his way back down the trail.

Sunoya took one last look around that awful place. Her eyes lingered on Noney's young and beautiful face uncovered by rocks, eyes staring at the sun. Sunoya reached down and closed them.

Then she scooped handfuls of gravel on Noney's face and ran.

10

Inaj's mind was all rage at his renegade daughter—he re- fused even to think her name. He'd bet she intended to ren- dezvous nearby with the bastard who stuck a baby into her belly, the Soco—where else would the girl run?

So he plunged upward in a huff, paying no attention to his men. Flee to the Socos, his own daughter!

"Ow!"

He threw a hand at whatever jabbed at his head. *What the hell was that?*

He felt the outside corner of his right eyebrow and his fin- ger came away bloody.

"Ow!" Left eyebrow!

Inaj hit at it, and swiveled his head in all directions.

"Ow!" Now the top of his head.

His men were chuckling, even his sons Wilu and Zanda.

Inaj looked straight up and saw a blue jay fluttering in his face. He cuffed at it, and it dodged.

"What the hell?!"

The men were laughing out loud now.

"Shut up! What is this damn thing doing?!"

The blue jay whirled in midair and dive-bombed him.

Inaj flailed the head of his spear at it and missed foolishly.

The bird fastened on his nose with both claws and pecked fast and hard at his forehead.

Inaj bellowed. Then he remembered he was a warrior and slapped his own nose. He nicked a feather out of the jay's tail as it squirted off.

"What in hell?" he shouted.

The jay landed on the branch of a pine tree and gibed at him. "Shkrr," it said, "shkrr."

"Bastard thinks he can make fun of me?" Inaj hurled his spear at the jay, which simply bobbed to a higher branch and watched it sail below him.

"Ja-a-ay!" it screeched, a shrill cry from high to low. "Ja-a-ay!"

"He's lecturing you now," said the round son, Wilu. The other son, Zanda, was hard-bodied.

Inaj whirled on Wilu and stalked toward him, brandishing his war club.

Wilu backed up. Laughter choked in the men's throats and died.

The muscular son, Zanda, said in a sharp tone, "Chief!"

"Too-li-li!" shrieked the jay. "Too-li-li! Too-li-li!"

Inaj turned and took a long look at the bird. "To hell with being mocked." He glared at his sons. "Let's move."

❖

Sunoya stopped in the cover of the last trees before the ridge and looked down. "Spirits, help us," she murmured. She could see Inaj and his comrades on the trail below. And when she stepped into the open, followed by Dak and Mother, Inaj might easily see her. She looked at the sky and cried out, "Immortals, help us."

An idea came to her. *A woman followed by two dogs—we won't look like Noney.* And a sadder idea: *When he finds Noney, he'll stop thinking about us for a while.* She shook her head to clear it and stepped cautiously into the open, peering downward.

Suddenly Inaj flicked a hand at his head. He waved at it over and over. After a moment he stomped off the trail and threw his spear at . . . some pine needles?

Sunoya laughed. She understood. She broke into a run for the top.

❖

Inaj brushed the pebbles off his daughter's face. He looked at her—dead, dead, dead.

He threw up on the mound. Incapable of words, he let out a croak as from a dying raven. He lay down, one arm in his own vomit. His body heaved up and down with emotions. Grief, rage, grief, fury, grief . . . He yelled. He beat his fists on the stones that buried his daughter's body. He kicked his feet. He roared like a man impaled on a spear.

Then he lay on the grave, silent, utterly still.

Wilu edged forward and touched Noney's fingers. Zanda looked contempt at his brother.

After too long Inaj got onto his hands and knees and said, "Sunoya did this." His voice scratched like a mountain of sliding gravel. He started taking the stones off Noney's body, one by one. He brushed the sand out of the creases in her eyelids and the corners of her mouth. He uncovered her shoulders and her breasts, which were hidden by her skin dress. He came to the belly—and jumped at the sight of the gaping wound.

He stared. His sons crept close and stared.

Inaj's rage froze, molten lava turned to ice. "Murdered," he whispered. "Murdered by that bitch!" he said. Again in a low, howling whisper, "Murdered."

Wilu and Zanda backed away, queasy.

"Because she can't have a child, she stole ours." He glared at Wilu.

The voice quaked, but the men couldn't tell whether it was shaken by rage or despair.

"Help me," Inaj growled.

Warily, the warriors uncovered Noney and lifted her.

Inaj slung her over one shoulder and stalked down the mountain, bearing his cold, stiff daughter home.

❖

That afternoon the family buried Noney in a proper way. Then Kanu gave them tea brewed from a willow root. To purify themselves from their contact with the dead, they drank it and then washed their bodies with it.

Afterward Inaj assembled his men and a dog packed with dried meat.

"My husband," Iwa said.

One by one Inaj threw words at his wife. "Our daughter has been murdered." He waited a moment and threw words again. "Our grandchild has been stolen."

Iwa murmured, "I . . ."

Inaj knew he was violating custom. A quarter moon of mourning was required after a death, the family cloistered in the house. What he didn't know was that his wife wondered whether he would bring back the grandchild or bash in its head.

His voice was low and taut. "Vengeance rampages in my heart."

11

Sunoya sang softly to the child, an old song, a song that spoke of the joys and griefs of life, all of it.

Stop that, said Su-Li.

Sunoya stopped and eyed him. Then she stroked Dahzi's hairy head.

If they hear you, said the buzzard, *they'll trap us in here.* He was perched on a rock outcropping at the mouth of a cave, sniffing into the darkness for Inaj and his men.

"I know you don't like caves." This was their second night in one.

You're one of the People of the Caverns.

"And you can't stand being shut in. But before we get to the Socos, we're going to have more nights in caves."

Sunoya put Dahzi, the Hungry One, on one of Mother's tits. No one else paid attention. Dak gnawed on his piece of dried meat. Mother dozed and sometimes growled at Dahzi.

You're not taking this seriously.

She saw his words painted in lurid colors in her mind. She said, "You said they're far behind us."

Maybe they're moving tonight, Su-Li said, *catching up.*

"No." She looked into Su-Li's eye and thought her calm made him back him off a bit.

They're fast and we're slow, he said. *If you were sure I'm wrong, you wouldn't be whispering.*

Sunoya reflected that it was odd that, though he didn't have a voice, Su-Li could take a tone with her.

Tomorrow we run like hounds toward the Soco village, said Su-Li.

"All right." She cradled Dahzi and rocked him. She gazed into his face in a dreamlike state.

Finally she stroked Su-Li's feathers. "The Immortals forbade me to bear a child, and then gave me this one."

❖

When Sunoya ducked out of the cave the next morning, she gave thanks to Thunderbird again. Though the little party had climbed higher and higher into the mountains, the weather was still warm. "Doesn't feel like Falling Leaf Moon," she told Dak. "The day is good."

She had the elk robes for blankets, but both days and nights were the temperature of a cave, and that was a blessing.

She looked up at Su-Li, high as the tops of the nearest balds. He flashed a warning to her: *Get going.*

They trundled down and down and on downhill. "Not fair," mumbled Sunoya, out of breath. "Downhill hurts my legs just like up."

Still, at midmorning they stood and gawked at the Soco River, the only big stream they had to cross. It was running full and wild.

Su-Li landed on her shoulder. "The Immortals, are they abandoning us?" Sunoya said.

They gave you this child for a reason, said Su-Li.

Sunoya eyed the raging river. The rain had swelled it, and the warm days were melting snow off the summits.

It's not deep here, Su-Li told her.

"But it's rough." She hesitated. "I might fall." She thought of the waves jostling her and the slippery rocks on the bottom and clutched Dahzi a little tighter.

There's no better ford downstream, said Su-Li. *I've checked. Look upstream yourself.*

The river was a huge, frozen waterfall. It was beautiful, high as a hill, sparkling like a thousand suns.

She looked at her companion. "Right. No time for sight-seeing."

I'll see how far back they are.

Sunoya gazed at the river and thought. Once her people had lived at the seashore, so the old story said, until they were driven out by a larger tribe. In those days they paddled about the water like turtles, and some swam underneath the surface of the sea, like fish. The Galayi were still strong swimmers. But people said you could go into a freezing river in a cold moon and lose your mind and drown.

Sunoya looked from Dahzi in her arms to Dak, lapping at the edge of the water. She took a deep breath, swallowed a horrible glop of fear, and set to work.

When Su-Li wheeled back toward them, she was done. Dahzi lay facedown, lashed to Dak's back and bawling. She'd wrapped him in fur as well as possible, but he wanted only to be held. "I carry you," she told him softly, "and we both die."

Su-Li landed on the sandy bank. *Get going!*

Sunoya looked back at the turbulent water, glinting with threat.

Inaj will rape you and kill you, said Su-Li.

"Let's do it," she said.

The first step was immersion in a painful world. The cold—Sunoya wanted to bellow. The ache in her legs—breath clotted in her throat.

Dak swam alongside, looking at her, trusting her. So far the baby was dry.

Sunoya scooted one foot forward. She wanted to holler and wouldn't let herself. Then she picked up the other foot and took a firm step. She shouted for her own benefit, "I don't get across, he dies, too. Go!" Six steps, eight steps, ten. A wave splashed high as her right breast, and her nipple pinched until it hurt.

Ten more steps and she grabbed onto the trunk of a dead tree stranded in midstream. She gripped a limb hard and hoisted her bottom onto the trunk. She sat for a moment, the water only up to her calves. Then she realized that, with the wind, she was still cold. Very cold. She slipped off the trunk.

And went under.

The current was a maelstrom. Her body was down, sideways, up, down—and then was flung underwater beneath the trunk. She reached up blindly and found a limb with her hands. She grabbed it but couldn't pull her head above water. *Air! Air! I'm going to die.*

A monster heaved her upwards by the shoulders. She beached on the trunk.

A war eagle retracted his claws from her hide dress. Su-Li was twice the size of a buzzard, and she could read his thoughts.

"Thank you," she wheezed.

I can't carry you, but I can give you a boost.

When she got her mind and emotions sorted out, he said, *It's shallower at the downstream end, and you won't be sucked back under the tree.*

"I can't do this," she said.

You have to. He turned his handsome russet head across the river. Both dogs stood on the far bank looking back at her, panting. *You hear Dahzi bawling?*

She crawled to the downstream end and, before she could think, flung her feet at the bottom. Waist deep.

In two dozen steps she was sprawled on her belly on the sand. She doubted that anyone could feel this cold and be alive. She crawled to Dak, unstrapped Dahzi, turned him over, and held him tight.

He hollered.

She mumbled, "I'm not warming him up . . . I may be freezing him."

Wrap one of the robes around you. Her spirit guide was back in Su-Li's familiar shape. She liked him that way.

And let's get moving.

"I ca—"

Sunoya passed out.

12

Su-Li watched nervously as the shadows stretched from the western mountains onto the water. Once in a while he glanced up toward the frozen waterfall. The slanted sun lanced light onto the branches of the laurels along the bank and the ice above. *Not a bad place sometimes, this Earth.*

He had done all he could, covered Sunoya and the baby with elk robes. Even partly wet, the robes held some warmth. Beyond that, he had to wait, which was driving him crazy. *Damned fear.* It was the true affliction of the realm between the upper and lower worlds, Earth.

He watched Inaj and his six men picking their way down the steep clay trail, its surface not quite dry. When they got to the river, Su-Li, Sunoya, and the dogs would be directly in view.

His brain whirled around, searching for ideas. He could hope for darkness, but it would probably come too late. He could hope that Inaj would make camp back from the river and not see the fugitives through the trees. He mocked himself. *How desperate you are.*

He nudged Sunoya with his beak. He pushed at her face until he made her blink.

"Hunnh?"

We've got to get going. They're almost here.

"Hunnh-hnn?"

Sunoya!

Suddenly, Inaj and his men appeared on the opposite bank. They pointed toward the helpless band. A couple of them shook their spears. One jumped up and down. Their pack dogs milled, eager for excitement.

It's over.

Su-Li felt a great infusion of sadness, like a dye in his blood. *Maybe they won't kill her,* he thought.

But Inaj will still rape her, he told himself honestly. *Hopeless.*

He missed the Land beyond the Sky Arch. *So why am I not glad for this chance to go home?*

He stepped onto the back of this human being he liked and flexed his claws into her. Anything, anything to get her to try.

Across the river two warriors jumped into the water up to their knees and dashed back out. All the men looked at each other. "Let's go. It's almost dark!" yelled Inaj. He shooed the dogs into the water. Then the whole gang jumped in and waded forward.

CR-R-ACK!

Su-Li jumped. *That sounds like thunder.* He looked around and saw geysers of water shooting up at the bottom of the icefall. The entire upper half of it was gone.

CR-R-ACK!

The lower half avalanched into the river. The ice looked like mountain goats running off a cliff.

Inaj and his men looked around and gawked at each other. Su-Li could almost see them wondering, could almost hear them asking each other what those world-shattering noises were.

They were standing in the middle, the deepest part, when the first ice blocks hit them.

Some ice was the size of pebbles, some as big as fists. Other pieces afloat were the size of human heads. A few bergs were as huge as the canopies of oak trees.

Ice floated downstream like a herd of sheep, bunched up, bumping. It knitted into a force as unstoppable as a landslide.

Inaj realized at the last instant what was bearing down on him. He screamed at the others and hauled himself onto a block bigger than he was.

It flipped and dunked him.

He fought his way back to the surface, got his feet under himself, and was clobbered again.

Underwater he lost sense of direction for a moment and was sure he was going to die. When a drifting piece of ice slammed him against the bottom, he figured out where to plant his feet.

Coming up for the second time, he sucked in half a world of breath and looked desperately upstream. A berg as big as a hillock was bearing down on him.

He launched himself into the air, pricked the ice with his knife, and clung like a spider.

The berg rocked, crunched, and ground against other pieces of icefall. Panicky, Inaj scrambled to a better position on the top and used his knife tip as a flimsy anchor. He looked back at his sons and the others and got an impression of an arm here, a head there, but could identify no one. Imperiously, his chariot swept him downstream.

13

Inaj crept along the bank on his side of the river, the near side, through the darkness, crawling over and around and through downed trees, boulders, and eddies. He kept going. Moving kept him warmer than sleeping. He cursed with every step.

He found his sons and two others shivering around a fire on the riverbank. Apparently two were missing, and all the pack dogs were gone. Faces were glum. They'd lost all their food, all their gear, half their weapons, and a third of their man strength.

"Get whatever sleep you can," he muttered. Like the others he stretched out close to the fire. All night he flip-flopped back and forth, like he was on a spit, broiling one side and freezing the other. He woke up feeling like he'd been hunted down, cut up, and roasted.

"Let's find them," he ordered. He crossed the river—easy now that an ill fate wasn't striking at him—and started searching downstream.

The Galayi code was fixed. Warriors never left the bodies of their comrades to be mutilated by enemies or desecrated by wild animals. They buried them respectfully and moved on.

As Inaj found nothing and nothing and nothing, not even

the corpse of a dog, he turned grim. He told himself that his fellow soldiers were cursed with the fate his daughter had barely escaped. Under his breath he wailed his apologies to his two comrades for this unforgivable sin, sending them naked, empty-handed, even mutilated into the Darkening Land.

Late in the afternoon the four survivors gathered back at the fire. No one had seen any sign of the missing men. They were drowned or crushed by the ice.

"Maybe they are with Those Who Live in Flowing Waters," said Wilu.

Inaj kept himself from giving a snort of disgust.

Galayi people told stories of these small creatures who lived in creeks and rivers, commonly called The Little People. They were said to be beautiful, shaped just like Galayis but only knee-high. Though often mischievous, they had magical powers and would help Galayis who got lost or into other trouble. Their special power was protecting Galayis who performed the purifying ceremony Going to Water. Sometimes these little people appeared in desperate battles and saved the Galayi from defeat. The Little People were tricky, though, and you had to be careful in your dealings with them. If you tasted their food, for instance, you would never be able to eat human food again.

As a boy Inaj used to look for the Little People near rivers, and he had spent an entire teenage summer hunting for springs where they might live, because the places water emerged from the earth were sacred. He still hoped to find one. But he had no patience with a man who appealed to them for help. His creed was that a warrior depended on his arms, legs, and heart, and those alone.

Before the men could get started on their tales of the Little People, he told them curtly, "Sleep while the sun is still up."

Then he disappeared into the forest. Shortly after dark he came back with the hind leg of a deer in each hand. "I got these without Little People helping," he said. As his warriors ate, he could see their energy coming back and their spirits rising.

When the meat was gone, Inaj stood up, looked at the river, and said, "Let's go."

"Now?" said Zanda.

Inaj glared at him. He didn't like having his decisions questioned, even by implication.

"They have a day's head start on us," he said, "and they're getting near the village. We'll make it up by walking through the night. And you won't get so cold."

Zanda took a step back.

Now Inaj grinned at his men recklessly, and his eyes glittered like ice. "Let's run this murderer down."

❖

Just go, said Su-Li.

Sunoya wasn't sure. "It's a full day away," she said. "They might catch us."

Get moving, returned Su-Li.

She pursed her mouth. The Immortals had chosen her for the task of saving the child of prophecy, delivering him to his father. Why? What if she couldn't do it? She flexed the fingers of her right hand, the one that bore the curse no one knew about, except herself.

You know the one thing Inaj says that's true? Su-Li went on.

"No." Her voice sounded petty and resentful, even to her.

When your life is at stake, don't dither.

He flashed that red-yellow eye at her. *Go!*

"Okay, you listen to me," she said. "Fly to the village. Go to the hut of the Red Chief." That hut's door would be outlined in red, for victory. "Make your rasp at Ninyu. He'll know who you are—everybody knows. Tell him to bring help."

She turned her back and got down to business, lashing their robes and remaining scraps of meat onto Dak. Without looking at Su-Li, she planted one foot in front of the other and tramped the downstream trail.

Su-Li lifted off. He would do his job.

"I'm worn out," Sunoya crabbed out loud.

From the height of the mountain Su-Li told her, *You are a medicine woman on a sacred mission.*

She padded faster.

❖

Inaj's power was more than strength and endurance. It was the ability to inspire other men to them.

He and his four warriors ran all night, slept for a little while in the first warmth of the morning sun, and ran again. Stride, easy stride, long-legged stride, stride forever. Inaj believed he had strength enough to turn a seven-day trek into three days. The Soco village was a two-day walk down the river from the ford. He thought he and his men could catch any woman, even after a day's head start. He pictured the village. If she got there first, she would poison everyone against him.

Every couple of hours he called a pause to drink out of the river. At these times he said very little.

"Today we do it."

"We're going to get them."

"I never wanted anything so much."

Stride, stride, stride.

❖

Damn this mortal realm! Su-Li flapped hard downriver and cruised to Ninyu's house. He was not only the Red Chief, Su-Li knew, but Tensa's father and the Hungry One's grandfather. The buzzard was anxious—fear, the cursed drumbeat of life on Earth, made him want to wring his own neck.

In the middle of winter the family would be sitting close to the warmth of their fire. Sunoya said Ninyu had pale hair and white skin. Some of his fellow villagers were leery of him. But in a fight he was a dervish. The warriors of his village had made him Red Chief because he awed them, and half-frightened them.

The buzzard saw the hut with the red-framed door and landed on the mud roof. The curs scurried over and yapped at him. Su-Li hated dogs. He knew it was unbecoming for a spirit animal to hate any Earth creatures, but dogs were pests.

Su-Li a-a-arked at the smoke hole and blew the smoke away with his wings. It would probably be the strangest halloo Ninyu had ever heard. The albino lifted the flap, looked at the buzzard with ironic eyes, and conjured up a half smile. "Sunoya's spirit animal," he said, nodding to himself. He carried his club. *If that didn't kill you, his sickly white skin would scare you to death.*

Su-Li couldn't think what to say. *How the devil am I going to get this done fast?*

He nodded his head up the river several times, the way the people did when they wanted to point. Ninyu came into the open, looking puzzled. A good start. But the Red Chief searched all around with his eyes. *No, no, follow me.* Even good human beings were slow to catch on. Su-Li pecked the door flap.

Red Chief Ninyu held out his arm, Su-Li landed on it, and they ducked inside.

Ninyu's wives and children chattered and shrieked and retreated to the back wall.

"I don't know what's happening," said Ninyu, "but this has to be Sunoya's new spirit animal. He's trying to tell us something."

Tensa regarded Su-Li suspiciously. Spirit animals were oddities, sometimes useful, but in the view of practical men not to be trusted.

Su-Li sailed to the ground and hopped around the center fire to Tensa. He stood sideways to the young father and fixed him with an eye. *Pay attention!* Unfortunately, Tensa couldn't read the buzzard's thoughts.

He pecked Tensa's belt knife. The young man jerked it out and threatened Su-Li with the edge.

"No!" said Ninyu.

Su-Li nodded his head to the knife several times. He felt like an idiot, like he was bowing to war, the greatest curse human beings had invented.

The two men, two wives, and all the children looked at the buzzard with frightened eyes and open mouths.

Su-Li hopped to where a spear hung from a wall on thongs. Not caring whose it was, he flapped up and pecked it. He looked at the two men. He flapped up and nudged it again.

Ninyu got an idea. "Su-Li, where is Sunoya?"

You're catching on!

The buzzard hopped to the door flap, nudged it open with his beak, and looked back at the two men. His eye was baleful.

They followed him out.

A dog charged Su-Li from the back of the house. The bird skittered up the wall hissing and clucking. Two dogs scratched at the wall as if they could climb. Su-Li screeched at them and launched himself into the air. *This place is maddening.*

He hurled a reminder at himself—*Sunoya!* He made a raggedy turn back to fly over the heads of Ninyu and Tensa. When he knew he had their attention, he flew to where the river trail merged into the village, flapped back to the two watchers, swooped low over them, and winged back to the trail head again.

"He's telling us Sunoya is up the trail," said Ninyu.

"And in trouble!" said Tensa.

Now Ninyu let out a war cry that hurt every ear in the village. Tensa ducked back into the house to get his other weapons, and his father's.

Men popped out of their houses pulling on their moccasins,

grabbing a club or a spear in each hand. Ninyu and Tensa whirled their war clubs over their heads and led the charge up the river.

14

Sunoya felt like she was running on legs that were twigs, bending and about to break. She'd always been fast, able to outrun all the girls and half the boys. She told her body to remember now how it felt, gliding over the grass . . .

She crashed to one knee and nearly crushed Dahzi in the muddy track.

The two dogs ran on a dozen strides, stopped, looked back, and whined.

She got the aching knee propped underneath her and checked on Dahzi. The poor creature was whimpering but not squalling.

"Good boy, good boy," she said. The poor child hadn't had a sip from Mother from dawn till now, midmorning. He dozed sometimes when she walked, but most of the time Sunoya trotted and Dahzi squirmed.

She hoisted herself and trotted forward. "This is stupid," she rasped.

She tripped on a rock and splatted down again.

Su-Li circled high overhead. She didn't have to look up to see him. She could feel him. She rumbled forward.

He landed on her shoulder. *The Soco men are coming,* he said. *They will protect you.*

"Go back and look for Inaj and his devils," she told him.

Don't have to, said Su-Li. *I just saw them from overhead. Right behind you.*

She started to fall and caught herself. She ran a dozen steps, put off asking, and ran fifty steps. Then she decided not to ask at all. What did it matter how far back her enemies were? She would run until she fell into the arms of the Socos or collapsed onto the hard earth and waited to be pierced by a penis or a spear. She ran, ran, ran.

You will survive, said Su-Li.

She shook her head violently. That wasn't what she wanted to hear.

The child will survive.

The cry came from behind. "Woh-WHO-O-O-ey! Woh-WHO-O-O-ey! AI-AI-AI-AI!"

Sunoya tumbled straight to the ground.

"Woh-WHO-O-O-ey! Woh-WHO-O-O-ey! AI-AI-AI-AI!"

It was the Galayi war cry, famous far beyond these mountains and feared everywhere. Strong and determined soldiers of enemy tribes, even when they had superior numbers, heard this cry and quailed. One or two would run. The Galayis would charge, hurling the cry at men's hearts. A half dozen more would run, and then entire phalanxes would break out of cover like hunted birds and flee.

And the Galayi men would kill them from behind.

Yes, they can see you, screamed Su-Li into her mind. She confused it for a moment with the wild hissing that came from his throat.

She got up and staggered forward.

"Woh-WHO-O-O-ey! Woh-WHO-O-O-ey! AI-AI-AI-AI!"

The cry made her blood turn to snakes. The first syllable was low and mysterious, the second high, eerie, ululating, the last a short woof. Then four roars of terror.

She ran but she wobbled.

"Change to an eagle! Take the child!" The words were a plea.

This is your mission, said Su-Li.

She ran crookedly.

"Woh-WHO-O-O-ey! Woh-WHO-O-O-ey! AI-AI-AI-AI!"

Su-Li launched off her shoulder and wing-flapped high and fast.

The Soco men are coming, too, he said. *Not far.*

Sunoya started to ask which crew was closer. Then she cackled at herself. She knew.

She weaved sideways, banged a shoulder into a tree, got her footing back, and ran.

Why not die running?

The child of prophecy, the medicine bearer . . .

Dak stopped and cocked his head. Suddenly he sprinted back, barking like an entire pack.

"Woh-WHO-O-O-ey! Woh-WHO-O-O-ey! AI-AI-AI-AI!"

Dak barked louder and sprinted harder.

Sunoya started to turn and look but caught herself. As she forced another step forward, pain ripped through her right thigh.

A spear plonked into the wet earth in front of her, quivering.

Sunoya grabbed its shaft to cushion her fall.

Now, even more fierce with elation, "Woh-WHO-O-O-ey! Woh-WHO-O-O-ey! AI-AI-AI-AI!"

Sunoya crashed onto a hip, protecting the child, and then spraddled onto her back.

Su-Li landed on his mistress's belly and faced Inaj. The Red Chief was out in front and in full charge. "Woh-WHO-O-O-ey! Woh-WHO-O-O-ey! AI-AI-AI-AI!"

He raised his war club. A few strides and he would crush Sunoya's head.

Su-Li hissed a warning.

Inaj laughed. "Her damn buzzard!" The words swirled with mad laughter in his head. "When I rape her, that will get rid of you. Then I can watch her die at my leisure." He cocked his war club.

"Ow!" The buzzard had grabbed his forearm.

He planted his feet and knocked the buzzard away. Except the damn bird didn't go.

Inaj dropped the war club and snatched it out of the air with the other hand, a trick he'd practiced hundreds of times. He roared in Su-Li's face and swung.

He found out how hard it is to hit a bird with a club.

On the ground Sunoya laughed out loud. "You can't even whip a bird!"

"There's one easy way, bitch!"

He jerked loose the knot that held up his breechcloth and leggings, and stood naked.

"Look at that!" Sunoya shouted, pointing. "Su-Li, eat it! It's barely a snack, but eat it!" Even to herself her laughter sounded insane.

Beyond Su-Li she saw Inaj's other three men charge up, bearing the certainty of death.

Su-Li swooped and pecked at Inaj's manhood.

Inaj hopped around and hollered.

Sunoya yawped out her own version of the Galayi war cry. *Why not?* "Woh-WHO-O-O-ey! Woh-WHO-O-O-ey! AI-AI-AI-AI!"

An answering cry came—"Woh-WHO-O-O-ey! Woh-WHO-O-O-ey! AI-AI-AI-AI!"—from the other direction.

Wilu, Zanda, and their companion veered off the trail and into the woods. Inaj took a look and scrambled after them.

In a moment Sunoya was surrounded by a score of Soco soldiers.

Tensa bent over her. "Sunoya, are you all right?"

She giggled. *Hell, no, I'm probably bleeding to death.*

She sat up, lifted Dahzi, and said, "Tensa, I present you a great gift. Your son. We call him Dahzi, the Hungry One."

Tensa took the child and held him up. The new father's face transformed, as from moon to sun. He hoisted the baby high overhead.

"Father," said Tensa, "this is my son!"

"Noney's child?" asked Ninyu.

Sunoya sidestepped the question and its terrible answer. "Look," said Sunoya, "the fingers of his left hand are webbed." Ninyu came and peered. All the men's eyes fastened on the webbed fingers.

In the forest Inaj grabbed Wilu by his breechcloth and hauled him down. He wrenched his son's spear away and spit out a fierce whisper. "Silence!"

He crept downhill. Cataracts of rage heaved him forward. *I will kill Sunoya.*

From the trees he saw the girl who pretended to be a medicine woman still sitting on the ground, surrounded.

Tensa—goddamned Tensa!—stood over her and held something high.

Inaj peered, commanding his brain to understand.

A naked baby. A boy. His damned grandson.

His rage cocked his arm and snapped it forward. The spear hurtled out from the green pine needles.

It pierced Tensa's back, slammed through his body, and sprayed blood out of his chest.

Tensa stood still for a moment, held by nothing more than sunlight. Then he collapsed onto Sunoya's legs. She screamed, and caught Dahzi in her arms.

TWO

Coming Apart

15

It was unspeakable. The Soco soldiers bore Tensa's blood-drenched body into the village, singing a song of grief for a fellow soldier.

Sunoya was limping from the rip in her thigh and woozy with fatigue. Ninyu carried his tiny grandson. Sunoya's heart sang a bass grief for Tensa and a treble rejoicing that she and the baby had set out on a difficult journey and arrived alive. As she asked the Immortals to guide the spirit of the fallen young man to the Darkening Land, she thanked them for the miracle of saving the life of the medicine-bearing boy child. Her emotions poured up and down, waterfalls going opposite directions. Her legs wobbled.

Tensa's sisters rushed out of their house and raised up cries of grief so intense Sunoya couldn't bear to listen.

A neighbor woman three times as old as Sunoya saw that the medicine woman could barely stand up and led her into her own house, helped her lie down, poulticed her wound, and gave her some food and water. Then she went out and came back with the child and Mother, and put Dahzi at the dog's tits.

When Sunoya was a child, this crone had been a neighbor, and she was gabby. Sunoya liked gossipy women and mustered up the energy to get her to chatting. "Five daughters in a row, then finally a son, one only son, now he's gone, ain't it awful?"

The woman wandered in her talk. From the blessed comfort of a borrowed pallet Sunoya asked what kind of adolescent Tensa had been. "One of them boys with high ideas, the kind people call noble and lotta families hope for. This un thinks maybe Ninyu hoped his son would become a White Chief." Of the three chiefs, most people thought White was the highest station.

The crone shook her head, as though people were foolish to want such high things and meddle in such impertinences as government.

Mother pulled away from Dahzi and wandered outside.

Sunoya forced another question from her weary throat.

"Yes, one of Ninyu's daughters is nursing. She has a boy nearly two. My grandchildren, they're grown already. Got me two great-grandchildren, one on the way, and I hope a passel more to come."

Bleary with fatigue, Sunoya snuggled Dahzi closer and gave herself up to sleep.

The baby sucked at the dry deer hide that covered her breasts.

❖

Time had never jangled so hard against itself. In the afternoon Ninyu and his family buried their only son properly. In the evening they enclosed themselves in their house to mourn. They grieved the loss of a *yuwi*, a being of spiritual energy, a unique life.

The next morning, hesitantly, the family gathered around their home's center fire and marveled at the new grandson in Sunoya's arms. Each of them felt the finger-webbing, each murmured, "The child of prophecy," and added phrases of hope.

Sunoya took a risk. "The Immortals have given him to me to raise," she said. "When they gave me Su-Li, they forbade me to have children. Because they intended me to bring up this medicine bearer, and train him for what he should be-come."

They studied the medicine woman uneasily. Ninyu took three or four deep breaths and settled it by saying, "Of course, you will be his mother."

So they made the other practical arrangements. The younger wife, Detala, was already giving Dahzi a breast. "And that boy is as hungry as his name," she exclaimed. Everyone agreed to tell Dahzi, when he was old enough to talk, to call Ninyu "Grandfather" and address his wives Detala and Nuna, which meant "awl" and "potato," as "Grandmother."

"And he'll call you 'Mother,'" said Detala to Sunoya.

Su-Li rasped from the smoke hole at the top of the hut. Ninyu looked up at him. The buzzard didn't like to be con-fined, but he wanted to hear.

"Naturally, you and the boy will live with us," said Ninyu.

Sunoya felt a sting of fear. She opened her mouth for a quick refusal when Su-Li interrupted in her head. *Accept. Too dangerous for us to live alone.*

Sunoya considered, but she was still uneasy. "Ninyu, I can-not let any man . . ."

"We remember the old stories. If you have a spirit animal, no man touches you."

Su-Li a-a-arked.

You will be a virgin and a mother! Thunderbird's words rang in her head.

Sunoya felt the tears come and then ordered them back. To weep with joy in a household drowning in grief—that would be thoughtless.

She looked at Ninyu's bleached face. She felt a swirl of fear and joy. From childhood Ninyu's face had scared her. "Thank you," she said. "I am honored, greatly honored, to be mother of the medicine bearer, the child of prophecy. Also honored to be taken into the home of the Red Chief."

No one spoke for a moment.

Sunoya checked the zadayi disc inside her dress. In the action it had flipped over. She turned it red side out.

Then she reached over and put her hand on Ninyu's arm. "How are you?" she asked him. It was out of line to ask, except that medicine people had certain privileges.

The chief's face rippled like darkening water. "Our family lost one *yuwi* and gained two."

She knew that he was only putting the best face on things. In any man's heart a newborn grandson would not make up for the death of a grown son.

After the week of intense mourning, the family took Dahzi to the village's Medicine Chief, who gave the boy a special blessing, carried him in a circle around the village, announced his name as Dahzi, the Hungry One, and led an honor song for the child of prophecy. The family joined in first, then all the people. They had heard rumors of the miracle child, but now they saw him for themselves, and smiles were broad. Most were glad that they, the Socos, and not the Tuscas, were given this boy. Su-Li flew slow loops above the celebrants.

Sunoya watched on tenterhooks. The Medicine Chief looked so decrepit that he might drop the boy. At the end of the song she clasped the child to her breast.

Ninyu raised his voice above the hubbub. "I have something to say."

People stopped talking. The Red Chief took Sunoya by the sleeve, strode to the middle of the circle so everyone could see them and hear him.

"Tensa has been murdered by the Red Chief of the Tuscas. That will lead to war between our villages. I tell you, though . . . I tell you that my son's death has awakened my heart. I will not lead such a war. Here and now I retire as Red Chief of the Socos."

He put his hand gently on Dahzi's forehead. "My new grandson is a medicine bearer. I hope that he will be able to turn every Soco's *zadayi* back to victory."

He walked to his own house with Sunoya, his wives, and his children trailing.

He waited until after supper to spring his next surprise on Sunoya. He took her out into the night air where they wouldn't be overheard. Su-Li rode on her shoulder.

"Sunoya," said Ninyu, "I want to ask for a great act of kindness from you."

In the darkness she couldn't read the eyes in his white face.

"I have spent my life on war, and it has brought me to grief. I am forty winters old. I'd like to follow the path of my own grandson. I want to spend the rest of my life learning medicine. Will you be my teacher?"

Sunoya was stunned. "I am much younger than you."

"Please."

She was taken aback to hear the word *please* from a great man. "Of course."

The moon caught his eyes, and she could see the light in them.

❖

During the next moon, the Moon of Short Days, by ancient custom the villagers would have gone to the Grandmother Sun Dance at the Cheowa village. However, the White Chief, Red Chief, and Medicine Chief talked it over and decided to stay home this year. After all, a War Chief of one of the villages had actually killed the son of their War Chief.

Instead of attending, the village sent a delegation of the three chiefs and well-armed men to register their protest at great council. If they did not get satisfaction, they would declare war on the Tuscas.

For Sunoya it was a horror. Here was what her dream had

predicted, the ruining of the Cape of Eagle Feathers, and all the misery that would follow.

Yet it was inevitable. She herself could not have gone and danced, drummed, and sung with Inaj, the murderer of her child's father. She would not have exposed the baby to the wrath of his vengeful grandfather. Inaj's spear had set these consequences in motion.

When the three chiefs and the soldiers left for the ceremony, she was already sure that she and the Galayi had only one hope, that the child of prophecy would somehow save them.

So she spent the Moon of Short Days tending to her son. She was not the Medicine Chief here, and did not bear the daily obligations of that position. True, the Soco Medicine Chief was not a shaman of Sunoya's power. In his lifetime he would make only one journey to the Land beyond the Sky Arch. By the beat of her drum and with the help of the *u-tsa-le-ta*, Sunoya could soar to the land above and seek the counsel of the Immortals.

Sunoya was satisfied with her position—she felt honored. As the second most powerful medicine person in the tribe, behind only Tsola, she was given responsibility not for her village but for the medicine bearer. In him, and through the blessings of the Immortals, her special abilities would bear fruit.

For now, she enjoyed the routines of taking care of Dahzi. When he wet himself or soiled himself, she changed his blankets and stuffed the inner bark of the cedar tree in them as an absorbent. She played with him. She babbled with him, napped with him, held him.

She also reveled daily in commonplace activities she had missed during her years devoted to training as a shaman. She played sister to Ninyu's grown children, and co-mother to their children. She gossiped with his wives, especially about who was courting who, which woman was pregnant, and which man was slipping around with whose wife. She helped prepare food, sew clothes, clean the house. She mended cuts and scrapes, soothed feelings, settled squabbles, and helped make their home a happy place to live. Though she was forbidden to love a man at night and start a child in her own belly, she took pleasure in the sounds that told her that other women were doing that. She happily watched the children grow, especially her own son. *Son*—that word rang in her heart.

Before the end of the Moon of Short Days the delegation came back with the inescapable news. They had demanded that Inaj cover Tensa's bones, that is, make lavish gifts to his family as recompense. Inaj had defied them. He had declared to the council that he wasn't the murderer—Sunoya was. She killed his daughter and stole his grandson. Publicly, loudly, he declared that he would kill this evil woman and reclaim his progeny. If he had to shed the blood of all the Soco villagers to get justice, he would do it.

The council ended in acrimony, the ceremony in disarray.

"Don't worry," said the White Chief. All three chiefs were sitting with Sunoya, Ninyu, and the entire family. Detala had served the adults sassafras tea. "Socos stand up for each other. We will fight Inaj if we have to, however we have to, for as long as we have to."

The Red Chief put in, "We do think you should take some precautions. I'm sorry to have to say this. Inaj will sneak first, attack second. One of your relatives, men you trust, should stand guard on Sunoya and the baby every moment of every day. When Sunoya walks through the village, when she sleeps, even when she goes to the river to pee. Every moment."

"Agreed," said Ninyu.

The Medicine Chief said, "What can your spirit guide do to help?

Su-Li said, *Tell them I'll keep watch from the skies. Anything else is between you and me.*

Sunoya said, "He has the eyesight of an eagle and a nose that's even sharper. He can smell enemies from the tops of mountains. He'll keep a sky watch for us."

"Good."

Sunoya smiled at her buzzard friend. He'd also enjoy being aloft, not sitting around trapped in a hut.

When the chiefs left, Ninyu said, "It's all right, Sunoya. We are honored to take care of you and the child."

She thought, *No, it's not all right being watched every moment. It's like being in prison.* She said, "You're very kind to us."

❖

Within a week a Soco man out hunting deer got a spear through the belly. Though the killer took the spear away, no one had any doubt who was responsible.

Within a moon two women gathering rose hips along the creek were kidnapped. One moon later they straggled into the village. Their tale was rape. They said their bellies could be full of children by any number of men, Tusca men. One added, "Probably Inaj."

The chiefs of the Socos did the inevitable. They declared that Inaj's acts demanded much more than satisfying the cry of Tensa's spirit for redress. This was no longer just a matter for Tensa's clan or the need for balance in the world. "We are at war," they declared, "with the Tuscas."

That meant their new Red Chief was now the village governor. No Galayi band had ever been at war with another.

Sunoya and Su-Li conferred quietly with Ninyu. "Do anything to stop this declaration of war," Sunoya said. "It will delight Inaj. It will make him all-powerful."

Ninyu said, "I am no longer a chief—this was bound to happen."

Word spread as fast as storms blew across the land. A runner came from the Cheowa village, begging the Socos to revoke the declaration.

"Did you tell Inaj the same?" the Red Chief asked.

"Yes."

"What did he say?"

"Inaj mocked me."

A runner from the Cusa village came with words even more urgent. The Cusa village was traditionally a place of sanctuary. They never entered into war for any reason, and offered refuge to any person being threatened. The messenger reminded the Soco chiefs of the great commandment of the Immortals when they created the People of the Caves, that no Galayi might ever shed the blood of another. He begged them to consider what punishments the Immortals might rain down upon the tribe if two bands made war on each other.

The chiefs told him to go home without even repeating this foolishness to the Tuscas. The Red Chief said, "The land is already aflame with war."

"Now Inaj is laughing," Sunoya told Ninyu. "He's laughing at us, laughing at the world, laughing at the Immortals."

Ninyu asked Sunoya, "How long will Inaj go on?"

"As long as we don't turn Dahzi over to him. You've got to do something."

"There's nothing I can do. For the moment, Ahsginah, the Evil One, reigns."

16

W hen spring came, the two warring villages risked going to the Planting Moon Ceremony. It was the dance
that brought full bellies to the people for the entire year—the
corn crop, ground, was a staple during the winter. Besides, no
one would dare violate the truce of these sacred dances.

"Still," said Ninyu, "we'll keep two guards on you and the
Hungry One all the time."

As soon as they made camp along the river above the village, an old man brought Sunoya a message. "Tsola wants to
see you tonight. You and the child."

Sunoya smiled. She knew this old man for what he was.

She had made a full day's travel carrying Dahzi already today, but for Tsola she could walk another hour up to Emerald
Cave. "Eat with us and we'll go."

"We'll wait until dark," said the old man.

The two guards were mystified when Sunoya told them
she and the child would be going to the Emerald Cavern that
night with the old man. They were more scandalized when
she said she'd be taking the child, and petrified at the edge
of the camp when the old man began to change. Fingers to
claws. Arms to forelegs. Skin to fur. Face to muzzle. Teeth to
fangs.

The panther turned to the guards. "Just follow and keep
calm. I see well in the dark."

In the middle of the night, though the Cavern knew neither day nor night, Tsola held the Hungry One, the child of
prophecy, and giggled. Sunoya laughed. She wasn't used to
seeing the Wounded Healer act this way. Tsola even held the

child toward the fire, for his sake, though she preferred the cool of the Cavern, and the darkness.

Sunoya reached up and stroked Su-Li's feathers. He still disliked caves, especially this vast one, and he could travel to the spirit world without Tsola's help.

Tsola got an extra blanket, wrapped the child tighter, and sat a few steps from the embers. "I have something on my mind."

"Talk her out of it," said the panther, Klandagi.

Sunoya frowned at him. She was used to Klandagi's voice, human with a hint of growl, but this was abrasive.

"I'll take this tone with her if I have to," said Klandagi. "It's my job to save her. The people need her."

"Let me tell Sunoya," said Tsola.

When Tsola finished her proposal, Sunoya was rigid with fright. Tsola uncovered the child's face and looked at it, waiting for Sunoya to say something.

After a long pause, Klandagi spoke instead. He howled like a beast, a wail of woe. Then he said, "If you do this, the clansmen of the chiefs you offend will rise up and kill you."

His mother gave him a stricken look.

"All I will be able to do is die trying to protect you."

Tsola seemed to go away for a moment.

"When the tribe loses you, it loses everything," the panther argued.

The Seer composed herself and answered evenly, "If I don't do something, they've already lost everything."

She let them sit on this notion. Klandagi padded to one of the clay-covered walls, stood up with his back against it, and scratched his spine, mucking his glossy coat with mud.

"I have to do my work," she went on. "Sometimes being the Seer is hard. I can't just wait and hope that this baby—"

Knowing his mother, Klandagi said, "And what are you *not* saying?"

Tsola sighed, looked long at the child, and said, "I love to wear the Cape. Wear it and hear its music. That is the legacy of the Seers."

Klandagi eyed his mother hard.

Tsola said to Sunoya, "What are your thoughts?"

"I . . . I don't know. It's daring." She cursed herself for being mealy-mouthed. "Seer, it's . . . You just can't."

Tsola blanked her face with thought—Sunoya was amazed at how smooth and beautiful the face was—and after a few moments snapped back to them. "When I took on this task, I accepted everything that goes with it," Tsola said.

Klandagi said, "It's *their* problem."

Tsola's eyes shot a plea to Sunoya. Her pupil and friend pursed her mouth and drew an idle pattern in the cave floor with a finger. After a while she said, "Well, then, let's figure it out."

Tsola motioned for Klandagi to join them. Her son didn't move.

"Listen to me," she called across the room to him. "I'm not going to live forever." Seers and their families had the gift and burden of living for a hundred and thirty or forty winters. "I've always had the power of the Cape. The people have always had the benefit. It's my calling."

Klandagi rumbled from the wall, "Think of what the people will lose."

"They need the Cape."

The man-panther curled his lips in thought, then walked forward and coiled next to his mother. His tail snaked up and down on the ground like a rattler.

After a few minutes of talk the two women grew excited, and Klandagi was helping out.

For more than a day, except that daylight was unknown in the Cavern, they chased ideas, tested possibilities, anticipated difficulties, devised and threw out tactics, created strategies.

Tsola roasted some deer meat Klandagi had brought in his jaws. He complained about cooked flesh being pallid stuff.

At last they considered themselves finished. All three were exhilarated and frightened. Tsola said simply, "Then I will see you tomorrow afternoon." The time of the Council of the Planting Moon.

Sunoya nodded and rose.

"We will change everything," said Tsola. Her face hadn't looked so young in Sunoya's lifetime.

"One way or another," said Sunoya.

Su-Li launched from her shoulder and wing-flapped through the corridors of stone, longing for oceans of air. Sunoya picked up her son. Alongside Klandagi she padded after her airborne companion.

17

At dawn the next day Sunoya shook her head and opened her eyes. The faint light crept through the leaves of her brush hut. "This is it," she told Su-Li. Her voice sounded weak even to her.

The buzzard had nothing to say.

She propped herself up on an elbow on her pallet of buffalo hides and peered at him. She poked fun at herself. "How come, no matter how early I wake up, you're always aiming that eye at me?"

The red-gold eye glinted.

Dahzi stirred and cried. Sunoya picked him up and rocked him. "No need to wake everyone," she said softly. The rest of the family was in brush huts on each side of her. He wailed again.

"You're hungry. Okay. I'll go next door and wake folks up and get you something to eat."

When she came back, she put Dahzi on a knee and fed him corn mush. "You know what?" Sunoya said to her son. "Today is Momma's big day." She spooned him another mouthful. "Momma and Grandmother Tsola are calling up a regular thunderstorm of change. You just watch."

A buzzard couldn't smile, in amusement or otherwise, but Sunoya thought he wanted to.

Su-Li squeezed his perch with his talons, fluttered his wings, and gave her a look. She knew he didn't like being trapped in the hut. "So you're hungry, too."

She tapped her shoulder. With one flap Su-Li landed there, and she stroked his feathers. "My guide," she said and gave him a wry smile, "red-faced and eats the dead. You get along, then."

She reached for a piece of dried meat and lifted the hide door of the low hut. Su-Li waited. "Dak," she called. The dog rumbled up for the meat. Sunoya tossed it far out the door, and the dog pounced on it.

Su-Li hopped out the door awkwardly and took wing before Dak noticed him. Every day they went through this routine. Su-Li couldn't be killed—*he* wasn't mortal—but it wouldn't be fun to get his tail feathers pulled out, or his wing broken.

Back in the dimness Sunoya held up her hands and looked at them. She was feeling wild and crazy. "I was born webbed," she said. Even alone she didn't mention that both hands were once like that. She picked up Dahzi and shushed him. "You're webbed. Together we're going to change the world. I'm starting it today. I'm going to raise you to finish it. And if I mess it up, well then, the people will remember me as a failure the size of Bald Mountain."

Holding Dahzi, she crawled through the low door and looked up into the bright sky. Her eyes lanced up to the buzzard, his wings angled up as he glided down to the river. The crisp light of the early sun glinted on their black and silver undersides.

❖

Su-Li raised his beak from the river water, and falling drops gleamed. He took a couple of awkward steps—the ground was a graceless place—flapped his wings, let his scarlet head slide forward, and lifted off. After a night cooped up inside, winging into the air made his blood pump. The sky was his escape from the world of mortality. It was limitless.

Su-Li spread his wing tips and arced to the left. He sliced across the river, looking down. He could do this service for Sunoya easily. With all the Galayi assembled here for the ceremony, she wanted him to keep an eye out. Gathered together like this, over a thousand strong, the Galayi were probably safe from other tribes, and surely no one would violate this sacred ceremony. But because of Tsola's plans for today, Sunoya asked him to keep a double-sure lookout.

Su-Li wing-flapped higher, so he could see far up and down the river. Four clusters of houses dotted the stream over a couple of miles, thick-walled buildings of wattle and daub. Sunflowers and knotweed grew on terraces, corn closest to the river. This was the home of the hosts, the Cheowa.

Between these villages clustered the camps of the other three bands, each several hundred people. They slept in brush huts and slurped food down fast, eager to spend as much time as possible visiting relatives and friends, flirting and courting, dancing and singing.

Su-Li sailed as slowly as he could, cruising one by one over the mountain slopes behind the camps and villages. He flapped his way across the river and lifted on the warm currents that swooshed up the mountainsides. He saw no signs of enemies.

As he cruised over the main Cheowa village at the mouth of Emerald Creek, he stayed high. He looked down at the council lodge and wondered how Tsola would fare there this evening. He had a sudden memory of a boy in one of the camps flinging a stone at him with a slingshot yesterday. *Idiocy.*

The life of these particular human beings grieved him. They lived in ignorance, fighting with each other and with all the other animals.

He let the warm winds carry him above the ridge and up the creek. No signs of danger. He could see a louse in a person's hair, and smell more keenly than that. There was no way he could miss enemies crawling close.

He flew on to the Cavern and the Pool of Healing, checking on Tsola. Three figures walked slowly down the trail toward the mouth of the creek, where the big village was. Su-Li would keep a close eye on their progress.

He sailed on to the mountain divide behind and rose in widening circles, higher and higher. He relished the cool air, the sun on his red skin, and the lift beneath his wings. If he did not have a mission from Sunoya, he would have roamed the sky for the sheer pleasure of flight. From here he could see mountain ridge after mountain ridge. Though he couldn't see it among the hills east of the mountains, the Tusca village sat there, a week's walk away for human beings. Over one ridge to the south and a day's walk along the river was the Soco village, and much further southwest the Cusa village. He could have flown to all of them, spent the night in a tree in the Cusa village, and then winged back in half a day. Freedom to roam.

At last he drifted back down the ridge on the other side of the creek. No danger anywhere, and the three figures continued their slow pace to the creek and to the council ground.

He coasted toward the camp of the Socos, where his companion lived. She was walking slowly toward the main Cheowa village, going to the council early. She looked up at him and held up her arm as a sign. He spiraled downward and landed on her shoulder.

All safe, he told her.

She cleared her throat and answered in words. "Except in the hearts and minds of human beings."

Su-Li said without words, *The Wounded Healer is on her way.*

18

"Every step is an adventure," said Tsola.

"A threat," corrected Klandagi. He walked alongside her in his panther shape. He enjoyed this irony. What an odd sight his family was—a woman about a hundred winters old making her way down the trail alongside Emerald Creek, her younger daughter of about seventy winters, and a black panther. He had no time to savor it, though. His eyes, ears, nose, his entire being were hunting for danger.

His mother, the Seer, fingered her daughter's sleeve on one side and rested a hand on the cat's back on the other. She wore a blindfold.

The panthers of this country were tawny, but Klandagi preferred to garb himself in the color of the felines of ancient stories, black as obsidian, dark as his heart. He wasn't used to being scared, and he hated it.

He was nervous about what was behind him, too. He had decided it was essential to protect the medicine bearer, so Dahzi was wrapped in a robe and held in the arms of Klandagi's other sister, deep inside the Emerald Cavern.

Tsola knew how upset her son was. Even blindfolded, she planted her feet with a firmness that said, *Never mind that now.*

She gave a giddy little laugh. Strange and wonderful—she was truly in the outside world. For decades she'd lived deep in the Cavern, visiting only its mouth to see her family, and then only in the dark of the moon. The world of the Cavern opened the door to wonders of the spirit world but deprived her of the joys of Turtle Island. In place of the open air, the far-reaching sky, the smells of blossoms, the sounds of birds, the wind, she had solitude, darkness, confinement, and sterility. Except near entrances, nothing grew in caves.

She was grateful for her son and daughters. Since she'd been a mature woman before she became the Seer, she'd had a husband and children.

Sunoya had a harder road to walk, a child but no husband, and no experience of love between a woman and a man.

"Tell me what everything looks like." This was to her daughter, Kanesga.

The panther interjected, "Su-Li is circling above us, keeping a sharp eye out."

Tsola cuffed him, half affection, half exasperation.

After a moment Kanesga began to describe the craggy ridge tops, the green mountainsides, the new growth on budding trees and bushes.

"Planting Moon," said Tsola. She had not planted, felt the loamy earth in her fingers, in more than half a century. She felt girlish.

Kanesga drew a word picture of the blue sky and dazzling white clouds that cupped the mountains, and multitudes of birds fluttering from tree to tree. Of all Earth's creatures, aside from her own people, Tsola loved birds the most. *Maybe I'm lucky to be blindfolded. Seeing might be overwhelming.*

She felt her son's back muscles bunch up in irritation, but disregarded it. It only meant that Klandagi cared about her, and he had a right to be worried. Only she could understand her wild feelings. She loved the Emerald Cavern, but hadn't realized how much she missed the rest of Turtle Island.

"Is the village in sight yet?" One foot after another, toward her native place.

"When it is," Klandagi muttered, "they'll be able to see us."

All these years, only an hour's walk away, her birthplace. She looked forward to hearing children playing and dogs yapping. She imagined the women huddled up and talking comfortably as they kept one eye on their broods. She wondered if the scents of hundreds of human bodies would disagree with her nose. The odors of the Cavern were earth and water.

Kanesga started to picture for her the sun falling toward the western mountains.

"Too much," said Tsola, her voice pebbled with joy and pain. Too much because she yearned to see the sunrise and would never be able to. Even the glints of sun around the edges of the blindfold hurt her eyes.

"Tell me what my face looks like." She hadn't seen herself reflected in water since she became the tribe's Seer.

Kanesga thought her mother was lovely, but she knew better than to tell her so. "You look like your name." The word tsola meant "tobacco."

"I'm like a leaf all wrinkled and hung up to dry." They chuckled together.

"Far enough," said Klandagi. From this curve in the creek he caught a glimpse of an edge of the village.

"The trees." The two of them led Tsola off the trail and over broken ground into the pines on the mountain slope. Klandagi said, "I'll be back."

He padded toward an outcropping of rocks, head gliding from side to side, golden eyes glinting as they searched for prey, or for enemies. At the outcropping he slipped with cat grace between some rocks, found a crevice, and coiled where he could peer down.

In the tangerine light of sunset the village looked normal, except that the men were gathering by the council lodge. Klandagi took his time and surveyed the scene carefully. Only his tail told of his edginess. Wariness was his way. Enemies were his job. And he hated this risk.

He pivoted his head smoothly and looked back. He had grown used to his strange family. All of them were ancient, though their bodies still looked youthful. Most of their children and grandchildren lived downstream in the village, but seldom came to visit. He felt more strange yet—more at ease being a cat than a human being.

Klandagi turned his head toward the village again, let his eyes flick over the entire scene, and then focused on the council lodge. It was a round, thatched roof with open sides. He marked swift ways in and out, and noted the nearest cover. His mother thought only of the triumph she hoped for. Klandagi saw the hazards. He forced himself to consider, now, the potential for catastrophe, the danger to the very life of the Seer.

People milled here and there. Children ran around, and some tried to ride the pack dogs.

The lodge was almost full now. He identified the four groups of chiefs treading slowly toward this once-a-year council. He noted with satisfaction that twilight was seeping into the valley. *Darkness will favor us.*

Klandagi bounded back to his mother and sister. Keeping his voice neutral, he said, "Let's go in."

The Seer smiled at him.

Klandagi had been making this transformation for decades, and it was almost instantaneous. Perhaps someone might have seen a hint of swirling dust, or felt a stirring in the air. A vigorous-looking and well-armed elderly man gazed back at his mother, took her arm, and led the way, alert as any hunter.

19

From the back row of the Council House, in the shadows, Sunoya watched Talani, the Peace Chief of the host Cheowas, make his slow way through the crowd to the council circle and his place of honor beside the fire. This was the sacred flame kept since the first people came to Turtle Island. Seeing that the creatures there needed fire, Thunderbird hurled a lightning bolt into a hollow tree and set it on fire. The Immortals also sent down messengers to teach the people to preserve this fire with powerful prayers and a special ceremony. It was kept alive every hour of every day by wise men taught these ways.

Talani was aged, and like all the Peace Chiefs dressed entirely in white—shirt, breechcloth, and thigh-high boots of deerskin tanned the color of old bones. A cape of white feathers wrapped him, his badge of office. In his left arm Talani carried his white stone pipe, and in his right he cradled the wing of a white crane. His white hair was piled elaborately on top of his head, making him seem by far the tallest man among the Galayi. Men of the Long Hair clan liked to make great displays of their hair.

Sunoya and Tsola were counting on the old man, the most admired of the White Chiefs, though no longer strong in body. The twelve chiefs sat together around the fire, sunwise: White, Red, and Medicine.

Su-Li touched Sunoya's cheek with a wing. Three elderly people, one of them blindfolded, were coming toward her. Sunoya made room and whispered greetings. No one noticed them in the smoke and shadows.

The old chief filled his pipe in a deliberate way, picked up an ember from the eternal fire, dropped it onto the sacred to-bacco, and drew the tobacco spirit into his lungs. Then he puffed it up to the sky and spoke the ritual words that asked that this smoke, which was his breath and his prayers, be carried high beyond the Sky Arch to the ears of the spirits.

His words formed a sculpture as elaborate as his hair. The Galayi loved oratory, and Talani had won his place as White Chief with the beauty of his speech, like the music of rain.

He addressed the four directions, and the special powers that lived in each. "These are the four pathways of the people," he said, "which meet here at the sacred fire." He gestured to it with his pipe.

He prayed eloquently for all the Galayi who lived in the green center, here and now. "We people are living in hard times," he said, "hard times, hard times." These last words were a dying melody.

"For the first time in the memories of the grandfathers of the oldest men," Talani said, "we are at war with each other. These are such times as bring the Black Man of Death to our young warriors; grief to their wives and children and parents; hunger during the long winters; impoverishment to many families; and worst of all, a sickness of spirit to all Galayi people."

Talani raised his voice to a high pitch now, and his speech took on the singsong of a climax. He bemoaned living his time as chief as a man painted blue, mired in sadness and defeat. He prayed that his grandchildren would paint themselves in white, live in continual happiness. He bade all Galayi to turn their faces to the red east and to fly like eagles into the rising sun and to victory.

After a long moment of silence Talani passed the pipe sunwise. Everyone admired his eloquence.

Now each of the three chiefs from all four bands would smoke the pipe and ask the smoke to carry all Galayi prayers to the spirits. All the people gathered behind these leaders would send similar prayers up to the sky.

Sunoya grimaced. Not every heart was good, not every prayer was for peace, and most of the prayers were feeble.

She sucked at her anger like a burned spot on her tongue.

The pipe made its way around the circle. A puff or two for each chief and brief prayers. All of the Peace Chiefs and War Chiefs were men, two of the four Medicine Chiefs women.

Sitting next to Sunoya, slowly, subtly, Klandagi transformed himself from an elderly man into a black panther. She looked fearfully at Su-Li on her opposite shoulder. The buzzard seemed to chuckle as he told her, *It's fine, no one is paying attention.*

Inaj took the pipe, smoked, and presumably prayed. Sunoya wondered what sacred thoughts could live in the mind of a man like him.

When the pipe had made its circle, Talani rose to speak again.

Before he uttered a word, Tsola whispered, "It's time." The Seer, Sunoya, and the panther got to their feet and made their way to the sacred fire. This violation of protocol was so flagrant that Talani was stunned into silence. Whispers scratched their way around the room. Su-Li squeezed Sunoya's shoulder, left talon, right talon.

When people got a good look at the intruders, they dropped their jaws. Tsola was blindfolded, steadied on one side with a hand on the back of a black panther. On the other side Sunoya bore a buzzard on her shoulder and held Tsola's arm.

Courtesy swerved like a drunk. A child cried. People spoke aloud. Some of the twelve chiefs half-rose—not a single Peace Chief or War Chief had ever seen the Wounded Healer. Every head craned toward the slight figure of the tribe's Seer.

Sunoya didn't know which was bigger, astonishment at the unprecedented appearance of the most powerful chief of the nation, or fear of the black cat.

"She's not blind," stage-whispered several people. "It's just that the light hurts her eyes."

"Look at the bundle."

Tsola carried in one arm a bundle of white buckskin, held in reverence.

They threaded their way to Talani. Tsola set the bundle gently in front of the fire and asked, "May I smoke?"

It would never have crossed Talani's mind to refuse this request from the Seer.

Tsola puffed ritually. The panther stood beside her, flicking his tail. Sunoya resisted touching the deerskin wrap again. Klandagi had dreaded taking it out of the Cavern. His predator hearing brought him people's whispers.

"Look at her dress."

"She's amazing."

His mother's entire appearance was a declaration. Her daughters had woven a dress from the inner bark of the mulberry tree and dyed it emerald. They rubbed her high moccasins with clay until they were a deep red-brown. They dyed a red stripe in her silky, silver hair from forehead to waist, to show that she was of the Paint Clan, the traditional clan of medicine people. They made her a blindfold and colored it with brown and yellow stripes on the top and bottom and a broad band of green down the middle.

Klandagi was tickled to see the awe on the faces of the chiefs. Green signified Turtle Island, brown was the color of the underworld, and yellow represented the realm above, where the spirits dwelled. Only the Medicine Chief of the Emerald Cavern, the Seer, had the power to travel freely in all three realms, and show others the way.

She handed the pipe to Sunoya, pushed a little on Klandagi's back, rose to her feet, and faced everyone. Seeing her full on, people oohed and aahed.

The Seer said to Sunoya, "Please give me the bundle."

Her heart pounding, Sunoya did. She murmured, "Forgive us, Powers."

Tsola unfolded the deerskin, lifted out the Cape of Eagle Feathers, held it high overhead, and turned it slowly in a circle in front of all eyes. The feathers were the reddish brown of the war eagle, with a wing sewn on each side of the front opening. The eagle's golden head made a cap for the one person who had the authority to wear it, the Seer.

The people were wonder-struck. This totem was as old as the Galayi people themselves, given to them when death first came to the living creatures of Earth. It was a symbol of their great pact with the spirit beings. Over all the generations since, only the Seers had actually laid eyes on it.

Klandagi knew the people didn't understand its true power. Some had even believed it to be an idle tale for children. He knew his mother would not put the Cape on, not as it was now.

The Seer began to speak of the totem. "Every Galayi has heard of the Cape of Eagle Feathers, but you do not know that its power has been spoiled. I want you to see for yourselves," she said. In a mottled voice she added, "And smell."

Klandagi looked at the chiefs' eyes when they heard that word. Anyone could see right away that the Cape was spotted with blood and blackened with mold. But Klandagi doubted that their noses were keen enough to pick up the putrid odor.

Now the Seer called upon her own eloquence, even finer than Talani's. "This Cape," said the Seer, "was given to the Galayi people by the spirit beings who live beyond the Sky Arch. It is our means of communication with them."

She hesitated. Every Galayi knew this tale, more or less, but surely none ever dreamed they would ever hear it from the Seer herself. "The Seer is caretaker of the Emerald Cavern. One of the responsibilities of the position is to fold yourself in the Cape at appointed times and listen to the wisdom the spirit beings have for us. The Cape has been our font of wisdom."

Klandagi's legs itched to spring. He could smell danger. He liked attacking and hated waiting.

"Now we have lost this power. For us the spirit beings are distant and weak. We are like a man lying at the bottom of a lake. He can see the sun vaguely, but it has no meaning to him. Like him, we are dying."

She paused, letting them think about it.

"There is worse. The Cape is made of the feathers of the war eagle, as you see, and it binds the eagles to carry our prayers to the spirit beings. Since we are without it, the eagles do not help us. Why are we living in such a pitiful way? You need wonder no longer."

Now her voice burned with intensity, and she did something stunning. She switched away from the formal style of the Galayi language used for prayer and council speech to the idiom of everyday talk. After her earlier avian flights of beauty, these words sounded rough as an axe breaking a stone, a spear thunking into a tree.

"We are walking in darkness because we commit acts unworthy of the Galayi. I can barely bring myself to utter these next words." Now her voice frothed with disgust. "We fight against each other. We kill each other. And in that way we have destroyed the Cape."

Klandagi and Sunoya snatched and held their breaths in the same moment. Tsola was taking a terrible risk. No one had ever spoken like this in council. Would it make her words repugnant to the people, especially to the chiefs? Or shock them into realization?

Klandagi growled and looked the chiefs in the eyes. *See how lethal I am.*

"Today I am taking an unprecedented step, showing all of you this totem. I do it to bring a lightning bolt of understanding to our minds: We must strive to find a way to restore the Cape, or persuade the Immortals to give us another one.

"The first step is to return to the basic virtue of all Galayi. None of us may kill another—not ever, not for any reason."

Tsola turned and looked at the Soco War Chief, then at Inaj.

Klandagi gathered his feet beneath him. He flicked his eyes up at Su-Li. The buzzard was ready, too.

The Seer went on in smoldering words. "The fault lies with the Red Chief of the Tusca band. The fighting need never have started, except that to feed his thirst for vengeance, and his ambitions, he instigated it."

Klandagi watched Inaj. The man was still as a star, just as the panther would be in the moment before he struck. *Your damned ego.*

The Seer took a deep breath, switched back to formal language, and made her voice into a great call to all the people. "Grandparents and grandchildren, mothers and fathers, sons and daughters, let us now all join together. Let us pledge ourselves again to what it means to be a Galayi. Let us all promise never to shed the blood of any other Galayi again."

Klandagi knew the worst would come now. Tsola would loose a whirlwind wrath and never be able to stop it.

"To cleanse ourselves of wrongdoing, to renew the Cape of Eagle Feathers and reestablish our connection with the wisdom of the spirits, we must take one action, and do it today. This step is severe but essential. If any Galayi has slain another in the last winter, his War Chief must step down now. Tonight. Then his band may elect a new man."

Murmurs rumbled through the room like wild river rapids.

"I call on the Red Chief of the Soco band to speak." She chose him because he'd been elected only recently, and might waver. She stepped sunwise around the circle and handed him the white pipe.

As though opening the door to words will matter to them, thought Klandagi.

As Tsola passed Inaj without a glance, the Tusca War Chief felt rage like howling winds in his guts. He almost grabbed the Seer.

The Soco chief lifted the pipe to the sky, and he seemed to consider it. When at last he spoke, his voice quaked. Inaj wanted to throttle him.

"I regret these moons of enmity between tribesmen."

Liar, thought Inaj. *You like fighting as much as I do.*

"Like all the Galayi people I yearn to see them come to an end."

Inaj heard an undertone in his enemy's voice that hinted at other feelings. *But you are a coward and will not speak them.*

"I don't know whether this is the right step. It may be. In the hope that it is, I step down as Red Chief of the Socos."

Are you getting in line to be a revered elder? I would have crushed such a weakling easily.

The Soco chief seemed to ponder whether he had more words. Even the manner of his pause was self-effacing.

The hush was transitory and precious, like the last glimmer of bronze light before the sun gives way to darkness.

Inaj leapt to his feet and broke the silence. "You know nothing," he barked at the Seer.

People were so shocked they barely knew why. Because a Galayi was interrupting a speaker in council? Or because he was insulting the Wounded Healer grossly?

Inaj's words crawled forward in a tone so low the people could barely hear him. "You know less than nothing." He spat on the ground at Tsola's feet.

Klandagi held himself back against a surge of energy.

"Seer, Wounded Healer, under any title you are a relic of a time long gone, and good riddance."

Tsola tore her blindfold off, stepped close to Inaj, and glared into his eyes. Klandagi flinched, and then realized the council house had grown dark.

Inaj's fury carried him on. "The world does not wait for fools. These times require the strength of a warrior, the commitment of a warrior, the courage of a warrior. Peace makes weak men. . . ."

"Shut up!" the Seer said.

For a moment violence throbbed in the air.

"Sit down."

Inaj did. Then he had a second thought, rose, and stalked off.

The river rapids of murmurs ran again. Klandagi checked the Soco chief's eyes. The man was so scared he was about to fly away in all directions at once. Klandagi turned his head to follow Inaj's exit. He despised this chief, but respected him. Inaj strode straight away without looking back.

In a calm voice the Seer put everything in Talani's hands. "I think the two chiefs have stated their thoughts, one on each side. May the other chiefs now decide the fate of our people." She passed the pipe to Talani, put a hand on the panther's withers, and sat down.

Klandagi rotated his head from side to side, eyeing every face. Fortunately, the human beings could barely see. *Will there be a fight?*

He felt his mother's hand on him, half for her comfort, half to hold him back.

"I will win," she whispered.

"Or be exiled or killed."

Sunoya put her hand gently on the Seer's.

Talani passed the pipe, inviting the other chiefs to speak. Klandagi's muscles began to relax. The tone of most speakers was uncertain. The words of the White Chief of the Socos were blunt. "All of us know that the Seer is telling the truth. Her remedy is the right one—to cut off two gangrenous fingers." Then the other chiefs chimed in with reluctant acceptance of the Seer's proposal.

Sunoya smelled success, but all was still up to Talani.

When all the chiefs had spoken, Talani's words were quiet and soothing. He said that the leaders of the people were agreed that the Red Chiefs of the Tusca and Soco bands must step aside. He suggested that the bands could choose their new war chiefs here at this ceremony, so that everyone could see that good will now reigned.

Sunoya said softly to the Seer, "You did it."

20

The drum seemed to thump the news to every ear. People gathered around the dance, and they heard it. Others walked the trails toward their camps or to the dance ground, and they heard it.

"The Seer is here!"

"She made the Red Chief of the Tuscas stand down."

"The War Chief of the Socos, too."

"I can't believe it."

Men and women smiled too much. Children didn't understand, but they played with more spring in their steps.

From a distance, upriver and down, all heard the drum, the beat that would not cease for a moment, day or night, until the last dance ended on the last day. For the moment its rhythm was a simple heart thump, the pulse of the ceremony, the people, the earth.

The anticipation of the dance made everyone happy.

When musicians felt the readiness, the beat changed—a quick-footed, loose-bodied figure flew from drums and tortoiseshell rattles.

This was the Monster Dance, robed and masked bogeymen

jangling into the circle of the people. Most represented enemies from nearby tribes in caricature. The chestnut masks were elaborate and wild. Teeth stuck out of mouths like fingers, gleaming white and stained with blood. A nose ring was big enough to pass a head through.

The monsters dashed at adults and lunged at children, but their crazy legs always made them stumble or veer off in another direction. The victims laughed and screamed at the same time, but never got caught.

One figure was a ghost, his mask the crinkly leaves of a wasp nest, the bottom of the nest a sneaky mouth. He wandered about making eerie sounds.

Several of the masked dancers bristled with vulgar sexuality. Two men displayed long-necked gourds as penises and scrotums. One dancer had arranged a buffalo leg bone as a dangling phallus, a buffalo tail dangling on each side, the bottom tufts of hair tied into globes.

The women laughed and pointed and made rude jokes about the size and usefulness of the dancers' actual equipment. They gave the monsters names spontaneously—Scrawny Dick, Mouse Tail Dick, and so on and so on.

Everyone found these antics hilarious. The crowd favorite was a monster who had built a little bellows that emitted a huge, watery, farting sound. Whenever he sounded off, the children giggled and screamed.

Suddenly, Sunoya dashed into the center of the circle, waving her arms wildly and stomping her feet. Any shaman could play this role, and Sunoya felt grand. "Tell me your names!"

The monsters fell silent.

"Your names!" Sunoya roared like the winds in the Moon When It Blows.

One by one, the robed figures answered with the names assigned them by the women, Crooked Dick, Skinny Dick, and more like that.

"Why did you come to this dance?"

One monster yelled, "To stick our spears into your men."

The others bellowed, "And our pricks into your wives."

Immediately they ran at various women, grabbed their breasts or bottoms, got behind them and pretended to hump them.

Sunoya whirled to face the musicians, raised her arms, and made her hands quiver. The drums and the rattles boomed and clattered a mad, deafening beat. Everyone screamed. The masked enemies cringed, fell to the ground, and covered their ears. The music banged to a climax and stopped. The monsters ran off into the night.

With the dance ended, a single drum thumped the soft heartbeat. People talked while they waited for the next ceremony, mostly about who would be the next war chiefs. They didn't have to say that everything would be better now. That's what set the tongues wagging, the feet moving, and faces smiling.

No one knew where the two fallen chiefs were—sulking, they supposed.

An elegant figure slipped from the darkness, accompanied by daughter and panther, and sat on the grass with all the people.

Whispers hissed around the circle—"The Seer! The Seer!"

People gawked. This was a memory to keep for their grandchildren.

Then the drums tapped out a new rhythm. Feet, hips, and shoulders began to jiggle. The Eagle Ceremony began.

21

Sunoya's exultation was too great even to speak. Walking back to the Emerald Cavern, she clung with two fingers to the Seer's sleeve. Though the Seer called her a friend, Sunoya always saw something majestic in her mentor, something that set her above others.

"I am just like you," Tsola said, "except that my job is harder."

Their conversations were often like this, the Seer responding to Sunoya's thoughts.

Sunoya felt keenly aware of everything, Tsola's daughter and panther son alongside her, the sounds of the night, the warm, moist air. Above, she saw the pale ghost of the new moon, fainter than light caught in a cobweb. She almost misplaced a foot and leaned on Tsola. She felt grateful for the night vision of the Seer and the panther. Su-Li perched on Sunoya's shoulder. He was blind in the moonless night, too. *New moon, the time for beginnings*.

Now, from the gentle shush, Sunoya knew they were coming to the place where Emerald Creek flowed out of the Healing Pool.

They circled around the water toward the house where Tsola's daughters lived. There they all sat by a low fire and took a little parched corn together, with some roasted buffalo meat. Visitors to the spring brought gifts of food in gratitude for the remedies.

"You won a great victory," said Sunoya.

"We have barely begun. This is the time to talk about the bigger task. It falls on you."

Sunoya felt like her teacher had struck in her the belly.

"The Immortals would never have listened to us as long as we were fighting among ourselves," Tsola went on. "Now we have a chance to renew the Cape, or get a new one.

"I don't know how to do it." The Seer let these words sit. "I will pray every day for the Cape to become clean and strong. But my thought is, that's not the way. If I'm understanding prophesy, a daring person will get a new Cape for us."

The thought lightninged through Sunoya. "Dahzi."

"I think so."

Dahzi, powerful enough in medicine to go beyond the Sky Arch and persuade . . . ? Sunoya said in a quavery tone, "My son such a hero?"

"I think so."

Sunoya was elated and scared.

22

Inaj built a fire in a cave. He used the fire in his belly to run down a doe, throw her to the ground with his hands, and twist her neck until it snapped. He fed himself, he simmered, and he thought. Before the memories of the grandfathers of the oldest men, his people had lived in caves like this one all the time. He spent each Hunting Moon camping in caves, to take male deer with his spear and provide for his family against the long winter. On raids against his people's enemies, and some-times against the damned Socos, he and his warriors made their camps in caves. The old stories said his people had come onto the earth through caves. He was comfortable here.

He watched the deer backstrap broil on the end of a stick,

watched the fire change it from living flesh to fodder for his blood. He didn't think, but only attended to his rage.

After two days of this brooding he fixed on an idea. He made a clandestine trip that night to the cluster of wickiups his own band occupied. He didn't waste time visiting his family. He sought out Linita, whose name meant "puppy." A feisty fellow, eager to please, a little off in the head, too young to be married, just right.

He took this boy to the cave and had a talk with him. This youngster got the name Linita because as a small boy he liked to imitate his own puppy, going about on all fours and begging for food scraps. The boy thought it was funny. Now he had one strength, that he loved to go into battle, and one weakness, that his thoughts were a little twisted.

Linita listened carefully, his mouth hanging open in that way he had, an off-kilter smile. When they were finished talking, Linita stayed in the cave, and Inaj walked back into his own camp and his own wickiup.

His family and friends remarked afterwards that, whatever Inaj had done while he was gone, it had evidently purged him of ill feeling. Now the man who had once been Red Chief was as jovial as anyone had seen him. He told jokes, he slapped backs, he had a good time. He walked with everyone else to the ceremonies each night and danced with vigor.

Iwa was thrilled to see her husband easy and happy. She had feared the worst, but now he seemed a changed man. She felt a new respect for him.

❖

The next morning the retired Red Chief of the Socos left his wickiup early and walked to the creek to pee.

His wife found him an hour later and sent up a wail the Soco people would never forget. They ran to the poor woman and found her soaked in his blood. His throat was slit. He was pierced through and pinned to the ground with a spear that might belong to anyone. His tongue was cut out. The dead chief's penis was cut off and stuck in his mouth.

A gang of Soco warriors grabbed their weapons and dashed to the Tusca camp. They knew who hated this chief, and they intended to make Inaj pay.

But the fallen Tusca chief sat quietly with his own family, in the open, in front of their wickiup, eating a little seed cake for breakfast. Everyone in the camp had seen him all morning—he had always been right there.

The Soco warriors surged with fury.

"The killer has to be Inaj—we know it."

"Impossible," said Iwa. Their neighbors said the same.

Inaj sat by his fire, relaxed, chuckling at the whole thing.

Tusca warriors ran up bristling with weapons. Young men jostled each other. Insults were exchanged. Before long a Tusca man was on the ground, head bleeding, skull caved in by a Soco war club.

In an instant two dozen more Tuscas rushed to the scene, their spears and war clubs raised and ready.

Now Inaj exerted himself. He faced down his own warriors. "Stand back! There will be a time!"

He commanded the Socos to get out of his camp while they still had their lives.

They did.

That afternoon the Tusca warriors met and re-elected Inaj as the Red Chief.

Late that night Inaj visited Linita in the cave. The boy greeted the chief happily, eager for the congratulations he had earned.

Inaj stood on one side of the fire and looked down at his instrument. He watched the youngster misinterpret his smile. He considered which of his weapons to use first.

He squatted, and Linita made the normal gesture of hospitality, thrusting out a cup of tea.

Inaj whacked his hand. The cup flew into the darkness.

The Red Chief seized the boy's arm. He fixed Linita eye to eye and gradually forced his hand into the fire.

Linita screamed. He tried to pull away, but Inaj held him. Linita flopped like a speared fish, but Inaj forced his fingers deeper into the coals.

"Fool," he said. "Dupe. Idiot. I have used you for my purpose and now I throw you away."

He cast off Linita's mangled hand.

The youth backed away on all fours, cowering and simpering.

Inaj stood up and glowered down.

"If you ever come back to our village, I will tell everyone who made a craven, sneaking attack on the great Red Chief of the Socos. I will tell his clansmen loudest of all. They will hunt you down, kill you, and feed your guts to the dogs."

Linita scurried deep into the cave. *I meant to gain favor. I . . .* He turned and slithered through a narrow crack. *Let me go, please let me go.* He crawled deeper into the earth.

Inaj watched him worm away.

The Red Chief smiled with satisfaction. Now he could concentrate on leading his men. He said to the walls of the cave, "We have to protect ourselves against the Socos, don't we?"

THREE

One Kind of Love

23

A mother's first duty was to teach her child what it meant to be a Galayi—to understand where you came from, how you arrived on Turtle Island, how to live a proper human life, and how to prepare to pass beyond into the spirit world. Throughout his boyhood Sunoya took every chance to help Dahzi learn.

One sultry afternoon she found him at the little creek where it chattered into the Soco River. He sat with his moccasins off and his legs in the water up to his knees, his guard behind him.

Spying carefully, Sunoya saw that the boy was playing with a water beetle.

Sunoya looked at Su-Li on her shoulder. He read her thought and flapped off to the top of a nearby snag. He didn't like being near the ground, and he could help spot danger from up high.

She slipped her moccasins off, scrunched her bottom down next to Dahzi's, and dunked her feet in the cool water. "Do you know the water beetle is a deep diver?"

"Yeah, I watched it, and I . . . I think I found out how. Look!"

The ten-year-old held the beetle underwater between thumb and forefinger and squeezed gently. Tiny air bubbles popped out.

Dahzi let the beetle go, and it scooted away.

"See, it packs air for its dives!"

Sunoya stopped herself, thought, and said, "Hmmm, I was going to tell you how Water Beetle created the world."

"Water Beetle created the world?!"

"Yes, but there's another story you need to hear first."

"I want to hear about Water Beetle!"

Sunoya, however, was a keeper of great knowledge, and she knew how to impart it.

"You almost squashed a little water beetle when you had no reason to. That has been the source of a lot of trouble in this world."

Dahzi dropped his head.

"Do you know that people and animals used to talk to each other, just like you and I do?"

Now Dahzi perked up.

"That's the way this world was made. We're animals, too, you know. Our word that means person, *ani-yuwi*? The animals and plants have names like ours. The deer are almost the same, *awi-yuwi*, the birds are *tsiqua-yuwi*, and the trees are *tluhu-yuwi*. So all of us, we have a spark of the original flame, which is spirit energy—*yuwi*."

She saw that she'd lost Dahzi.

"You want to hear about when the plants and the other animals all went to war against the people?"

"Yeah!"

"Well, the people were acting disrespectfully, like you did to that water beetle. You know how your uncle teaches you boys to throw spears, so that one day you can kill deer? And when you're bigger, elk and buffalo? You shouldn't kill more than your family needs to eat, plus some for old people who can't hunt anymore, and you know you're supposed to say a prayer when you kill one."

"I know the prayer."

"Sing it for me."

Dahzi sang,

Deer, I have shed your blood, and beg your pardon.
Deer, I take your flesh, and beg your pardon.
Deer, your flesh gives life to my children.
Deer, I thank you for your flesh.
Deer, I thank you for your life.

Dahzi added in speech, "You say it because if you don't, Little Deer follows you home and makes your joints sick and you're all crippled up."

"That's right." Sunoya was glad Dahzi's uncle was teaching him the right way. "Have you ever seen Little Deer?"

"Yes! He's the king of the deer, totally white, and he's only about knee-high. I saw him!"

In fact, only the greatest masters of all the lore of hunting had ever seen Little Deer on Earth, and no living Galayi had.

"You want the story?"

"Yes!"

"All right, people were killing more deer than they needed and weren't paying their respects. Same with the elk and buffalo. People tore up the beehives, too, because they were greedy for all the honey. And they ripped whole plants out of the ground instead of just taking the parts they could eat and leaving the rest of the plants to grow again next year."

She took a good look at Dahzi and couldn't tell whether he was sad or bored.

The storyteller plunged on. She'd lost him once, but not again. "All the animals except humans got together and voiced their complaints. Since they all thought human animals were being selfish, they agreed to send sickness and ailments against people. The deer, for instance, gave people arthritis, and the ticks gave them fevers.

"They also agreed to do much more. They sent messengers to the plants and said, 'Let's all go to war against the human beings. They're arrogant and want everything for themselves. If we band together, we can wipe them out.'

"The plants talked it over. According to their old stories, they were essential to the survival of all the people, deer, bears, birds—every animal. If the plants didn't breathe, none of the animals would be able to breathe—that's what the stories said.

"The king of the plants was a very old chestnut tree, and he offered a better idea than going to war against people. Instead, the plants could make a deal with them that would make both the plants and human beings stronger.

"So the plants got together with the chiefs of the people and made an offer. 'Here's what we want from you—spread our seeds everywhere. Take them and plant them in good places, places they aren't growing now. If you do this, the world will be covered with plants everywhere.'

"'And what will you give us in return?' asked the chiefs.

"The old chestnut had that figured out. 'We'll give you parts of ourselves for food,' he said, 'just like we do now.' He paused dramatically. 'And much more. We'll make medicines for you. We'll grow things in our leaves and stems and roots that will cure you from illnesses that animals attack you with.'

"The people chiefs consulted and decided this was a good deal.

"'In return,' the old tree reminded them, 'you have to plant us everywhere.'

"So they made a deal, and the plants didn't join the animals in the war.

"Then the people had to work things out with the angry animals. We promised the deer to say the prayer that you know. We promised to give a Bear Dance every year to show our respect, and a Buffalo Dance—you've been to both of them—and other agreements like that.

"Finally, the world was at peace. But people still had to accept one punishment. Because we acted like we thought we were more important than anyone else, we couldn't talk to animals or plants anymore. We still can't."

"That's sad," Dahzi said. He picked up another water beetle and watched it crawl around his hand. Then he dunked the hand into the water and let the beetle swim away.

"When you don't act right," said Sunoya, "you pay."

❖

"Dahzi," said Sunoya, "time to study."

"Aw, Mom," said the teenager.

Several of his fellow players grinned at him.

Su-Li wing-flapped off Sunoya's shoulder and toward the skies. He didn't like human squabbling.

"Just a little while longer," said Dahzi. "One goal."

They were playing the stickball game, where one team threw the ball forward with netted sticks until they scored a goal at the other team's end. Dahzi wanted to play for the Soco team the next time they were challenged.

He was frustrated. His mother and grandfather were stalling him. He wanted to go on a vision quest. He wanted to go to war. He wanted to get rid of the damned guard who hung around him every moment. But to go on a vision quest you needed to be prepared and put on the mountain by a medicine man. This village had two medicine people, his mother and grandfather—Ninyu had long since been appointed Medicine Chief. Both were saying no to him.

He hated thinking about it.

"How about one more goal and I tell all of you a story?" She got a lot of hangdog looks. "You'll like it. It's about sex."

Now she got some shrugs and smiles. "Go score your goal."

She sat down next to the guard who still went everywhere with Dahzi. Since the year Inaj outwitted Tsola and Sunoya at the Planting Moon Ceremony, the Tuscas had attacked with hardly a pause, and the Socos had fought back.

Sunoya was tired of the whole situation, and beyond tired. Everyone was, except apparently for Inaj. Sunoya felt like she was marching her life to funeral music.

She was also tired because this young man was a huge responsibility, the center of her duty not only as a mother but as a medicine woman. He would eventually answer the great question of her life. In the end would she wear her rawhide disc with the blue side out, for desolation? Or red for victory?

Unfortunately for her the guard didn't boost her mood. His duty of watchfulness forbade talking.

When the boys had scored their goal (Sunoya didn't notice which team did it), they walked down to the river with her, drank, lounged on the grass, and listened to the story. They all knew some of their people's old stories, like how Buzzard shaped the country where the Galayis lived into high mountains and deep valleys; how the turkey got his gobble; how the rattlesnakes took revenge on the people, and then gave them a song that would cure snakebite; and many stories of the Little People, who stood only knee-high to a human being and lived in the rivers and owned powerful magic. But they didn't know any that were sexy.

Su-Li landed and took a place on Dahzi's shoulder now. Dahzi was the only person, aside from Sunoya, that Su-Li would touch. The buzzard liked stories, and he liked seeing boys get their egos tweaked.

"A young man named Namu was feeling very lusty," Sunoya began, "and he got a clever idea. When he saw the women leaving the village to go to the river and bathe, he decided to sneak along after them and see if he could find a way to send his *do-wa* into one of them."

The boys giggled.

"So he folded his *do-wa* up, packed it in a pouch, and carried it in on his back.

"A bluebird flew alongside and teased him. 'What's that you have in your pack?' asked the bluebird. 'Is that your *do-wa*? Your *do-wa* as long as twenty snakes tied together in a string? Your *do-wa* as big and strong as the tap root of the tallest tree? And your balls as big around as your head? Is that what you're carrying in your pack?'

"Namu didn't answer. The bluebird knew very well what was in there."

The boys were looking at Sunoya with strange expressions.

"Well, men were different then—that's the point of the story.

"Namu crept through the laurels and got down to where he could walk in the river. When he could see the women around the bend, he slid back into the trees and parted the branches for a peek. The women had left their dresses on the grassy bank, and they looked very beautiful. Maybe he liked the young ones better, and his eyes spent some time caressing their breasts and thighs. Every woman, though, even the oldest crone in the village, looked desirable to Namu.

"As he watched, he imagined how good the place between their legs would feel to his *do-wa*. Imagining this, he unfolded his *do-wa* slowly, and imagined some more, and he began to feel like he was dreaming.

"He slid his *do-wa* gently into the river and let it drift downstream. But it floated on the surface.

"'That will never do,' the bluebird said. 'The women will spot that thing right off.'

"Namu drew his *do-wa* back and tied a stone to the head. Slowly, he fed the *do-wa* back into the river, and it slithered downstream. This time it ran along the bottom, well-hidden.

"'That won't work either,' said Bluebird. 'How's it going to get up where it needs to go?'

"So Namu reeled his *do-wa* back in and this time tied a smaller stone to it. When he floated it back into the water, it was perfect.

"Down along the current and beneath the ripples his *do-wa* drifted, sneaking up on the women.

"What Namu didn't know was that these women had seen this trick before and were wise to it. In the past they just got out of the water, pretending they didn't notice anything. But this was one time too many.

"The old crone said, 'It's Namu—I saw him peeking out from behind the laurels.'

"The prettiest girl of all said, 'I've had it with men doing this. Let's teach him a lesson.'

"The old crone gave a wicked grin, grabbed her deerskin skirt, and picked a certain thistle with it.

"The other women giggled and watched in fascination, half afraid they knew what she was going to do.

"She took the end of Namu's *do-wa* in one hand and with the other she stroked it gently with the thistle, handling the bristles carefully with the hide.

"Namu immediately got lost in sensual delight. This was wonderful beyond wonderful.

"What he didn't know, but the women did, was that the milk in the thistle was poisonous. Inch by inch, it was making Namu's *do-wa* numb. When he couldn't feel anything on a section of flesh, the old woman would pinch it off and throw it to the fish. She worked her way right up to Namu pretty quickly, feeding the fishes as she went. When she got to him, he had dozed off in pleasure.

"The old woman left him with, well, about the length men have now, and let him sleep. So they say."

Dahzi gave his mother a wicked eye. The boys shrugged and wandered away.

Su-Li jumped from Dahzi's shoulder to Sunoya's and made a rasping sound.

"Are you laughing at me?" she asked the buzzard.

He didn't answer.

"Or them?"

I have a do-wa, *too,* he said, *but it was never forty feet.*

24

Jemel was a Moon Woman. She'd known that since she could remember, and it never bothered her. In fact, she liked it.

The people told all sorts of stories about Moon Women and how crazy they were. The first Moon Woman got the name because she stared at the reflection of a full moon in a pond until she lost her mind, walked into the water, and drowned. Most of the stories, though, were about women falling in love with men—wildly in love—and what trouble that brought everyone. One Moon Woman got so crazy that she ate her children. Another turned into a coyote and did nothing but howl at the moon for the rest of her life.

Jemel had heard these stories as often as any Galayi girl did. However, her mother changed everything—she made a point of subverting the teachings. According to her mother, these stories were just a way of getting women to give up whoever and whatever they really wanted. They made love seem like something that made you crazy—it took you over entirely, body, mind, and spirit, and brought you to a terrible end. Mother pointed out that the Galayi word for "moon," *u-do-su-no,* was very much like the word for "crazy" or "lunatic," *u-nah-su-no.*

Mother had another way of undermining the stories, maybe

a better one. It was common Galayi wisdom not to get too excited, not to hope too hard, not to be eager, not to display emotion, and in fact not to feel it, to damp it down. Mother deliberately taught Jemel the opposite. When Jemel wanted something—a cloth sash for a dress, paint for her face, dyed porcupine quills to make a decoration—Mother always said how great that would be, and reminded Jemel constantly of how much she wanted it. Sometimes Jemel got what she wanted, and experienced a big vibration of thrill. Sometimes she didn't, and disappointment burned her gullet.

When Jemel got hurt that way, Mother would say, "This is life. Pain and joy—both are real, both are sharp. Feel all of each one. Then you're alive. If you mute the pain, mute the joy, you're a ghost shadow."

Mother also said the stories about Moon Women were a way of making girls marry men they weren't interested in. Most Galayi marriages were arranged by the families. A love match was rare, and usually an object of sly smiles and predictions of woe.

"Jemel," her mother said a hundred times, "what you love, doesn't matter what it is, or who it is—that's your heart and spirit, that's you. Don't let anybody talk you out of it, don't let anybody get in its way. Otherwise you live with a hole in your heart."

Then she would give the little girl a kiss and say, "The one I love is you."

Jemel was her mother's only child—her sisters came out of her father's other wife—and she got lots of attention.

Until her mother died, when Jemel was twelve.

As Jemel got a little older, she started putting together a bigger picture than what her mother actually said. She came to understand that Mother had been unhappy all her life. *What if I wasn't Mother's biggest love? What if she wanted someone else and didn't get him? Or something else?*

The child Jemel had gotten hints of the story, but the teenage Jemel asked questions and put it all together. At sixteen Mother had fallen madly in love with a man her own age. Both families were dead set against the marriage.

In the end Mother's lover was sent to another village to live with relatives. On the journey something happened to him, and he was never seen again. Mother was trapped into marrying her older sister's husband. But Jemel, said some of the whispers, was the daughter of Mother's lover, not her husband.

This kind of arranged marriage was the Galayi ideal. The man Jemel was raised to call "Father," Katya, was a good husband and a good father. But he was like the other men of the village, and apparently all the Galayi people. He loved his wives in an amiable way, and the marriage turned into a sort of bargain—we'll have sex sometimes, we'll make a family, and we'll run a household and raise children, make a good life. There was no wild attraction in Katya's kind of love. Passion was ruled out. Even today Katya had a comfortable marriage to two of Mother's sisters. Grown children lived with him, and plenty of grandchildren. It was a contented life.

What Jemel wanted—she knew this by the time she was twelve—was a grand romance. She kept her mouth shut about it. She'd already heard that she was a lunatic.

The hardest part of her life so far was waiting three entire winters after she turned twelve and watching her friends become women and be courted, while she remained a child.

She learned from the experience. She watched her friends flirt with various men, their own age and older, and saw the pointlessness of it. They liked some suitors better than others, disliked some, may have dallied with some, being careful about the time of the moon. But a feeling of ritual and convention infected the process. These weren't affairs of the heart—they were a kind of commercial display. The woman went to the man considered most appropriate.

Jemel thought long and hard about how her friends could play such a foolish game, how they could marry into comradeship instead of passion. Maybe they were thinking that they could still have fun with anyone they wanted in the bushes. Jemel thought that was a dumb way to live. She didn't understand it, and she didn't want to.

❖

Before Dahzi could slip out of the house, Sunoya said, "You said you wanted to learn the *aktena*. Your grandfather said he'd teach it to you. Go right now—he's waiting for you by the river."

The boy's body language said, "Aw, Mom." He wanted to practice the ball game or work on his weapons skills. Learning medicine felt like a bore. Almost all the men his age—he was nearing twenty—had gotten their visions, had gone to war. They were *doing* something for the people.

"Don't forget what your life's calling is," she said to his disappearing rump.

Waste of breath, Sunoya and Su-Li said to each other at the same time.

"*Aktena* is want you want to learn?" asked the albino shaman with a sly smile.

"Yes," said Dahzi. After a moment's thought, he really was curious about this one.

"It won't get you a lover," said Ninyu.

"I know. It's for women to make men fall in love with *them*."

"You might call it love," said Ninyu. "All right, sit down." Dahzi's guard stood nearby and kept his eyes and his ears on the world at large.

"You generally do *aktena* at the new moon, because the spell lasts until the next moon begins. Enough time to have a lot of fun in the bushes. Here."

He handed Dahzi a smooth, rounded river stone used for

grinding and spread some apple seeds on the big flat stone in front of him. "Grind these up," Ninyu said, "very fine, like dust. They have to go into tea without being noticeable."

Dahzi set to it. The potions, charms, and other things he learned couldn't remain theoretical. He had to be able to make things that worked. Or he supposed he did. He wished he was learning to fight. If he got to be War Chief, he could get even with the man who had made his entire life miserable.

After a while, Ninyu said, "That's very good. Now pour it into that tea." He set a clay cup in front of Dahzi, with a little sassafras brew in the bottom.

The youth stirred the two together and saw that the seed powder wasn't conspicuous.

"Now the woman must put some of the blood she makes once every moon into the water."

Dahzi gaped at the medicine man.

"You won't have to explain to any woman how to do it. Every woman wears a piece of mulberry cloth at that time to soak up the blood—you know this—and she can wring a few drops in."

Ninyu enjoyed the look on Dahzi's face. He was a good-looking boy and needed to be inched down once in a while.

"Any kind of tea will do." Ninyu pantomimed a wringing motion and then handed the cup with mock ceremony to Dahzi.

"That's it. You want to do some drills?"

The question caught Dahzi rising to run off.

"I guess so." He sat back down.

"You need to drill," said Ninyu. "Every potion and charm your mother and I have taught you, they have to be done exactly right. When you're calling in the big powers of the spirits, you can't make a mistake. You could get the lot of us hit by lightning, or make every woman in the village barren."

Sunoya had said the same. Dahzi wouldn't have stayed with

Ninyu any longer, but he had decided that today was the day to ask again.

"So I guess I'm a medicine man." He held up the webbed fourth and fifth fingers of his left hand.

"You were born to it."

"And medicine men go on vision quests."

"Sure. Extra sure."

"Then I want to go now. Let's do the work."

"Why now? What's your reason?"

My friends have all done it. They're getting war honors. They're getting women. They're not babied by a guard.

"It's just time."

"The spirits decide."

"If you ask them."

"Is this about war honors?"

"You know it is." A man needed the medicine of a vision to fight, to risk his life in the face of an enemy.

"That's not your path."

"I choose my path."

Ninyu reached out and touched the webbing between Dahzi's fingers.

"Is this the Medicine Chief talking, or my grandfather?"

Ninyu felt uneasy. "Why do you want to fight?"

"You know," Dahzi said. War honors were the beginning of manhood and the door to marriage.

That didn't satisfy Ninyu. "What enemy do you want to fight?" There were plenty of raids against the coastal people to the east and the prairie people to the west.

Dahzi spat it out. "My other grandfather."

The words fouled the air, like a rotten smell.

"He's evil. He killed my father with a spear. He beat my mother so bad I came early, and she died giving me birth. He wants to kill me."

Ninyu said, "Inaj is the reason our village and theirs have been at war since you were born."

"He thinks I'm the reason—that's what I hear."

"An infant making people kill each other, how likely is that?"

They were quiet for a moment. Ninyu felt like he couldn't breathe. His grandson breaking the greatest of taboos, to kill another Galayi. His grandson destroying the power of the child of prophecy.

He said with forced calm, "Inaj is not Ahsbingah, you know. He's just a misguided man."

"I want to kill him. That is what I owe the Soco people, for twenty years of trouble."

"It would destroy you. Never mind that he would kill you. If you won, your spirit would die."

Dahzi made a bitter face. "I choose my path."

Ninyu quelled his feelings. "But not with my help."

Dahzi stared into space, looked at his guard, and twisted his mouth.

❖

Jemel held still while one of her mothers pinned her hair high on her head, creating great sweeps and loops of glossy black. Earlier Jemel had scented her hair with mint leaves and rubbed it with oil. Jemel was draped shoulder to ankle in her first dress woven of mulberry bark, beautifully dyed. The women of the family had prepared for this event well in advance. Tonight was the ceremony when their daughter announced that she had become a woman. The sign of her new status was her hair and dress.

Jemel led the way out of the house and began her procession around the village. Her family followed, and her mother lifted up the first voice in the honor song. Her entire family raised their voices, too, and then neighbors and other families joined the parade. Soon half the village was walking behind Jemel and the other half singing along. It was the first great occasion of any young woman's life. On the walk she glowed with her secret. She intended to find passion.

Over the next few weeks Jemel stood outside her family's home, as custom required, and received men visitors in the evenings. She found that she liked being courted. The attention flattered her, and at the same time it tickled her. But this courting didn't matter. She was playing, waiting for the one man she would be crazy about.

One evening when she was flirting with several men, a youth walked up and joined in. She'd seen him around the village but had never paid attention to him—it was the young man who never went anywhere without a guard, Dahzi, the son of the medicine woman Sunoya. Suddenly she saw him in a new way. His body was lithe, his smile teasing, his eyes soulful. She had no idea whether he could give her what she wanted, to be loved greatly, to be adored.

During the next quarter moon she kept an eye out for Dahzi, learned his habits, put herself where she could watch him without being seen. It was an exciting game. Just looking at him made her chest get tight.

Dahzi started coming around every evening, sitting in the circle of the men who surrounded her, or sometimes behind them. She never spoke to him, never let her eyes make contact with his, never let herself appear to notice him.

By the time of the new moon he was staring at her the way a sunflower gazes at the distant sun.

❖

Dahzi watched his mother prepare the potion. She poured hot water into a cup, dropped something into it, and set the cup against the wall of their house to steep. Dahzi thought he recognized what Sunoya was dropping in, some red vegetable scrapings.

"You're sending someone on a vision quest."

"When they go on a quest, women prefer having me guide them."

Dahzi knew what the vision path was. Tonight was the full moon, the time to begin. A male seeker would wear nothing but a breechcloth and moccasins. He took nothing with him, not a weapon, not a robe. He left between first light and dawn and went wherever his heart took him. He found a place that was solitary—it was important to see no one else. This place should feel good and right. That was all the shaman could say about it.

Dahzi didn't know much about the customs for female seekers.

"Is the tea for the seeker or for you?"

Sunoya looked up at her son. She was intrigued—he was showing interest in a woman's quest. "Me. I follow along on the quest. I see what the seeker sees."

"I want to seek."

"I know you're impatient for your chance."

"Sure." His tone told a bitter story.

"When you're ready emotionally, either your grandfather or I will be glad to help you. It will be an honor."

Dahzi pictured himself performing the ceremony. A small space, with no room to walk around. No eating or drinking. During the day he would pray to the spirits for a vision. When he wanted to, he would sing a song. The spirits liked to hear Galayi voices raised in song.

He had pack-ratted bits of information from his friends. He knew how. He was ravenous to go, ravenous to get an animal helper, ravenous to earn a name.

"I *am* ready," he told his mother.

She stirred the potion and said nothing.

"Mother, I want to go on the mountain now. Will you help me or not?"

"Not yet," she said. "And not your grandfather, either."

"Why not?"

"Hating Inaj is not a reason to seek a vision."

She wondered again: *One grandfather is Ninyu, a good man, a man of medicine. The other is Inaj. Has Dahzi inherited both? Are good and evil warring within him?*

25

Silence was all he needed, absolute silence. He slipped out from under his fur robes, went to the door, opened it, and slid into the darkness of the night. Toma sat back against the wall, groggy as usual. Instead of tapping his shoulder, in one quick motion Dahzi stuffed a squirrel skin into his mouth. Then he bound the guard's hands with leather thongs. The hide absorbed Toma's protests almost entirely. In moments Dahzi was gone.

He was very satisfied. The family's two dogs were in the hut, accustomed to people going out at night to pee. Dahzi was always glad to be away from dogs. Even Su-Li, if the buzzard woke up, couldn't follow him in the darkness.

Dahzi started up the Soco River, his mind entirely empty about where he might go. He felt happy, his legs springy. He kept thinking, *No guard*. He was elated about that. He would never need a guard again—he could take care of himself.

About dawn he saw some stony cliffs rising above the pine trees on the other side of the river. When he studied the cliffs, he realized that a war eagle's nest hung over the edge of one of the lower shelves.

Perfect. The eagle felt like a good omen.

He splashed his way across the river. Since he first crossed it on the back of his mother's pack dog as a newborn, he'd waded it at low water several times. The river was rising now, the spring runoff flowing in, and he had to swim a few strokes in two different places.

Odd that he was leery of dogs. Maybe he picked it up from Su-Li. The buzzard had seen them in packs, and said they were vicious.

On the far side he scrambled up the mountain like he'd seen elk bound up. He climbed above the shelf with the nest and looked at the home of the war eagles.

It was empty—too early in the year for the grown birds, eggs, or fledglings. He noticed several feathers in the nest, white near the quill tip, brown below. He thought they were beautiful. He knew, though, why the people didn't gather them for decoration. One of the old stories told about a man punished by the eagles for approaching their nest. He was a long way above the nest, and above danger.

So. He would do his own vision quest. Was he not the medicine bearer? Why would he need help?

He chose his small space, prayed and sang all day long. He kept an eye on the weather, though. Sodden clouds were bunching up on the peaks and ridges. By mid-afternoon he could smell rain, and the drizzle began just as the sun dropped out of sight.

He began to wonder whether he should have done this by himself. His mind shook a finger at him—arrogant.

He dreaded the night. Since he had a bare chest and no robe, the wet and cold could be miserable.

He shook his head sharply. The danger was not the rain or the temperature—it was the distraction. *I have come to get a vision, see an animal helper, and earn a name. My mind must burn with my intention.*

Within an hour he began to shiver. In two hours he was shaking uncontrollably. He ordered his mind and spirit to ignore his foolish body. Instead they ignored his will. He knew that he was to watch for a sky parade put on by the spirits, but no sky was visible. He couldn't even see clouds, but just a shapeless, shifting, formless gray mush of nothing.

Hours and hours of shaking. He gave up hoping for a vision. He thought only of getting through the night.

At dawn he appeared at the door of his home. His mother and Ninyu were outside, waiting for him.

Dahzi started to stammer something out.

"We know what happened," said Sunoya. "Come inside and I'll make you some tea, and then some food to break your fast."

Dahzi liked the fire even better than the tea. He wished he could take his skin off and spread it out to dry and warm up.

He looked at his hand and noticed that the cup was the same one his mother used to brew something yesterday for another seeker. "What did you make tea from yesterday?"

Ninyu said, "You're putting off what we have to say to each other, so I will say it. You suffered terribly from the rain and cold. Your mind got preoccupied with earthly matters like staying warm, staying alive. You didn't have any energy to seek a vision."

Softly, "Yes."

"You disobeyed us. You dishonored us."

Now firmly, "Yes."

Sunoya said, "You dishonored the spirits. That's why they didn't come to you."

Dahzi didn't dare look his mother and grandfather in the eye.

"When you come to him with a proper attitude," said Sunoya, "your grandfather would love to put you on the mountain."

"That's true," said Ninyu.

Dahzi didn't hear the words. He told himself, *I'm ashamed. I'm angry. I'm afraid of losing my chance at Jemel.*

26

Jemel sat herself down and talked sense to herself. Good sense? From a devoted Moon Woman? That was funny.

Her mother had told her the way to get a man's genuine love, and to connect two bodies and two souls. Also, her own body told her how. It was time. She wondered whether, in true Moon Woman style, she should be flagrant about it. She decided that deviousness was also the Moon Woman style. *Anything and everything*, she thought, *as long as I do it all the way.*

When her group of men dispersed one evening, she asked Dahzi to stay a moment. Walking away, the other men traded smiles and odd looks. The request could be innocent, for a woman her age might ask a young man to do her various small favors. She could ask for turtle shells for making rattles, or for the tips of deer antlers to hang from the hem of her skirt and clatter when she danced, or other things. Intriguingly, the request could also indicate where her affections pointed.

The oldest man said, "I don't think so," glancing back. He was about thirty winters old and had one wife.

"Of course not. He's much too young," said a second, eyes straight ahead. This fellow, whose wife had died bringing forth their first child, had taken a fancy to Jemel.

The young lady herself said to Dahzi, "Meet me on the water path tomorrow morning—I want to show you something."

Dahzi was so stunned that he could only nod.

She watched him walk away. He'd seemed sulky the last two nights, but she didn't care. Her mind was made up.

The next morning Jemel told her mothers that she was going with two friends to get some watercress. She was fond of watercress leaves, not to put into soup or stew as her mothers used them, but to eat alone and fresh, as soon as possible after being plucked from the water. The watercress grew thick in a certain place a couple of miles up the creek, so her mothers expected Jemel to be gone all morning.

Jemel started along the water path with her friends, and when they came upon Dahzi and his guard, she invited him to join them. In a little while she pulled Dahzi off the path, under a huge weeping willow that overhung the creek. "Wait," she ordered the guard. Jemel's girl friends walked on, giggling.

Dahzi started to ask whether they were going to gather branches—women used the pliant willow limbs to make baskets—but something stopped him from speaking. He later decided that this hesitation saved him from a good deal of teasing.

The moment they were fully in the dense shade of the branches, Jemel put her arms around him, put her lips to his, and showed him a new use for his tongue.

Abruptly she paused and held him at arm's length. She eyed him hard and said, "I am a Moon Woman. You know what that means."

Unable to speak, Dahzi nodded yes.

"I want you. I want to fill you with passion and get passion back from you."

Dahzi nodded again.

"Do you have big feelings to give me? If you don't, tell me now, and we'll act like this never happened."

Dahzi squeezed out three words. "I love you."

She cocked her head and waited.

"I adore you," he said.

She pulled him to her, kissed him, reached for his breech-cloth, and . . .

That's how Dahzi's sexual education began. Jemel knew nothing from experience but had a lot of tips from her mother. Her body guided her to the rest. They loved each other every way people can.

Hours later, Jemel led Dahzi back to the edge of the village. He was so dizzied he thought he couldn't have found his way home without her. The guard idled along behind them. Dahzi hated his presence more than ever.

That evening he went to her parents' house before the time for suitors. She came out to sit with him. He felt like every eye in the village was trained on him. "I went out to cry for a vision," he said.

"I know."

"I saw nothing."

"I heard that."

"I can't try again until the next new moon."

She knew what he was telling her. He wasn't a man yet and couldn't ask to marry her.

"I don't care about any of that. We mounted the panther this morning. Wherever it goes, we'll ride it."

Dahzi nodded, accepting.

Soon her other suitors arrived.

❖

After she'd been hearing the gossip for about a week, Sunoya decided she'd better do something. She made some of the honeyed seed cakes Dahzi liked so much. When Dahzi came back from his morning excursion, she took him down by the river, a cool place they liked to talk.

After he'd eaten two of them, she said, "You like Jemel."

He nodded. She gathered he was tongue-tied.

He believes he loves her, Su-Li said quietly.

"Lots of boys like her," she said. "Men, too."

Jealousy made a ring of fire in Dahzi's heart. He swallowed the rest of his cake and said, "She loves me. She told me so."

Sunoya took thought. Without words she said to Su-Li, *If I try to cut off this flirtation, he'll always yearn for her.*

Yes, said Su-Li.

"She looks like a nice girl," said Sunoya. "Medicine bearers can marry."

"Yeah," said Dahzi.

Sunoya eyed him, thinking, *He's not wide-eyed about his destiny as a man of medicine. Not anymore. And he's not a boy now.*

"Unless you want a spirit guide, like Su-Li."

"I don't think so," Dahzi said. He ate the last bite of his seed cakes and rinsed his fingers in the river.

His do-wa *doesn't think so,* said Su-Li.

"I worry about your future."

"You can count on this much. Jemel and I are going to get married." *Unless one of the other suitors gets her.*

"When?"

"I don't know. Look, there's something I have to explain. Big passions don't happen very often. That's what we have."

"Dahzi . . ."

"Wait. I know. I know the stories about Moon Women. I know the usual stuff about going with big feelings." Now he looked at her with flame in his eyes. "But I also know about passion. It's real. I didn't know until now."

"Dahzi . . ."

"Mom, listen to me. No one who's lucky enough to have this big feeling will walk away from it."

"Dahzi . . ."

"Mom, you don't know. You're a virgin."

She flinched. The way he spoke to her was . . .

Easy, said Su-Li.

Sunoya controlled her breathing. "It might happen. But so much else has to happen first."

"Right. I have to get a vision. I have to get a name. On the next new moon I'll do that." He couldn't wait. She might choose someone else. "I'll be a man, and Jemel and I will be together. We're not asking permission from anyone."

He let her see that in his eyes.

❖

Sunoya waited. For two days she noticed that Dahzi and Jemel came back to the village about midday, not together, but one shortly after the other. She wondered how Jemel gave her family the slip so easily.

Dahzi found the morning's breakfast still on the coals and wolfed it down. He'd been away since dawn. Sunoya watched him with a smile.

Then he stretched out on his robes for a nap.

"My son," she said, "I want you to have whatever you want. If you want Jemel, I want her for you."

Now he opened his eyes, held hers briefly, and closed them again.

"I wonder if you're forgetting that you were born to be extraordinary."

He looked at her and she held up her webbed fingers to show what she was talking about.

He closed his eyes again.

"Tsola and I believe you were born to be the one who gets another Eagle's Cape for the people."

"Mom," he said in disgust.

"I know about prophecy," she answered. "Ninyu knows. Tsola knows."

Dahzi sat up. "Mom, I'm only thinking about one thing, getting a name and getting Jemel. After I marry her, my future might be . . . besides Jemel, I don't know, some fairy tale. But Jemel and I love each other."

He threw himself down and turned his back to her.

❖

Sunoya thought about it. She mourned about it. She talked with Su-Li about it. On the second evening she did what she had to do. She walked gently to Jemel's family's house and slipped by the girl and her group of suitors quietly. If Dahzi shot her a look of alarm, her back was to it. She ducked into the open door and greeted Jemel's parents. Invited, she sat. She asked for the pipe and sent puffs of smoke to the sky. *This smoke my breath, this smoke my prayers.*

She took confidence from Su-Li on her shoulder. Then she spoke the words that had to be spoken.

The next morning at first light, before Jemel could slip out again to meet Dahzi, her father and brothers marched her out of the village.

After he waited half the morning by the water path, Dahzi came home. His eyes were heat lightning flickering. "Where is Jemel?"

Sunoya heard a tone her son had never used to her before. She sighed a little sadness, like a sip of death.

"Her father and brothers have taken her to live with relatives."

Now Dahzi's voice was a lash. "Where?"

"The Cusa village." She watched him absorb the news. "You know it doesn't matter where. She'll be well guarded."

He gave a curdled cry. "Why-y-y?!"

"Because you are too young, both of you. You especially. You can't support a wife and children, not yet. In a few years you'll be a good hunter, or a good medicine man, and you can have a family. Not yet."

"Damn it, I—"

"Dahzi!" She cut him off sharply. "Be glad her father and

brothers simply left. They wanted to give you a beating. First I tried to talk them out of it, then I had to use a threat."

Everyone knew medicine people could make good on their threats.

He let out a roar.

"Get a vision. Earn a name. Become a man. Make a life for yourself."

He bellowed and stomped out.

FOUR

A Strange Journey

27

Dahzi woke up to the shush of the river and the lilac twilight. He didn't know where he'd been all day. Stomping and rampaging until he exhausted himself. Cursing Jemel's family. Cursing his mother and his fate. He hoped he hadn't cursed the spirits, but he couldn't remember.

Now he had a reality to face. He didn't want to go back to his house, the place where he grew up, but hunger and cold drove him there.

He didn't speak to anyone. He ate, went to bed, and ate again without even the words "thank you." He didn't sleep that night. Instead he tossed and turned, fretted, steamed, stewed, and somehow around the edges of his fury thought things over. He wanted to do something so dramatic that the whole world would give him Jemel.

That morning he watched for his chance, rolled up his pallet of robes and tied them, and picked up his spear. He hadn't yet made himself a war club.

He strolled casually out of the village and headed up the river. He had made up his mind. He was going to kill Inaj.

Kill his grandfather! Kill the man who led a war against the Socos, Dahzi's people, for nearly two decades. Kill the man who killed his father.

Yes, slaying another Galayi was *the* forbidden crime. But Inaj did it. Maybe Dahzi inherited the desire to kill.

His mother said being born with webbed fingers controlled his destiny. Maybe having the blood of a killer in his veins controlled it.

And it will make me a hero.

The trouble was, he didn't see how to get close enough. This was the planting season. Inaj was probably at home—the governor of a village had to stay home most of the time. Dahzi couldn't even think of marching straight into the Tusca village and killing its chief.

On the other hand, Inaj might be out leading a raid, maybe against one of the tribes that lived along the ocean to the east. Again, maybe the raid was against the Socos. He'd stolen women right out of the fields before, just to mock the villagers.

The truth was, Dahzi didn't know where Inaj was. But he knew where he would be in half a moon. Then the entire Tusca village would migrate west over a couple of ranges of mountains and turn north to the headwaters of the Soco River and over the divide to the Cheowa village. For the Planting Moon Ceremony. So Dahzi knew where his chance would come.

He walked in a foul mood for a day and a half and came in late afternoon to where the trail from the Tusca village met the river. He looked lingeringly at the big waterfall which had saved his life, and his mother's life. Twenty winters ago, when Sunoya managed a difficult ford of the river, Inaj and his men jumped in right behind her. As they were crossing, the frozen waterfall collapsed into the river and swamped them.

Dahzi took the trail along the right bank of the river and angled up alongside the waterfall. It was beautiful now, full of sprays where it splashed against rocks and spumed away downward, catching glints of sunlight here and there. It almost improved his mood.

Above the waterfall the mountain got steep and the trail was slow going. Dahzi walked up high above the falls, back down to them, and up again. He stood and peered ahead to the ridge, down to the falls, and around the woods. He imagined the ambush, one bloody fantasy after another. In the end he thought this might be the place.

He walked to the ridge and then angled up the brushy slope. He'd seen shadows in an outcropping of limestone that meant a cave. That would keep the spring showers off and would provide shelter while he waited. He needed to check the lay of the land thoroughly. He needed to spot hiding places. And he had to practice with his spear—he would get only one try.

He knew it was wicked. But maybe he was born to it. He knew the odds were long. He didn't care. Heroism and Jemel beckoned. Wickedness? Death? Without Jemel there was no life.

Dahzi made snares from the loose bark of vines and caught a rabbit on the first day. The second day he went hungry except for some tea. On the third morning he waited quietly near the river at first light and watched the deer come to water. When a buck stepped close, he let fly with his spear and hit it right behind the shoulder blade. In a flash he jumped on it and cut its throat with his blade.

He stood over it with strange feelings. Jubilation, because he had done it—this was his first deer. Elation, because now he had food, enough to last him until the Tuscas arrived. Regret, because he had killed.

He reminded himself that no animal died before its time. Deer resurrected themselves from their spilled blood. He knew that. He sang the prayer that would appease the king of the deer.

Then he set to dressing out his kill and carrying the meat up to the cave.

That night, when he was roasting the liver, he suddenly became aware that someone was sitting on the boulder behind him.

Dahzi's heart jumped in his chest.

"Never mind me," the fellow said. He talked fast, like he was jittery. His accent was Tusca, which didn't ease Dahzi's mind.

"How did you get here?"

"Back in there, yes, back in there." He pointed into the recesses of the cave, and Dahzi saw that a skinny man might slip through. He wondered how big the cave was.

The stranger worked his lips, making little sounds that weren't quite words, and then were. "I sleeps here a lot."

Dahzi moved so that the firelight shone on the man. A slight figure, unkempt, badly dressed, and filthy, grinning with an odd enthusiasm and bouncing up and down on his haunches. Sometimes Galayi went crazy and lived alone in the woods. Maybe the fellow was one of these.

Dahzi extended the rest of the liver to the man on the tip of his blade. "Want something to eat?"

"Don't get much meat."

The man reached out with a mangled hand. The four fingers were glued together, the skin melted, maybe by a burn. The thumb opposed them like the claw of a crab.

The fellow held the meat with his claw, inspected it from all angles, and stuffed the whole thing into his mouth.

A crazy hermit, thought Dahzi. "What's your name?"

"You call me Paya." It meant "crab." He seemed to be warming up to the idea of a little conversation.

"But what's your name?"

"People used to call me Linita. 'Cept I'm not nobody's puppy anymore, and don't hardly see many people. Don't tell a soul you saw me, not a soul. Or where you saw me, especially not where." He tossed out words like a quick-tapped drum.

Dahzi thought fast. "I'm Crooked Eagle." Dahzi felt guilty about this lie, which was a claim that he'd had a vision of an eagle. Still, he couldn't tell his real name. This was a lie with style, and surely the Crab Man didn't matter. Dahzi had liked seeing the eagle nest and the feathers, and hoped he'd really see an eagle on his next vision quest. Foolishness, he knew.

He noticed that the Crab Man carried a skin bag full of something flung over one shoulder. "What's in the bag?"

Paya's eyes jumped from side to side in panic for a moment and then turned canny.

"Mushrooms," he said. "Want some?"

"Yeah." This felt weird to Dahzi, but it pleased him, and he liked mushrooms. He liked the childlike Paya.

The Crab Man stuck out a handful. Dahzi slid them onto his stick and wound a strip of deer fat between them. The odd fellow took a stick and did the same.

Too soon the mushrooms were gone. Dahzi eyed the bag. He could see Paya had a lot more of something in there, but he said nothing.

"I go to the villages, I trade mushrooms," said the Crab Man. As he spoke, he bounced up and down in his squat. He started making some tea.

This claim couldn't be true. At least no one came to the Soco village trading mushrooms—they were too common to pay for. Dahzi looked the Crab Man over carefully.

"I trade 'em to the shamans for their medicine," the fellow said.

A bigger lie. Dahzi knew well what shamans used, and they didn't use mushrooms.

Dahzi decided to test the child-man. "You know Mena?" That was the Medicine Chief of the Tuscas who replaced Sunoya.

The Crab Man shook his head. "Don't go to that village. Can't stand Inaj." He dipped himself some tea but didn't offer Dahzi any.

From the way he said it, Dahzi thought he was terrified of the Red Chief.

"Why?"

"Not to talk about. He done me bad, enough to say. Now I stay clear of him, way clear."

It struck Dahzi that the Crab Man must know this piece of country very well. Maybe he'd help set up the ambush.

Paya piped up happily. "You can sleep here tonight if you want."

Dahzi had been sleeping here, and thought he could do whatever he pleased, but said okay.

Eventually they curled up on opposite sides of the fire.

❖

In the morning Paya was gone. Dahzi built a fire and roasted some deer meat. Today he'd also start drying it.

Suddenly he heard odd noises from the depths of the cave. Like footsteps, but scraping. And along with it, panting.

He stuck his head through the narrow opening at the back of the cave. For a moment he saw nothing in the gloom, and then Paya's face appeared, grinning. In a moment the rest of the Crab Man popped up.

"Got something down here—oughta come see," Paya wheezed out. He snatched a big stick from behind a boulder and wriggled out through Dahzi's peep hole. Before Dahzi could even jump back, Paya stuck the stick in the fire. It was covered with pine pitch, and it blossomed into a torch.

"Come have a look-see," the Crab Man said. He pedaled back into the darkness fast on his hands and knees, and Dahzi followed the same way.

In moments they were looking over a precipice. Dahzi could see sloping walls, but the bottom was darkness and mystery.

"Long way down," Paya said. "Deep as maybe ten men standing on top of one 'nother. Watch."

He grabbed a vine, leaned his weight on one arm, and started backing down the steep slope. About ten steps down he wedged the torch into a crevice, gave Dahzi a wild grin, grabbed the vine with both hands, and dove into the darkness. "C'mon," called an echoing voice.

Dahzi decided to climb down as far as the torch and have a look. He took a double-fisted grip on the vine and looked to see how it was fastened at the top. He couldn't tell. *Oh well, it held Paya.*

He squeezed the vine hard and stepped down sideways, watching where he put his feet. The limestone was slippery.

When he got to the torch, he peered over, expecting to see nothing but blackness. Paya was standing at the bottom and held up another torch. Dahzi wondered how he'd lit it.

"C'mon down," said Paya, "it's easy. Fun, too. Just put one foot after 'nother."

Hell no, Dahzi said to himself.

Studying the slope, he saw that the drop wasn't sheer. The limestone was broken up, making steps here and ledges there.

"C'mon, there's secrets to see."

Now the Crab Man was showing off. Dahzi would have bet that no one else had ever been in Paya's cave.

"C'mon, c'mon!"

Dahzi did.

He clambered too fast and almost lost his footing a couple of times. Even by the faint light of the torch he could see that the holds were plenty good.

When he planted two feet on solid rock and let go of his choke hold on the vine, he felt heat. Behind Paya was a low blaze, beside it a pile of tinder and wood, and beyond that a big heap of charcoal and ashes. The Crab Man had been coming here a long time and had this place well outfitted. Dahzi wondered why. He'd never seen mushrooms growing in caves, not beyond the entrance areas.

"Follow me," said Paya, "follow me. There's stuff you won't believe."

Like a man struck dumb, Dahzi followed the blaze of the torch. They went through a low, tube-shaped passage—*Like the body of a snake,* Dahzi thought. It gave him a chill. The tube seemed almost to swirl at the end, and then it opened into a chamber. Dahzi had the sense of wonders both marvelous and terrible looming in the vast darkness.

Paya led him eagerly to one area. It had a floor flat as a prairie, a ceiling as flat as the floor, and a forest of slender stone columns between, like little trees of rock pushing down against a solid earth and up against an immovable sky.

Dahzi reached out and stroked one. To his surprise it was cool, slick with moisture, and smooth. Where he expected to feel strength and tension, he experienced a sensual delight.

"Lookee here, too," said Paya. He touched a knee-high jut of stone with his toe. "Shaped just like a you-know-what, ain't it?"

A big do-wa, thought Dahzi, *but still a* do-wa.

"Come along here, boy."

Dahzi followed in the Crab Man's footsteps, pacing among graceful columns.

"Here-here-here."

Paya held the torch high so Dahzi could see. A whole wall looked like cloth, undulating smoothly down like it was draped over a woman's breasts, belly, and hips.

"You could spend days just in this room, you could," said Paya. "I've done years here, and I ain't seen it all. But one thing . . . You gotta see this right now."

Dahzi followed the Crab Man in a state of mind he did not understand. It was exhilaration, or ecstasy, like hearing a forest full of leaves, each one singing as it fluttered. The question of whether he should trust this odd fellow flickered across his mind like a shadow of a bird in flight and disappeared. Paya was a friend.

They walked a good way across what seemed to be the

same big chamber. Then they went around a corner and he could see light from the outside world, not a lot, just a little coming through a crack in the rock, but enough to make him feel better. Oddly, Paya crawled up the crack and scraped at something near the outside edge with his knife. He looked back and saw Dahzi watching him, then clambered back in a hurry, like a kid caught nabbing sweets.

They walked on through the chamber. The space was narrowing down, like going from an enormous stomach to a gut. They treaded through a narrow passage, then an area of broken footing, then a low alley. Finally they had to crawl, and at the last, slither.

When Dahzi got on all fours again, he heard . . . water. Running water. He could hardly believe it.

Paya led him a few steps to the bank of an underground river—and stepped in.

Dahzi looked at the torch, wondering how long it would last, and where Paya might have another stash of torches.

The youth waded into the cool water. He was filled with excitement and fear.

Paya doused the torch in the river.

Blackness. Astounding, absolute blackness. Dahzi felt like he was floating through space and slowly turning head over heels.

"Ain't never seen nothing like this, huh?" said Paya. The Crab Man cackled. "If 'seen' is the word."

Flutterings in the heart and mind. Gurgles in the gut. Surges of emotion. Wild beating of the heart. Then huge pulsations of fear lifted him up and crashed him down. Dahzi drowned in panic. He suffocated in terror.

He heard himself scream, and then realized that the scream was entirely in his mind.

Infinite darkness. Blackness like a world of its own, filling all the space that keeps the stars apart. There was no sun, no moon, not even the faintest glimmer of any heavenly body. A universe of blackness.

They stood there for . . . Dahzi hadn't a hint of an idea how long. Days, moons, winters. They stood until . . .

The mind knows a place beyond terror, and Dahzi found it. It was a surrender to the center of dread, where every horror had come to pass, and there were no more.

He stood for a long time in that place, too.

At last, as though he knew Dahzi had found a bizarre kind of rest, Paya took his hand.

Dahzi's world changed—a warm hand. The Crab Man led him downstream.

They glugged along, and the plish-plash of the water made two points of orientation in an empty world.

Dahzi heard the river begin to hum, like it was running faster.

"This is going to be somp'n exciting now," said Paya.

He shoved, and Dahzi pitched into nothingness.

At first he thought he'd fallen off a mountain. He ker-plunked into water. Maybe he'd fallen a body length.

Now they seemed to be in a pool of still liquid. Dahzi discovered he could stand up, though the water came to his collarbone.

"Learning somp'n new, ain't you, boy?" Paya pulled Dahzi on.

Before long he said, "Close your eyes." He waited. "Honest now, be they closed?"

Dahzi closed them. Nothing could be darker than what he was seeing.

"Now cover them tight with your hands."

Why not?

Glee squeezed Paya's voice upward. "I got you a fine surprise."

Dahzi followed his strange friend, trusting, in truth in a

state beyond trust. He felt like he'd been swept out to sea in a basket and had given himself up to the thrill of the ride.

Step after step. Dahzi couldn't tell what was changing, if anything. The water lowered little by little to his waist, and then his knees.

"Open your eyes."

Blasts of light.

They stood in a big lake, which was a dazzling radiance. Sunlight streamed in from one side. It was astounding. Sometimes Dahzi had resented the blistering rays of the sun—here the sun seemed a blessing beyond imagination.

It came through a huge shaft angling gently up, a window on the world ruled by Grandmother Sun, who was now unreal. The opening on the mountainside was big enough for a dozen elk to walk through side by side.

"I've found some things out in my years here," said Paya. The words skipped like stones across water.

Gradually Dahzi's mind accepted the reality of this light, just as it had adjusted to the grasp of darkness.

Paya led the way to the shore and to another pile of firewood and several torches. Dahzi thought, *We don't need the torches here. Maybe they're for the trip back.*

"Build a little fire and I'll get us a treat," said the Crab Man.

Dahzi set to the work with flint. Paya waded to a shallow part of the pool and squatted. He was perfectly still, his hands in the water. Dahzi wouldn't have thought Paya could stand so still.

As Dahzi blew the first embers into flame, he saw Paya fling his arms upward, and a shadow flew from them. Whatever it was splatted onto the rocky shore and did a white dance there.

Paya squatted again and waited. Dahzi stoked the fire and watched in amazement. Before long another something sailed up from Paya's hands and did the flop-dance.

The Crab Man splashed his way to his catch, crabbed along the shore to the fire, and presented it for Dahzi's inspection.

Fish. At least they imitated real fish, except they didn't have eyes. Little bumps stood where their seeing organs should have been. And they were an eerie white, pale as fragments broken off a full moon.

Paya gutted the unnatural fish, skewered them on one of his sticks, and held them over the flames.

"Think they're ghosts, do ya? Your tongue, it will tell you different."

The flesh had a delicate taste, but savory. Dahzi's mind rummaged around for what the taste was but could come up with nothing like it.

"Flesh, yes, good flesh. This is somp'n, ain't it? We could catch more, eat more, but there ain't that many. The lake don't grow so many. Little flesh, little flesh.

"Follow Paya now, and you'll get a sweet treat for the eyes."

They splashed across the lake toward the entrance of the light. As they waded, the Crab Man's eyes flicked about. The eyes looked like the crazy flight of bats through the air.

"Stay here," said Paya. "You stand right in this spot now. Be back quick."

He climbed into the shaft and looked for . . . Dahzi couldn't imagine what. Eventually, he plucked something with his fingernails and dropped it into the bag he'd tucked into his belt.

When he'd worked his way back to Dahzi, the Crab Man said, "Right on now, right this way." He seldom walked without talking, like his feet made his lips go.

He stopped at the edge of a deeper pool gouged into the lake. The bottom was oddly mottled with stones that looked like broken and discolored egg shells. That was a bizarre setting for one of the most beautiful flowers Dahzi had ever seen. It was white as a lily, with long, curly petals, shimmering delicately on the bottom on the pool.

"Very ginger now," said Paya, "reach down and touch it. Very ginger."

Dahzi did.

He looked at Paya gape-mouthed.

The Crab Man giggled and giggled, sending out hee-hees like birds scared out of trees. "Stone, yes. Oh, stone, it's a flower of stone. Did you ever?"

His tone took an edge. "Easy now, don't you break it. Paya, he's been watching 'em, there's a few more, but far as I can tell, takes years to make one, years. Don't break it now. Ginger. Give this place love, yes, give it love."

28

Love took the form, that night, of storytelling around the fire. Coming and going, the two of them had passed so many turnoffs and alternate passages that Dahzi couldn't have kept count of them. Paya had several stories for each byway—perhaps hundreds or thousands of stories about the cave.

They ate the meat of the deer and Dahzi soaked up Paya's tales. He felt even hungrier for lore than for food.

Finally the Crab Man wound down and rolled up in the deer hides he used for blankets. He summarized the day's events with these words. "Folks know there's a whole world above the earth—that's the world of the sun and moon and stars. It's a world they all, well, it's enchanting, ain't it, and it has the Sky Arch beyond." He sighed, and let an undertone of secret pleasure creep into his voice. "But they don't know there's a world beneath their feet, now, do they? Don't know that, no. Takes a different sort to explore that world, and a different sort to love it."

"How big is the cave?" said Dahzi.

"Who knows? Big as the mountain, be my guess. Think on

that, the whole mountain, all the way from the Cheowa village to where the trail from the Tusca village comes in."

Dahzi pictured it—a monster of a cave, maybe hundreds of holey fingers under a stone bulwark where you'd never guess, and maybe lots of ways in and out.

"Way it happens, seems like, the water, it comes down from the sky and runs through the ground and makes all the passages this way and that." He made a snaky motion with one hand. "That's the way Paya figgers it, anyhow."

"How long have you been here?"

"Come the Planting Moon it'll be nineteen winters. Ain't wanting to go nowhere else, no, ain't wanting to. Got my cave."

Dahzi took the plunge. "What happened between you and Inaj?"

Paya sat up and glared at Dahzi. "Rude," he said. "I told you, no talk about. Don't."

The Crab Man laid back down and turned his back, declaring he was on his way to sleep.

But this was important to Dahzi. He said, "Inaj did something terrible to me. You can't imagine."

Paya rolled back over, fixed Dahzi with his eyes, and held up the mangled hand. "This he done to me."

Dahzi waited, to give honor to Paya's pain. Then he said, "Inaj killed my mother and my father." Dahzi didn't see anything in Paya's eyes, no glint of recognition of who he was.

"The bastard will be coming right by here on the way to the Planting Moon Ceremony."

Paya rejected the hint. "You stay away from that. He's a bad man. Because of him I can't live with my family."

Banished then, as Dahzi suspected.

"You want to fool with him, you get away from my cave. Stay away."

Dahzi was willing to bet, though, that he could get Paya to teach him the secret places of the mountain, maybe even

places where passages of the cave led to the surface, and an assassin could hide.

Soon Paya was wheezing, and the rhythm of his breath carried Dahzi off to sleep.

The next morning they went straight down into the cave
again. Dahzi wanted to go back to the underground lake, but
Paya bubbled, "I've got more for you to see, much more. Years
worth of seeing in this cave."

They poked through so many passages that Dahzi had no
idea where they were. He marked in his mind how easy it
would be to get lost down here.

Dahzi watched for light creeping in, anything that would
indicate another way to the surface, maybe close to the trail,
maybe offering a sly angle toward striking at Inaj. They saw
one huge opening in the earth. Paya threw a stone up, and millions of bats swarmed into the air and up the shaft. The boom-
ing made the roar of river rapids seem tame. Paya cackled, and
a hundred steps beyond was still cackling.

That night Paya seemed too tired or irritable to tell stories.
He gobbled up his food, brewed some tea, and again didn't offer Dahzi any. With his cup he scrambled outside. Dahzi followed, but the Crab Man ignored him.

Then Paya made a high-pitched moan of ecstasy. Dahzi
followed his eyes to the sky. After some moments he saw two
falling stars at once. Paya moaned higher and louder. Dahzi sat
beside him and watched in silence. It was a rain of falling stars,
and it seemed to go on half the night.

Finally Paya turned to crawl back to the cave. He said, "Tomorrow this un'll be going away for a few days. Must trade
some mushrooms. Planting Moon time, the shamans want 'em.
Must trade."

❖

He was gone when Dahzi woke up. *So what am I going to do
today?*

He looked at the entrance—*Whoops*, said his head, *both entrances, one to the world of light and one to the world of darkness.*

He knew he was going to go into the cave alone.

I can slide down the vines, take a torch, and walk down the river to the lake. I know how to do that. Yes, I do.

He wanted to have an adventure, and he wanted to check out a suspicion.

He worked his way down the vine a half dozen steps and jammed his torch into a crevice, just as Paya had. He looked over the drop. It seemed a lot darker this time.

He eased down the vine, clamping hard with both hands. Step down, good ledge, foothold, big step now, down and down.

Until he fell.

He blinked his way back to the world, flat on his back, his head smarting. He could see the flicker of the torch above.

He chuckled.

He thought about it and decided that he hadn't fallen any farther than from tree branches that were just out of reach. He just happened to land smack down on his back, and his head took a rap.

He laughed. He guffawed at himself.

He found Paya's embers, half seeing his way, half sensing, and finally kneeling down where he felt the warmth. He built the fire up and looked around.

It seemed like this was Paya's home, more than the cave entrance above. He had a good supply of firewood, a deer stomach suspended from a tripod for cooking, a hide wrapped full of wild onions, rose hips, lots of mushrooms in another wrap, a little dried meat, and some shriveled-up fat tucked away in a pouch. Paya also had some clay pots, bowls, and cups here, a couple of spare knives, extra moccasins, plenty of elk and buffalo hides with the hair still on, and some tanned deer hides. Looked like he really did trade something to someone.

Dahzi lit a torch and followed the familiar way to the chamber filled with slender stone columns. When he got there, he was again stunned by now lovely the columns were. The world below the ground truly was as beautiful as the world above.

He found his way to the stone that draped like cloth, and this time he ran his hand down it sensually.

Soon he got down to business. He walked to where light came through the crack first, set his torch down, and climbed up toward the fissure. He was dazzled by what he found. The stone near the entrance was covered with lichens in a rainbow show of colors, orange, chartreuse, purple, yellow, and other hues. He looked carefully into the crevice where Paya had stuck his knife. More lichens, with a patch scratched bare. Dahzi craned his neck to get the best look possible at the bare spot. From the hints of color around the edges, it looked like Paya might have scraped away some scarlet lichens.

"Hah!" Dahzi said aloud. He was pleased pink with himself. If Paya wanted to keep his secrets, he shouldn't have done his gathering in the sight of one of the few people trained in the magic of plants.

Then Dahzi reined himself back. *Suspecting isn't knowing for sure.*

He wanted to get some of these red lichens for himself. But where? They were called *u-tsa-le-ta*, and both Zadayi and Ninyu used them to take dream journeys.

Shamans drank the *u-tsa-le-ta* in tea. That's probably the tea Paya hadn't offered to Dahzi. The stuff was forbidden to anyone but medicine men.

Dahzi looked around the crack. He saw a lot of lichens, but not the scarlet. If Paya was trading *u-tsa-le-ta* to the shamans, he might have picked a lot of the cave clean. It would be valuable stuff. Still, lichens grew back.

So Dahzi would search the big air shaft that opened onto the lake.

❖

Dahzi carried a torch down the underground river this time. He didn't need to repeat Paya's version of the thrills of walking in absolute blackness. Soon he began to hear the shush of water moving faster, and then the cacophony of it crashing over the waterfall. He would never forget the scare of Paya shoving him over, or the great surprise of the soft landing in the pool below.

Soon he stood at the top of the falls. By torchlight he could see that they were barely taller than he was. He fidgeted at the top. He eyed the route he and Paya had climbed back up two days ago, but he didn't think he could manage it holding the torch. No choice then.

He held the torch high and jumped.

He blubbed to the surface of the water with a roar in his ears and absolute blackness for his eyes. Gingerly, he touched the end of the torch. Hot but wet. He muttered at himself and groped his way forward. The Immortals gave people eyes for a good reason.

This time he came into the light from the air shaft gradually. It made the entire lake an impossible shimmer, perhaps a mirage. He thought of the blind fish and the stone flower and wondered what other miracles he would find if he explored. But he had a job to do.

He splashed toward the air shaft, one time stepping in suddenly over his head. He clambered out of the water and up the incline toward the surface of the earth, what he'd always thought was the real world. Near the entrance the rock turned into a garden of lichens, colors brighter than usually seen outside.

He found his way to the exact spot where Paya had scraped. There was the same evidence. The residue was red. Paya was gathering *u-tsa-le-ta*.

Dahzi thought, *Naughty boy*.

Now to find some. Maybe, being watched, Paya hadn't searched thoroughly.

In fact, Dahzi found the red lichen almost at the mouth of the shaft. It was a nice piece, half the size of an oak leaf.

He had a strange feeling about it, a sense of hypnotic pull. He looked toward the world outside, with its sunrises and sunsets and green plants and skies full of birds and woods full of leaves and berries and animals. He had a job to do there, too. Maybe he should climb out of the cave and check it out as a possible location for an attack on Inaj. Find out where the trail was, and where the Cheowa village was. He didn't even know what side of the mountain this entrance was on. It could be in the wrong direction, or it could be exactly what he needed for his revenge.

He put his palm on the *u-tsa-le-ta*. He felt power in it. He could go to Paya's fire and make tea.

All right, Dahzi told himself, *one job at a time.* He started scraping at the lichens.

29

The tea was sweet and tangy and made him sleepy. *Why not?* he said to himself. He stretched out and relaxed.

Before long he woke up and realized that he was lost. A forest. This forest was dense, heavy, overhanging—it turned the world to twilight and shadows. He was at a fork in the path, and he didn't know which way to go. Down each byway he could see another fork, beyond that another. Suddenly his mind raised high, and he could see miles of dense forest, the way a raven, a buzzard, or an eagle did. With his strange vision he could see through the thick canopy of branches and leaves, could see all the paths and all the choices in the paths one after another, as many choices as there are days in a lifetime. No end to it, and no way, ever, to be sure what way to go.

He was back under the canopy of trees, back on a single path. Where was he trying to go? He couldn't remember. A great pang tore through his chest. Then he told himself, *I don't remember, but I will. I'll remember, or I'll recognize it, or . . .*

But he doubted that, doubted himself. Almost forgot himself as a self.

He tried to think, but every thought was cut off by the word *lost.* It echoed throughout his being, like that was the first breath he ever breathed, and every breath after.

A thought slapped him. *Running from somebody, I'm running from somebody.* Or was he? He wasn't sure.

His legs moved willy-nilly in some direction or another. He didn't tell them to move—he was only a passenger on the boat of his legs. This way he floated, that way, any way. Everywhere the forest was oppressive. It hung over him like clouds of catastrophe. It created darkness that kept him from seeing where he was going.

One step ahead of his foot a crack opened in the earth. As he gaped at it, it opened wider, to four times the size.

He leapt and landed on the far side.

The crack groaned and doubled again in width.

Now he wondered if he was on the wrong side. *No way back now.*

He turned forward to try to see where he was going. He would always be lost unless he could see.

Then he noticed. Low bushes of every kind lined the path, and in the closest one on his left nested a black snake.

No, the black snake was one of the leaves.

No, all the leaves were snakes, their heads weaving, their tongues flickering in and out.

All the bushes turned into snakes, thousands or millions of black snakes. Every twig of every tree became a snake, heads undulating back and forth, eyes wild with malice.

He thought for a moment, *Black snakes are not poisonous— their bite doesn't kill.*

As the thought formed, though, so did the answer. Their weapon was not poison—it was terror.

The snakes struck. They didn't touch Dahzi, but only darted their heads toward him and snapped their fangs in the air inches away.

He screamed.

He turned and started to run. The crack in the earth had turned into a canyon, and it was full of snakes.

A snake wrapped itself around his neck and wound its head to glare directly into his eyes. Its muscles oozed around his throat.

Dahzi gazed into the snake's eyes hypnotically. He saw a dance of . . .

The world lurched.

Dahzi felt himself seized bodily and hurled through something, not air, maybe through realities.

He materialized next to a fire and a couple of figures. He bellowed. All in the world he could do was bellow.

Tsola said to Klandagi, "Praise the spirits, he's still alive."

FIVE

A Dangerous Mission

Maybe Dahzi slept for days, except that in the Emerald Cavern there were no days and no nights. From time to time he sipped some broth. When Tsola got him to eat soup with a little meat, she began to talk to him.

"You're lucky to be alive."

"Ummm." He could barely bring his mind to focus on what was around him.

She fed him some more soup. "You were about to be killed."

The snakes, he remembered. The snake around his neck, the snake in his face. "Yes." He was surprised at the faintness of his own voice.

"Not only your body killed, your spirit killed."

"Ummm?"

"Perhaps we'd better wait to talk."

She fed him in silence, and he dozed off.

When he felt strong enough to sit up and stay up, he looked around. A fire. Meat spitted over it. The ordinary tools of living. The walls of a cave. The face of a beautiful old woman looking into his face. Lying next to her, a black panther.

She put her hand gently on the panther's head. "Don't be afraid of Klandagi. He's on our side."

Dahzi began to form a dim realization. "Where am I?"

"In the Emerald Cavern."

He nodded. That meant something to him, the great shrine of the Galayi people, so this must be . . .

"Let's start over. I am Tsola, the Seer."

Dahzi nodded. "And Wounded Healer," he murmured. It was coming back.

"Yes. And this is my son Klandagi. Today he's presenting himself in his panther form."

Dahzi knew. Sunoya had told him, others had told him. But it was a jolt to see.

"How did I get here? I was lost."

"You did a very foolish thing, went to a very dangerous place, and I had to bring you back."

Dahzi tried to sort that out and failed. "Did something dumb."

"Yes. You made tea from *u-tsa-le-ta* and drank it. You knew better. Ninyu and your mother taught you better."

"Wasn't clear, felt confused."

"You're not a child anymore. It's time you get some clarity and act like you have it."

"I, uh . . ."

"Here's how we start. How did you get into the cavern, and how did you find the *u-tsa-le-ta?*"

He realized he needed to tell the whole truth. He started all the way back with how he sought a vision and failed. Then he told how he fell in love with Jemel and was denied her, how he ran away from the village. As he went along, the story got less jumbled.

"I had a crazy idea of what I was going to do. I was going to kill the murderer of my mother and father, the man who has brought twenty winters of misery to the people. My grandfather, Inaj."

He looked into Tsola's eyes, wondering, and saw that she was waiting. He let the spasm of rage pass.

"I thought if I did that, Jemel's family would let me marry her. They'd have to. I would have been a great hero."

Klandagi snorted with contempt.

Tsola spoke softly but firmly. "You would have been a great fool. Instead of saving the people, you would have pitched them to greater misery."

"I wanted to be a hero."

"You speak like a boy. It's time to act like a man."

"I'm not a man yet. I don't have a vision, I don't have a name."

"Yes, well, by madness and luck you've ended up where you can get both. And become a hero."

She saw the light animate his eyes for a moment, then give way to fatigue. "Get some sleep. Then we'll talk more. A lot more."

While Dahzi slept, Tsola and Klandagi discussed the problem. They needed a great mission accomplished, and had only a boy to do it.

"I have to prepare him and I have to motivate him."

Klandagi said, "If we don't launch him now, we probably won't see him again."

Tsola pulled at her chin. "He has to choose the mission. We can't force him into it, or trick him."

"His mind is on the girl, not on saving the people."

"He has powers he doesn't know about."

"No way for him to know." Klandagi said. "Also, he's thinking with his *do-wa,* and he's going to keep thinking with it."

"I sense something more there. He really loves her. Maybe she really loves him."

She sounded touched by the idea. Man-woman love, to most Galayi, was a piece of bad luck. But Tsola had always been intrigued by the idea.

Klandagi jumped up and started to pace. He forced himself

to stop and looked across at his mother by the fire. He made himself go back, lie down, and speak. "Here's one thing I've learned as a panther—human beings overthink things. When you're an animal, you know inside yourself what has to be done and you just do it, right now. Leap on that deer. Get away from that buffalo. Kill that mother coyote and get the pups. You act. You might be fine, you might get hurt, you might die, but you act."

Tsola regarded him thoughtfully. "In this case that would mean?"

"Light a fire in the boy and send him out. Now."

"What if he fails?"

"Then he was never the medicine bearer. But I believe he is—look at his left hand again. He'll find a way."

Tsola nodded. "All right."

❖

"How many days have I been in here?" said Dahzi.

"We don't pay attention to days and nights in the Cavern," Tsola said.

"Is the Planting Moon Ceremony going on now?"

"We have more important things to think about."

He was getting strong. She'd taken him on a good walk in the Cavern yesterday. Klandagi kept saying it was time.

"Here's what happened to you. You had a big piece of good luck and bad luck. You wandered into the Emerald Cavern, without knowing it. Paya found you—he goes everywhere here, everywhere but one. Like a fool, whether he meant to or not, he showed you the lichen. As far as I know, this is the only place it grows.

"You recognized it—you'd seen Ninyu and your mother with it. You made the tea and drank it, and you didn't just have dreams. Ninyu gave you the apprentice's version of what happens. You traveled to the Land beyond the Sky Arch."

Disbelief flushed into his face. "The Land beyond the Sky Arch doesn't look like that."

"Actually," said Tsola, "it doesn't look like anything. Its form is spirit, not flesh. But we're human beings, and when we visit there we see it as physical. That's the way our minds are."

"Until I got there, I pictured it as the most beautiful place in the universe."

"It's whatever is in your mind is at the time. You were scared, so the Land was scary."

She watched Dahzi turn that over in his head.

"You are afraid of snakes, so you were attacked by snakes. What you saw tells us nothing about the Land beyond the Arch and everything about you."

Now he shook his head. He didn't think so.

"You need to remember this. You have remarkable powers. You were born with them. If an ordinary person drank that tea, someone who isn't a shaman, he would have awful dreams and wake up with a bad fever. You took the journey—only a few of us can. I brought you back."

Dahzi made a face, but she could tell that being special pleased him.

"What do you mean," he said, "you brought me back?"

"When I saw you were in trouble, I drummed myself across the border between this world and that one. I do it often, to consult with the Immortals. I grabbed you and brought us both back."

"That was the scariest thing of all."

"And it left you depleted, exhausted," said Tsola. "That won't happen when you learn to come and go properly."

"I . . ." He made a strange face. He didn't like this conversation.

"Why don't I let you be alone for a while? Go for a walk

if you want to. If you get lost, I can find you anywhere in the Cavern."

When he got back, he was excited. "I found the river."

Klandagi gave Tsola a look that meant, *He doesn't know what's waiting for him there.*

Tsola gave him food and tea. "Dahzi, we have to talk seriously. You have a mission, a big mission, something that has to be done for the people."

Dahzi waited. Her guess was that he was half excited and half stubborn.

"Your job is to get a new Cape of Feathers for the people."

There, it was in the open. All her attention was on the boy's eyes. What was in them? Excitement? Anger?

"What are you thinking?"

"When I was born, Inaj killed my father."

"Exactly. The tragedy of our time."

"Especially for me. His crime controls my life."

"Go on."

"For twenty winters, because of what he did and kept doing, a guard followed me everywhere I went. Now, because of his crime, you want me to set out on some huge mission."

"Yes."

"Doesn't anyone care what I want?"

Tsola looked at Klandagi. Holding his eyes, she took time to think this through. Finally she said, "This is not because of your grandfather. He's just the instrument. This is what you were born for." She picked up his left hand and stroked the webbing gently.

"I don't believe my hand is my fate."

"You can embrace the call, or you can resist it."

"I embrace Jemel and resist other people's ideas for my life."

"Damn it, boy," said Klandagi in his gravel voice. "Don't you understand? You can have everything. Do something great for your people. Be a hero. Be admired. Have the woman you love. Be a leader."

Dahzi set his face.

"Here's the main thing," said Tsola. "If you embrace your calling, it can be good. Grand. If you resist it, the calling will hound you."

Dahzi's face set itself harder.

"We can talk about it later," she said. "Time to sleep."

But when Tsola and Klandagi woke up, Dahzi was gone.

31

Dahzi waited in the shadow of a big boulder just above the entrance to the Cavern, watching the house and the Pool of Healing. The Pool, fed by a spring below the mouth of the Cavern, had three or four visitors. An old woman was showing them how to use the healing waters. If Dahzi remembered right, the helpers were Tsola's daughters. Tsola lived in the Cavern, her son guarded it and her, and her daughters ministered to people who came for help.

Dahzi had been taught the patience of a hunter, and he used it now. He crouched in his shadow and didn't stir. He got hungry and thirsty, but he stayed perfectly still. *I myself am a shadow.*

Visitors—they were a good sign for Dahzi. Galayi people came to the Pool mostly when they were at the Cheowa village for the Planting Moon Ceremony, just an hour's walk away. If the ceremony was going on, or about to start, his mother would be there. His mind added, *Inaj will be there*, but he tried not to pay attention.

He waited for full darkness, all the time listening for footpads from inside the Cavern. He didn't want to get caught, especially by a panther.

When everyone was gone or in the family's house, Dahzi slipped down to the pond, lay flat on his belly, and drank deep. He was ferociously thirsty, and he could use some healing.

Then he made his way down the mountain to the village. He did it the hard way, in the underbrush. Klandagi might be watching the trail.

By midnight he could peer down on the houses and council lodge. No dancing—the ceremony hadn't started. But the Soco village might have arrived already. He circled the Cheowa houses, found a log, eased it into the river, and floated gently downstream.

Yes, there were the brush huts of his village, at their usual camping place.

He shivered until first light. Then he padded quietly among the huts until he found Sunoya's. He scratched the door flap and said, "Mother."

She peered out, then leapt out and embraced him. Su-Li jumped off her shoulder and lit on the hut. He didn't care for gestures of affection.

"Mother, I need to sleep."

She pointed to her own blankets.

He wrapped up. *Warm and safe.*

❖

When Dahzi woke up, his mother had tea and corn mush ready for him. He ate and drank greedily. He kept giving her sneaky looks, wondering when she'd ask where he'd been. She didn't ask, which was a relief.

Su-Li croaked at him. The buzzard's eyes looked, as usual, like he was teasing.

Dahzi teased back, "Is that your wisdom for today?"

Then he noticed the shadow hulked by the door. "Who's that?"

"Your guard," said his mother.

Dahzi suppressed irritation. "Mother, I'm done with guards."

She sighed and said nothing.

"Mother!"

"It was never my decision, it's what the family wants." She paused. "And they're right."

Dahzi huffed out his exasperation.

"Son, Inaj is here for the ceremony. His warriors are here. He can probably guess revenge is on your mind—it would be on his. I can't think of a worse time to be without a guard."

"If I was a child."

"The bravest warrior in the tribe isn't safe against an ambush, or an attack by a dozen men."

Su-Li a-a-arked.

Sunoya said, "Why is this so important to you?"

"I am a man. I want to be treated as a man."

"Then do your vision quest, earn a name."

"Tsola says I have to do a different quest, much harder."

"Tsola?"

"Yes."

His mother didn't ask. "Then you do."

"You're all messing around with me."

"What are you talking about?"

He reacted to the edge in her voice. "All of you. You treat me like a child. You say I can't have Jemel." Now his voice curdled. "I have a life! It's mine!"

Su-Li rasped out a quick, harsh sound. Sunoya could feel his anger. She deliberately made her voice gentle. It wasn't the Galayi way to speak harshly, especially a son to a mother, or a mother to a son.

"Is Jemel everything?"

He dropped his head and appeared to find something fascinating in his crossed legs. "Mother, please don't tell me about Moon Women, or about the madness of love."

She shrugged.

"It's rare, but it happens, and it's beautiful. I can barely tell you how I feel when I'm with her."

"And she feels the same way?"

"She started it. Her mother was a Moon Woman, and brought her up to live this way."

"That's why her relatives took her all the way to the Cusa Village. That's why she's not here."

Dahzi looked lightning at her. "We will be together."

"Her relatives will stop that."

Su-Li fluffed his feathers and squeezed Sunoya's shoulder in impatience.

Without words Sunoya asked him, *Is this passion real, or is he thinking with his do-wa?*

Both, said Su-Li. *His do-wa is marching a hundred steps ahead of his brain. But the passion is real.*

It is also love?

Yes.

Sunoya pursed her lips and thought.

Someone scratched at the door.

She gave Dahzi a nervous look and called, "Come in."

An elderly gentleman ducked through the door flap and gave them a kind smile. Looking again at Dahzi, he said, "Am I intruding?"

"You are an honored guest, Grandfather," said Sunoya. "Would you like something to eat?"

"Thank you," said the gentleman. He sat by the morning fire, moving with remarkable suppleness and grace.

Sunoya felt relief spread through her like a blessing, and she knew Su-Li felt the same way.

She said, "Pusa, this is my son Dahzi." Then she turned her back to hide her smile. She was thrilled to see him, and flabbergasted.

"Welcome, Grandfather." It was a term of respect given to any elderly man, and this man was unmistakably important.

Pusa spooned mush out of the bowl Sunoya gave him and kept his face carefully blank. Sunoya knew he didn't really like to eat anything but meat.

Me neither, quipped Su-Li.

Sunoya frowned at him.

When Pusa finished, he said to Dahzi, "I bring a message to you from Tsola, the Seer."

"What?" His tone was barely respectful, and Sunoya gave him a look.

"She has asked me to offer you a path of action that will help the people and win you Jemel."

The silence was unnerving. Dahzi's mind swirled with confusion. He'd run away from Tsola. She'd told a stranger about his predicament? And this stranger was to set things right?

"This is a hard task," Pusa went on, "and the rewards are huge. If you agree to take it on, the Seer will give you a name. When you complete the first part, you will get a vision quest to the Land beyond the Sky Arch and a gift from Thunderbird."

Su-Li rasped. Sunoya could feel his amazement, and he could feel hers.

"And when you are finished, Tsola herself will ask Jemel's parents to give her to you as a wife."

Dahzi worked his Adam's apple up and down. *Unbelievable.* His eyes flicked from his mother to this stranger.

Barely able to control her voice, Sunoya said, "Dahzi, I know this is surprising. But you can trust Pusa. He is the Seer's closest confidante."

Dahzi murmured, "Tell me what you want me to do."

"It will take some telling. Sunoya, would you make us some tea?"

Su-Li fluttered onto Dahzi's shoulder. Sunoya jumped up, broke sassafras roots into a deer stomach, and tonged in some hot rocks from the fire. "Ready soon."

Pusa said to her, "Maybe you'll send Su-Li outside to watch. Let's make sure we're safe."

Dahzi thought, *This man is scared, too.*

Sunoya sent a silent query to Su-Li. When she got his answer, she said, "I think Su-Li should hear what you have to say."

Pusa inclined his head to her wisdom. "Then let's move outside where we can all see, and be sure no one is close enough to hear us."

They did.

Pusa asked, "Who is this man?"

"Toma, a relative we use as a guard. He is trustworthy."

Pusa nodded. The guard moved a few steps off. His eyes constantly flicked over the entire camp.

Sunoya handed them steaming cups of tea. Pusa looked long at the young man. "This is a big mission."

He was glad to see the embers of defiance in the boy's eyes.

"First, you must travel through all the land of the Galayi people and gather one hundred and eight wing feathers of the war eagle. You may not capture or kill any eagle. Take the feathers only from nests. You'll find out how hard this is. Awahi will tell you about eagles."

Awahi was an elderly man from the Cusa village, Eagle Voice, here to sing for the Eagle Dance in a couple of nights. His name meant "eagle voice."

"Gather only the finest and most beautiful feathers. That will show your devotion. When you have enough good ones, and perhaps some extras, take them to Awahi for a blessing, and then to Tsola.

"You must hunt these feathers entirely alone, and you may not visit your mother, Jemel, or anyone you know except

Awahi, Eagle Voice, until you have collected them all. Hunting to feed yourself is part of the task.

"The sooner you get the job done, the sooner you can begin the second part, and the sooner you can be married."

He let all that sink in. So far he could see only fire in the boy's eyes.

"Any questions?"

"What about the man who stole feathers from the war eagle and got punished?" It was a story even children knew.

"Awahi will teach you an old prayer that will placate them. More questions?"

"I do all this alone?"

"Yes. But you may meet people along the way who will help you. Nothing wrong with that. Any more questions?"

"No." The youth was beaming.

"You cannot visit Jemel."

"Yes."

"So. Now. If you agree, Tsola has already picked a name for you. I will give it to you as soon as you commit yourself heart and soul to gathering the feathers."

The youth gave his mother a look that said, 'I told you so.'

"I promise to do my best to bring Tsola one hundred and eight beautiful feathers." His words thrummed with energy. "If my mother will make me a *zadayi* disk, I will come back wearing the red side out."

"Then I give you the name Tsola has decided to honor you with. You are Ulo-Zeya, The One Who Dwells in the Clouds."

Dahzi gasped. Sunoya and Su-Li tingled with wonder. It was an enormous honor, the title of Thunderbird himself, the model for all winged creatures in both worlds, of time and of eternity.

"When you present the feathers to Tsola, she will tell you what the rest of your mission is. It is the shortest in time, but the most difficult and dangerous. When you succeed, she will speak to Jemel's family on your behalf." He didn't need to say that no Galayi family would refuse such a request from the Seer.

Three people and one buzzard sitting against the hut wall, elated and on edge, held each other's eyes.

"Tsola offers you two bits of advice. Be careful about telling anyone you're on a mission for the Seer. It would bring you enemies. And use only the name Zeya."

It meant "dweller," an equivalent of "citizen," a name of no distinction. Dahzi mouthed his new name, Zeya. He liked it.

"Your true name would attract too much attention. What else do you need to know?"

"When do I start?"

"Hunt first. Dry meat. Take a pack dog."

"Dogs makes me nervous."

"And Su-Li nervous," said Sunoya.

"All right," Pusa.

"I will make a disc for you," said his mother.

"Wear it with the red side out," said Pusa, "to show you expect victory."

"I have a question," said Sunoya. "Can he take a companion?"

"Who?" said Pusa.

"May Su-Li go with him?"

Zeya, Pusa, and Su-Li were astonished at the question.

Pusa considered, worrying one earlobe with his fingers. Finally he said, "Does Su-Li want to go?"

Sunoya looked across and into the eyes of her companion, still sitting on Zeya's shoulder. She said, "Yes."

Pusa said, "Then I think it's a good idea, on one condition. Su-Li may not help Ulo-Zeya find nests or gather feathers. That he must do on his own."

"Yes," said Zeya.

The old man clapped his hands and grinned. Then he

reached out to the earth and rolled forward onto all fours. He looked into Zeya's eyes with a strange smile. His eyes took on a look of great concentration, and his body began to change. Claws oozed out from the ends of fingers and toes. Hair turned into fur. Teeth stretched into fangs and crept onto his lower lip. Eyes switched from brown to a scintillating gold. Last, a human head flattened and grew a muzzle, and the face became feline.

Zeya squeaked out, "Klandagi?"

In a low roar the panther said, "May the spirits be with you, my son."

Zeya stammered, "T-t-thank you."

32

When Klandagi disappeared among the brush huts, Zeya stepped around and squatted beside his guard. "Toma," he said, "I'm sorry for what I did to you."

The guard gave him an odd look but said, "I understood."

Zeya gave back a big smile. Over twenty years he'd gotten to know the guards well. They were all relatives and clansmen.

"You can go. I'm finished with guards now."

Sunoya came close. "It's all right, Toma. He's right. No more guards."

Zeya grinned at his mother.

Toma was a rotund fellow of about forty, not a warrior or hunter of any particular distinction, but a good father, a good husband, and a man was who overly fond of good food and ribald jokes.

He hesitated. This was something new.

"Come on," said Zeya, "let's all tell Grandfather Ninyu together." Ninyu and his wives were in the brush hut next door.

"Okay," said Sunoya. "He'll be glad not to have to spend every morning making a guard schedule." She was pretending to feel a lot lighter than she did.

"Now that you don't have to baby-sit me," said Zeya, "what are you going to do?"

"Go deer hunting," said Toma. The bands had carried ground meal and dried meat as they walked to the ceremony, so everyone now longed for fresh meat.

"Me, too," said Zeya.

He scratched on Ninyu's door flap and heard a call to come in.

"Want to come hunting with me?" said Toma.

Bending down to the low door, Zeya said over his shoulder, "I have to go alone."

❖

Zeya's first decision was to hunt well away from the camps. The forest around the encampments would be filled with hunters right now, so the deer were scattered elsewhere. He took enough food for a couple of days, walked up the river toward the mountain pass, and followed a creek running off a far ridge.

He felt light. His feet wanted to skip. For the first time in his life he was wild with freedom.

That evening, a full day's walk from camp, he found tracks that showed where deer came to water. He eyed the route they had to follow downhill to get to this spot. He backed away, leaving as little scent as possible, worked his way up the mountain, and found a limestone outcropping that overlooked the deer path. Then he stretched out, watched, enjoyed the sun, and thought.

What did he need to do to come back with 108 feathers, wearing the red zadayi outward? What did he need to learn to be the best possible hunter, so he wouldn't waste his days searching for food? What did he need to do to arm himself against enemies?

He had to learn all he could from Awahi, the man who sang to eagles, for sure. He would also trade somehow for a war club and get some practice using it. He knew the trick was to swing the head so that it had some real force at the moment of impact, and not just be a falling stone. He would get a start on learning that skill.

Waiting was a good time to think, but Zeya found his mind drifting away. He wasn't much worried about any of these difficulties—they seemed trivial. Instead he fantasized. He pictured himself in the blankets with Jemel. He imagined the first child they would have. He imagined several people greeting him respectfully as The One Who Dwells in the Clouds, especially Jemel's mother and father, who had acted scornful to him. Also one of her older brothers. That fellow wanted to become Red Chief and carried himself with an arrogance that put him far above Zeya. But below The One Who Dwells in the Clouds.

Somehow Zeya got lost in his fantasies and woke up chill in the middle of the night. If the deer had come in the twilight, they were gone now.

Between first light and dawn he remedied that. Two does pranced lightly down the path, stopping every few steps to sniff the breeze. Though Zeya was upwind of them, maybe they caught a remnant of his smell from yesterday. They acted wary, so wary that he risked a throw before he should have. His spear struck true. One doe down, the other bounding away.

He sang the prayer that would keep the king of the deer from making his joints swell, cut off the meat he needed, built a fire, and started drying it. His adventure was off to a good start.

In three days he was back in the Soco camp and in his mother's hut. She almost burst into tears when she saw him.

"What's wrong, Mother?"

"Oh, Toma went hunting with two of his nephews and didn't come back. It made me afraid for you."

"Where did Toma go?"

"He'll turn up tomorrow."

"Can't Su-Li find him?"

"No luck with that yet."

Zeya was sorry, but he had a plan for today. He had to go to the Cusa camp and talk to Awahi.

❖

"Grandfather, the spirits have called me to find one hundred and eight eagle feathers. I am asked not to name the purpose, but please believe that my heart is good."

Sunoya told the man who sang to eagles, "He's telling the truth. He's walking the red path."

The old man was sitting in front of his brush hut, facing the morning sun. He looked so frail that Zeya wondered how he managed to sing vigorously for several hours. When he sang, he accompanied himself on an instrument made of one string stretched on a length of wood. His own body seemed to be made of no more.

"A hundred and eight?" His voice cracked, which it never did when he was singing.

"Yes, Grandfather." He threw a look at his mother.

She got up. "I'll leave you two to talk."

Awahi watched her go, his lips twitching and damp. Su-Li pivoted on her shoulder and watched the two of them.

"Maybe you can do it," Awahi wheezed, "maybe you can. Do you know how the war eagles nest?"

"I know nothing, Grandfather."

"Each pair mates for life. Here at their home during warm weather, they build three or four nests at different aeries, sometimes more, all very high and hard to get to, so they'll be safe from predators. Like you. They like rocky ledges, usually, and they make the nest bigger across than a man is tall, and higher than his waist. Some years they use one nest, some another."

He smacked his lips together oddly. Zeya felt a great distance between himself and Awahi, Eagle Voice, a chasm made by the passing of winters.

"They are here now. Every spring they rebuild whatever nest they choose for this stay, with twigs, moss, bark, and grasses. Then the female lays eggs, usually two. Now she's sitting on them, while the male hunts and brings her food. He likes the balds for hunting, not the valleys, where the thick forest blocks his vision."

Zeya gaped, but didn't even think of speaking.

"After about one and a half moons the eggs hatch. Then the birds take turns, one stays home and the other hunts for the whole family. Most of the time the bigger chick will live and the smaller will die, sometimes killed by its brother or sister."

Zeya almost exclaimed at that.

"The nature of every animal is different," said Awahi, "and every one is what it should be.

"After about another two moons, the baby bird will be fledged out enough to fly. You may enjoy watching the young in their first flights. Then the mates teach their offspring to hunt. And finally, like all good parents, they kick him out so he can make a life for himself somewhere, and they head south for the winter.

"Right now the mother is sitting on the eggs. If you go near the nest, you'll be attacked by two birds whose wings spread further than you are tall. Their killing dive is the fastest movement of all the animals. Their talons can bring death to a wolf." He gave a wry smile. "You'll want to try the nests they are not using this year."

Zeya's fears relaxed a little.

"You know about the one pair near your own village."

"Yes, Grandfather."

"Near my village there are four nesting pairs, and I'll draw a picture and show you where they are. In the mountains above the Emerald Cavern"—he inclined his head to indicate that he meant the ridges right above where they sat—"there are three pairs. And near the Tusca village"—he paused, gave Zeya a sad smile—"dangerous for you, there are two."

He slipped into his hut and came back with deer hide and some charcoal from the fire. He sketched quickly. "This is the Cheowa village." He drew the creek leading to the Pool of Healing and the entrance to the Cavern, and the ridges above.

"You can see this nest"—he made an X—"if you walk the ridge top and then look down to the right of the first creek." He diagrammed the location of three nests along these ridges, and then made a more elaborate picture with four nests marked near his home village. "I don't remember much about the nests in the Tusca region. I was there only once as a very young man. They're in the first mountain range as you travel toward the Soco River, that's all I know."

❖

"Su-Li," she said, "I don't think we've let Zeya see your yes and no."

Sunoya smiled at her son. "This is really complicated." To Su-Li, "Show him no."

From his perch on the snag the buzzard shook his head back and forth with comical exaggeration.

Sunoya chuckled. "Do you think you can guess yes?"

Zeya said, "Why didn't you tell me? All these years . . ."

She shrugged. "We didn't need the signals. You do. Now he's going to teach you some more complicated ones."

Su-Li glided down like he was going to land on Zeya's extended arm. At the last moment he cut a sharp turn and wing-flapped off straight back the way he came. Then he landed in the top of a snag, looked at the two human beings, and beamed a message down to Sunoya. *What does he think that means?*

"Okay," Sunoya said to Zeya, "this is the first signal, and he wants you to guess, see how well you two communicate just by intuition."

Zeya considered, *Straight toward me, straight back.*

Sunoya looked at her son quizzically.

"Uh," said Zeya, "he's telling he wants me to follow him that way fast."

Sunoya made a face. When she transmitted Zeya's guess to Su-Li, he shook his head back and forth and gave out the loudest croak Zeya had heard from him.

"Exactly the opposite," said Sunoya. "That signal means danger is coming from that way."

Zeya mumbled, "Danger coming from that way."

"Now, Su-Li, show us that one again."

Su-Li repeated the maneuver, ending up on the snag.

"Big one. Swoops right down at you, doesn't land, and flies back the way he came, that means there's danger coming from that direction."

Zeya nodded.

"He feels grumpy about doing this," said Sunoya. "He says it's our fault we have to make up these dumb signals. We messed things up so human beings can't talk to the other animals, or understand them."

Zeya knew the story, the time the other animals got mad at people and decided to send diseases against people and wipe them out. Except for the intervention of the plants, it would have worked. When human beings made peace with the animals, they still lost the ability to talk to other creatures.

Sunoya said, "Now, how can you tell him, 'Go the way I'm showing you'?"

Su-Li lifted off the snag, zoomed right at Zeya like he was

going to land on his arm, and at the last moment veered sharply off to the right.

"You see it?" said Sunoya. "That's the way you *should* go."

"The way I should go," repeated Zeya.

Su-Li ran the maneuver again, this time cutting off hard to the left.

"You understand?" said Sunoya.

Su-Li landed on Sunoya's arm.

"Now give him a signal for, 'There's a cave over that way,'" said Sunoya.

Su-Li cocked his head, then cocked it another direction. He hopped onto the ground—they knew he hated being on the ground. He picked up a rock the size of a small finger joint in his beak. He flew up, circled, and hurtled back toward the youth.

Zeya stuck out his arm in the routine way, wondering what on earth was going to happen.

Su-Li flapped and hovered at the last moment, didn't land, but dropped the stone into Zeya's hand. Then he flew off up the hill.

"Yes," said Zeya, "the stone means a cave, and he's flying toward it so I can follow."

Sunoya checked mentally with Su-Li and said, "You got it."

They went over the signals several times. "Your life could depend on knowing this," said Sunoya.

At long last they looked at each other, tired. Zeya said, "Are we finished?"

Sunoya thought and said, "One more. Su-Li, give him something that means, 'You've completely misunderstood what I'm telling you and are doing exactly the wrong thing.'"

The buzzard nodded his head a couple of times and launched from Sunoya's arm. He flew well up the mountain. Sunoya wondered if he was thinking something up. Suddenly he whirled and dived straight toward them. At the last moment he flung his wings out against the wind for a quick stop. He hovered for an instant above Zeya's hand and deposited a gob of white goo in his cupped palm.

Zeya hooted.

"Now follow through. What direction is right?" said Sunoya.

Su-Li wheeled another way.

"So the gob of droppings followed by a new direction," said Sunoya, "that means, 'You're headed the wrong way, dumbhead, follow me.'"

33

Toma whimpered. He despised himself for it, but he was beyond all self-control.

Inaj slid his obsidian blade firmly down Toma's inner thigh. Toma gave a little yip of pain. A finger's length of blood oozed out.

With even greater concentration Inaj made another cut, creating an L from the end of the first cut. He looked Toma in the eye. No exclamation of pain this time, but Inaj could see that his subject wouldn't hold out much longer. With a sure hand he made a third cut back up Toma's thigh. Then he gripped the bleeding flap of skin and slowly pulled it back.

The victim screamed again, a ululating wail.

"I hate that sound," said Wilu.

Zanda snorted.

Inaj looked up into Wilu's face. He said, "It's unworthy of

206 ❖ Caleb Fox

a man. But you can steel yourself so you don't hear it, if you want to. I myself enjoy the screams."

When Inaj got to the end of the parallel cuts, he kept pulling, tearing away the untouched flesh near the groin. When he exposed the red muscle beneath, he said, "There's the real meaning of 'naked man'." Toma's other thigh already showed a patch of nakedness the size of a man's hand.

"We know there are things you haven't told us," Inaj said.

Toma babbled. Every time he tried to talk a lot of gibberish came first. Inaj was disgusted by him. Gradually, the man had made enough words that Inaj and Zanda pieced some of it together. Toma had only heard part of the conversation, he claimed. Guard duty was watching, not eavesdropping.

Zanda said, "Let's go over it again, what we know. Klandagi came in the shape of an old man."

Toma nodded.

"He left in his panther shape."

"Y-e-e-s."

"He gave Zeya a mission."

Toma nodded.

"To gather eagle feathers."

Another nod.

"Why?"

Toma shrugged.

"You didn't hear that?'

Inaj gave the ripped skin a vicious little tug.

Toma wailed. Tears ran down his face. "No," he said in a quaver.

"He's supposed to gather the feathers alone."

Nod.

"No guard."

A shake of the head.

"What's he supposed to do with them?"

A shrug.

Zanda said sharply, "Why are they doing all this?"

Another shrug.

Inaj said, "I don't think you've told us everything."

He started a new cut, this time straight across the knee cap.

A good while later, having shed a lot more blood but learned nothing more, Inaj stood up and handed Wilu the obsidian blade. "Entertain yourself with him, then kill him."

"Let's just kill him," said Zanda.

"I want to watch Wilu play with him," Inaj spat out. He sat on a small boulder.

Wilu made a cut under one of Toma's nipples. By now the man was too weak even to whimper.

Zanda smiled at his father.

❖

As Inaj, Wilu, and Zanda walked back to the Tusca camp, Inaj said, "To be hideous to your enemies"—this was one of his favorite lines—"what would be more enviable?"

Wilu paid attention. His admired his father and followed him in order to learn. And he felt slighted. When Inaj stepped aside as Red Chief of the Tuscas—he wanted to give himself entirely to fighting—he had not supported Wilu as the new Red Chief. He had spoken for Zanda, and Wilu's younger brother was elected. Wilu pretended not to mind.

Sometimes his father's fierceness made Wilu quail a little, and he was ashamed of that. A warrior's greatest strengths were to be relentless and fierce.

Inaj smiled at the night. "You know," he said, "Sunoya and Ninyu have just made their big mistake."

Zanda and Wilu nodded.

Inaj seemed to be thinking out loud. "I will send four men against the whelp who pretends to be a medicine bearer."

"Father, let me kill him," said Zanda.

"Maybe," said Inaj. "I will send three other men first. We know where the nests are. Our warriors can find him." They walked several steps while Inaj thought.

"You and I, though, we will go on a visit to see my brother in the Cusa village. Hah! The sanctuary village."

Cusa was well known as a peace band. If any person committed a crime, the victim's clan brothers would go after him. But if the man reached the Cusas before they caught him, even if he was from another tribe, he was given sanctuary. Then the wrong would have to be set right without a beating or bloodshed. Inaj despised the Cusas. They lived deep in the southern mountains, far from the enemies to the east or west. According to Inaj, they let the other bands do their fighting for them.

"Hah! Won't my brother be surprised." Inaj had never visited the Cusas. "And a fine irony. When the pretender brings the feathers there to seek a blessing, if he lasts that long, you will make him a gift of death."

34

Earlier that same morning Zeya, the man once called The Hungry One, now Dweller-in-Clouds, packed his travel gear in two slings, on one side a hairless elk hide and two pairs of moccasins, on the other a wrap of dried deer meat. He was his own pack dog, but it was a modest load—Zeya meant to move fast.

Zeya adjusted the slings on his shoulders. He paid no attention to his mother, who could tell stories about old times forever. He picked up his spear and his war club from where they leaned against the brush hut.

His mother hugged him and gave him a kiss on the cheek. "Don't forget. From here to village edge your name is Dahzi. Every step after that, it's Zeya."

"Yes, Mother."

She held him at arm's length. "People will see you leave. You never know what . . ." She avoided speaking of Inaj by name. "People don't know who Zeya is. Pays to be wily." One last hug. "Go."

Zeya held out his arm. It was a delicate moment. "Su-Li," he said.

"When you're out of the village," she said, "I'll send him after you. It's good to keep some things secret."

Zeya strode away smiling. He liked his new name. For several days he'd been calling himself Dahzi Zeya jokingly. He liked it. *Hungry Citizen.*

He intended to hunt feathers and not deer. He could gather wild onions, rose hips, chestnuts, acorns, and other wild food as he went. He didn't need to take the time to stalk deer, butcher them out, and dry the meat, so he told himself. Zeya would hunt feathers on a thin belly, he would use the urge in his stomach to drive himself harder. He would have 108 feathers before anyone knew it—he would stun Tsola with the breakneck speed of his triumph.

His fellow villagers looked at him as he walked past. A few nodded, no one spoke. He had been disgraced when Jemel's family marched out of the village to keep their daughter away from him. Probably they thought now that he was headed to the Cusa village to try to see her, and be humiliated again.

Let them think so. Deception is good.

But cover his trail? Walk the hard way through the forest instead of taking the trail? He didn't think so. He didn't expect anyone to follow him. If they did follow on such a well-traveled trail, they wouldn't be able to pick out his moccasin prints from scores of others. And when he crossed the river, he would lose them. He chuckled. The imaginary "them." His mother was a worrywart.

He was walking his own path. Awahi had said to try the nests right around here first. But Zeya had a burning to go back to the spot where he had sought a vision and been shamed.

He'd seen feathers in the nest below. There he would turn shame into conquest.

❖

That evening Inaj, Wilu, and Zanda followed Awahi away from the ceremony. The old man loved to sing to the eagles—it was his calling—but it wore him out. The dancing would go on far into the night. The custom at the Planting Moon Ceremony was to dance all night and sleep half the day. Right now Awahi would wrap himself in a robe and doze a while, and at dawn walk back to his camp with his relatives.

He padded over to a place where he could drink from the river easily, and where thick tufts of grass would make his rest good.

As he lay on his belly slurping up the sweet, cool water, hands grabbed his arms. He stood up of his own accord. He had no fear of enemies—who would attack the Galayi when all the warriors of all the bands were gathered together?

When he saw Inaj's face, his stomach knotted. Everyone knew the former Red Chief, the man who had kept the people at war all these years.

"What do you want from me?"

"You told Zeya, the Soco, how to gather eagle feathers."

"I taught him how to do it in a sacred manner."

"What will he do with these feathers?" asked Wilu. The son's voice didn't have the menace of the father's.

"He'll bring them to me for a blessing." The old man thought it best not to mention Tsola, who had humiliated Inaj at the great council nineteen winters ago.

"When?"

"During the Harvesting Moon."

"Where is he hunting nests first?"

Awahi hesitated. So far what he had said was entirely to Zeya's credit. This question sounded dangerous.

Inaj knocked him flat, sat on his chest, and began to choke him. "Quick, old man, don't think how to fool me."

Awahi looked into Inaj's eyes and saw evil. He held up his hands in a plea, and Inaj eased his grip.

Awahi turned his head back and forth to soften the pain in his neck. The end of his life? He was old and rickety. Death did not seem like such a bad idea.

"Old man, I know how to inflict pain, a lot of pain."

Awahi decided. Quickly, weakly, he squeaked out, "I gave him a map of some nests near my village. He'll go there first."

Inaj got up. Awahi lay still, afraid even of Inaj's eyes.

"Old man," said Inaj, "if you are wise, you'll tell no one that we asked you these questions."

Awahi nodded. Far inside himself he said, *I sent you the wrong direction and got away with it.*

Twenty steps away Inaj murmured to Zanda, "The old man is lying. The boy knows the nests near the Soco village. That's where he's gone."

35

Zeya was boulder-hopping along a ridge on a fine morning. He wore a necklace of eleven eagle feathers under his shirt, each dangling from a leather thong. The ones on the necklace were beautiful, and they were grouped into four on the right side of his chest and seven over his heart. The four represented the four directions, and the seven stood for the directions understood more fully—east, south, west, north, above, below, and the center, which is in the heart.

He was feeling very good about himself. At the nest below the spot where he'd tried for a vision, he'd found thirteen good feathers altogether, one for each moon in the Galayi calendar. That site now seemed to him a place of special blessings. He located two other nests not far away. They would have been within easy walking distance if the route hadn't been straight up and down, using hands and feet.

Then he had walked ten days to the mountains surrounding the Cusa village. He had a feeling that was the right area to try next. On the walk he'd gotten to know Su-Li much better. Every night they huddled in a cave and had a one-sided dialogue. Zeya couldn't hear Su-Li's half of the conversation, but he could guess it. He spoke his thoughts, watched Su-Li's eyes, and supplied the answer in his imagination.

"You're grumpy, aren't you?"

No answer.

"Is it because we spend every night in a cave?"

No answer.

"We're called the People who Live in Caves."

"A-a-ark!"

"I like caves."

They're full of snakes, spiders, and other poisonous creatures.

"The fire is cozy."

The sky has the warmth of the sun.

"It's safe in here."

You can't even stand up, and I have to walk to get out. Walk!

"You don't like doing this with me, do you?"

It's my duty.

"Well, these long years with my mother, away from the other Immortals, they're also your duty, and you don't like that."

Su-Li made a rasping sound, and Zeya wasn't sure what it meant.

"Except, you've actually gotten fond of her, haven't you? You love my mother."

Su-Li jumped onto Zeya's arm, put his beak right in front of Zeya's nose, and flapped his wings violently.

"Okay, that's a big no. I get it."

But he still thought Su-Li did, secretly. Maybe secretly from himself.

❖

Zeya was out looking for the nests near his own village. At the ridge top Zeya climbed an outcropping to get the best view. He thought he knew where he was. He looked up at Su-Li and saw that the buzzard wasn't signaling him anything.

Then he spotted the nest. It was huge, and built on a rocky spire that stood out from the cliff. He didn't see a bird on it. Even if the eaglet was too small to spot, one of the parents would have been on the nest, guarding the eggs, easy to see.

He whooped his excitement.

He angled down the hill to the base of the spire to figure out a way to climb it. He reached up to test a hold with his right hand.

A spear point slammed into his left armpit.

He fell and rolled downhill. The spear levered out, ripping flesh.

He came up on all fours and skittered behind a boulder.

He breathed. His hearing, his sight, his smell soared into full alert.

His eyes fixed on the spear lying out in the open, bloody. *That point cut through me a fingernail's span from my heart and lung.*

I'm still alive.

His eyes ate everything within throwing distance and saw nothing. *What the devil?!*

Alive but bleeding plenty.

My enemy knows where I am. I have to move.

His enemy was also somewhere above him. Which gave Zeya an idea. He slipped his spear across his back, through the straps that held his sling bags. He let his war club dangle from its wrist loop. He took a second look up. Impossible to climb. Except . . . except he needed the impossible.

Zeya reached high and slipped his hand into a crack. No good, too wide. He fished for a hold inside of it. No luck. He made a fist. Ecstasy—it filled the crack tight. He leaned his weight on the fist, walked his feet a couple of steps up the wall, jammed the other fist into the crack up higher, stepped up again, and grabbed a high handhold. In an instant he was on top of the boulder. His eyes made a survey in a circle. Still he saw nothing.

He slipped his sling bags off and climbed the cedar that hung out from the top. Still nothing.

Suddenly a man sprinted out of an outcropping, straight toward Zeya's perch. Caught in the branches of the cedar, Zeya couldn't get off a spear throw.

A Tusca. Inaj has sent someone to kill me.

The man stood near the boulder for a moment. The big rock was shaped kind of like a mushroom, wider on the top than the bottom. His foe had only a nub of an ear on the right side, maybe from an old wound.

Nub Ear let out a war shriek and charged around the boulder to the downhill side and . . . found nothing.

In a moment Nub Ear reappeared beneath Zeya.

Zeya smiled to himself. His mind spun with thoughts about what the man must be thinking. With any luck, he was looking for Zeya in every direction but up.

I'm hidden right above you.

Thought, breath, pumping blood—all were vined together.

But what if he does look up?

Quiet as a cat, Zeya climbed back down the tree. He wondered if Nub Ear would find a way to climb the rock. He listened for scraping noises, sounds of hard breathing. None. He peeped over the edge and saw nothing—Nub Ear must be back under the cap of the mushroom.

If the bastard tries to climb up, I will ram my spear down his throat.

But nothing.

Still, Zeya had an advantage, the high ground. Also, he knew where his enemy was.

Zeya went to all fours on the boulder. If the man made a move . . .

Now he saw one moccasin foot sticking out. Nub Ear was looking, listening, thinking.

Zeya remembered to clamp his left arm hard to his chest. He couldn't wait forever—he was oozing blood. Several of his eagle feathers were already soaked.

Su-Li flew closer and circled.

They didn't have a signal for, *If you pissed, you would hit your enemy on the head*.

And it wasn't quite that way, yet.

Zeya wanted to holler, "Why didn't you spot the danger?" He knew the man must have been concealed, lying in wait.

He crouched, tense, nerves like plucked strings.

He had an idea for an attack, a wild one, more a howling urgency than a plan. The moment Nub Ear stepped away from the boulder, Zeya would pitch himself directly on the man, knock him down, and before he knew what was happening, cut his throat.

Fears fluttered through his mind like bats. Nub Ear had every advantage on him. Bigger, stronger, heavier, more experienced in war, and most of all not so scared.

The foot moved.

A shoulder appeared.

216 ♦ *Caleb Fox*

The foot and shoulder circled the boulder clockwise.

Carefully, creeping, Zeya circled with them. *He must be looking for my tracks!*

On the far side of the boulder, back where he'd climbed up, Zeya could see more of Nub Ear. His enemy was looking all around. Then, survey completed, he stooped.

Maybe he sees one of my footprints in that bit of sand between the rocks. He'll see that the tracks end and he'll realize . . .

Nub Ear looked up.

Zeya hurled himself into the air.

Nub Ear shouted and started to roll.

Zeya's hip whacked Nub Ear's shoulder. They bounced apart and scrambled to their feet.

Nub Ear grabbed for his knife.

Zeya cocked his war club.

Nub Ear darted inside the club's arc, making it useless. He thrust at Zeya's belly.

In desperation Zeya flung a forearm at the slashing blade. He felt a fierce burn along his lower ribs.

He dropped his war club and jerked out his knife.

Su-Li seized Nub Ear's neck in his talons. The claws dug in. Blood streamed. Nub Ear bellowed.

Before he could think, Zeya rammed his knife into the man's belly.

Unbalanced by Su-Li, Nub Ear toppled backward. Gripping Zeya's knife hand, he pulled his enemy down on top of him.

Zeya jerked his knife out and buried it in Nub Ear's chest.

Su-Li fluttered into the air and perched on the boulder.

Straddling his enemy, Zeya looked into Nub Ear's eyes, turned his head, and vomited into the sand.

36

This time Su-Li found a cave for Zeya, signaled the way to him, and watched impatiently until Zeya got the bleeding stopped with a piece of soft hide.

Su-Li brought in dead grasses, twigs, and small limbs for a fire. He himself disliked fires. When he'd finished, he plucked some dried meat out of one of the sling sacks, dropped one piece on Zeya's forearm and the other on the ground for himself.

"You wonder what I'm thinking about that man. He knew what I'm doing, seeking out nests. Looks like he even knew which nests."

Su-Li just looked at Zeya.

"I can't stand the dark." In the last of the day's light Zeya got out flint and lit Su-Li's kindling.

Zeya bit off pieces of the jerked meat and contemplated Su-Li, or his mortality—neither of them was sure which.

"Do you think Awahi gave me away?" *Chew, chew, chew, swallow.* "Looks like it." More chewing. "But it doesn't feel right."

Su-Li cocked his head sideways at Zeya.

"Awahi guessed why I want the feathers. I could see it in his eyes. He wants the Cape of Eagle Feathers restored, too." Zeya felt of several thoughts and spoke one. "He loves eagles."

They finished their meat. "So who told Inaj? What did he know? What *could* he tell?"

Su-Li did a quick flip of his head to the other side and looked at Zeya with that eye.

"We don't know, do we?" He swallowed the last of his

meat. "But we know the bastards will be waiting for us ahead, don't we?"

He pulled the elk hide over his body, used his hands for a pillow, and closed his eyes.

❖

Zeya spread out his eagle feathers for Paya to see. After plundering the nests of the Cusa region, he had forty-nine.

"Oh! Oh!" cried the crabbed-over man, jumping up and down and circling the elk hide. Zeya was displaying the feathers just inside the mouth of the cave, where the wind wouldn't disturb them. Su-Li sat on a rock projection in the mouth itself, where he could fly away.

Zeya grinned at the buzzard. Paya looked like a toad hopping around.

The little man threw furtive glances at the spirit animal. Su-Li glared back.

"Yes," Zeya told Su-Li right in front of Paya, "I know, you're not sure we should show them. But Paya is a friend."

The Crab Man beamed at Zeya, who thought, *I bet he hasn't had a friend in twenty years.*

"Paya showed me the cave," said Zeya, "and all its beauties. Isn't that right?"

"Yes, yes, Paya did, I did."

"And that led to all the good things that have happened. It gave me this mission."

"Yes-yes!"

"And besides, Paya knows this mountain backwards and forwards."

"Yes-yes!"

"I should say inside and out. Underneath and on top!"

Paya giggled. "Yes-yes-yes-yes!"

"And I bet he knows where the eagle nests are."

The little man hesitated. "Maybe. But they're, they're, they're dangerous."

"Sure they are. But I have Su-Li to protect me. He flies up high and looks around—you know buzzards see everything—and warns me if there's any danger."

"Umm, umm, umm." It was a squeaky, frightened sound.

"Do you like the feathers?"

"Yes-yes." He grasped one gently and lifted it into the light like a pearl of great price.

Suddenly he dropped it. The feather arced its way to the floor of the cave.

"Blood," said Paya. His voice was curdled.

"I used to wear some of them around my neck," said Zeya. "When I got scratched, I bled on them."

He picked the feather up. "I've been meaning to clean them. Feathers can't be hurt by water—they're made to get wet. May I use some of your water?"

Paya barely nodded.

Zeya dipped his fingers into the gourd Paya kept in his rocky camp home and stroked the feather gently. "See now, it's good as new."

He offered it to Paya, but the stooped man wouldn't touch it.

"Paya, this is what I'm hoping. Tomorrow you will show us the three nests on this mountain. You know where they are, don't you?"

Paya gave a meek nod.

"And you won't even have to go near them, I promise. You can show us from above, a long way off."

Paya nodded but didn't say anything.

"So that's yes?"

"I'm scared," said Paya.

Zeya was prepared for this possibility. He drew out a fine obsidian knife with a handle made of a bear jaw, the one once owned by Nub Ear. It was better than his own, but he felt spooky about keeping it. "If you'll help us, I'll give you this," he said.

Paya took the knife. He held the edge so that it gleamed in the half light. He inspected the strength of the binding, handle to blade. He beamed like a kid. "Yes-yes," said Paya.

❖

It wasn't an easy morning. The first nest sported two eggs and a mother sitting on them. The second involved a scramble so much up and down that Zeya could barely keep up with the bent-over Paya. And when they got near the next, so close Paya was trying to point it out with an extended finger, Su-Li came wing-flapping hard at them.

He swooped directly over their heads, made a turn sharp enough to shave a head clean, and sped right back where he came from.

Zeya frowned. He ran it through his mind several times, but it came out the same way every time. "There's someone over by that nest. Someone who's waiting for me and wants to kill me."

"Oh-oh-oh," said Paya. He scurried back the way he came.

"Wait!" called Zeya. They weren't within range of the enemy's spear yet. They didn't have to run like ducklings home to mother. They could plan something.

Paya was scampering up and down boulders and rock faces like a lizard. No chance of stopping him. Zeya trailed his friend as fast as his weary bones would carry him.

Except that Paya disappeared.

Zeya got to a long, open stretch following the ridge, and there was no sign of Paya.

The only cover was the forest on the mountainside a hundred feet below. Would Paya hide in the woods? From Zeya? Why?

Su-Li glided down so fast he made Zeya jump. The buzzard picked up a big pebble in his beak, floated onto Zeya's shoulder, and dropped the pebble into his hand.

Again, Zeya sorted through the signals, and again there

could be no mistake. A cave. But that didn't make sense. The cave was a half day's walk away.

Wait. Maybe I better follow Su-Li.

Paya was holed up in a tiny opening. At first Zeya thought he was sucking his thumb like a baby. He was in fact whimpering, and that did not endear him to Zeya.

Then Zeya took a look deeper into the cave. He would never have identified this oversized crack as an opening into the mountain. But there was a passageway.

He took a few steps into it.

"No!" cried Paya. The Crab Man grabbed Zeya from behind by the shoulders and pulled him to the ground.

Zeya started to growl at Paya and thought better of it. The passage turned here, and the shadows were deep. He got onto his hands and knees and groped.

Paya grabbed him by the feet and wouldn't let him crawl forward.

Su-Li perched on the highest rock, barely over Zeya's head, and peered into the three-quarter darkness.

Zeya stretched out. His hands groped forward and felt nothing. Which made his stomach do a flip.

"There's a vine," said Paya.

Zeya felt around and found nothing.

"Come back and light a torch," said Paya.

Torches. Zeya should have known.

Paya showed off his spot. It was a sinkhole twice as wide as a man is tall, and deep enough that Zeya couldn't see the bottom. He tossed a pebble in. Only after a full breath in and out did he hear a splash.

Su-Li croaked.

A vine dangled from above and dropped into the darkness. "Does it reach the bottom?" asked Zeya.

"No," said Paya. "You have to know how to climb up and find the end. Good water down there."

Paya hooked his damaged hand onto the vine, curled his legs around it, and swung across. He let go of the vine, dropped to the cave floor, and let the vine swing back to the middle. He grinned across the chasm at Zeya.

"You're stuck."

Paya cackled, pulled a long stick out from behind a boulder, hooked the vine, and sailed back.

"Feel the vine," he said.

Zeya slid his hands up and down. Every couple of feet Paya had gobbed on pine pitch, to help with climbing.

"Why do you go back in there?"

Paya hung his head and scrunched his shoulders. "You know." He would never stop exploring the underground world.

"Some setup you've got," said Zeya. "Lots of setups, I bet, all over the mountain."

He looked at Su-Li and all around at this hidey-hole. There were plenty of torches, bedding, gourds of water, and lots of mushrooms, wild onions, dried berries, rose hips, and the other food Paya liked.

"Let's start a fire," Zeya said. "There's things I have to tell you." *For instance, I've put you into danger.* But he didn't say that.

Soon a flame was cheering the hole up, and Zeya was heating up a rock to make tea. "How many houses do you have in this cave?" he asked.

Paya shrugged.

"How many entrances are there?"

"Paya has found many-many, but there are many-many more to find, to find."

"Okay, I have to tell you something important."

The Crab Man gave Su-Li a furtive glance, and Zeya a look just as sneaky.

"The man who has come to kill me, he was sent by Inaj."

"Inaj!" The sound was more like a hawk of phlegm than a word. Paya got onto all fours like a beast about to flee.

"Please," Zeya said, and put a hand on his friend's shoulder. "It's all right. I have an idea."

He tonged a fist-sized rock from the fire into the hanging bag, poured water into it, and dropped in half a handful of dried berries.

"I talked to my mother, Sunoya. You remember my mother?"

Paya quailed a little.

"You remember?"

"Yes."

"She heard you disappeared when all the big trouble happened at the Planting Moon Festival. Remember that? When the Seer humiliated Inaj and he got kicked out as chief? And then all of a sudden the other Red Chief was dead and Inaj was back in?"

Paya stared into his lap.

"Remember?"

"Yes."

"Mother heard Inaj told you to stay away. That's what your relatives thought."

"He told me, he told me never to come back to the village or he'd tell people something and get me killed."

After his outburst Paya seemed chastened.

"It was Inaj who hurt your hand. Inaj is the reason you live all alone. The reason you have no family. The reason your hand is a claw. Isn't that right?"

"Ye-e-s-s."

"Paya, that man who's out there waiting, the one trying to kill me, Inaj sent him. Why don't we get even with Inaj? Get back at him a little bit?"

❖

Zeya hopped along the ridge, up onto one ledge, down onto another. When he got high, he visored his eyes with one hand and peered toward the nest. But he was really watching Su-Li.

As Zeya asked, the buzzard was circling above the nest. When he floated over the assassin's hiding place, he dipped a wing for a moment and then reasserted his circle. Nothing unusual about a buzzard hovering around. If the enemy changed places, Su-Li would give the signal again.

Zeya worked his way to a low spot in the ridge and then up toward the nest. About a hundred steps away he stopped and began, apparently, to inspect the country thoroughly. He studied the rocks and trees in every direction until he got the sign he was waiting for from Su-Li. The assassin was on the move, sliding toward his prey.

Zeya turned and trotted fifty steps back. Then he stopped and studied the scene again. He couldn't see his foe. One of his advantages was that the enemy had to move slowly and stealthily. Zeya was free to walk openly, skip, run, or do whatever else he wanted.

In that fashion they worked their back to the crack in the rock that hid the cave. Zeya always knew where the assassin was. But now came the tricky part.

He sat on a high boulder above the crack, laid his spear down, and leaned his back against the rock. He was angled halfway between flat and the noonday sun. He closed his eyes to three-quarters and pretended to sleep. Instead, he was watching Su-Li very closely.

Being bait made his skin prickle.

When it came, a thrill of fear bolted through Zeya.

The killer sprinted straight toward him, in the open. On one side of his head his hair fell to his waist. The other side was shaved clean.

Zeya vaulted off the rock, leaving the spear, and ducked into the cave.

Trapped. Please think I'm trapped.

Half-Shaved Head stopped and crouched behind a rock.

He studied the dark hole. Zeya could see him peering intently, but apparently the shadows were too dark.

Zeya stuck his head halfway out and jerked it back.

Footfalls!

Zeya quick-footed around the corner into the darkness. As he grabbed the vine, he shouted, "Leave me alone, you bastard!"

He swung across the sinkhole, dropped lightly to the ground, and jammed the vine into a crack. He grabbed his waiting war club and whirled, ready to . . .

What's wrong? Where is the bastard?

Creeping forward, Zeya supposed. Cave dark had scared Zeya, too. But the man's eyes would have trouble adjusting, like Zeya's did.

Half-Shaved Head came forward on all fours, carrying a long-bladed knife.

The bastard's being careful, too careful.

Sure enough, the assassin stuck a hand into the empty air and sat back on his haunches.

If I had my spear now, I could kill you!

Half-Shaved Head turned to go back.

At that moment Paya drove a shoulder low into the assassin. Half-Shaved Head bumped backwards, teetered on the edge, seized Paya's hand, and plummeted into the darkness.

Paya tumbled after him, screaming.

❖

Zeya shouted, "Paya! Paya!" He shouted himself half hoarse.

He stared across at Su-Li. His mind was tumult. *No*, he had to tell himself, *the buzzard cannot hold the torch as you slide down*.

Slide down, though, was exactly what he had to do. Into the darkness.

Paya is down there.

Into the darkness.

"I'm going," he said to Su-Li. He knew the arguments the

bird would give him if it could talk, or rather if he could hear it. The same arguments his mother would give him—"Your mission is more important than anything. Don't risk the people's welfare for a single life, not even your own."

He didn't care. He grabbed the vine, swung across, and lit two torches. Maybe he could go down one-handed for a ways and stick one into a crack and see. The other he would leave as a beacon.

He wrapped his legs around the vine, gripped it hard with one hand, and started sliding.

It wasn't as hard as he feared. He got down one man-length quickly, then two. He stopped and looked around. No crack for the hand-held torch.

Down he slid again, before worry could paralyze him. Down, down.

He peered toward the water he knew was down there somewhere. He could see nothing, absolutely nothing at the bottom. The pool below was the infinity of night without moon, without stars, without hope.

He swung a little from side to side and—hey!—he spotted a place to jam the torch. That would ease his way back up, and it would soothe his spirit.

He swung vigorously and bumped the side too hard and had to grab hold quick. Carefully, he squeezed the torch handle and rammed it in deep. He tugged at it to make sure. Then he let go and pendulumed out across the sinkhole, and back, and back.

When he stopped, he leaned out and looked down harder. Still nothing but darkness.

He started sliding down with both hands. The bumps of pine pitch felt good.

The torch tumbled end over end, down, down, down, dunked headfirst into the water, and went out.

Downward lurked absolute blackness.

His first impression was that he was a leaf in a wind, blowing to the sky, to the earth, sideways, every which direction.

He closed his eyes. He spoke out loud and firmly. "Your legs are below you. Your hands are above you."

He opened his eyes. He looked up. There burned the beacon. The world he knew hung by that flickering light.

He descended. Why, he didn't know.

He stopped and tried to picture what he'd seen by the light of the falling torch. Maybe a hump in the water. Maybe the hump was a back, maybe not.

Fear prickled him. Where was Half-Shaven Head?

He might be anywhere.

He twisted on the end of the vine. He looked at the back. He studied the rest of the water. He studied the lower walls. He decided to descend.

His feet slid off the end of the vine.

He hollered.

In a great hurry he muscled up and got his legs wrapped around the vine. His arms wouldn't last long.

Then he remembered. Paya had said the vine ended above the water. You dropped into the water and then climbed up the wall a way to reclaim the vine. Paya probably had a hooking stick stored there.

Maybe Half-Shaven Head had climbed up and was . . . He eyed the walls right around him and then took several pulls to get higher.

"Paya!"

No answer.

"Paya!" Three more times. No answers.

His arms were getting shaky.

I am somewhere in the blackness between stars, clinging to the illusion of a vine. If I let go, I will die. If I wait for the assassin, I will die.

He inched up.

It got harder. And harder.

He forced himself. Legs loose and then up very fast, good grip. He learned to rest his arms by clamping the vine in his armpits, alternately.

Repeat. Repeat. Repeat. *If you want to live, do it again.*

He looked up and saw that the darkness was eased by a flame. In that faint light, on the rim of the sinkhole, he saw a shape that might be Su-Li.

Zeya said, "Help me."

Su-Li a-a-arked.

"Help me."

He looped the vine under his right arm, behind his neck, and pressed the left side of his head against it. He let his arms drop. He said, "Arms, can you do it?"

No answer.

Suddenly Su-Li launched off the rim and floated down to Zeya. They looked at each other. Zeya wasn't sure what he was really seeing, but he could hear the slow beat of the buzzard's wings.

Then Su-Li fell downward.

Zeya felt like he, too, plummeted into the blackness. But only his heart dived. He wondered if Su-Li was frightened by the darkness. At least the assassin couldn't kill an Immortal.

In a moment Su-Li reappeared, flying the tightest of circles in the hole. The lower part of the vine dangled from his mouth.

Zeya pulled hard on the vine several times to get higher. He wanted to see what was happening. He couldn't imagine. Saved or killed?

At the top Su-Li disappeared behind a boulder. Zeya heard rustling. Then he felt the vine rise up into his crotch.

Su-Li hopped to the rim, looked down at him, and squawked.

Incredulous, Zeya let his weight sink onto the loop in the vine. It was like sitting in a kid's swing. He chuckled. Swings were made of vines.

A while later, rested, he pulled up until he could see the rim at eye level. It was out of reach. He swung back and forth. He wasn't high enough.

Three more good pulls. He swung again. Maybe enough.

He kicked out for his best swing, sailed toward the warm light—now it looked bright as suns—and flung himself into the air.

He hit the rim with his belly. He began to slide. He pawed everywhere for purchase with his hands.

He felt himself start to topple backwards. Just then a toe found a jutting rock, just enough of a bump . . .

He planted his palms flat on the rim and with the greatest exertion of his life muscled himself onto the rim.

He collapsed and lay flat.

He might have slept except for one thought. *Paya is dead.*

37

Zeya made the long walk toward the Tusca village in low spirits. He had eighty-one war eagle feathers wrapped in his hide, almost all good ones. But he couldn't stop thinking about Paya.

He also couldn't stop fretting. Su-Li rode the air above him constantly, keeping a double-sharp eye out for miles around. Zeya had nearly been killed twice, and now he was walking toward the village where his mother grew up and where he normally would have lived all his life. It was also the village where his great enemy lived, his grandfather Inaj. He had never laid eyes on it.

He topped the ridge on the west side of the valley and looked down on storied territory. On the grassy slope below his mother had been hit by lightning. And there, as she died, he had been born.

Far beyond, by the river in the valley below, he could see the tip of the village.

"The one place I can't go," he said out loud. An odd feeling rummaged around in his chest. *For my entire life my grandfather has been threatening to kill me. And now he's going all out.*

So he left the trail, angling across the slope toward the forest below. He would make a wide circuit to the north, around the Tusca village and toward the five nests Awahi described, in the mountains on the far side.

Still, he was sure. *The one place they're bound to be waiting for me is here.*

❖

Zeya made a fire for his cave camp and started broiling strips of back strap on a stick. Today, for the first time in all his quest, he'd killed a deer and now intended to take time to make meat. He tossed the liver to Su-Li, who pecked at it.

"You like that, don't you? I like this. Let's take the next two days off and dry this meat. Let's take the next two weeks off. Let's quit this mission before we get killed. I mean, I get killed." Sometimes he forgot Su-Li was immortal.

He took a big bite, chewed it, and studied Su-Li. "So what are you thinking in whatever language you speak that I can't hear, much less understand? You're thinking, I hope this kid gives me time to find the murderer who's waiting out there."

He swallowed and bit off another big piece. When he'd finished it, he said, "That's the plan. I'll stay here tomorrow while you search. And the next day, too, if you want."

He spiked more steak onto his skewer.

"Do you think Inaj knows where we are? Think he knows I killed his first two men? Does he know you're my secret weapon?"

Su-Li shook his head in the motion that meant, *No, uh-uh*.

Zeya laughed. Su-Li hardly ever communicated that way. Zeya had almost forgotten he could do it.

"So go out tomorrow and tell me where I meet my fate."

At sunset the next day Su-Li came back and perched high in the mouth of the cave.

"Well? Where is the killer?"

Su-Li shook his head no.

"No killer? Oh, sure."

Su-Li shook his head no.

"Okay, seriously. How many nests did you see, all five?"

Su-Li dipped his head down and back up.

"You know which one they're hatching eggs in?"

Su-Li nodded yes.

"How many killers did you see, five?"

Su-Li shook his head.

"Four?"

No again.

"Three?"

When Zeya got to one, he was really scared.

No again.

"You saw none?"

Yes.

"Not any?"

Yes.

"That's terrifying."

Yes.

"It means they've outsmarted us both."

Su-Li squawked.

"You're probably saying, 'Damn right they did.'"

❖

Zeya walked toward the last nest in euphoria and dread. He'd left it for last because it was the easiest one to get to, and he'd be worn out by the time he got there.

Su-Li flapped, glided, and soared across the sky all day and saw absolutely nothing.

At the first nest Zeya was sure he and Su-Li were fooled by some demonic trick and he was about to die. He got nine good feathers there, and a pleasant breeze blew the sweat off his body. Fifty feet away from the nest he suddenly whirled back on it, spear cocked. Still nothing, still no one. He didn't know what to think.

At the second nest he found seven nice feathers—up to 105 now. No matter where he cast his suspicious eye, he saw no trouble. The world was a lovely shape of jagged mountains, rolling hills, shining rivers, and endless reaches of green trees. The breeze was dancing and fresh, the sky innocent of clouds.

At the third nest he found six feathers, giving him three more than the minimum required. But nearly a dozen of his feathers were scraggly, and the Cape deserved the best he could find.

Besides, something was wrong. Life as he knew it was hard, never pungently sweet and exhilarating, as it seemed today. Something was always hidden behind the facade. The last nest pulled him with a mysterious force.

When he got close, he saw that it was probably the biggest nest he'd seen, wider and longer than two buffalo robes laid side by side. It was in good condition, tight everywhere. The eagles must have used it only last year.

He walked around it gingerly, hands on the sticks for balance. He couldn't walk around a lot of the nests, because they literally hung over their ledge on three sides, and the fourth was a vertical wall.

His inspection made him smile. At least a dozen feathers were caught in the twigs or bark or moss. This was a big find.

He laid his spear on the lip of the nest, pushed himself high, and raised a heel to clamber up.

Twigs crackled in the center of the nest. A human head poked up.

Dazed, Zeya noticed that the face had a long chin with a knob on the end.

Frozen, Zeya watched the hands lift a stick to the mouth.

Zeya heard a *pffft!* sound and felt a stabbing pain in his belly.

He looked down and saw a dart hanging there.

The world tilted.

Zeya fell. Limp legs hit the ledge and crumpled. His body toppled backward into the air, and the air was dark.

❖

Su-Li dived.

The assassin stepped awkwardly across the springy nest and peered down at Zeya.

In despair Su-Li saw that the youth wasn't moving. He'd fallen two or three times his own body height onto a steep, shaley slope.

Su-Li steepened his dive and fired despair into fury.

Knob Chin lowered himself off the nest onto the ledge and started climbing carefully down toward his enemy's body.

He couldn't have made a bigger mistake.

At full speed Su-Li raked talons across his face.

The enemy screamed and tumbled head over heels. He hit the slope on one shoulder, and his momentum rolled him over Zeya's body.

Knob Chin tried in a befuddled way to get to his feet. Su-Li hit him again, a sharp stab of beak to neck.

The victim wailed in terror, looking around frantically.

Su-Li saw that he hadn't dealt a mortal blow. The neck wound was bleeding freely but not pumping blood.

Su-Li turned in the tightest wheel he could and hurled himself like a spear at Knob Chin's back. At the last moment

234 ❖ *Caleb Fox*

he spread his wings, caught air, and plunged his talons into the bastard's shoulders and neck.

Knob Chin screamed. He clutched at the buzzard's legs and tried to rip the talons out. Su-Li laughed wildly in his mind.

Suddenly the warrior tried something else—he threw himself downhill and rolled.

Su-Li let go and fluttered up. When Knob Chin stopped and hoisted himself onto his knees, Su-Li swooped at his face. The assassin screeched in horror. He batted at Su-Li's talons, but the buzzard got both shoulders.

Knob Chin rolled again, a momentary reprieve. Then he did the only thing that could save him. He ran downhill. Ran pell-mell. Fell, rolled, banged himself up, and ran some more.

Su-Li attended to Zeya. The young man was breathing. As far as Su-Li could tell, he hadn't broken his neck or back, not even his arms or legs.

The dart had fallen out somewhere along the way. The wound barely dribbled blood—it was a deep slit. Su-Li sniffed at the wound, and then he knew the danger was not bleeding or infection.

Luckily, he also knew someone with the knowledge of how to treat poisons.

38

Zeya saw things, he heard things, and none of it made any sense. The Darkening Land, he supposed, didn't make sense. He floated through enough sounds and pictures to believe that he was being carried. From the mud of his mind a memory grogged into consciousness. The Darkening Land was seven days' travel to the west. Then everything made sense.

You had to be carried on the journey, because the dead couldn't walk.

❖

Zeya swam up and up and up and at last his face broke through—through water or fog or something else?—into the light.

It was the most beautiful face he'd ever seen. Her skin was red-gold, like any human being's, but her hair was yellow. Her eyes were blue. She was stroking his face with a cool, wet rag.

She spoke, and her voice was a soft, sighing wind. "Hello, Ulo-Zeya."

He drifted into her eyes and beyond them to a place where he could see nothing and was lost and . . .

❖

He was riding a river and it was liquid fire. He rolled, he swelled up and down, and the hot waves washed over him.

Water splashed onto his hair.

Cool, sweet cool. "Co-oo-ool," he murmured.

"Yes, Zeya, it's cool," said the sighing wind voice. "You need it."

He so wanted to see her blue eyes that he forced his own eyes open. The world he saw didn't make sense. It was all water and sky, and the water was falling, not like rain but like rivers. *I am lying in a river that runs straight down,* he thought foolishly, *from the sky to the earth.* The Darkening Land is a strange place.

Blue Eyes stood up and reached for something. She was a complete human woman, delicately sculpted, utterly beautiful, and from tip to toe she was knee-high.

She held a cup to his lips. "Drink this," she said.

He sipped. Inside he laughed. *How much fun the Darkening Land will be,* he thought, *when I can stay awake to see it.*

❖

A-a-ark.

A-a-ark.

A-a-ark.

Zeya began to think . . .

Su-Li?

He blinked himself awake.

Croak.

Su-Li!

Zeya lay flat, and Su-Li perched on a rock an arm's length above his head.

"Hello," he said. Speaking felt strange. He craned his neck left and right to make sure he could move it. He stuck an elbow out and propped himself on it. He studied the buzzard. "You're immortal," he said. His mind fumbled its way forward. "So this isn't the Darkening Land. It's the world of the Immortals." He couldn't think of its name.

"Yes," said a familiar female voice, "we are Immortals. But you are still on the Earth, the in-between realm."

Zeya gaped at her. Knee-high, that was right. Tiny, perfect features. Yellow hair. A face of amazing beauty.

She sang five notes, middle, high, quick-low-and-high, middle.

Six, ten, twelve human beings walked over to them. All were knee-high and, though most were men, stunningly beautiful.

"The Little People," he said.

"That's your name for us. It's fine."

"You sang," he said.

"In here it's a good way to be heard."

Then he noticed. Here a bass note underpinned all sound, a low roar. Everywhere—to his left, his right, above—he saw water falling.

He focused his attention. Rock walls honeycombed with rooms. He was sitting near the falling water at the front of one room, which went many paces deep into the wall.

"That's right," she said. "We live behind the waterfall. We also live in the rocks on either side of it, and above and below."

"Who are you?"

She thought for a moment. "Call me Saylo."

The name rang like musical tones, "say low," like speak softly.

"Would you tell me what's going on here, Saylo?"

"Tomorrow. Meanwhile, drink this."

He drank and slept.

❖

"Tell me."

Saylo looked at Su-Li, took a deep breath, and launched in.

"Su-Li came and asked us to help you. We know the cure for the poison."

"Poison?" That was medicine man business. The man who attacked him was a warrior.

"Did you get a good look at the weapon?"

"Saw a stick, nothing that looked like a weapon."

"It's something new Inaj and his men invented. A piece of hollowed-out river cane. They put a wooden dart in the end and glue on thistle to make it fly straight. The wood is whittled very sharp, and the tip dipped in poison."

"Nasty," said Zeya.

Su-Li rasped.

"Your friend said, 'The human talent—instruments of death.'"

Zeya mulled this over. "The bastard shot me with a poisoned dart."

"Then we brought you here. He got away."

Su-Li croaked.

"He says your enemy might have come back to finish you off."

The buzzard croaked again.

"He also says, 'I got the assassin good.' The poison would have killed you by nightfall."

Su-Li spoke again.

"Su-Li says, correctly, that if the poison had been brewed

by a powerful herbalist, like Ninyu, it would have killed you before he even chased off your enemy."

"How far away were you?" asked Zeya.

Saylo pursed her lips and thought. "We Little People are everywhere."

Zeya focused as much on the movement of her lips as on the words she said. He still felt woozy.

"It took a long time to get the poison out of me?"

"No, we took care of that immediately, while you were still on the mountain. Since then, I've just been treating your fever."

"Fever?"

"From the wound."

"Where are we?" He would have said anything to keep her talking, she was so lovely.

"We're in one of the big waterfalls that make the Galayi land so beautiful. Where exactly is it? Let's just say that if you left here today, walked half a day away, turned around and walked half a day back, we wouldn't be here. The waterfall wouldn't be here. Everything you see or hear or touch here would be gone. Or invisible to you."

Zeya swallowed. "That's hard to take in."

"I know you're trying to keep me talking. I like you, too."

He reached out, picked her up, and tried to kiss her.

She stuck a finger in his eye.

"Ouch!" He set her down, shamefaced.

She glared at him.

"You're cute when you're mad."

She stuck a finger in his other eye and—*blink!*—disappeared.

Su-Li shook his head.

"Yeah," grumbled Zeya, "if you could talk, you'd say, 'How dumb can you be?' "

❖

Zeya slept for a long time. Twice he woke up for a moment, realized his eyes were sore, and went back to sleep. When he heard someone clearing his throat with a tiny sound, he sat up and paid attention. A very old man, a Little Person, stood next to him.

"I'd appreciate it if you'd lie down," said the old man. "I don't like your head higher than mine."

Zeya laid down and knit his hands behind his head.

"My name is Ralo." He spoke in a deep voice. "You won't be seeing Saylo again."

Zeya nodded his acceptance. He was held by the sound of Ralo's voice, soft as fern hair and very low, a contrast to Saylo's birdlike tones.

"Please don't think we're prudes. We know you think Saylo is pretty, and she likes that. The Little People love beauty of every kind." Ralo wore a glistening white robe with lilac trim.

"We even know you're feeling disloyal to Jemel because you felt desire for Saylo. There's nothing to be embarrassed about.

"It's just that, we Little People are immortal. We don't do the thing human beings do to reproduce—we have no need to make more of our own kind. Understand?"

Zeya nodded.

"Also, what you see here is like shadows made by your hands and fingers on a rock. It isn't really here. I'm not really an old man, or young woman, or girl, or any age or gender.

"When you're here, you see beauty. Because beauty is the purpose of our existence. It's natural and right to be attracted to beauty.

"I hope I haven't confused you. Now I'm afraid I must bid you good-bye—we all must bid you good-bye."

"I like it here."

"But you can't stay. No one can. Or I should say, those who stay become Little People."

"Become Little People?"

"Anyone who eats our food becomes one of us. You haven't eaten anything since you've been here, except for some broth made from meat that Su-Li brought in. Broth made from flesh." The old man shuddered. "Our food is celestial. If you ate it, you would be one of us."

Zeya looked around. He had never even imagined a place so lovely—water spilling silver through the air, light softened by the spray, and everywhere the beautiful Little People themselves. "That doesn't seem so bad."

"Your mission is important. To you. It's who you are, and this is who we are."

The old man cocked his head, winked, and turned away.

"Ralo!" said Zeya. Ralo looked back. "Thank you."

"You're welcome."

"Thank you for taking care of me, Saylo."

"You're catching on," Ralo piped in Saylo's voice. "And you're a smart aleck. A very likable one." In a deep, male voice he added, "When you go, take that nasty weapon with you."

39

I'm sick of this," Inaj said to Wilu and Zanda. "Let's go do some flaking."

Boredom, boredom, boredom. The sons could read their father's face the way a dog could read pee. Inaj was tired of sitting around with his brother Vaj and family. He'd rather spend the afternoon up the creek. This morning Vaj had told them about a place there with some flint. He could see the boredom, too.

To Inaj his brother lived an incomprehensible life. Almost no hunting, a few snares to set, a lot of lounging around while the women harvested and gathered, or sewed, way too much fussing over his grandchildren, and worst of all, talking interminably— Vaj and his women did nothing else. It irked Inaj.

Yesterday had been a particular trial. The women were picking corn, and Inaj wanted to do something. It wasn't hunting season yet. Normally Inaj would have instructed the young men in war arts, but they were lackadaisical about such skills in the Cusa village. Inaj suggested the men could gather cane for more blow darts—anything but sit around.

Vaj, a jovial man with a big belly, agreed. But he kept finding reasons to stay home. It was clear that he liked sitting outside the hut enjoying the sun more than anything else. All afternoon he told Wilu and Zanda stories about adventures he and Inaj had as boys. In the evening he started a game with his grandchildren. They watched the fireflies and identified or imagined patterns. Sometimes one would see a rabbit flicker for a moment, or a raccoon. When the twelve-year-old grandson saw the Hunchback constellation, which the Galayi used to mark the North Star, Vaj picked the boy up, gave him a bear hug, and acted like the youngster was the smartest thing on earth. Inaj was disgusted.

Wilu understood this family better than his father did. He found a life of pleasure tempting. Sometimes he wondered about his father's love of killing and his thirst for power. But Wilu had no intention of taking the Vaj path. He wanted to be Red Chief one day. Zanda had won the election last time, but another would come and his legendary father would swing votes. Inaj demanded total dedication.

The three carried their weapons—even that was questionable behavior in this village—and started up the river. "Good to be away from these vain Cusas for an afternoon," said Inaj. He could never forgive them their pride in being peaceful.

A hundred paces beyond the last hut a creek ran into the river, and the knapping site was above the head of the creek.

Maybe the noise of the two streams was why Wilu and Zanda didn't hear the footfalls. But their father did.

Knob Chin was walking like an old man. He had big scabs and one wound still open on his neck and shoulders. He gazed dully at Inaj and murmured, "Chief."

"Fool!" said Inaj.

They had some trouble getting Knob Chin to the site, but Inaj tongue-lashed him upward. This man, one of Inaj's most trusted warriors, chosen to be the first to use the blow dart in battle, now padded along like an invalid. When they found the flint, he lay flat on a boulder while Inaj, Wilu, and Zanda worked.

Inaj's questions were merciless.

Knob Chin threw words back. "I am sure he's dead, damn well sure."

"You—"

Knob Chin was testy enough to interrupt the Chief. "The poison, it went into him deep."

Inaj didn't bother to look up from the spear tip he was flaking. "So you say. I keep reading the story in all those scabs. Maybe a story more truthful than the one your tongue tells."

He held the spear tip up to the best light. Making a fine one was skilled work, and he liked it.

From the corner of his eye he saw that Knob Chin's eyes were pleading. That was good. Humiliation was an effective tool, one of Inaj's favorites.

"I would feel a lot better if you had brought me his head. That was your assignment."

"I told you—"

Inaj interrupted. "Yes, the bird." The word came off his tongue dripping with contempt.

"The buzzard. You see what he did to me."

Inaj saw. "He tried to take your head off." The Chief gave

Knob Chin a smile that suited a warrior who had been defeated in battle by a bird.

"Zanda, it's interesting, isn't it? Who would think Sunoya would give up her spirit animal, even for a short time?"

Zanda made a grunt of assent and kept his eyes on his work.

Inaj gave Knob Chin a big grin. "Now we know why your predecessors didn't come back."

"Well, I'm back."

Inaj took a last look at his handiwork and said, "This is a fine point." He stood up. "Let's get you to the village for some sanctuary." He mouthed the word ironically. "You need it."

Knob Chin watched the Chief start down the creek, rubbing the edge of his point with his thumb. No doubt it was a sharp edge. Knob Chin was glad it wasn't meant for his flesh.

❖

Su-Li flew straight at Zeya, made a sharp pivot, and flew straight back toward the Cusa village. Then, so Zeya would be sure, he repeated the signal.

Zeya got it—an enemy in the village.

He left the river trail and scrambled through the trees up the mountain. Then he sat on a high overlook and looked down. Not that he could see any enemies from the distance. That was Su-Li's job.

All the way up the mountain his mind simmered with frustration. He looked forward to getting to the village. He had all the feathers. He had killed two assassins and escaped the third. Now he wanted Awahi to bless the feathers and let him take them to Tsola.

Su-Li squawked.

"All right," he said, "yes, I want to see Jemel, too."

Su-Li squawked again.

"Okay, I'm crazy to talk to her. But I can't." Those were the terms of his mission. But he could watch her, from a distance.

"So what enemy is here? Another one of Inaj's assassins?"

Su-Li shook his head no.

"So who?"

The buzzard waited.

"Do I have other enemies in the world?" He steamed. What had he done to deserve this? Then he thought. "You mean Inaj is here? Himself?"

Su-Li nodded his head yes.

Zeya took in this news. Finally, he said, "I need to sleep." He found a grassy spot and stretched out on one of his hides. He was bone-weary, weary of travel, weary of loneliness, weary of climbing to aeries, weary of fear, weary of killing. He didn't get any sleep.

❖

Su-Li crouched on the young man's shoulder. In the middle of the night he didn't take to the sky—too risky to fly in the darkness.

Zeya had a job, but couldn't help wondering where Jemel was. What hut did she sleep in? Did she like these relatives? Was she being courted? Was she slipping into the bushes with another man? Or more than one? Jealousy simmered in his gut.

He cursed himself for not concentrating on what needed to be done. After a while he knew where the two village guards were standing, one upriver and one down. He whispered, and Su-Li nodded his head yes.

Zeya decided to go in noisily, scuffling his feet, whapping branches, and calling, "Friend," in a loud whisper.

"Cusa?" asked a disembodied voice. The guard had taken cover, but he knew the approaching figure was a Galayi.

"Soco," said Zeya. "I've come to see Awahi."

The guard showed himself, a moving shadow among still shadows cast by the moon.

"Friend!" said Zeya again, walking forward. "I need your help."

The guard jumped at the sight of Su-Li. Zeya spoke a few words. The man nodded and was gone. Before long, he came back with Awahi himself.

"Is it really you?" said Eagle Voice. "Did you get away from his assassins?"

"By luck."

Awahi gave him a look that said, 'Not all luck. Couldn't be.'

The older man wheezed, "It's dangerous here," and started toward his hut.

"It's dangerous everywhere," said Zeya, following.

"Yes, but did you know Inaj is right in this village?"

"I know."

"With his sons Wilu and Zanda." If possible, the old man seemed skinnier, no more than a few twigs.

Zeya muttered a curse. Su-Li corrected him with a nip on the ear.

Awahi held up a hand for silence. Zeya was afraid the dogs would bark at the buzzard smell, but none did.

Back in his home, Awahi said, "Want to eat?"

Zeya was cold and empty-bellied. He tucked his weapons into a corner and asked for tea and meat.

Awahi rasped, "Inaj has been here for half a moon. He's pretending to visit his brother, but he's really waiting for you. He didn't think you'd live this long. On the other hand, he's thorough."

Awahi handed Zeya some dried meat, and Zeya shared it with Su-Li. Zeya hadn't had meat since the dart stuck him.

"After you left before, he came and asked me questions." Awahi didn't sound happy about it.

"What did you tell him?"

"That I told you how to gather feathers in a sacred manner."

"Anything about Tsola?"

"Nothing."

But something was bothering the old man.

"He demanded—you know how that beast makes his demands—to know what nests you would go to first. I lied to him."

"I didn't go where you told me anyway."

"Praise to the spirits that you're alive."

"I have to sleep," said Zeya.

Awahi thought and said, "You are an honored guest. To have you in my home is a blessing, and you may stay as long as you like. But I'm frightened for you." He cast a nervous eye at the spear, club, and blow gun.

"I'll stay inside all day tomorrow."

"Inaj, Wilu, Zanda, and the third assassin, the one Su-Li attacked but didn't kill, they watch this hut all the time. They've probably also asked the guards to keep an eye out, adding gifts to win loyalty. They may already know you're here."

Zeya and Su-Li looked at each other.

"Also, in the daytime you could stay inside, but even you have to go out to pee."

"Then I'd better get the blessing and go," said Zeya.

"It will be a privilege to bless the feathers. Did you get enough?"

"Plenty."

"Good. I'll bless them, and you can rest until the Hunchback constellation says first light is near, then slip away."

"Okay."

"Remember, nothing can happen to you in this village. The peace chiefs don't kill—they do worse." Awahi chuckled.

Zeya knew the penalty, banishment, living completely alone the rest of your life. And it was rigorously enforced by all bands. He thought, *You end up crazy as Paya.*

Then Awahi said, "Something important. One of Inaj's sons may kill you tomorrow. But if you kill him . . ." And Awahi told him what had to be done.

❖

Su-Li flapped up to Awahi's smoke hole. The buzzard ratcheted his head in several directions and saw nothing. "Fly away at the first hint of light," said the old man.

To Zeya, Awahi said, "A man walking with a buzzard on his shoulder is a little conspicuous."

Zeya slipped away in the last of the darkness and met Su-Li where the guard had stood.

"No guard here," said Zeya. Both of them wondered whether the guard had left his post to tell Inaj and get some kind of reward.

Zeya had thought his plan through out loud back in the hut, Su-Li nodding approval or disapproval and Awahi pitching in with an occasional bit of advice. Zeya was eager to get it done.

He sprinted along the trail downriver. The two sacks over his shoulders, one full of feathers and one with a little dried meat, bounced clumsily. The spear and the war club were awkward in Zeya's hands, and the blow gun rubbed against his butt. But he needed distance. He wanted to get downriver, the direction away from the Emerald Cavern. He wondered if they would suspect. If no one followed him, he would circle the long way around to Tsola.

Just as the sun came up, he found a rocky outcropping where his tracks wouldn't show and slipped off the trail. He hid his club and spear under a log. A little way off, he stored his feathers and meat in a pine tree. Then he walked into the river.

Easily, quietly, he floated along. Within a hundred paces he saw a hiding place, a dead cedar that had fallen into the river during the spring flood and now, at low water, was stranded on a sand bar.

He lay in the water, his eyes raised just over the trunk, his face hidden by branches. He could see fifty paces of trail with no obstructions, and he had glimpses of more than that. It was very unlikely that anyone would see him. If his pursuer was watching with care, his eyes would go up the hill.

Zeya could see Su-Li, and that was essential. The spirit buzzard was making tight circles above the river. He hovered, facing Zeya, showing that he knew where his comrade was and was doing his part.

Now Su-Li straightened from his circle and wing-flapped straight down the riverbank. When he got to Zeya, he turned in a tight arc and flapped back up the river.

The signal from the first learning session. *An enemy on my trail*, Zeya said to himself. No surprise. *Now tell me where and how many.*

Su-Li lowered one wing for an instant, then flapped again.

Zeya's breath stuck in his neck like a stone. *Close! Just a few hundred strides up the river. If he's been coming carefully, he was after me from the first moment.*

The sprint had saved Zeya.

He had a nasty thought—he ought to go back and kill the guard. But he wouldn't.

Su-Li made a tight turn and flew back toward Zeya. As he passed the spot where he'd lowered a wing the first time, he made a clean glide, wings straight out.

One enemy. Zeya wondered whether it was Inaj, Wilu, or Zanda.

Su-Li began circling again.

Within moments a figure came into sight, trotting. Zanda. He was a man on the make, younger and stronger than Inaj, and even colder of heart. Everyone talked about Zanda being the bloodiest warrior in the tribe, to impress his father.

My uncle the killer, Zeya thought. It was head-spinning to see that one of his uncles was hunting him, that an uncle planned to cut off his head and give it to his grandfather.

As Zanda passed, Zeya saw the spear and club in his hands,

the blow gun stuck into his belt at the back. *So he'll use a sneak attack if he can,* Zeya said to himself.

He waded softly around the tree, crouching and making no splashes, and eased into a swimming position in the water.

Immediately he saw that Zanda's trot was faster than his float. He frog-kicked his legs gently. He needed to keep up. *If Zanda looks back, I'll turn into a beaver.*

The first time the trail cornered to the right, so that Zanda couldn't see around it, Zeya's uncle walked softly up the hill a way and looked ahead with care.

Zeya floated past him. Now he knew it might work.

❖

He was in position. It hadn't been easy. He'd floated past two right-hand curves before he saw good cover. Just around the bend a small creek flowed into the river, and above that a big eddy. In the eddy stood a batch of cattails, straight and tall.

He went into the cattails on hands and knees. Zanda would leave the trail before he got to the cattails, and come back just below them, his attention downriver.

It would be an easy shot. Zeya had practiced with the blow gun every day of the journey from the waterfall of the Little People to the Cusa village. He had gathered the herbs Ninyu taught him and made a poison, which he thought he'd never do. He was ready.

Part of him didn't like it. A dart from behind, a poison instead of a mortal blow with the hand, face-to-face. But his grandfather had tried to kill Zeya in every way.

Zeya had to end it. His job was to get the feathers to Tsola. He was doing that for the people. He would kill his uncle the surest way he could.

❖

It was taking too long. Zeya's eyes focused on each part of the forest, from the corner to the creek. Back and forth, slowly, he inspected every nook and cranny. He wanted to be able to spot a still man, a creeping man, a man hiding behind trees.

No matter how careful Zanda is, this is taking too long. Doubt pinged in Zeya's chest. Had he figured wrong?

Overhead Su-Li wing-flapped fast, straight downriver, pivoted, and flew straight back up.

Yes, yes, an enemy coming from upriver, I know about Zanda.

Su-Li did it again. Zeya wondered why.

He needed to see a little better. He crouched, his eyes at water level. The cattails were thick here. Gradually, gently, he raised up. First a hand span. Then another. Soon he was out of the water to his neck, then his shoulder blades. Now he was half visible, but he could see better. Zanda wouldn't be looking for an attack from the river.

Pain raged through his back and left shoulder. He yelled and tumbled backwards, letting his blow gun fall.

He heard a wild thrashing through the river shallows.

Live or die!

He glimpsed a spear floating on the water, blood-tipped.

As he struggled to his feet, he saw something whirl toward him. He flung himself sideways.

The war club whacked the water where he had been.

He dived. Though the water was only thigh-deep, it cushioned the second blow to a mild thump on his leg.

Zeya pulled his blow gun out. Then he cursed himself for an idiot. *How do you blow a dart underwater?*

Zanda grabbed him around the torso and heaved him out of the water like a hooked fish.

Zeya kicked and hollered. He bit Zanda's ear.

Zanda dropped him.

Zeya found his feet and faced his enemy.

Zanda stepped inside the length of cane. He laughed the hearty laugh of the triumphant. A war club against a flimsy piece of wood. He reached out, grabbed one end of the cane, and started bending it.

Crack! Splinter!

Zeya was holding a twig. He started to toss it away.

Zanda leapt, grabbed Zeya by the throat, and crushed him to the bottom.

Zeya looked at his murderer through the distortion of water. He could see big scars caused by the pox. He could see a madman's eyes. He couldn't breathe.

He kicked, but the water took the force out of his blow.

He wriggled and writhed, but Zanda was too strong.

He looked at Zanda's face. Darkness was creeping in from the edges of his vision.

Idea. One last idea.

Zeya had a shard of wood in his hand.

He slipped the tip of the broken cane toward Zanda's neck, right at the small hollow just above the collarbone. When it was almost touching, with all the strength he had left, he rammed it into the flesh.

Zanda grabbed his throat with both hands. He stood up, and Zeya went right with him, gasping for breath. Zanda tried to yell, but it came out as a gargle.

Zeya whacked the butt of the cane with his palm. It sank in.

Zanda uttered an awful sound that blended coughing and vomiting.

Zeya whacked the cane one more time.

Zanda spasmed and collapsed.

Zeya's mind ran riot. *You're a warrior,* part of him said.

You're a lucky moron, said another.

How did he figure it out? called another voice.

Who gives a damn? called another.

Su-Li rasped.

Zeya put his hands on his hips and caught his breath. "Yes, I know," he said, "you were trying to tell me Zanda hadn't gone into the woods, he was coming right along the river. In the river." He looked back along the trail and at the cattails. "I don't see how he figured it out." He shrugged. "I never will."

Su-Li hopped forward, awkward as ever on the ground, and tapped Zanda's neck with one wing.

Zeya pulled the splintered cane out. He inspected the tip. *Very little blood for the end of a human life.*

Su-Li tapped the neck again.

Zeya looked at the small puncture wound, nothing dramatic, but enough.

He snapped his mind back to Su-Li. "I don't want to do it."

Su-Li touched the neck.

Awahi had told Zeya last night, "Whichever of the sons follows you, if you kill him, cut off his head."

Su-Li agreed—he'd nodded yes.

"That's repulsive!"

Awahi grabbed Zeya's shoulders with both stringy arms. "You need to show Inaj you're a worthy adversary."

Su-Li nodded a more vigorous yes.

"This won't be over until Inaj is dead. No one has ever intimidated him. No one has ever made him quake inside. If you kill Wilu or Zanda, that's your chance. Do it. Make him know. You are to be reckoned with."

"All right," Zeya had said.

But now, standing over the mortal remains, he said, "It's gruesome, I can't."

Su-Li tapped the neck.

"All right, all right," he said. He went to work with his knife.

❖

The village tittered with reports and rumors. Jemel meant to get the real story. She strode up to Awahi's fire. On such a hot day the old man had cooked outside and was sitting in the shade of his house eating his supper. He lived off the gifts of people still young enough to hunt, to plant, to snare, to gather. He was Eagle Voice—he'd devoted his life to something worthwhile. Jemel respected him. But right now she was mad.

"They say Zeya came here to see you." Her lover's reputation had spread village to village, and everyone knew the boy called Dahzi was now the man called Zeya.

The old man looked across his spoon at her, bewildered. After a moment he said, "Sit down, my dear, I'll get you a bowl."

"I don't need anything to eat. I want to know what's going on."

Out of courtesy he set his bowl down. "I know it's hard. You got whisked off to live here when your folks threw a fit about Zeya. You feel like a castoff."

"A prisoner," she corrected.

"You're an admirable young woman. What do you want from me?"

"They say Zeya was here last night, stayed over with you. I want to know why. Where is he now? What's he doing?"

"And why didn't he come to see you?"

"Why didn't he take me out of here?"

Awahi nodded to himself. He had lived long enough to learn that telling the simple truth is easiest for everyone.

"Zeya came here to get me to bless some eagle feathers. He's on a big mission for the Seer."

"What?"

"He's gathering eagle feathers for a gift to the Immortals. I'd best not say more."

Jemel decided not to pressure the old fellow. After all, she was holding something back, too.

"He's a special man, your Zeya."

She looked daggers at him. "Don't flatter me. Tell me what's going on."

"You know Inaj is here."

"And his sons." Her voice was like an astringent medicine. "Including the one who is now Red Chief."

"Inaj sent some men out to kill Zeya." He moistened his lips with his tongue. "Zeya killed them instead."

He saw something move behind her eyes, like fish in a stream, but then the daggers came back.

"Why didn't he take me away?"

"The Seer ordered him not to make any contact with you or his mother, not until he's performed this mission."

"And then?"

"He didn't say. If an old man's eyes can see, though, he loves you."

"He should have come to me."

"Then his mission would have failed. Do you love him?"

Among the Galayi this was a question not ordinarily asked—too close to saying, "Are you crazy?"

"We are passionate for each other. If we have to live in another village, we will. If we have to live in a cave, we will. If he dies, I will throw my life away like a dirty rag."

Awahi looked at her in fascination. He had not seen a Moon Woman since he was a teenager. That one was a queer old woman with only dogs for companions. Awahi never found out what happened to the man she loved or why she had no family then.

His mother told him that was what love did to you. To Awahi Jemel didn't seem full of love—more like a buoyant ferocity.

He felt a pang of compassion for her, and great curiosity. "I don't know what else to tell you, my dear."

"Where has he gone? When will he come back?"

"I must not speak of his mission. I'm afraid. Today Inaj sent Zanda on Zeya's trail, to kill him. I hope he survives."

Jemel felt a stab of fear. Zeya . . . Then she wanted to throw mocking words, but she pulled herself back. *Hope he survives.*

Ridiculous. It made her blood shriek against living like other people.

A-a-a-ark!

Her head shot upward. It was only a buzzard, but they never called out. Then she saw. Something big swung from his talons, swung by its . . . hair. She squelched an awful thought.

The buzzard flapped straight across the village common and dropped whatever it was carrying in the middle. It bounced three times and rolled to a stop.

She sprinted toward it. Somehow she kept from screaming, but dread gushed from her fingertips to her toes.

A head, yes, it was. She fell to her knees and threw up.

Someone ran up beside her and lifted the head by its hair.

The most horrible cry she'd ever heard fought its way out of Inaj's throat, colored by every ugliness in the world.

Dangling from his hand, the head circled slowly. When it turned its face to Jemel, she saw it was Zanda.

Jemel's eyes danced with elation. Inaj's blazed with rage. They loathed each other.

SIX

Flying Between Worlds

40

Zeya was exhausted. He'd been walking for two weeks, and a lot of the time he'd been running. He hadn't stopped to hunt but had only eaten what berries, nuts, and roots he found. Worse, he'd slept badly. The faces of the men he'd killed floated through his dreams. Though they seemed stoic, their eyes glinted dark with evil. Their lips, floating disembodied, told him at great length how they or their clansmen would take revenge. Zeya heard the words but didn't understand them.

When he woke up in the morning, he said to himself, *That's all childish nonsense.* He didn't need to do anything but hurry to give the feathers to Tsola. If he needed protection, Su-Li would provide it.

But he was never easy, ever weary.

❖

He stood on a high ridge and looked across a wide valley at the Emerald Peak. He was west of the mountain and further west of the Cheowa village at the mouth of the creek. In fact, he was on Thano hunting grounds. He thought, *Dangerous for any Galayi, but not as dangerous as being among my own people.*

He was sure that Inaj was having the trail to the Healing Pool and Emerald Cave watched. More murderers.

"Does coming from the back side eliminate the danger?"

Though it wasn't really meant as a question, Su-Li shook his head no.

"So how do we get there alive?"

He had discovered over the last couple of moons that many times the best thing to do was nothing. Sit and think. Maybe an idea would come to him. Maybe he would see something. He wanted to get closer to do his watching and thinking.

"My friend, would you see if it's safe to go down this mountain and across into the woods?"

Su-Li raised his wings to lift off.

"Find a cave for tonight," Zeya said. They'd reached an accommodation. Zeya slept every night in a cave, and Su-Li slept in a snag overlooking the entrance.

Su-Li glided downhill.

"I'd be dead without you," Zeya said to the buzzard's tail.

❖

This time Zeya wasn't dreaming the faces of assassins. He was sitting and playing cat's cradle with Jemel in front of her parent's house. She laughed when he said something funny, but laughed kind of wildly. Once in a while she would glance off toward the trees. Zeya swallowed hard. One of her lovers was there, he knew that, waiting in the woods for him to go away so he could . . .

Then he realized.

He shushed her.

When they were absolutely silent, he could hear . . .

Whispers!

Whispers? He came half awake. He couldn't make out . . .

A hand clapped onto his mouth.

His blood rushed. He twisted, broke free, and took a blind swing at the darkness.

"Hold your tongue!" said the low voice.

He swung again.

A hand seized his arm. "Quiet!"

He recognized that voice . . .

"It's me, Paya. Mind the noise."

Paya?

A hand pushed around in the embers of his fire. A twig burst into flame. By its light he could see . . . Paya.

"I thought you were . . ."

The hand clapped back over his mouth.

"Shut up," Paya said in a wheeze. "We've got to get away from here. They're lying in wait for you outside."

"Su-Li would see them."

"Not asleep, he won't. Let's go."

"We're trapped!"

"Not hardly. There's a little passage back here. You never learn, and neither do they."

The passage turned out to be tiny. Zeya had to shove his two bags ahead and slither through on his belly.

Beyond the squeeze and around a corner, Paya lit a torch. They walked and crawled for a long time, waded for a while, and came to one of Paya's small camps, this one on the bank of an underground stream.

"Want to eat?"

Zeya put an arm around the Crab Man's shoulders and embraced him. He guessed no one had done that in twenty winters.

"Want to eat? Paya thrust dried meat before Zeya's eyes. He could see embarrassment on the Crab Man's face. He took the meat and chomped on it greedily.

"You want the story," said Paya. Pride filled his voice. "Ain't hardly no story. I knew a way out. At the bottom of that pool, yes, a way out."

Zeya shook his head in amazement.

"You mighta guessed that Paya knows every crack and

crevice of this cave. I found that passage, it's underwater, I found it before. You can feel the water moving and follow it. The other fella, he didn't feel it, he laid there and died."

"You swam out the bottom?"

"Yeah, Paya did. And that other fella, if he'd been able to see me or known any way at all, he'd a still laid there and died. Scared to swim down into the blackness, most people. Yes, they are, scared."

"You're a good man."

He'd never seen Paya smile so big.

"How'd you find me?" asked Zeya.

"That was easy. The Seer, she's expecting you about now, and she looked and looked. That one, she can see every bit of the Emerald Cavern in her mind. You and me, we have to go looking and find each nook and cranny. But not that one. She can see every little piece of it. She told me where you was and to come get you."

"So we're in the Emerald Cavern."

"For certain. This un hardly ever leaves it."

Zeya resisted hugging him again.

"I saved you, I did done."

41

Y ou have days and days to sleep," said Tsola. "I'm very excited now."

She shook him lightly again. Zeya sat up, blinking. She actually kissed his cheek.

"Magnificent," the Seer said. "Zeya, what you've done is magnificent. I see you've turned your *zadayi* red side out."

He gave half a smile. The *zadayi* was an accident. He wondered if she'd thought he couldn't bring it off. He wondered if she knew how close he'd come to failing.

The panther got up, padded closer, and curled up next to his mother. Su-Li came along for the ride, rocking up and down on the panther's shoulders. Apparently, the magical animals were friends.

Zeya gave Klandagi a sour look. "Panther disguised as a nice elderly gentleman, you threw me into the fire."

"I am a nice elderly gentleman," Klandagi said in a river-rapids roar, "and that was a good deed."

Su-Li croaked. Zeya wondered whether the buzzard was saying, "Right!" or "You don't know how many times this fellow almost messed it up."

"Su-Li told me what happened," Tsola said, "and I told Klandagi and Paya." The Crab Man smiled and lowered his head, embarrassed.

Zeya was glad he didn't have to go over the story—every bit of him was worn out, even his tongue.

"Have you guessed what's next?"

"Too tired. My brain's not working."

"Then take this thought to the land of dreams with you. You will travel to the Land beyond the Sky Arch and present the feathers to Thunderbird. With them he will make a new cape for the Galayi people."

"Whatever you say." Zeya got a pallet, laid it near the fire, and rolled up.

His last glimmer of consciousness was a wish. He'd rather go to see Jemel than travel to the Land beyond the Sky Arch.

❖

Zeya couldn't tell whether he slept for days and days—how could anyone know, deep in a cave? He sat up and looked around by the faint light of the fire. He did feel rested, even restless.

"Hello, Son."

It was his mother.

He grabbed her and hugged her.

"A-a-a-ark!"

Zeya laughed. He'd nearly knocked Su-Li off Sunoya's shoulder in his enthusiasm. "I apologize, Sir Spirit Buzzard."

"A-a-a-ark!"

He held his mother at arm's length and looked at her face. It was furrowed and shriveled. She looked ten winters older.

"Mom, what's happened to you?"

"It's nothing." She stroked Su-Li's ruff.

"She didn't tell you," said Tsola. "She's deeply connected to Su-Li. Without him she wastes away."

"But he's back now," said Sunoya, stroking him.

Zeya grinned at her. "You came fast to get him."

"Actually," said Sunoya, "I came to kiss you and send you off to the Land beyond the Sky Arch. It is the journey of a lifetime."

He looked at Tsola. "Now?"

"Are you ready?"

"I'm famished," he said.

Klandagi rolled to his feet, stuck his face in a corner, padded over to Zeya, and from his jaws dropped a big deer roast.

Zeya gaped at it and said, "I think I'll cook it."

"Don't cook my part," said Klandagi.

When they finished eating, Zeya said to Sunoya, "Is it time?"

"It's time."

"We have to swim there," said Tsola.

"Swim beyond the Sky Arch?"

She laughed. "No, swim to the Emerald Dome. You haven't heard of it. Sunoya knows, she's been there. Only Medicine Chiefs go there, to start their journeys. It's a beautiful and miraculous room, but the main thing is, it's a launching point, like a high rock for a bird to start its flight."

"A-a-ark!"

Zeya said, "Do you want to go home, Su-Li?"

The buzzard looked from face to face.

"Funny, you're not answering me. Well, anyway, Sunoya needs you right now."

"There's something you should know," Tsola said. "The people closest to you, all of them, have given you certain gifts. I can't tell you what they are, but they're waiting for you beyond the Sky Arch. You'll need them there."

"Am I crazy for doing this?"

"Let's go," Tsola said.

❖

"Take all your clothes off," said Tsola.

Zeya hesitated. He could hear rustling, and he didn't want to see a hundred-year-old woman naked. Not that he could see a thing in this absolute blackness.

"Don't dally," said Klandagi. "I have all my clothes off all the time."

Zeya did as he was told.

The world he had now was sounds. He could hear Klandagi's breathing. The stream nearby, flowing. Tsola's feet as they padded here and there. He could feel a very gentle stirring of the air in the cavern, but he couldn't hear it.

Tsola splashed into the water. "Follow me downstream," she said. "It's underwater part of the way. Do you feel disoriented?"

"Very."

"Darkness does that. You can't get into trouble underwater as long as you go downstream. Don't turn around and try to swim upstream, that's all that matters. You'll run out of breath."

"Okay." He could feel a squirming in his guts.

"When you run into me, stand up. It will mean we've come back to the air."

The squirming turned to terror.

"It's best if you don't think about it. Remember, your mother did it, every Medicine Chief has done it. Relax and don't worry. Let's go."

He heard her step into the water.

"Reach your hand out to the left."

He did and she took it. Then he remembered that she could see in the darkness, and was embarrassed.

She gave his hand a little tug. "This way."

He hesitated.

"Go!" roared Klandagi.

He put one foot into the chill water, and then the other.

She pulled him and they splashed gently along. "In a moment we'll come to a wall."

After a few steps she put his hand on the rock. "I'm going to let go, then swim underwater. You follow."

She did. Taking an enormous breath, he dived in.

42

*A*ir. *I need air.*

He swam. *Alive, but no air.*

Tsola's voice sounded inside his head. *Relax and don't worry.*

He made a deliberate effort to relax his body and make the swimming motion easy. *My mother did it. The hundred-year-old woman in front of me is doing it.*

He imagined himself as a turtle. He peered into the dark, watery universe with turtle eyes, he thought with a turtle brain. He felt what it was to be an aquatic animal.

I need air. His chest was swelling with desperation. *Turtles take a big breath and hold it, too. They're easy with keeping breath in and swimming along.*

He told himself that the current was helping him. *Yes, I can feel it.* He kicked his feet and swept his arms back, going faster. He had liquid arms and legs, boneless, like a turtle's. He made his head flow back and forth, like a turtle's. Sometimes his turtle claws scraped the sides. *Am I in a tunnel?*

What I'm touching, it might be stars, it might be fish, and I may be beyond the moon. I may be in the depths of the ocean.

His turtle body spun. He lost track of which way was up, which was down, which was sideways. After a pang of fear, he discovered he didn't care.

He gave up. His body was turning, and, yes, he might gulp water instead of air.

His head banged into flesh. Rising, he discovered that he was standing back to back with Tsola. *I was swimming upside down!*

He touched her in the dark with his hand. That made him hope it was her back he'd bumped into.

She took his hand. "Now we walk."

They did.

"Now we swim again. This one's not as long." She gave his hand a squeeze. "You'll know when you get there."

She was gone.

He didn't want to do it. Fear dribbled down his body like icy rain. *I can't do it. Crazy to throw myself into the arms of fate like that. I've seen dead men the last few moons. Dead men live inside my skull now. I can't do it.*

He looked around. He felt the blackness more than saw it. *I am standing alone, deep in the earth, absolutely blind and helpless.*

He ducked his head under and went.

Topsy-turvy, turning round and round, and now it was worse than before—he had vertigo. He couldn't control his body, couldn't control his mind. He could identify nothing of the universe.

He began to sense light.

He thought to open his eyes.

In the center of darkness a faint spot of light!

An illusion, idiot!

The light grew, it widened, it reached out to him, it welcomed him.

I'm dying!

Light engulfed him, bright as a sky. *But there is no sky down here!* It was like blackness flip-flopped, and in its place was the center of the sun.

He stood up.

Light everywhere. Green light.

Impossible. He was in a room that was half a dome, cupped above by limestone, held below by a lake. The water was dark green, the air light green. Here, deep in the mountain, light was banished—yet the room was bright. The stone ceiling was a green sky.

Tsola smiled and said, "Welcome. Now you see why my home is called the Emerald Cavern."

❖

They sat on the bank entirely naked. Tsola was building a fire. She kept all the materials for a camp here, including food, firewood, and utensils. Zeya noticed a drum, and next to it a pile of the scarlet lichen, *u-tsa-le-ta.*

"We don't wear clothes here. The Immortals require us to be our undisguised selves."

Zeya was surprised that it didn't bother him, and that in her way Tsola was beautiful.

He said to her back, "How can you swim all that distance? I could barely do it."

She half-turned to him and said, "Well, I'm used to it, and I age at about half the normal rate. I'm in my fifties."

"Half?"

"All the Seers do that, and their families. It's a secret, and you must keep it. The waters of the Healing Pool? Within the cave they have even greater powers. Anyone who drinks that water every day ages slowly."

"That's why you don't let all the people know."

"We would be overrun. Only the Medicine Chiefs know, and one of them will be the next Seer."

Zeya couldn't take it all in. Finally, he said, "What makes the water green? What makes the light?"

Tsola shrugged. "Why question miracles? Just enjoy them."

Zeya nodded. He watched Tsola set up a tripod of sticks above the fire and hang a buffalo stomach from it. He looked around, and now he noticed bones here and there on the banks of the lake. "What are those?"

"Human skeletons."

He watched her drop heated rocks into the water into the buffalo stomach. He said, "I don't get it."

"Could you swim back through the tunnels, the way we came?"

He thought of the force of the current, how it swooshed him along, yet how near he came to running out of air. "No."

"Medicine people come here to make the journey to the Land beyond the Sky Arch. Some get here and can't cross the threshold. They won't go on, and they can't go back."

She dropped a handful of *u-tsa-le-ta* into the hot water.

"How does the seeker go on?"

"He dives down into this lake and doesn't come back to this place."

"How deep is it?"

"As deep as life and death."

"But the seeker doesn't come back?"

"After you've been beyond the Sky Arch and gotten what you went for, the Immortals send you back to my home in the cave. Klandagi and Sunoya are waiting for us there."

Zeya pondered this. "How do you get back?"

"A secret way."

"And the ones who don't go beyond the Sky Arch?"

"You see them there." She gestured to the skeletons. "Fortunately, over many generations, very few have failed. But from here, Grandson, there is no turning back."

Zeya got up and walked around the bank of the lake. The light was eerie, the beauty was woven of fantasy, and his destination was macabre. He stopped and looked down at the bones of a human being. He wondered about this man or woman—he would never know which.

He looked into the eye sockets of the skull and into the cavity where no consciousness lived. He wondered about the person's experience of ordinary life, sun, wind, water, food, family, fun. He thought how it all had turned to phantasms day by day, as someone lay here and starved to death. Probably the last days were chimeras of dream, mere imaginings, shadowed and cold.

Fear. My enemy.

"The tea is ready."

He walked back to Tsola, and she handed him a cup.

"It will take me to another world," he said.

She nodded. "Take your mind ahead of your body."

"Paya gets it for you, doesn't he?"

"The dear Crab Man. He gathers it and sells it to me and the other Medicine Chiefs. Only to us."

"What do you use it for?"

"Everyone has to go to the Land of the Sky Arch for the first time through the bottom of the Emerald Lake. After that, he or she can go just by saying the right prayers, drinking the *u-tsa-le-ta,* and drumming his or her way across."

Zeya nodded. That was what his mother did sometimes, and that was why she treated her drum as a sacred object.

"Drink," said Tsola. "Then we will begin the ceremony."

❖

Zeya turned into a crystal. His mind, all of his being, was shafts of light reflecting in more directions than the sky has stars. Colors he had never imagined shot through the inner space of his angle-cut head. Each color showed itself in a fanfare of hues, far more than had names in any Earthly language. The colors swirled continually, and he was floating in them, as he had floated in the cavern itself, with no sense of which way was up or down. Nor did he care.

He watched a display of greens. Yes, there was the light green of new buds, the forest green of leaves and pine needles, the dark green of the sea, the silver-green of leaves along the creeks, and thousands more. He could distinguish between the greens of different grasses, and between the eager new grass of spring and the weary grass of early autumn. He was lost in greens.

So it was with purples. He recognized the hue of violets, of certain moments in sunsets, of larkspurs, irises, and harebells. He was also bathed in reds, yellows, blues, and oranges, in colors he could name, in colors he had never seen or imagined. He was lost in radiating light, and lost in time.

After a dozen breaths or a dozen lifetimes, Tsola tied the bag of feathers to his chest. Then she took him by the arm. He got up and went willingly. For him every direction was ecstatic. He was pleased to discover that his legs worked. He wondered where they were going and hoped that when they got there, he would be able to recline again and watch the grand display.

He felt the water on his feet and knew it for what it was. Up to his knees, his groin—he wondered if he could shoot his *do-wa* all the way across the lake, now that the world was freed from logic and limitations.

Up to his ribs. Tsola said, "Keep your eyes closed. Dive. Find the bottom. Let the current take you to the opening, and keep swimming down."

He did. More ecstasy. His fingers found the rocky bottom, and he followed the slant down. Soon he began to feel the motion of water flowing, and he let it guide him. When he felt the water pulling him faster, he gave himself to the current and to the colors ricocheting around his mind. He saw the lights against the night sky instead of the bright day. The water rushed fast—he felt like he was falling, falling, that was good—this was his journey.

It came to his mind that he had no air. The lake was a waterfall now, and he would never be able to swim up it. Maybe there was air below. Or maybe he would die. That was good.

When the time came, he didn't fight his lungs. They made a great spasm, sucked in the death-giving water, and Zeya died.

43

Zeya woke up in . . . Had he woken up? He could see nothing in any direction, left, right, ahead, back, up, even down. Was he conscious? He abode in absolute darkness.

He waved his arms. He kicked his feet. He tucked his head to his knees and rolled himself like a ball. He waved his hands at the universe. He could move, so he must be awake. The odd part—the impossible part—was that he was in a world with nothing else, or at least nothing else that he could see, smell, touch, hear, or taste. Nothing.

Fear zinged tremolos through him, body and soul.

He looked around again. His eyes brought him nothing. *I am in utter nothingness.*

He put his hand on his heart like he would have put it on

Awahi's zither. He wanted to stop the vibration and end the sounds. They were terror aborning.

Terror equaled death.

He rolled his body in several directions. Nothing.

He swam through emptiness as he would have swum through water. Nothing.

He shouted. No sound.

He spoke softly. No sound.

He reached for the pouch at his neck to get his flint to strike a spark. No pouch—he'd forgotten he and Tsola came through naked. But something strange. His neck felt feathery. His touched his face with both hands. They felt feathery. *I'm carrying the feathers somehow.*

He couldn't worry about that now. Tsola? Where was she? Nowhere.

The Land beyond the Sky Arch, where was it? Surely this could not be where the Immortals lived. He had a strong sense, an absolute conviction, that what lived here was nothing. Not nothing in the sense of all things being absent. Nothing as a solid entity itself. Nothing as the jam-full population of an impossible place.

Then how was Zeya here? He could breathe, he could think, he could move.

Impossible. This place was an impossibility. To be here was impossible, impossible, impossible . . .

What on Earth . . . ?

Well, this isn't Earth, that's for sure. He smiled.

Smiling reminded him. Tsola had told him, "If you get scared, talk to me. I'll be alongside you, and I have experience with this journey."

"But you aren't here," he said out loud, although no sound came out.

I am, she said in his mind.

He jumped. From here to places beyond the furthest stars he felt alone. Nothing inhabited in this world. Yet someone was inside him.

"Help me," he said.

What do you want?

"Not to be scared."

Tsola said, *Is that why you spoke? You are afraid?*

"Of the dark," Zeya said, hanging his head.

Yes, the darkness goes forever, said Tsola.

"Is that what we're doing? Making me face my fears?"

You overcome fear by doing something. What are you going to do?

He was completely bewildered. He said, "Give me light."

Immediately, he was surrounded by bright stars. He saw no sun or moon, but a shimmery star-glow, faint as moonlight reflecting off water, allowed him a kind of sight.

Yet he saw nothing, nothing but the light itself.

It felt ridiculous, but why not try? He said, "Give me company."

Immediately, people clustered around him. His mother. Tsola. Klandagi. Paya. Jemel. And a stranger.

Somehow he knew he couldn't touch them—these beings were insubstantial. He stood and looked at Jemel. Their eyesight seemed to create a winding cord of connection, mind to mind, heart to heart. Feeling traveled through that cord like blood, and it said without words, *I love you.* He was happy.

Sunoya said—no words traveled through the air, all were in his mind—*Zeya, I introduce you to your father. Tensa, this is your son Ulo-Zeya, who was known as Dahzi as a boy. Zeya, this is Tensa, who died so that you might live.*

Never in his life had Zeya wanted so much to embrace someone. The joy he felt at his father's presence was like a huge spring of fresh water leaping from the ground.

"Someday I want to talk to you," he said.

Tensa said, "Someday you will."

Zeya looked happily at everyone. "Walk with me," he said.

A path had appeared among the trackless stars, a path of flat stones wandering off to . . . where? He didn't know. He was full of joy now, and in his delight he knew that these stones were for him, they were a way laid out only for him, they were his journey.

He started stepping from stone to stone. They were set a little apart, but no more than an easy stride. Walking along them was simple and pleasant. With every step he saw new stars ahead, more light, more excitement. He laughed.

He turned his head to share it with his company of loved ones, and two of them were gone. Paya had dropped out for some reason. And Klandagi.

Oh well, he told himself, *it isn't their path. It's mine.*

The departed often leave gifts, Tsola said.

"Gifts?"

You'll see.

He turned back to the path and saw that it was getting more complicated. The stone steps were a little further apart, and not quite in a straight line. He eyed them carefully, saw what would work, and started skipping along the stones. Hop left, hop right, hop to the left. It was fun.

He went quite a way before he looked around again. Jemel and Sunoya were skipping along behind him. They looked content, but their eyes held knowledge he didn't have.

Behind them was no one. His father and Tsola were gone. Dropped out.

I suppose their paths branched off in some other direction. He hadn't seen any other stone paths. He thought, *Maybe their life directions aren't mine to see.*

He looked back at his path and at once was absorbed. Now it was changing, intriguing. The stones were set farther apart and at odd angles, so that you couldn't actually stand on a lot of them. All you could do was jump forward, plant your foot momentarily, and quickly leap to the next stone.

The challenge was irresistible. He strode forward, he sprang, he leapt, he teetered, and he sprang again. As he went farther, the path got trickier and trickier. He couldn't stop now—he would fall. He leapt and cavorted and played his way along.

At last he came to a large, flat stone and stopped to rest. Then he saw why it was a stopping place. The next stone was set too far away. No one could jump to it.

Yet. There was something curious in the space itself. It was like a dust devil, but in a world without dust. It was a congruence of breaths of air, of energies. If he could figure out exactly where to put his foot, he might . . .

A sense of loss lanced him. He turned around. His mother was gone now. Only Jemel stood with him. Her eyes were songs, one of love, one of grief. Tears streamed down her face.

He understood with all his being. He had to go on. Ahead of him was his way, the path made for him. Though it would get harder and harder, it was his joy, it was his one true life.

But it was not Jemel's way, not Jemel's life. Hers led in some other direction from here. He could not see the direction, or even say for sure that it existed. But she saw it and would take it now.

He knew. He looked at her with a longing and a grief beyond all imagining.

Then he turned his back, looked hard at that convergence of energies. Yes, yes! Incredible! He did see where he could put his foot. He stepped out, felt for its tricky purchase, and . . .

44

Zeya stood in a crazy version of his home country. Mountains jutted up in every direction, but steeper than in his homeland, and thicker with pines on the high slopes. The lines of the ridges were sharper and wilder, the peaks higher, and they were covered with snow.

Snow? But the land was in bloom. He looked down again at the hills and valleys. They were lush with mountain ash trees, yellow birches, hemlocks, red oaks, and other broad-leaved trees in full glory. The dogwood trees in the wide valleys were in bloom, and the fields were wild with flowers.

Everything was altered. The grasses were pink, the rivers orange, and the sedges along their banks turquoise. The rhododendrons flung out blossoms in mad colors, scarlet, fuchsia, and canary yellow. The rocks of the hills glittered like gemstones. Above them the sun was rising, and its globe was silver.

He laughed. A very gaudy version of his home.

He was standing on a high aerie, a rocky point that offered a vista in every direction of whatever country this was. A nagging thought popped up clear, and he grinned at himself. How could he see the flowers of the low valleys from here on top of the mountains? If this was the Land beyond the Sky Arch, his eyesight was extra-powerful here. He liked that.

The sky above the peaks was a faint lilac. He found that he could look directly at the silver sun without hurting his eyes. He thought the color was terrific.

It's rising, said Tsola's voice inside his mind, *except that it never comes up. It's always rising.*

He laughed out loud at that notion—what else could he do?

Suddenly he heard song and looked around. The sky below him, close to the trees, was filled with birds. Taking his time, he spotted warblers, scarlet tanagers, sparrows, owls, chickadees. *Where are the ravens?* he asked himself, and then saw a sprinkle of them on a ridge across the way. He raised his face high, made a wish, blinked, and saw the big birds he loved, the ones that rode the winds far above the trees and even above the balds—a half dozen hawks spread out, a pair of war eagles near a nest, and on the eastern horizon a lone buzzard.

He felt a glow in his chest. "Okay, if this is the Land beyond the Sky Arch, where's Thunderbird?"

You'll find him, said Tsola.

It was eerie, talking to someone inside him.

His cheek got a sharp itch. He reached up to scratch it and touched feathers. With a jolt he remembered. *These must be the feathers for Thunderbird.* He felt both his cheeks—feathers. His forehead, chin, neck, all feathers. Was he wearing the beautiful feathers? Weird beyond strange.

He reached for his nose and put his hand on something horny. A beak? He opened his mouth, stuck a finger in, and bit himself with his own beak.

A quaver of fear ran up and down his spine.

He raised his hands and looked at them. The right hand was a talon. The left hand, the one with the webbed fingers that marked his life path, had turned into a claw, like that at a crayfish.

What on Earth? His nerves were all drums and rattles.

No, Tsola reminded him, *not on Earth*.

He looked at his feet. They were paws.

The drums and rattles crescendoed.

His legs were those of a big cat. His body was a black panther's.

Worse, he had a second set of arms. Or rather legs, panther legs, with paws.

"Hello," he said out loud, "I'm scared."

You're all right, said Tsola.

He surveyed himself. His upper legs were a panther's. His arms, a separate set from his front legs, ended in a talon and a claw. His chest and belly were a panther's, like his hind legs. From what he could tell his face was a bird's.

"What's going on?"

You're beginning to discover your gifts.

"You mentioned gifts." His tone was quavery.

Yes.

"Better tell me."

Klandagi gave you the body of a panther, as you can see. You will be able to run fast on your four legs, faster than any person, faster than any animal in the forest.

Zeya waited. He wondered why he'd need to run in this land.

Paya gave you a human arm with a pincer, like his. It was the best he could do, and his dear heart is in it. I gave you an eagle leg with a talon. I also gave you the head and neck of an eagle. Your eyesight is amazing.

The drums and rattles were frenzied-wild now.

Su-Li gave you the beak of a buzzard. You can smell as well as any creature on Earth.

"What do I need to smell?" Then, "Why don't I have wings?"

You haven't earned them. But you will.

He pondered. Two companions were left out. "What about Jemel?"

She gave you a human heart. A vessel of love, said Tsola between his ears. *Your love for her, your love for yourself, your love for life and everything in it.*

Zeya nodded. He felt odd. It must be a blessing to receive these marvelous gifts but . . . "And my mother?"

She gave you courage. Whatever comes to you, you can face it calmly, clearly, optimistically.

Zeya nodded. What was she *not* telling him? What was here to be afraid of?

You'll discover that, Tsola said. *And I gave you one additional gift, one that is the special ability of shamans. With practice, you will be able to see beyond illusion to truth.*

Zeya nodded. He was overwhelmed, disoriented, discombobulated. The drums and rattles were screaming.

Tsola said, *What would you like right now?*

He told the drums and rattles to shut up, and they eased off. He settled himself down. "I'm alone. I'm thirsty. I probably should eat."

Walk down to the stream and drink.

He looked at his airy perch, and no hands to hold on with.

You'll find that panthers are more agile in steep, rocky places than people. Just go.

He leapt from his perch to the ground. His strength felt terrific. He flexed his claws. He would be a great hunter.

By the way, you don't need to eat. No creature eats any other in this land—they are all immortal. You will never be dahzi. She chuckled. *Good thing you left your old name behind, Hungry One.*

Zeya pranced down toward the creek, thanking Klandagi for his body and its power. He leaped to the tops of outcroppings. He climbed high in a tree and viewed the world from a limb. He padded through the forest with the confidence that he was the most powerful beast of all. He let loose a roar and discovered that it was a bird's screech.

Oh well. He chuckled at himself. His mother had always told him to know himself. Right now that was a little tricky, but fun. As he bent to drink from the creek, he heard a snarl from behind him. He looked back and heard yapping and growling sounds from the left. When he turned in that direction, the sounds came from the rear again. He put his back to the creek and swiveled his head, his panther body poised to spring, his eagle eyes able to pick out every detail of the forest.

Tsola's drum sounded in his head.

Dogs, that's what he heard. A pack of dogs with patches of every color, brown, black, liver, tawny, blood-red. Spotted, striped, brindled, they blended into the forest uncannily. He couldn't tell how many, but there were lots. They jumped and crawled over each other like maggots on a corpse.

He shot his eyes in every direction for a tree. Bushes aplenty along the bank, but no sturdy limbs within leaping distance.

The snarls and growls rose to barks. The dogs crawled closer. *They're like leeches,* he murmured to himself, *dangerous leeches.*

He considered getting behind them with one huge bound. Too far. The pack was like one big predator, constantly shaping and reshaping its mass, creeping ever closer.

An ice glob of fatalism formed in his chest. He'd always hated dogs.

Time to act.

As he sprang, he felt his bleakness undercut his strength. He landed in the middle of a whirling mass of canine attackers. He felt teeth tear at his legs and belly.

He bounded again, and the pain in his hindquarters screamed of dogs hanging by their teeth. He hit the ground running fast, but he had to slow down, twist, and shake off the dogs. As two fell off, others snapped onto him. He spotted a sturdy branch, leaped, and caught it with his forepaws. A gleam of hope powered him up.

Then he had to swing himself around to get rid of the brutes and their clamping teeth. Brutes, even if they were small. He raked one with a forepaw and watched the blood spray as it fell. He whacked another off with a backswing. He started to bite the third one before he remembered that he didn't have panther jaws, only a yellow beak. He clutched the damn thing's throat with his talon and squeezed until it let go. Then he kept on squeezing. When he dropped it, the cur fell like an empty skin.

He was safe. The dogs could snap all they wanted to, they could leap at him, they could make demonic noises, but he was above it all.

He decided to climb higher. When he raised his body, he discovered that he couldn't push off his left rear leg. It was dead. He looked and saw that he'd been hamstrung.

I can climb anyway. With one back leg, two front legs, and his arms, he clawed his way up the oak to the highest branch that would bear his weight. There three of his panther legs curled under him, ready for action. The fourth dangled uselessly.

Tsola's drum insisted on being heard.

He looked at the dogs. *I can outlast you.*

Can I really?

He told his head to shut up, laid his head on his forepaws, and watched the dogs. He wondered if they would go away in the darkness, or stay all night. He looked at the sun. Then he remembered. Tsola said the sun never arced across the sky in this world. It always sat on the rim of the mountains, rising. Was that possible? It hadn't moved since he arrived.

He watched the dogs. They circled and snarled. The sun stretched out on the mountain ridges, brilliant silver, utterly still.

Zeya felt a new weight inside his strange body, a familiar one, despondency.

"Tsola," he whispered.

No answer, but he heard the drum.

"Tsola!" he said louder.

Silence.

"Tsola, where are you?"

Nothing.

He wailed, "I am abandoned."

Now desolation descended upon him. Needing company, he began to talk to himself. *Dark is never going to come. The dogs*

*are never going to go away. I can only hobble on three legs. I'll never
get away. I knew all along—I'm finished. I'll never see Jemel again.*

He put his head down on his front paws and closed his
eyes.

Sleep didn't come. Self-talk clattered at him. In a small boy's
tone he said, "I'm going to die of thirst up here. Or starve."

Zeya said, "You can't starve. Tsola said you'll never be hungry in this land."

"Well then, thirst to death," said the little Dahzi voice. "Tsola
has abandoned me."

"You can hear her drum."

No answer.

"Your mother gave you the gift of being calm, clear, and
optimistic."

Dahzi snickered.

"Why don't you take a nap?" Zeya told Dahzi.

He realized he had never felt so tired. His body and spirit
were buried under mountains of fear, despondency, despair.

He never knew how little or how much he slept. When his
eyes opened, the sun was still rising. The dogs still paced and
growled beneath the tree.

Tsola's drum spoke to him. The young man once named
Dahzi muttered, "Surrounded by death. How long before I'm
eaten?"

Zeya said, "Why don't you do something about it?"

Dahzi and Zeya both looked down through the same set of
eyes.

"Do you know who you are?" said Zeya. "Use your gifts.
Go down there calmly, clearly, expecting the best."

Dahzi wasn't sure. "I'm scared."

"That's the point."

He rose up on three legs. "All right." He wasn't sure what
he was doing as he climbed down, staying off his bad leg. Did

he want to do his best and let it come out however it would? Or did he just yearn to get it over with?

As he got lower, the dogs barked louder and leapt higher up the trunk. He watched them from just out of reach. There was a clear pack leader, a one-eared, tawny female. The other dogs snarled, but they were watching her to see what to do.

Zeya felt a change in himself, a firmer heartbeat. *I want to fight.* It wasn't a matter of winning or losing, but some other feeling.

He dangled a forepaw. A brown male with a white-tipped tail circled the paw at a distance. From time to time he glanced over at the leader. One-Ear kept aloof, watching.

White-Tip leapt, roaring.

Zeya swatted him away. The strength in his foreleg felt good, but he had to keep a tight grip with his one good back leg.

White-Tip tossed up a storm of barks, threw himself up again, and got the same result.

A split second later a black female let out a flurry of barks and hurled herself up. She got teeth into Zeya's fur, and he had to sling her hard left and then harder right to get rid of her. He felt the rake of her teeth.

That gave Zeya an idea.

It also gave One-Ear a thought, apparently. She edged closer. She didn't swarm with the others at all, but stayed apart and watched intently. She was no more than two bounds away. He wondered what her mind made of him, bird head, panther body, and panther smell. He hoped the smell would win.

Zeya dangled his right paw toward the thronging animals, teasing. Some jumped at the paw, and occasionally he felt a wet muzzle. When a brindle got its head high enough, he slapped it hard.

One-Ear leapt when his foreleg was flexed the wrong way.

He knocked her the way she was already leaping but couldn't claw her.

She circled, tongue hanging, maybe laughing. She would strike again soon.

When she was on his right, he cocked his head to the left, hoping that she would think of a panther's eyes, straight ahead, not an eagle's eyes, on opposing sides.

One-Ear took the bait.

Instead of whacking her away, he seized her body, drew her to the limb, and clamped her with both forepaws.

Her head was a whirlwind of teeth, all trying to get at his feathery neck. She flung savage roars into his face. Her body was writhing fury. He locked his good leg to keep his balance.

He sank his talons into her throat.

Blood spouted. Her roars turned to whines and squeals.

He squeezed. At the same time he scissored at her windpipe with his pincer.

Her body sagged.

His talons squeezed a final time, and his pincer tore her throat out.

He let her drop. One-Ear's body *pflumphed* into the dust. The pack backed away, mewling. Within instants they slunk away.

Tsola's drum punctuated his victory.

❖

When he woke up, he needed a few moments to realize that he was back on his aerie. He gaped at the mountain world spread around him in every direction. He marveled again at the perpetual sunrise. He stood up to stretch and discovered that his hind leg didn't hurt. He felt his neck—the feathers weren't even ruffled.

What did you learn? said Tsola inside his mind.

"I won," said Zeya, something atavistic in his voice.

What did you win?

"A fight to the death."

What did you conquer?

"Dogs that wanted to kill me."

Maybe you'd better sleep.

"I will."

❖

He awoke floating in darkness.

He spoke. He heard nothing, not human voice, not bird call, not panther roar. He yelled. If he made a sound, emptiness ate it up. Yet somehow, deep inside himself, was Tsola's drum.

Then he had an unexplainable feeling. He was trapped. He had to get out. Out! Out right now!

He swam through the air, if this place had air. Faster, furiously he swam. Except that he didn't seem to move.

Maybe he had no way to tell. He had nothing to judge by, no places he could go toward or away from. Maybe he should swim again.

Am I a spider dangling from a long thread? He reached gently over his head with a paw. Nothing there. He groped left and right. Nothing there. Beneath his feet. Nothing there. What was holding him in place?

He screamed in terror. And heard nothing.

Tsola's drum massaged his mind.

Something real, where is something real?

He had a brainstorm. He reached a paw to his own throat. The paw eased through the air and touched nothing.

He felt for his belly. He had no belly, or hindquarters, or head, or . . . He groped gently for his *do-wa* and found nothing but empty space.

He could not scream in terror. No throat to scream with. No tongue. No lips.

He slowed somehow. A realization slowed him. Dim at first, very dim. Shapeless as a mist that went on forever. Coalescing slowly, consolidating into a shape-shifting cloud.

I am a consciousness without a body. A consciousness without a world. A consciousness alone in the universe.

He assessed things. *This is a dream.* Except that it wasn't. *It's a dream.* Too real for a dream. He gave an order. *Whatever you are, get out of here.*

❖

He shook his head and was perched on his aerie.

He said aloud, "I told it to go away and it did." He shook his head in amazement. Now Tsola's drum sounded like a companion.

He made himself turn his head and take in the view all around. How spectacular the world looked from here. He laughed. Spectacular and weird and funny. What could be weirder than a world that disappeared when you told it to? What could be funnier than being a panther-bird? "Oh, world," he said, "you're a joke when you aren't a terror."

Not bad, said Tsola in his head.

"Was it a dream?"

You tell me.

"No dream is that real."

Right. Describe to me what's happening to you.

"My mind is a little wobbly right now."

Do it.

He told her about the pack of dogs, and then about the . . . He didn't know what to call it. "Maybe the experience of absolute aloneness."

Are these fears of yours? Long-time fears? Dark-of-the-night fears?

"It feels like they've always been inside me."

So they are.

❖

Zeya walked down a winding path, but he couldn't feel the ground beneath his feet. He felt like he was walking on fog. Four slender trees lined the path on the right side in elegant order. Each one was as tall as five men, and spaced about twenty steps apart. Grassy fields spread behind them. On the other side of the path were tangled woods, wild with weeds, bushes, trees, the normal jumble of a forest. He didn't care about that. He was drawn to the perfect symmetry and beauty of the trees on his right.

He walked toward them to the beat of Tsola's drum. A man stepped out from behind the first tree. He stood at attention and as Zeya approached, cocked his spear. It was Nub Ear, the first of Inaj's assassins. His torso was still bloody from the knife Zeya buried in him, and he had the unseeing eyes of the dead.

Zeya felt twisty-creepies crawling up and down his spine. Deliberately, he disregarded the fear and said, "You're not real. You're a villain from my dreams."

Nub Ear lowered the spear and stepped back behind the tree. As Zeya passed, he could see nothing behind the tree but air.

Half-Shaved Head, though, jumped out from behind the next tree with fierce energy. His skin was loose and sagging from his watery death. As when he toppled into the pool, he held his knife ready.

Zeya said, "If you stab me, I won't feel it."

The sentinel beside the next tree was Knob Chin, holding a blow gun. To Zeya's surprise, his eyes were also glazed with death. The wounds Su-Li gave him must have turned foul.

"Don't pretend," said Zeya.

He came to the last of the trees, and Zanda stepped out, dangling his war club and spinning it in a tight circle. His throat was still bloody, and a shard of cane as long as a human hand jutted out from it.

"My uncle," said Zeya, "shame on you."

Zanda disappeared.

❖

"Tsola."

Yes.

"They're my monsters."

Think so?

"I'm creating them."

Then do something about it.

❖

Zeya sat on the bank of the river, occasionally dabbing his beak into the water. In the slow-drifting current he watched the perpetual sunrise, the colors waving with the gentle swells. He grinned at this absolutely incomprehensible world. He loved it.

Off to his left lay a log thicker than his leg and longer than his body. It was half hidden in weeds and covered with furry green moss. It gave the impression of being ancient, and more than ancient, a predecessor of Time itself.

Tsola's drum spoke of time or eternity.

Off to his right lay a log that, except for minor details, was identical.

They were both slinking through the grass toward him.

The slinking was very slow. He'd been sitting here, perhaps, for the time it would take to gnaw the meat off the bones of a captured rabbit, if rabbits died in this land, which they didn't, and if eagle-panthers ate here. The logs had moved in that time perhaps the length of Zeya's black, furred leg. The signs were small, certain grasses smashed, the tops of tall weeds stirring.

They were water moccasins, of course. For them to show their bodies as olive-colored was only the smallest change. He wondered if they would open their mouths and show the insides, white as the most brilliant clouds. He didn't think so. Showing their mouths was a threat. Instead they would just strike.

He took comfort in Tsola's drum.

He grinned. He wondered if he was crazy. He kept his head pointed forward, as a predator bird does, since it sees well to both sides but observes less well straight ahead. He never actually saw either log move.

He wondered if the logs would coil before they struck. He didn't think so. If this place had eagle panthers, why not fanged logs?

His mind felt calm. Truly. He almost believed himself, but his blood was rimed with ice.

He'd seen the same thing once. He watched two water moccasins sneak up on a bullfrog sitting at the edge of a pond. Their approach was so gradual, by such miniscule movements, that they not only fooled the frog, they fooled each other.

The joker Fate made them strike at precisely the same instant. Fangs sank deep into the frog from opposite sides. Snake bodies thrashed like limbs whipped by high winds. Each hunter was determined to exert its will, swallow its prey. Neither could.

The frog had no will.

The three of them fell into the pond and disappeared beneath the green scum, still thrashing.

Zeya was calm. He would know when. River water dripped from his beak, and he watched.

Two panther paws flashed at once. They bashed two snakes, which looked exactly like water moccasins now. While the snakes were dazed, an eagle talon seized one neck, a pincer the other.

The snakes coiled themselves around Zeya's feathered legs, but that meant nothing to him. He lifted the heads, each to the level of his opposing eye. He gazed into their white mouths. A little fear still thrummed through his blood.

He maneuvered the two heads together, gaping jaw to gaping jaw.

The snakes clamped—they bolted all their fury into each other. They metamorphosed into a single snake, poisoning itself.

Zeya set the writhing heads down and pinned them with a paw. He picked up their tails with his talon and pincer and tied them together. He inspected the knot, a job good enough to kill.

He examined the squirming, twisting heads once more. He felt elated. Smiling, he tossed the reptilian hoops far out into the river.

Nicely done, said Tsola.

❖

"They were my fears, all of them," said Zeya. He was happily perched on his aerie.

You weren't just the owner, said Tsola. *You were the creator.*

"I guess so."

They were your closest companions.

"I actually made them?"

Yes.

"Then I was in control and couldn't lose?"

You could. Your fear could have overwhelmed you, and you would have died not only in body but in spirit.

"I won."

Yes. With help from . . . ?

"Mom gave me courage, you gave me the power to see through illusions."

Exactly.

"Are we through with this?"

What do you want to do now?

"Meet Thunderbird."

As her drum tripled its speed, Zeya felt his entire body lifted off the ground by hurricane winds. Thunder banged, and he lost his mind.

45

W elcome," said Thunderbird.

Zeya quailed at the earthquake of his voice. Thunderbird laughed. He clapped his wings together, and thunder cracked the air. He laughed again.

"You look dizzy," said the great bird in a voice that was a mere roar.

He blinked, and sheets of lightning lit the world. Now Thunderbird really cackled. "Sorry," said Thunderbird, "I can't help showing off."

Thunderbird had wings with feathers of every color imaginable, and now Zeya saw that snakes lived in them. He flapped one wing, hurled a snake downward, and it forked into bolts. "Sheet lightning from the eyelids," he said casually, "and bolts from the wings." He paused for effect. "You can relax now."

Zeya took his hands off his ears and opened his eyes. Then he looked at his paws—they were again human hands. He had a human trunk and legs. He felt his neck and face—they weren't feathered. A necklace of 108 beautiful feathers of the war eagle rested in his lap.

"Take a seat, guest." Thunderbird fingered the feathers. "Tsola was right, you've done very well." Zeya was aware of her drum on the edge of his consciousness, a steady pulse that kept him in this strange world.

Thunderbird's tone changed. "You did so well she's honored you with my name. Just remember that you're the imitation Cloud Dweller." He paused. "Don't worry, I won't be watching you closely back on Earth. I don't pay that much attention to mortal matters."

Zeya couldn't help gaping at the bird. Each of his wings was as twice as long as Zeya's body. His head was the size of Zeya's chest.

"Don't you have something to give me?"

Zeya held up the necklace and spread it with his hands. The gathering of the feathers had been the first great adventure of his life, and four men had died trying to stop him.

"No speeches required," said Thunderbird. He plucked the feathers deftly out of Zeya's hands and inspected them. "Beautiful, aren't they? They remind me of me."

Zeya listened and thought Tsola's drum was advising him to say nothing.

"Look around you," said Thunderbird.

They sat in a nest constructed from cornstalks and padded with mosses. It was roughly circular, wide enough for twenty elk to stand on, and it floated on air.

"Not really," said Thunderbird. So he could read Zeya's thoughts. "To float on air, that would be cloud-dwelling, wouldn't it?" He chuckled at his little joke. "Walk over to the edge and look down. No, go ahead."

Zeya crawled over and looked down. The nest was like a disc perched on top of a gigantic finger. This finger was actually a stone tower higher than any of the mountains in the Land beyond the Sky Arch. Dizziness whirled Zeya around for a moment, and he clung to the tap of Tsola's drum for balance.

"Now what are we going to do?" said a human voice.

Zeya managed to turn without making his head tumble and look.

Thunderbird had transformed himself into a middle-aged man. He had pale skin, a head with only a fringe of hair, eyebrows that looked like black caterpillars, and another black caterpillar on his upper lip.

"Humor is reason gone mad."

Zeya was half confused, half revolted.

The new Thunderbird chortled. "Never seen skin this color, have you?"

All the human beings Zeya had seen were tawny, except for the albino Ninyu. Only the bottoms of fish and frogs had Thunderbird's white skin.

"And some men have thick hair on their lips and faces, they really do."

Galayi men had very little hair like that.

"But you aren't getting the joke. Now that I have no wings, only these puny feathers pulled off their wing bones, how are we ever going to get down from this nest?"

Zeya just looked at him.

"All right, dumb joke." He ballooned back into Thunderbird. Unlike Klandagi, he made the change in a eye-blink.

"Why have you come?" His voice was basso now, and his tone formal. "I want you to ask me properly."

"The Galayi people fell from grace. They broke the one rule the Immortals gave them. They killed each other. That brought the eagle-feather cape you gave them to ruin. I bring you these feathers with a formal request for a new cape."

"Granted. You really are a remarkable young man, even though I'm making light of it."

"Our Seer will wear the Cape and seek your wisdom."

"I know." Weariness lay under the words.

"And I request formally that you teach me all the songs of the Eagle Dance. Our singer, Awahi, is a good man, but over the generations we've forgotten many of the songs."

"More than you imagine," Thunderbird said. "I will put the songs directly into your mind. When you want to sing at the Eagle Dance back on Earth, open your mouth and the songs will come out."

"And I want to ask you some things on my own, things Tsola didn't tell me to ask."

"Go ahead." He sounded curious.

"Why is the grass pink in this world? Why are the leaves yellow, purple, orange—every color but green?"

"You like green?"

"I love green. It's the color of life coming back to the world."

"I could tease you by saying green is a color of death. A green leaf makes a yellow leaf inevitable. Life makes death inevitable."

Zeya blinked at Thunderbird.

"Remember my answers and think about them when you're back home. Hope for a good laugh."

"Do you really answer our prayers?"

"I'm answering Tsola's now, with the Cape."

"Do you really think about us that much?"

"Whether I do or not, thinking of me, thinking of this eternal world, asking for its power to be in you—all that gives you strength in your mortal world."

Thunderbird cocked his beak downward and considered. Then he spoke in a serious tone. "Remember, yours is a mirror world. I am the one true eagle. All of Earth's eagles are reflections of me. The same is true of everything that is. The permanent and enduring raccoons, ants, bushes, rivers, and mountains are here. The ones on Earth are shadows, and have the weakness of shadows. That is why everything on Earth dies, or deteriorates. Not so here."

"Why? Why did you make our world at all? Or why did someone make it?"

"What you're asking, you don't need to know. Your job is to live a good life as a human being. Besides, being serious is a bore. Let's have some fun."

Thunderbird grabbed Zeya in his talons and sailed off the nest. Tsola's drum seemed to beat faster, maybe in imitation of Zeya's pounding heart, or maybe as a tease.

First they seemed to take a tour of the Land beyond the Sky Arch. Its beauty was ideal. Buffalo and elk grazed in fields thick with grasses that were every color of the rainbow. Wild-flowers bloomed everywhere. Huge waterfalls gushed on the mountains. Bushes and trees bright with blossoms lined sparkling rivers. Zeya chuckled—he realized that the rivers sparkled in a sun that wasn't yet risen. The Immortals' land ignored such obstacles—it was perfect.

Then he realized that this was no tour. Thunderbird was circling on air currents that were lifting them higher and higher. The air was getting colder. They rose above the high-est mountains, and then above the clouds that puffed up to twice as high as the peaks, and then twice that high again. Zeya started shivering violently, and he couldn't seem to get enough air. He told himself, *Look at the sunrise. It's incredible—enjoy it.*

Just then Thunderbird dropped him.

Zeya plummeted. He felt twice as cold. Though the winds were terrific, he couldn't seem to breathe.

Above, Thunderbird flapped his wings. Snakes flew into the sky, and the air crackled with lightning. Thunderbird's laugh was almost as loud as the thunder he made. "Know terror!" he roared.

Zeya knew it in his fingers, his toes, his nose, his ears, his bones, and his blood. Panic pitched him this way and that and every which way. He became a blob of shimmering fear. He looked around at the beauty of the world. His eyes wanted to clutch it, because it was the last beauty he would ever know.

Halfway between the great heights and the death that awaited him below, Zeya grew calm. He knew the end of his adventure, and the knowledge gave him ease in his heart. He had nothing to fear.

He decided to pretend that he could fly—and made a discovery. If he flattened himself like a leaf descending from a tree, he could sail a little bit, almost like a bird, and he didn't fall as fast. In fact, he lost the sensation of falling. He floated. Toward the earth, yes, and toward death, yes, but he was floating. He was almost flying.

He looked and for the first time saw the ground rushing up toward him. A riff of fear clattered through him. He almost lost what little control he had, almost nosedived toward the rocks below. He eased himself out of the fear and back into his float.

Tentatively, he flapped his arms. They seemed to hold a little air. He flapped again, and, yes, air. It was a wonderful illusion— he was flying, he was a bird! He flapped again and again and learned . . .

He *was* flying! He could lift himself in the air! He could sail back upward! *I can fly! I'm going to live!*

He felt his vision change somehow. He didn't see ahead so well, but to each side he saw with a clarity that seemed incredible. He felt as though a world painted in fuzz was now turned into sharp lines and glowing colors.

He gulped. He saw a wing attached to his body—a wing on each side. He took a chance, tucked his head, turned it sideways, and looked down and back. Talons, and a broad, feathered tail. He studied the markings on his wings.

I am a war eagle.

He looked up at Thunderbird. The great bird laughed. Zeya soared up, and Thunderbird laughed louder. *Only a bird-god,* thought Zeya, *could make a laugh sound like thunder.*

I'm flying. As a child he flew in his dreams. *I'm flying in reality.* He chuckled. *I guess this reality.*

"Let's play!" roared Thunderbird.

Thunderbird whirled and flew at Zeya from the front. An attack!

At the last moment Thunderbird spread his great wings and

stopped in midair in front of Zeya. He held out his talons. "Grab on!"

Incredulous, Zeya reached out and held talons with the great bird.

"In this position we could kiss or kill!" roared Thunderbird. He blinked, and sheet lightning flashed.

"Close your wings!" said Thunderbird.

They both tucked their wings in and fell, locked together eye to eye.

"Diving!" roared Thunderbird. He let go of Zeya, turned himself beak down, flattened his wings to his body, and sped downward.

Zeya peered after him. "Why not?" he shouted.

He imitated Thunderbird's form and shot down. The winds were ferocious, and in Thunderbird's wake the turbulence was intense. Zeya watched his mentor and told himself, *That isn't a mountaintop rushing up at me—I'm not headed for those trees.*

He clutched everything within himself tight and hurtled down.

Just above the summit Thunderbird changed angle and followed the slope of the mountain down.

Doing the same—he hoped!—Zeya didn't get the movement exactly right and actually brushed a wing tip against a jutting rock. He felt some pin pricks and glanced back to see several of his feathers dart through the air.

Thunderbird flashed down to the river, let his huge wings flap against the water, and flung back a rainstorm at Zeya.

"Let me show you how to climb the easy way," roared Thunderbird.

He crossed the valley to the next mountain—what freedom they had, covering such distances! There he simply stuck out his wings and began to float upward. How could that happen to Thunderbird's huge body?

Zeya did the same, and the air lifted him, too.

"Warm winds rise," Thunderbird cried, "and cool winds sink down. Here the sun is always coming up, so the air's always getting warmer, and we can go up without working hard. What a deal!"

They rose in perfect quiet, a sublime upward sail without effort. In the time it would have taken to walk across Zeya's home village, they passed the mountaintops.

Thunderbird flapped out over the valley again and gave Zeya a mischievous look. "Let's go back to the nest. I have a surprise for you."

Zeya resisted saying he wanted to keep flying.

He watched Thunderbird and carefully made his first landing as an eagle, wings spread, body weightless, a gentle float onto the nest.

"A fellow might think you'd been an eagle all your life," said Thunderbird.

Zeya felt like strutting.

"Before the principal business at hand," Thunderbird said, "a request. Here is the new Cape."

"Gorgeous," said Zeya. It glowed with splendor.

"In return for this gift," said Thunderbird, "I would like the Galayi to initiate a new practice among the warriors. From now on, when a man performs a heroic feat in battle, his comrades will give him a beautiful feather from a war eagle, and the warrior will wear it as an emblem of his courage. From now on this will be the highest sign of honor in war."

The god-bird cocked an eye at Zeya.

"I will tell everyone," said Zeya.

"However," Thunderbird went on, "these feathers must be gathered without killing any eagles."

"Yes," says Zeya.

"Very good. You and I, we've gotten along famously, haven't we?" That mischievous look again, with something dark in it.

Zeya answered formally, "I could not be more grateful for what you've done for me."

"Perhaps now you'll do something small for me."

"Of course."

"Change yourself back into a human being, back into the young Soco man who came here as a seeker."

Zeya felt a thrill of fear. "I don't know how," he said.

"Just begin, and you'll know."

Zeya cocked his head sideways and looked down at his right talon. Inside himself, he told it, *Change*.

Claws fell off. Toes reappeared. The four-part talon started growing skin, and then melded together into a human shape.

Lifted by wonder, Zeya extended his right wing. *Change*, he told it without words. The tip of the wing started reshaping itself into fingers.

Zeya's eyes got huge, and he had to resist laughing.

Zeya made a mess of one thing. He converted his beak into a nose and accidentally back to a beak. When he thought he'd finished his face, Thunderbird handed him a cloth and said, "Blow your nose."

When Zeya honked his beak, they both laughed.

Still, Zeya got it done in short order. He looked down at himself in amazement. He studied the body he'd had all his life. Then he looked directly at Thunderbird. "Thank you. For me personally, this is the greatest gift of all."

"No," said Thunderbird, "for you personally *this* is the greatest gift."

Thunderbird seized Zeya with one of his huge talons and held him up to an enormous eye. He blinked, and sheet lightning numbed Zeya's brain. The bird-god pointed his beak to where Zeya's ribs met his belly and stabbed him.

Zeya felt warm blood run down. He managed to gasp, "What are you doing?"

"Eating you," said Thunderbird.

Quickly, the bird-god slit Zeya from sternum to crotch bone. Zeya felt the cold air of the heights seep into his being.

Thunderbird reached deep under Zeya's ribs with his beak and drew something out. Zeya's heart. It beat one last time in Thunderbird's beak, and the bird-god solemnly gulped it down.

SEVEN

Triumphs and Losses

46

Z eya suddenly lay by the fire in front of them, unconscious.

Tsola reached out and took the Cape from his loose hands.
Tenderly, she wrapped it in a painted elk robe. Then she stepped
back to Zeya, knelt, and turned his zadayi so that the red side was
out.

"Thank you," said Sunoya.

"That, what Thunderbird did, was terrible to watch," said
Tsola.

"I heard of it, but I never saw it done," said Sunoya.

Zeya stirred.

"You're Okay," Sunoya told him.

Pacing nervously, Klandagi said, "It won't help, not yet."

He was right, it wouldn't. Soon the world would rotate a
quarter circle to the left, or some direction, and her son's mind
would click in.

"You're all right," she said again.

"Zeya, can you hear me?" This was Tsola. "You're here with
your mother, and me, Tsola, Klandagi, and Su-Li. You're fine."

Both medicine women remembered the disorientation of
their own first trips across. They looked at each other with the
knowledge of how much more awful Thunderbird had made
this crossing.

"The greatest gifts call for the greatest sacrifices," murmured Tsola.

Sunoya gave her mentor a look. She didn't need lecturing right now. "You're fine," said Zeya's mother, stroking his forearm.

Su-Li said inside her mind, *He will be fine, better than fine.*

Still, he lingered in an unconscious or half-conscious state. Sunoya took Su-Li outside. While he looped up the sky, she sat and watched the twilight reflect in the Healing Pool. Tsola's daughters went about their business quietly. No one was here for healing right now. "Except," Sunoya said out loud, "for my son, the hero of the people." A hint of bitterness spiced her words.

And me. Being apart from Su-Li had weakened her. Her life energy was interwoven with his. She would have to spend time in the Pool. But now her son needed her.

Inside the Cavern Zeya finally woke up enough to reach down and feel his belly. When he didn't find a wound, he drifted back to sleep.

Later he whispered, "Thirsty."

Sunoya gave him broth. Klandagi said with a chuckle, "He won't want any more of that special tea for a while."

Zeya's first sentence was, "How long was I gone?"

Tsola spoke up. "Not even long enough for my arm to get tired from drumming."

Zeya blinked at his companions, the Cavern, and this world that was not beyond the Sky Arch. He shook his head as though to chase memories away. "I went a lot of places. I did a lot of things."

"I know," said Tsola, "I was there."

The panther raised his purr to a hum.

"I told Sunoya and Klandagi everything," said Tsola.

"I am in awe of what you accomplished," said the big cat.

Zadayi Red ❖ 307

Zeya shook his head again. Clearly, he didn't know what to make of that, or anything else.

"I died," he said.

"And came back to life a new man," said Tsola.

Zeya gawked at her. Then he closed his eyes and drifted back to sleep.

"We'd best take our time, talk to him only as he's ready for each part."

"Yes," said Tsola. She looked urgently at the Cape. "Waiting is hard. I'm dying to put it on."

❖

Piecemeal, Zeya came to understand what had happened. Or at least he listened attentively to what they said and marked it in his mind. He would ponder it in his own time.

"I guess I'm all right with the journey across," he told the two women, his mother and his teacher. "The enemies I met— the dogs, the snakes, all that—I created them myself. They were *my* fears, so I had to deal with them. I got the new cape." He looked at the bundle. And I got a gift"—the next words were hushed—"I can turn into an eagle."

Both women nodded. They'd been over and over these things.

"And I had to die to come back?"

"Yes."

"But when you went, you didn't die."

"No."

"Because . . . ?"

Tsola said, "Over time, you will know. You are still called on to do great things in the future."

"And a better man was needed to do them?"

Tsola chuckled. "You might put it that way."

"It's too much."

"Let's give him something," said Klandagi. He looked at

his mother and Sunoya. "Zeya, here's an idea, this will be good. Change yourself into an eagle. Do it. Right now."

Zeya looked at the panther hesitantly. He started to speak.

"Just do it," said Klandagi.

Zeya did, foot to claw, arm to wing, flesh to feather. "I can't imagine ever getting used to this." As though to convince himself, he pecked at his neck feathers, looked at his companions, and flashed his wings out.

"And what do you want to do now?"

"Fly!"

"Go to it."

The eagle hopped toward the cave entrance and launched into the sky. Su-Li flew with him, wing tip to wing tip.

"Bring him back soon," called Sunoya.

47

Winging over his home country was spectacular. He knew the Cheowa village, the path up to the Emerald Cavern, the trails to the Soco and Cusa villages to the south, and to the Tusca village in the east. He knew the mountains, he knew the rivers. But to see them as a pattern, how everything flowed together, was amazing. The landscape came together with a kind of sense he had never known. The river started in the mountains high above the Cheowas, came crashing down to the broad, flat valley where the houses stood, and wandered in snaky curves to the south. Halfway down the valley the stream turned fast and roily. In the distance he could see where the trail from the Tusca village dropped in and the river trail ran on south, with a sharp bend westward and then south again, to the Soco village.

He could see how the ridges came down from the balds. They divided as they descended, and a creek formed between each two ridges. A mountain, he realized, had a logic all its own.

What do you want to do? said Su-Li.

I don't know. Dweller-in-the-Clouds looked wide-eyed at his companion. *How are you talking to me?*

The same way you're talking to me.

We can communicate directly now, mind to mind?

When you're an eagle.

Believing—accepting this fact—was swallowing a big lump for Zeya. *Can you do this with Klandagi?*

When he's a panther.

I didn't know that.

No one else does. Best to keep some things to yourself. So what do you want to do?

They were gliding south along the river, not even flapping their wings. *Go see Jemel.*

She's back home in the Soco village, with her parents.

Let's fly.

Easily, comfortably, they flapped and floated down the valley. *How far can you go in a day?*

About a week's walk.

I can't believe this.

Do you realize we're flying down the route you took to get to the Socos twenty winters ago? Let's circle down, and I'll show you something.

Zeya hadn't realized Su-Li could be so chatty.

Here's what's funny, said Su-Li. *When you're a human being, you'll go back to thinking I can't talk. Okay, there it is. That's the waterfall where the caves of the Little People were, and were not. Also the frozen waterfall that shattered and saved your life when you were a tiny baby.*

Zeya had heard the story a hundred times, how he, Sunoya,

and the dog swam the flooding river and Inaj's men got bashed by the icefall when it crashed down.

The first time your grandfather tried to kill you, said Su-Li. *One of many.*

He'll never quit, will he?

No.

Zeya felt blood lust in his heart. He had to be honest. *I want to kill him.*

Yes.

But I can't commit a crime against the new Cape.

No.

They flapped along in silence.

Let's do something about your blood lust.

Zeya looked at him nervously.

Hunt.

They glided along the grassy hillsides. Su-Li saw the rabbit before Zeya did. *Dive,* the buzzard said, fast and hard. *Use your talons, not your beak.*

Zeya shook his head to clear it, and found out that didn't work with an eagle's neck.

Dive! said Su-Li.

Zeya did. He was thrilled at his own speed. He eyed the rabbit fiercely and felt in his blood the old fever of the hunter for prey.

He made a clean miss.

His wings carried him up while his heart sank. He didn't know whether the rabbit darted away at the last second, or whether his aim was bad.

Wheeling back toward Su-Li, he spotted a gopher. Without thinking, he hurtled toward it. He hit it with one talon but didn't get a grip on it. The gopher scurried off.

Another rabbit. Zeya used himself like an arrow plummeting to the ground. And this time he hit. The rabbit squirmed, but Zeya used his other talon to break its neck.

He arrived at the height of the mountaintop to fall in with Su-Li, rabbit dangling.

Dweller-in-Clouds? said Su-Li.

I am now.

Let's light on a bald.

They did. Zeya started to invite Su-Li to join him in eating, then interrupted himself. *Is this carrion?*

It is now.

Have you gotten to like carrion?

Mortality stinks, said Su-Li.

They fed.

As they lifted off, Zeya said, *Small but good.*

When you're a human being, you'll need more to eat.

They flapped downriver.

There it is, said Su-Li.

The Soco village, his home. Zeya glided sideways a little to get the best view of where he grew up. He felt his heart touched. He pictured childhood friends playing in the creek, racing across the fields to see who was fastest, giving and getting bloody noses. He remembered seeing Jemel for the first time . . .

After he got oriented, Zeya started wheeling in tight circles over Jemel's house. *That will be my house soon,* he thought. *I hope.*

Nothing. No sign of anyone.

Across the village he saw Ninyu walk away from his house, maybe to talk to someone or do one of a hundred chores. He felt a longing to see everyone again, his grandfather and grandmothers, aunts and uncles, cousins.

He let himself glide down toward Jemel's house—he was good at flying now. Still he saw no one from her family.

I think that's enough, said Su-Li.

Has our marriage been arranged?

That's a question to ask Tsola.

They winged back up the river. Zeya thought of the woman he wanted. She was a Moon Woman, full of wild feelings. He had no doubt that if she saw a man she wanted, another man, she would take him.

❖

Zeya was worn out by his flight and, from the look of the light outside the cave, slept from dusk one day to dawn the next. Or was it dusk the next? He went to the cave entrance, looked at the world, and saw that it was dawn.

"I'm starved," he told his mother.

She gave him plenty to eat.

"I think you need to understand better what happened on your journey," said Tsola, sitting in the shadows.

"I need to talk to Jemel."

Tsola started to protest but said instead, "Whatever you want."

"Inaj is looking for you," said Sunoya.

"I'll fly," Zeya said.

"He's got spies in the village," his mother said. "Count on it."

"Do you want me to go along?" said Klandagi.

"Tsola needs you," Zeya said.

Tsola was picking up the wrap that held the Cape. "No," she said, "I'll be in the Emerald Dome. It's safe there."

But Zeya had had a guard for too many years. "I'll be all right."

"You want Su-Li with you?" said Sunoya.

He kissed his mother. "You need him," he said, "and I don't."

"Fly," said Klandagi. "Fly away home."

❖

Where is Jemel?

Zeya watched the village from the top of the snag. People coming and going, children playing, dogs running around, young women walking to and from the fields to gather the last of the harvest, young men making spear heads and old men sitting with them, probably telling hunting stories. He knew many of the old women were sitting inside, near the light from the doors, sewing. They liked to be near the fire.

All day long he'd sat here—no sign of Jemel. Her family was here. Her mother, aunts, and sisters traipsed back and forth from the cornfields constantly. *Where is Jemel?*

Zeya was full of odd feelings. Jemel, himself, his journey, the future—everything tumbled around inside him like pebbles in a rattle.

Maybe that was why, for the first time, he felt funny about these routines of daily life. They were the patterns of days he had lived during his twenty years on the Earth. And they were good. He felt nostalgic about them. But he also felt separated. He was different. He murmured to himself, "Sitting here in the shape of an eagle—that's as different as things get."

More than his body had changed. His spirit had shifted, though he couldn't say how. His awareness was altered. Everything within the sweep of his vision seemed to him a blossom of mortality, bright and brassy and ignorant. The children who now played were on the way to turning into the old men and old women. The crops grew in the summer and died before winter. People gathered them because they lived by feeding on other living beings that they killed. The men slew the deer and sang a prayer asking forgiveness. The breath that carried their words bore the intimation of their own deaths, and their fear of it.

Even a seed bore the inevitability of death. Everything that lived died and became food, so that other creatures might live. It struck Zeya as a bizarre mixture of beauty and horror.

Where is Jemel?

He remembered to check the skies around him. Eagles had few enemies in this world, none he knew of, but he was still mortal. Klandagi reminded Zeya that Su-Li could not be killed, but the two of them could. Born to die.

The day itself was dying. The sunset oozed colors on the edges of the mountain ridges. The night would be cold.

Just then something caught Zeya's eye. His heart quickened. It was Jemel, walking away from the house toward the creek. It looked as if she was going where the women went to pee. But why had she been inside all day? Why hadn't she been working in the fields with the other young women?

She was with child.

He could tell by the way she walked. Though she wasn't near birth time yet, it was unmistakable.

Humiliation flash-flooded through his veins.

He intended to speak to her. He intended to challenge her.

❖

Jemel stilted toward the stream. She hated the way she walked. Her back hurt all the time, carrying this baby, and she felt like she had to hump each hip upward to get her foot off the ground to clomp forward.

She hated her life. When her father threw a fit about Zeya, she'd been whisked off to live with relatives in the Cusa village—no choice. The relatives clearly didn't want her around. Once they saw she was with child, they treated her like a pariah, and everyone in the village snubbed her. Everyone except Awahi. He was kind.

Then, suddenly, she was brought back here without any explanation. She might as well have been a pack dog. She had to go where she was told, no choice—"Just do what we say."

She was fierce to be finished with living this way.

She clung to one thread that kept her sane. She thought about Zeya. She fantasized about the passion of their reunion. She imagined the birth of their child, with Zeya properly there and performing the Going to Water ceremony. She pictured husband and wife hovering over the baby, cooing, enjoying seeing it learn to turn over, sit up, take a first step, speak a first word. She thought of herself and her husband getting up in the morning, starting the fire, eating breakfast together, and telling each other their dreams. Even more often she imagined what she would do with Zeya in the blankets. Thoughts like that were her salvation.

She allowed herself no doubt that they would be husband and wife. She was a Moon Woman, she had found her passion—she had found her life.

She shut out all challenges to her conviction except one. At night sometimes, in tatters of dreams or half-dreams, she saw Zeya dead. From the time Zanda's head was dropped into the village, these dreams romped through her sleep.

That day Inaj went wild with fury, and she exulted. But tales raged like fire through the treetops. They were only bits and pieces that came to nothing, but they twanged her fear.

Inaj had sent men to kill her lover. She wished she could kill him.

What Jemel did, in her dilemma, was build a dam against her emotions. She went through the days aloof, pretending. In the evenings she sat with Awahi. He was good to her, he knew her heart, he was a friend. Unfortunately, he had no information that would help.

Sometimes she found herself angry at Zeya. Yes, she knew that was stupid, and acting stupid only made her more angry. Sometimes she circled back in a bad temper to the old questions: When her lover visited the village to see Awahi, why hadn't he talked to her? As far as she was concerned, no explanation mattered. He should have found a way. She would have.

At night she lay in the blankets telling herself she'd been snubbed, perhaps abandoned. Fury volcanoed in her chest. Her passion pendulumed from love to hatred.

Now she wandered along the stream bank further than she

needed to. Finally she peed, and emptied the gourd holding the pee she'd made all day. But she needed more time out of the house. She hated the custom of confining child-carrying women to their dwellings. She wanted air. She knelt by the water, scooped it up with both hands, and bathed her face.

Just then a war eagle lighted in a dead tree nearby. She was surprised. The great birds usually stayed away from people. She stared. And then the bird spoke.

"Unfaithful," said the bird. "False-hearted. Deceiver."

The bird made its words more savage by using the voice of her lover. It went on cruelly.

"Traitor. Betrayer. Villain . . . ."

Jemel wailed to keep herself from hearing. She slammed her forehead to the grass, stopped her ears with her fingers, and screamed. Other words rasped forth, but she drowned them out.

When other women came running to see what was wrong, the bird flew off.

She told them nothing.

❖

Zeya lifted himself high into the air. The winds were gentle, his emotions turbulent. He flapped away from the Soco village hard and fast. Then he hesitated and glided. He wanted to visit with his mother and Su-Li. He wheeled about and coasted downwind toward the village. He yearned to talk to them more about what he'd seen and done in the Land beyond the Sky Arch. It was the most extraordinary event of his life—that was a wild understatement—and who could he talk to about it except for Sunoya, Su-Li, and Tsola?

Far off his eagle eyes saw Jemel clomp the last few steps to her parents' house. He hated seeing her struggle along with the burden of another man's child in her belly. She ducked into the house. He hated the thought that his rival, his conqueror, would soon be moving into that house—or already had moved in.

He executed such a sharp turn that he swerved down a few feet. He'd be damned if he'd go down into the village. What if he saw Jemel again? What if he saw her with her lover? What could he do, squirt droppings at the man's head? Or worse, at his back while he topped Jemel?

He set his beak toward the Emerald Cavern and flapped upwind. Tsola would console him. Maybe she would help him make a life there. Maybe he could become a sort of hermit, like herself.

48

With the Cape bundle tied to her back, Tsola swam to the Emerald Dome. There she hung the feathers up to dry, smudged them with cedar smoke, and waited. Every inch of her body prickled with eagerness. She hadn't worn the Cape in twenty years.

She cooked a meal and drank all the water she could. While wearing the Cape, she would eat nothing, drink nothing.

When the time came, she drank the sacred tea and donned the feathers. And again the ecstasy came. The universe began to sing. Though her predecessor had said he experienced the wisdom of the Cape in rainbows of light, it always came to Tsola in sounds. The music was extraordinary. It was made entirely of human voices, but voices that sang much lower and much higher than in the ordinary world. They made a floating, ethereal music, not of great harmonies, but individual voices each with its own melody. Somehow the voices melded into one vast song of infinite sweetness. It was not a music that could ever end. It was whole, entrancing, infinite, and exquisitely beautiful at each of its moments.

318 ❖ *Caleb Fox*

Sometimes she imagined that the voices belonged to every one of the stars, singing simultaneously of the limitless delights of the universe. Sometimes she heard the voices as the utterances of all human beings, every person of every place who walked the Earth now, everyone who had ever walked it, and everyone who ever would. And they all sang of love.

She sat and listened for several days, until the music felt complete. Then she gently slipped the Cape off, wrapped it in its bundle, ate and drank a little, sat quietly for several more days to steep herself in what she had heard.

When she had absorbed it, even though without words, she asked her wisest self to tell her what action to take in the world where she lived her daily life. She got an answer. Then she took the way that only she knew back to her home, her family, and beyond the mouth of the Cavern, her people, all human beings, and all the peoples of this planet, animal and plant.

By her own fire Klandagi waited for her, as always.

Whenever she came back from the experience of the Cape, she needed silence, not talk. Sound felt like an intrusion on her experience. But now she whispered to Klandagi. "What moon is it?"

He spoke softly, knowing her feelings. "The quarter moon, waning."

Her voice, even having a voice at all, felt strange to her. But she murmured, "Go to the Cheowa village. Tell the chiefs that I have the greatest news they will hear in their lifetimes.

"Then ask the White Chief to send messengers to the other three villages. All the people will convene at the next full moon." She paused, her voice tiring. "They must do exactly this. Each of the villages, including the Cheowas themselves, will camp a day's walk away from the great council lodge, and the three chiefs of each will come there with only ten escorts for protection. They will enter the council lodge without escorts and unarmed. Repeat that—without escorts and unarmed."

Klandagi started to ask a question, but she shook her head no. "Do exactly that."

He nodded, raised his purr into a low growl of assent, and padded off.

❖

Zeya dragged in, his spirit shredded. Tsola could see dejection radiating from him. She suspected what had happened. *Welcome back to human life*, she thought.

He told her the pathetic story. She didn't ask the obvious question—"Why are you sure the child isn't yours?" She thought he had to struggle with that one himself. Instead she said, "You are creating your own troubles. As you did in the Land Beyond. You know how to stop."

"When you consider . . ."

"Why don't you consider that Jemel is free? She's a woman of great passions, and she does what she pleases."

He hung his head.

More gently, she said, "Think about what *you* are doing."

He grimaced.

"You know."

Spending the words carefully, one by one, he said, "In the Land Beyond I fought enemies that I imagined. I created what I feared and fought to the death with it."

"Yes."

"Not smart."

"Correct."

"I'm jealous. Very jealous."

Tsola nodded.

"Why don't I stop? I know better."

"Because you're a human being."

"I *know* better."

"Zeya, over there you got big insights. But knowing doesn't solve problems. Use the knowledge to fight your demons."

"I have a big one that's outside."

"You do. But most demons are inside."

❖

Zeya circled high over the Soco camp. The morning was young, and he had updrafts to ride.

His mother was in one of those brush huts. He had not seen her since the catastrophe with Jemel, and he yearned to talk to her. His friend Su-Li was probably there, too—maybe they could fly together today. But Zeya couldn't bear to go into the camp, not yet.

He spoke to Su-Li in his mind. *Want to fly?* He got no answer, and wondered why. Maybe the buzzard was far away.

These last three-quarters of a moon had been a bad time. Klandagi was on his mission to gather the bands together. After his talk with Tsola—"Why don't you consider that Jemel is free?"—Zeya had nothing to do but fret. Live a hermit's life like hers in the Emerald Cavern? Tsola dismissed this idea in less than a breath. She let him live with her daughter's family at the Healing Pool and make himself useful for a short time, and reminded him, "You are the one of prophecy."

He hated those words.

He liked helping the people who came to the Healing Pool. Every moment he wasn't working, though, his mind was on Jemel and his humiliation. He spun through the days attending to the ill and injured, and despairing through the nights.

When the camps began to assemble for the great council, Tsola called Zeya into the shadows of the Cavern. "I have a job for you. Fly above the three Soco chiefs as they walk to the council lodge. Make sure they're safe from enemies."

"Having anything to do will feel better."

"And talk to Jemel. Go to her in human form and apologize for the terrible way the eagle spoke to her."

"I can't."

"Do it. Now."

He started toward the mouth of the Cavern and the daylight.

"Don't get absorbed in Jemel and forget the chiefs. They're expecting you. The fate of the people depends on what happens tomorrow."

He felt ashamed of himself. "Yes."

"Keep a sharp eye out for trouble. When the lodge convenes, sit at the smoke hole and listen to every word."

"Yes, but I . . ."

She held up a hand. "Go now. I have to prepare."

So he came here and wasted his time spiraling upward. He called to Su-Li again. No answer. What was going on?

To hell with it, he decided. He winged across the mountain into another valley and spent the day hunting. All the while, even as he ate, he cursed himself as an idiot. *I can't face Jemel. I have to face Jemel.*

Early the next morning he watched the three Soco chiefs wrap food in skins. He was out of time. He landed on a sandy beach along the creek, where he could watch for enemies. He changed himself into his human shape—he was getting quick at this transformation. He strode into the camp and up to the two brush huts that housed her family.

"Jemel," he called, "I want to talk to you." It was rude to bark out like that, but he couldn't help himself.

Her head stuck out a door. Then she was on her feet and run-waddling toward him. She threw himself into his arms. She kissed him with a passion that deluged the past and carried it off on a flood of emotion and sensation.

He forced himself to remember what had happened. With her enormous belly pressed against him, how could he forget? He pushed her back to arms' length.

"I have to apologize to you."

"Let's never do that. I love you."

"You don't know what I did."

"I don't care. Don't you see?" She cupped her bulging belly with her hands.

That was what he hated seeing. "I treated you terribly."

What was in her eyes now—hesitation?

"This is hard to explain. I . . . I came to you as an . . ."

That would never work. In a flash he knew what would.

"Unfaithful," he said in a harsh tone. "False-hearted. Deceiver."

He saw that she remembered. The war eagle face, the voice, the awful words.

"Traitor. Betrayer. Villain."

She backed away from him, as from a bear or snake. Her eyes were wild.

"You can't understand, I know."

"You're the one who doesn't understand!"

He was stumped. Then he got an idea. Skin turned to feather. Feet turned to talons. Nose and mouth turned to beak. The war eagle spread his wings and flapped to the nearest branch.

"Who are you?" she cried, frozen to the spot.

"I am Zeya, transformed. Who are you?"

Her knees trembled, but she found her voice. "I am the mother of your child!" She stumbled backward and then shouted, "How could you do this?" She ran.

Zeya's mind whirled like the wildest winds. *I . . . what?* He forced the words to add up. And then he realized.

He changed into human shape so fast feathers stuck out around his ears. He dropped down from the branch and ran after her. "Jemel! Jemel!"

She could only waddle slowly. Beyond her he could see the three chiefs lashing the food bundles onto a pack dog. He caught up fast and grabbed her arm. "Say that again. What you said I am.'"

She jerked the arm away. She glared him. She delivered the words like blows. "You are the father of my child."

"Are you sure?"

"Why aren't you? Has your imagination run away with you?"

"Yes." He saw it now. Just as he had dreamed up the enemies on his journey to the land beyond. "I was jealous. Crazy jealous."

She put her hands on her hips. "Idiot! Fool! Buffoon! Chump!" The smile on her face grew huge. "Jealousy scooped your brains out."

"Yes. I'm sorry. I love you. Supremely."

"You know how I love you? I wish you were inside me right now. So just say it straight out. Do you want to be my husband and this child's father?"

He wrapped his arms around her. They spent half an eternity kissing.

Then she pulled back and said, "Feel our child." She put his hand on her belly. "It's not kicking right now." She slid his hand indecently low.

"By the way, I have a new name. Luckily it's not idiot, fool, buffoon, or chump, though I deserve those, too. It's Ulo-Zeya, Dweller-in-Clouds. I want to be called Zeya."

Just then Ninyu walked up. "Grandson, you have a job to do."

Zeya drew back and looked from his lover to his grandfather and back. "Yes!" He told Jemel, "Yes to the future." To Ninyu he said, "Yes to the job."

He stepped further back, grinned at them, and began the process. Skin to feathers.

49

Tsola sat blindfolded by the sacred fire. In front of her lay an elk robe wrapped around something.

Three by three the chiefs found their way into the building by the light that came from all sides and sat cross-legged around the fire. Klandagi studied every one of them. He was his mother's eyes. Yes, they were required to come unarmed, and what the hell did that mean? The autumn day was chill, and every man wrapped himself in a blanket, where a knife or war club might be concealed. The panther saw no suggestive bumps yet.

Klandagi looked up. Tips of feathers showed that Su-Li and Zeya were perched at the big smoke hole, where they could hear.

Inaj strutted in last, trailed by the White Chief and Medicine Chief of the Tuscas. He had been Red Chief for three decades, except for a brief interval when he maneuvered his son Zanda into the position. And in that tribe the Red Chief was always the head man—had they not been at war with the Socos for twenty winters?

Klandagi wished he could jump Inaj right now and tear his throat out. With so formidable an enemy, a warrior would normally cut the heart out and eat it, to add its strength to his own. But Klandagi wouldn't touch a heart so foul.

Inaj seated himself at the far end of the circle, which put him only an arm's length from Klandagi's mother. The panther slid into the space and gazed into the chief's eyes.

Inaj smiled at Klandagi.

Curious, thought the panther.

"Everyone is here," Klandagi told Tsola.

She lit the sacred pipe and passed it. While the chiefs smoked, Klandagi inspected Inaj meticulously. Klandagi hoped his gaze would intimidate the chief.

When the pipe returned to Tsola, she acted without a word—she opened the elk robe and held up the treasure. "Thunderbird has granted us a new Cape of Eagle Feathers," she said. "The young man of prophecy, formerly known as Dahzi, now called Dweller-in-Clouds, crossed to the Land beyond the Sky Arch and brought back the Cape. It was an adventure that will be told among our people for generations."

Above the smoke hole, Su-Li said to Zeya without words, *Don't puff your chest up—she's doing enough of that for you.*

"That story can be told later. Right now, we have the Cape, and I have spent days listening to its wisdom, its guidance toward peace and prosperity. The eagles are ready to act as messengers to—"

"Don't waste my time," Inaj burst in. He stood up and sneered at all of them.

"Mother," Klandagi whispered. She gave him a tiny shake of her head—*no*—and put a hand on his haunches.

"I have something fascinating to show you," declared Inaj.

All the chiefs looked at each other aghast. No one but Inaj had ever interrupted a council so rudely. He was standing, his head far above theirs. His whole body language was scorn.

From underneath his blanket Inaj drew a shapeless mass of cloth. Suddenly, he threw it over Klandagi. Tsola jerked her hand out. The panther was trapped in a net.

Klandagi roared and clawed at the fabric. He writhed and twisted. All he accomplished was to get his claws caught, and the netting wrapped tighter around him.

Tsola reached for the net, but Inaj grabbed her arms.

She took two deep breaths and said, "Son, be still. No one will kill anyone here today."

Inaj chuckled. He declared, "Tsola the Seer brought us here to talk of peace. We've heard it all before. It meant nothing then, it means nothing now.

"So let me tell you something exciting. This council will in fact be a great triumph. Though our Wounded Healer disagrees"—he twisted the title into irony—"this will bring peace. And a great victory for me."

Now he turned and spoke directly to Tsola. "Thank you for asking us to come here unarmed. Thank you for asking us to leave our warriors a day's walk away." His eyes lit with exultation. "For my two hundred men are right here, they are coming out of the trees on the hillsides around this village. They await my command. If you tell your escorts to resist, they will be slaughtered. So let us have a truce for the moment."

Klandagi fought the net and roared.

"Here is my plan for peace. After tomorrow the Soco Band, enemies of the Tuscas, will not exist. First we will slay you three Soco chiefs and your ten escorts." He eyed Ninyu. "I promise you, you will never leave this village alive. Then we will take advantage of the truce to attack your camp tomorrow and seize your women and children. Your best men will be dead, most of the rest out hunting, the remaining few leaderless—the fight will be quick and easy business. Over the next quarter moon or so we will track down the rest of your warriors one by one and kill them—every Soco man we can find. Particularly, and with special pleasure, I myself will kill the young man who puffs himself up to the name Dweller-in-Clouds, he of the webbed fingers, the one who should never have been born."

Above, Su-Li said to Zeya, *Your loving grandfather.*

"But we are kind. We will take your children into our families. We will make your wives our wives. And we will feed these new mouths with the game from your hunting grounds." He waited. "That, and only that, will bring an end to twenty years of war. So in this manner, dear Wounded Healer, I, Inaj, Red Chief of the Tuscas, present you with the peace you yearn for."

"You're insane," said Tsola. Her voice was a dagger.

"Crazy with joy, perhaps," said Inaj. "Mad with the scent of conquest.

"Right now, I offer a choice to you chiefs of the other two bands, and your escorts. You may camp here peaceably today, tonight, and tomorrow. Or you may fight with the doomed Soco chiefs and warriors." He shrugged. "I don't care which. If you choose to die, we Tusca chiefs will simply take leadership of the entire tribe." He nodded, as though accepting an honor.

He looked outside. "The shadows show that it's nearly noon. My escorts are blocking your exit, and my army is gathering in the meadow north of the village. By the time they've assembled you must give us your decision."

He laughed and stalked out, leading his White Chief and Medicine Chief.

50

Tsola slipped her arms under the net, embraced her son, and lifted his prison away. She held him tighter and said "No, there are too many of them."

She felt his muscles ease off, but she could hear the fury in his breathing, and feel it radiating off his skin.

First Zeya then Su-Li fluttered down from the smoke hole. *We are here, Seer,* said Zeya.

"Join us in the circle," she said in words, "and transform yourself into human form."

Zeya did. The chiefs gaped—none had seen this new power of Zeya's. He held up his hand, reminding them of the webbed fingers. Su-Li perched on his shoulder.

Tsola smiled at Zeya's gesture, and nodded. "Who wants to speak?"

"I'll kill them all," said Klandagi.

"Act real," said his mother.

The White Chief of the Cusa band said, "We three will stay and fight with the Socos."

"Go slowly," said Tsola. "Let's be very sure. This could mean the end of the Galayi people."

"We three Cheowas will also stay," said their White Chief. His voice was thin with age.

"Thirty-nine men, some of you years beyond your time to fight, against two hundred. You will all die," Tsola said.

Everyone looked at her expectantly. Surely she had some guidance to offer at such a critical time.

But it was Zeya who spoke up. "Leave me alone beside the sacred fire, please. I have an idea." He touched Su-Li's talon to ask the buzzard to stay.

All but Tsola stared at this inexperienced youth. How could he . . . ?

The blindfolded Seer handed the pipe to Ninyu beside her, picked up the Cape, and stood. "Lead me outside," she said to Klandagi. All the chiefs followed her.

Zeya looked into the fire, raised his voice to the skies, and sang. Thunderbird had promised that when he needed an eagle song, it would come to him, and it did. Four times he sang it through. When he finished, he had an answer, though it didn't come in words.

Zeya stepped outside to face the doomed. He felt calm and clear. Su-Li lit on his shoulder.

"Lay down your weapons," he told the escorts.

"Rot in hell," said the biggest one.

"Lay down your weapons," Zeya said again in a simple way. "If any of you chiefs have hidden weapons, put them down, too."

A gnarly man with a scarred face spoke up. "We got no chance, and you take away what little we got."

"If you need a miracle," Zeya said, "you may as well ask for a big one."

He looked up at the trees. Dark shadows marked the leafless branches, where none had been before. Beyond the valley, V-shaped pairs of wings slashed the sky. *I see even more,* said Su-Li.

"We don't have long," said Ninyu.

Zeya looked carefully at the Tusca enemies.

In fact, Zeya thought, they did have a while. Some of the Tuscas were still painting their faces as their medicine guided them. Some were putting on talismans from their spirit helpers. One fixed the body of a raven on top of his head. Another tied weasel tails into his hair. Far to one side a warrior pulled the entire head of a buffalo over his own head and face. Those who were ready fell into a mob, picketed with spears and war clubs.

Zeya stepped up to the nearest escort, took his weapons out of his hands, and laid them on the ground. Then he turned to another escort. Klandagi caught on and accomplished the same with growls. Su-Li rasped at several of them. Quickly everyone was disarmed.

"Now," said Zeya, "no matter what happens, don't strike a single Tusca man, don't shed a drop of Galayi blood."

"No worries about that, is there?" said the big fighter.

Zeya's men tittered with weird laughter.

"No matter what happens," Zeya repeated.

By that time the Tuscas were ready. Inaj marched forth, his son Wilu beside him, and the mob tramped behind the two. Some whirled buzzing noisemakers over their heads. Then Inaj loosed the Galayi war cry, and all two hundred warriors joined in—"Woh-WHO-O-O-ey! Woh-WHO-O-O-ey! AI-AI-AI-AI!"

The escorts and chiefs eyed each other. Only one man of them expected to live.

"Woh-WHO-O-O-ey! Woh-WHO-O-O-ey! AI-AI-AI-AI!"

"Zeya," said Tsola, "before you go, I ask you a favor. Take off my blindfold. I want to see this."

"Last thing you'll ever see," said the gnarly man.

Zeya slipped the blindfold off and laid it in her lap. The Seer wove her fingers over her eyes, shutting out most of the light.

"Woh-WHO-O-O-ey! Woh-WHO-O-O-ey! AI-AI-AI-AI!"

"Are you ready?" said Zeya.

"It's all right to go to the Darkening Land," said the gnarly man, "but I wanted to walk behind a man, not a boy."

Zeya smiled freely. "You won't walk behind either one," he said.

The chiefs and warriors looked at each other and shrugged their shoulders.

Zeya walked casually toward the enemy, as though on an evening stroll.

"Woh-WHO-O-O-ey! Woh-WHO-O-O-ey! AI-AI-AI-AI!"

From behind, the chiefs and warriors saw Zeya begin to change. His black hair turned russet. His face became a beak and two golden eyes. He turned one of the eyes to his comrades and one to the enemy. His arms grew feathers and were wings. His legs turned to talons. He spread his wings wide—he was the biggest eagle they'd ever seen.

Exclamations burst from his followers. "I can't believe it!" "What the hell?"

Zeya and Su-Li lifted into the sky.

His comrades stopped. Some took heart. Some thought they were abandoned and their feet wanted to flee. Then Ninyu said, "Look!"

Eagles were circling above the meadow, hundreds of war eagles.

Zeya started his own circle, close to the ground. The flock of eagles swooped down and fell in behind him and Su-Li. They wing-flapped once around the Tusca mob.

The unarmed men gaped.

The Tuscas took no particular notice. Inaj and Wilu looked at nothing but the pitiful, helpless enemies they were about to exterminate. "Woh-WHO-O-O-ey! Woh-WHO-O-O-ey! AI-AI-AI-AI!"

Zeya said to Su-Li, *May an eagle who is sometimes a Galayi kill a Galayi?*

Su-Li said, *Let me do it for your mother.*

On the first pass he slashed at the Red Chief's neck with a talon. Bright red spurted.

There was no second pass. Su-Li swooped down from behind and dug into both of Inaj's shoulders with his talons. The chief leaned his head back and screamed.

Su-Li pecked the left eye viciously. Twice. Three times.

Inaj's screams filled the skies, and then were drowned out by the screams of his mob. Every warrior's eyes were assaulted by an eagle, sometimes two. Every warrior flailed at the war birds with their weapons, and no man hurt a bird.

Blood streamed down faces. Men collapsed onto the ground, holding their eyes and wailing. Some eyeballs squirted onto the bloodied earth.

Zeya watched a few warriors manage to run away. He noticed that his uncle Wilu escaped. It didn't matter. In the time a man needed to walk around his own village, the Tusca army was in tatters. Zeya looked around at his triumph. *No, the eagles' triumph.*

He coasted down and landed beside Inaj. Su-Li stood on the Red Chief's chest, talons deep in the flesh.

Zeya looked at the Red Chief writhing on the ground, blind, in agony, defeated. "Chief," said Zeya, "as a grandfather, you were despicable."

Su-Li reached down deliberately with his beak, plucked up the large vein in his neck, and bit it in half.

Tsola shut her eyes, thrust her arms into the air, and yelled, "Woh-WHO-O-O-ey! Woh-WHO-O-O-ey! AI-AI-AI-AI!"

51

Sunoya stopped and looked down the trail. Where it opened into a meadow, the remnants of the Tusca people wept openly, milled in agitation among their brush huts, or sat with their heads in their hands.

"They feel doomed," Zeya said.

He had sent a runner ahead with the news. A family without men to hunt and fight would starve, or be overrun by enemies. These people faced extinction this very winter. The nip in the morning air felt like a sharp warning.

"It's terrible," said Sunoya.

They deserve it, said Su-Li.

"No one deserves that," said Ninyu.

"We'll help them," said Zeya.

"I lived in this village for seven years," said Sunoya. Even though Inaj had driven her out.

Klandagi growled. They all knew his assignment. A few Tusca warriors were wounded but alive, probably hiding in the forest. Klandagi's mother was safe in the Cavern. "Guard Zeya," she instructed Klandagi. "He is the future. Protect him."

At the camp Zeya said, "Let's bring them all together."

When the people shambled into the common, heads down, feet dragging, Zeya spoke to them kindly. "I'm sorry about your men. You've heard the story—hundreds of war eagles attacked them." He hesitated. "I called those eagles to war."

He let that sink in and went on. "You know why. They were about to wipe out the Soco band. Your Red Chief said so in the council—bragged about it. But Galayi must not shed the blood of other Galayi, ever. That's how we will live from now on.

"Know that Galayi people did not harm your men. The eagles did.

"The other three bands have promised to take care of you. All the bands will come together tomorrow at the council lodge, the way we do for the Planting Moon ceremony every spring. Then all of us will bury your men with honor, on an east-facing slope, and with the ceremonies every Galayi deserves.

"After that comes the hard part. You will choose new families to be part of, or they will choose you. We will stay at the Cheowa village until every Tusca is taken in. Then the Tusca band will exist no more. That saddens me. The one who gave me birth was a Tusca. I grieve that the legacy of your Red Chief, my grandfather, Inaj, is hatred and mass death.

"Today let's rest, and I'll talk with you privately, anyone who wants to talk. Tomorrow morning we'll walk to Cheowa."

Zeya spent the afternoon and evening listening to Tuscas who wanted to tell the stories of their lives, to mourn the loss of husbands, fathers, and sons, to speak their dread of the future, to confide anything at all. He listened well and spoke little.

Sunoya watched amazed, stupefied. Her son. "I feel peculiar," she told Su-Li.

You raised him to be the one of prophecy, and he has exceeded all expectations.

"I could never have done it without you."

Thunderbird sent me here to help you.

"But I keep feeling like I'm losing something."

His greatness sets him apart, from you and all of us.

She laid out these important words. "I came through for my mother."

You did.

"All my life I thought maybe she was wrong." She looked at the last two fingers of her right hand, the ones webbed at her birth. "I thought maybe I was cursed."

She did right. You chose the good. I'm honored to be your companion.

She looked at him in shock. Her lips edged into a smile, and for a moment she felt weepy. Then the feeling came back. "I am bereft."

Su-Li said nothing.

"What will I do now? I'm only forty winters old. Our people, if they reach forty, live to seventy a lot of times. What will I do?

You are in the prime of life. You'll have grandchildren to enjoy.

Sunoya thought she heard something odd in his voice, but she didn't know what it was. She'd learned long since that he didn't tell her some things.

"I should be with Jemel," she said. She looked down the creek. She always found water soothing. "Would you like to go flying?"

Yes.

Again the odd tone.

"Why don't you go?" She looked across at Zeya, who was listening to people's sorrows. "I'd like to be alone for a while."

Su-Li looked into her eyes, turned his head away, and launched.

❖

Sunoya meandered along the creek. She didn't know what she wanted. Idly, she ate some rose hips, which she didn't particularly care for. She found some berries the bears hadn't yet gotten and sucked out their sweetness. She sat on a rock and dangled her feet in the cool water. Soon the creek would be cold—snow would cover the balds and on warm days melt into this running stream. She played in the bottom sand with her toes. She gazed at the leafless laurels across the stream and ruminated. Forty winters old, still vigorous and strong. *Forty winters, and I've done what I came to Earth for.*

As the afternoon got warm, Sunoya got sleepy. She wrapped herself in her shawl and lay down in the grass. The *shhh-shhh* of the creek sang her to sleep. She dreamed that she was a bird—she couldn't tell what kind—flying through a cloud. As a girl, when she dreamed of flying, it was exciting. Now the cloud changed everything. She couldn't see the Earth, she couldn't see the sky, she couldn't see where she was going. She flapped and flapped and flapped but never figured out where she was, or where she should be, or what direction she was headed. She whimpered.

Wilu stepped from behind a tree and stood over her.

She whimpered again. That was all right with Wilu. No one could hear her, probably not even if she screamed. No one would hear them, not this far from the trail.

He put a foot on either side of her, knelt, opened her mouth, and gagged her. She waggled her head and tried to yell, but too late. Her eyes gaped when she saw his face. He smiled down at her.

He forced her hands above her head and bound them with deer hide thongs. She stared at the badger tied into his hair, a black head with a white stripe and a small jaw of amazing ferocity.

He thought, *You'll find out just how ferocious.*

When she was secure, he stood up and put a foot between her legs, on her skirt. Now she wouldn't be going anywhere. "A virgin," he said.

Slowly, he slipped his deerskin shirt over his head. One at a time, he slipped off his moccasins. He drew his knife out of his belt and set it beside her neck, untied the belt, held the breechcloth for a moment, and let it drop. He leered at her with hatred.

He pulled a pouch off the belt, dug his fingers in, and rubbed his *do-wa* with bear grease. It was already hard, but he wanted her to see. He stroked himself several times, deliciously.

Then he knelt between her legs, picked up the knife, and pulled out the neckline of her dress. With the sharp blade he cut the dress delicately from her neck to her breasts, then to her waist, then to the bottom of her skirt. He let his eyes linger on her. "Your breasts are beautiful, not that I give a damn."

He rubbed her crotch with greasy fingers. He glared into her eyes, hoping to see desire, but saw only hatred. He raised her knees and thrust himself into her.

52

Sunoya pulled Zeya away from a widow and said, "I'm going to die tomorrow."

Disbelief slapped his face. He saw her dress cut top to bottom and tied with her shawl. He looked into her eyes for the truth and saw it.

He forgot everything else in the world. He couldn't hear the woman he'd just been listening to. He forgot about Klandagi, who was never more than one leap away from him.

"Take me seriously. I'm going to die now." Now her speech stumbled. "And I have a lot to do . . ."

She turned away from him and took one staggering step. He grabbed her. "Mother," he said with an edge, "what happened?"

She whirled on him like he was a culprit. "Wilu raped me. Just now."

"Where?" said Klandagi.

"Down by the creek." She waved a hand in that direction. Klandagi bounded off.

Zeya wrapped his mother in his arms.

Sunoya said, "I don't know if I have enough concentration to call Su-Li."

At that moment the buzzard hovered over her, then perched on her shoulder.

"Goodbye, friend," she said to him.

Zeya couldn't hear what Su-Li said back, but he could guess.

He knew the story. If any man ever had his mother, even by force, she would die. In a single day she would wither, grow ancient, and at the next sunset pass on to the Darkening Land. At the same moment she passed over, Su-Li would be whisked away beyond the Sky Arch. Sunoya knew, Zeya knew.

They sat and he held her. Through the evening they stayed there. In the last of the light Su-Li perched on her shoulder. *I understand,* he said. All night long they stayed like that.

In the morning Sunoya said, "I want to go to the bathroom." Zeya walked with her.

When they got back, she said, "I'm hungry." Somehow he found two honeyed seed cakes for her. He ate nothing. For her to eat and die, he to starve and live—it was unspeakable.

Word spread through the camp. The Tuscas packed up and left for the Cheowa village. People nodded to Zeya as they left, and no one spoke. He held Sunoya all day. Late in the afternoon she drifted out of consciousness. Zeya eased her down, lay beside her, and held her. Klandagi curled up nearby, and Su-Li perched on her arm.

When the sun spread itself along the ridge of the mountain, lunacy rattled Zeya. He stammered out, "How long?"

Then he smiled ruefully at himself for asking a question the buzzard couldn't answer with signals.

The buzzard perched on Sunoya's hip now.

"I'm going to stick out my hand and grab the sun and hold it in the sky," he said. His mind hurled crazy thoughts at him, and one was: *Stupid*.

When the sun was gone and only a little light lingered, Zeya said to Su-Li, "Will you be sad to go back?" Half of him despised the bitterness in his voice, and half of him didn't give a damn.

Su-Li turned one eye directly into Zeya's face, and it glowed. He said, *I love your mother*.

Zeya burst into tears. He snuggled into Sunoya's back and let himself rock with great, pitching sobs.

When the light was only a hint, and not even a hint, Zeya sat up and looked at the buzzard.

Su-Li said, *Maybe I love your world*. The spirit animal's head swiveled all the way around slowly. The two of them could barely see. *It's a terrible world. Time. Joy and horror, brutality and beauty. The death of every creature's life for another. It's love and murder, illness and art. It's unspeakable*. Zeya had never heard so many words in a row from Su-Li. He hesitated. *This what Thunderbird sent me to Earth to learn. I've fallen in love with the world of Time*.

Sunoya said, "My friend, you do go on." She chuckled soft and low. Zeya embraced her, kissed her cheek, clasped her hand, and looked back at Su-Li.

The spirit animal was gone.

For a moment Zeya couldn't breathe. He squeezed his mother's hand. He looked into her eyes—unmoving. He breathed. He closed the eyelids with tender fingers. He kissed the dead lips. He slid the zadayi from her dress and laid it on the outside, red side facing the world.

53

Klandagi didn't want to sit and watch his friend die. He raged to take care of the rapist.

He followed Wilu's footsteps easily enough, muzzle to the ground. When the scent led onto the main trail to west, the big cat felt sure the Tusca warrior was headed for his own village. Maybe he had belongings he wanted to collect. *And go where?* thought Klandagi. The Tusca people existed no longer. After what had happened, no other Galayi village would take in a son of Inaj.

The black panther loped along the trail, night eyes showing the way, nose up to catch another smell. In the darkest hours he caught it—a fire, used to keep a man without blankets warm. He followed it to the cave entrance.

He hesitated a moment, then let out the loudest roar he could.

He heard scurrying within, but saw nothing. He roared again and leapt to the entrance. Half a dozen steps back, Wilu crouched against a wall. He cringed and simpered.

Klandagi blocked the exit, but saw a hole at the back.

That gave him an idea. At the battleground Zeya had strictly prohibited the shedding of any Galayi blood. Klandagi considered himself exempt—he wasn't a Galayi now, he was a panther. Intriguingly, he had other options.

Making sure his voice filled the cave, he said, "You hurt my friend. I want to kill you, which would be easy. But Zeya and Tsola"—*amazing, I'm thinking of Zeya as one of our leaders*—"say one Galayi can't kill another."

He pounced forward and raked his claws down Wilu's arm.

Wilu whined.

"So," Klandagi went on, "the traditional punishment for rape is banishment. You live alone the rest of your life, you see no one, you're miserable. Very fitting, I think, worse than dying.

"I believe, though, that I won't take you before the council for a formal trial. I'll impose the sentence myself."

Wilu spasmed visibly.

"Get on your hands and knees."

Wilu didn't move.

The panther swatted his face and drew a drizzle of blood. "Don't try my patience. Get."

Wilu did.

"Go into that hole."

Wilu hesitated. Klandagi growled, and Wilu crawled forward.

The passage narrowed. Klandagi hoped it wouldn't dead-end. Though Tsola knew the entire Cavern—she could picture parts she'd never seen in her mind—he didn't.

Wilu emerged into a bigger space and half turned toward the cat, awaiting instructions.

This is delicious, thought Klandagi. *Either way will be satisfying.*

"Get going," said Klandagi.

"It-it-it's dark."

"Perfectly dark," said Klandagi happily. "Where we're going, you'll never see the light again." He roared, and Wilu scrambled away.

"Stand up like a man," Klandagi said. He realized that Wilu was so blind he couldn't tell that this chamber was high enough.

Wilu obeyed.

"Turn very slowly in a circle."

Wilu did.

"Stop. Walk straight ahead."

Wilu fumbled his way forward. Klandagi knew how scary it was to be walking underground, in an unknown and unpredictable place, and be totally sightless. He'd heard every one of the medicine seekers talk about it. He'd turned himself into a man and experienced the total darkness of a cave. Terrifying.

From time to time he had to tell Wilu to turn a little to the left or right. He hoped this chamber was long. He wanted the bastard to have plenty of time to feel the panic. And he heard running water somewhere in front of them. That would be the place.

After a while, when it was obvious, Klandagi said, "You hear the water?"

"Yes." The voice was a quaver.

"That's one of our underground streams. This is where you'll be spending the rest of your life."

Wilu wailed.

The cat savored the horror Wilu must be feeling, and would feel.

Soon Klandagi said, "Stop." Wilu did. "Kneel down." Wilu did. "Reach a hand forward."

Wilu put his hand in the water. "So you'll have enough to drink. Unless we go a moon without rain and the stream dries up. I'll bring food about once a week, unless I forget."

"You're going to leave me here?"

"Do you think you could get out by yourself?"

"No! No! No! No!" The voice was tremulous.

"Good. This is where you live until you grow old and go to the Darkening Land. If you call this living. You'll never be able to see anything real, but don't worry, your mind will provide pictures. Ants, bats, snakes, every manner of creature, real and imaginary. Your head will dream them up in bright color, day and night. Not that you'll ever know day from night again.

Your life will be a nightmare." He let it sink in. "Good-bye now."

Wilu screamed, *"No-o-o-o-o!"*

Klandagi padded a few steps off, dragging his nails so that Wilu could hear him, then turned back. "By the way, in case you decide to try to grope your way out, or take a chance and follow the stream? Oh, that would be delicious, swimming into a darkness without end, and without air. Just in case? Tsola will be able to see you at every moment, and she'll send me after you. To cut you up and bring you back to this fine place."

Klandagi walked off.

About a hundred human steps away he laid down to watch and listen. Wilu was sobbing. The tears went on entirely too long, and Klandagi got impatient. *Why not go on?* he thought. *I don't care which way he dies.* But he was curious.

When Wilu stopped crying, he called out, "Klandagi? Klandagi? Klandagi? . . . Anyone?"

Silence. The silence that would last forever.

Wilu sat still. Klandagi supposed he was thinking of it, between flights of pure terror. After a long while, Wilu pulled his knife out of his belt. He held it to his cheek for a moment. Then he raised it high and plunged it into his belly.

Klandagi padded back to him. The knife was thrust in fully to the hilt, the hand clutched tight on it. The wound would do the job before long.

He touched a paw to the hand that didn't hold the knife. Wilu's whole body jumped. He moaned.

Kalndagi said, "You're more of a man than I thought. Good-bye." The great cat walked off and kept going.

54

In the morning Zeya touched his mother's face and drew his hand away. He couldn't bear to feel her flesh cold.

Going hungry, he pulled the robe she lay on until it was on an east-facing slope. The work was exhausting, and he couldn't go any further. But just at that moment Klandagi came bounding across the valley. With his teeth and Zeya's ebbing strength, they got her decently high.

They sat and rested a few moments. "Stones," said Zeya.

Klandagi transformed himself into an old man—panthers had no fingers to grip stones. They covered her decently. "We'll leave her all the food I have," said the man once called The Hungry One. He looked around. "I don't know the songs," he said. The songs that eased the spirits of the dead and helped them on their way.

"I don't think we should sing them anyway. Her journey won't begin for seven days. Tsola will want to sing the songs herself."

Zeya thought about it. "You're sure."

"Yes."

He looked at the ugly, obscene stones that held his mother. "What now, then?"

"The people need you. Turn eagle and go."

"I think I'd better turn eagle and sleep."

They both turned, and both slept.

❖

Before the sun was high, the two of them stood at a gap in the ridge and looked down on the village. Hundreds of Galayi men and women were assembled outside the council house.

344 ❖ Caleb Fox

The building would never hold so many people, and many would have to watch from outside. Several chiefs were on their way, ready to make an entrance when the crowd was seated.

Klandagi said, "Tsola said to tell you this. You have to make your appearance in eagle form."

"No," said Zeya.

"And she said you'd say no. So I'm to tell you that it's a gift from Thunderbird to all the Galayi people. They need to see it, to feel the power given them through you."

Zeya nodded.

Soon he coasted toward the council building. People didn't take notice of him until he made a soft landing next to the smoke hole. Then some pointed and many laughed.

With wings still spread Zeya turned slowly to each of the four directions, showing his eagle self to all the people. Then, feather by hair, talon by leg, wing by arm, he changed himself into the young leader Zeya.

People buzzed and then roared. They cried, "Chief! Chief! Chief!"

Zeya slid down the mud-slabbed dome, and Ninyu gave him a hand to the ground. Jemel rushed up and hugged him tight.

"Come sit by the sacred fire," Ninyu said. "The people want you to be a chief. The chiefs want to make you . . . They'll explain."

"How silly," said Zeya.

"How necessary," said Ninyu.

"You'll do it," said Jemel.

"Yes," said Klandagi.

"All right," Zeya said. "Klandagi, will you go get Tsola? All of this—all—is her doing. Meanwhile the three of us will talk to people."

So they did. Each going his own way, they sat with as many people as they could. They listened to the never-ending laments of Tusca women who had lost their loved ones. They listened to women glad to have more children and a second wife coming to the house. Talked to men who worried about the coming hunt, and whether they would get enough food for so many mouths for the winter. Gathered children together and told stories. Several times Zeya told the one about how Buzzard gave the world its shape.

The other chiefs caught on and followed the example of Zeya, Ninyu, and Jemel.

Zeya encouraged everyone to eat heartily at midday. Not long after they finished, Klandagi led Tsola into the council house blindfolded, and the people assembled.

Zeya greeted Tsola, introduced Jemel to her, and sat behind the Seer.

"Join me," she said, and patted the ground beside her. Zeya did, feeling odd.

When all the chiefs were seated, she smoked the sacred pipe and passed it to Zeya. Feeling more uncomfortable, he smoked and passed it. When all the chiefs had sent their breath, their prayers to the sky as smoke, Tsola said, "Who wants to speak?"

Ninyu led the way with a canticle of his grief at the deaths of so many Galayi. Each chief took his turn, a chorus of loss and sorrow.

Tsola asked Zeya to speak of his mother. He did, and he then he plunged on. "I feel devastated. But I know that this single death, even if she was the most important person in my life, was small compared to what the people have endured. We abide in anguish today. We have walked in desolation since the day I was born."

Everyone knew the story of how Zeya's mother fled from Inaj, who then killed Tensa and launched twenty years of war.

"I ask us all to make the shed blood into life-giving water.

Let us find a way to make horror into wisdom. Let us use tragedy to make our spirits buoyant. Let us turn death into resurrection."

He fumbled for more thoughts, found none, and sat down.

Ninyu stood and said, "We can take Zeya's words and turn them into a song of hope."

When he sat down, Tsola waited for the other chiefs, wanting someone to add his voice. No one did—it was too soon.

So she told a story. How the word came to her of a boy born to save the people. How her friend Sunoya raised the boy to walk the path of prophecy. When the young man resisted, the force of life itself seized him and carried him into the Emerald Cavern and to the journey he was born for. How he defeated the assassins to gather 108 beautiful feathers. How he crossed into the land beyond the Sky Arch, encountered demons, earned an audience with Thunderbird, and brought the Cape of Eagle Feathers back to the people. How he brought a personal power as well, which they had witnessed the last several days.

"The nine remaining village chiefs have conferred," she said. "They are unanimous. At this time and in this place, I, the Medicine Chief of all Medicine Chiefs of the Galayi people, declare Ulo-Zeya, The One Who Dwells in Clouds, the supreme chief of the nation, the chief of all White chiefs, Red Chiefs, and Medicine Chiefs."

People cheered.

Tsola turned her blindfolded eyes to Zeya and smiled.

"I can't," he said softly.

"It's your destiny," said Tsola.

"I'm still foolish." He looked at Jemel, and they both thought of his bout of jealousy.

"We all are," said Tsola. "But you are chosen. Stand up and say something."

So he spoke to all his people. "I'm afraid you trust me with too much. But I will do my best to help you all."

They cheered louder.

Ninyu stood up. "Next week we will celebrate the marriage of Zeya and Jemel." Sorrowfully he added, "After many burying songs."

Jemel got up and showed off her belly. People laughed.

"I will sing songs in their honor," said Tsola, "and all the people are invited to join in."

❖

When the sun fell, Zeya and Jemel spent their first night together as a married couple in a house loaned to them by the White Chief of the Cheowas.

Sitting by the fire naked, they sang to each other the traditional song to bind their affections forever. Together they sang four times, "*Our souls have come together.*"

And alternately, four times, "*Your name is Jemel, you are born to the Soco people,*" and "*Your name is Ulo-Zeya, you are born to the Tusca people.*"

Then each of them warmed hands by the fire and tongued spittle onto their fingers. While they rubbed this spittle onto the others' breasts, they sang four times together:

Your body, I take it, I eat it
Your flesh I take, I eat
Our souls have come together
Your heart I take, I eat
O ancient fire, now our souls are meshed
Never to part

Zeya watched the firelight flicker on Jemel's face, her arms, her breasts. He was filled with love, with purpose, with dedication. They continued together.

Black spider, bind us in your web
Until I met her [him] I was covered with loneliness

My eyes had faded
I went along sorrowing
I was an ancient wanderer
Spider hold us together in your web
Our souls have come together

Ancient fire, hold us firmly in your grasp
Never let go your hold

They curled up together and slept.

❖

Jemel's cry startled Zeya awake.

"It's time for the baby!"

He bolted outside to get help. Against the darkness light was a breath in the east. He ran downstream to Ninyu's brush hut.

"The baby's coming!"

Ninyu's wives scurried upstream to Jemel.

Ninyu quickly prepared the sacred tea. He and Zeya walked in a stately manner to the river. Zeya looked for the moon, which his people called "sun living in the night." A fingernail of darkness chipped off its right edge. They passed the house of Jemel's tribulations and stopped at the river bend, within sight and sound of the house.

❖

In the house Jemel lay on hide blankets, catching her breath. The pains were terrible. Poles crossed and tied together slashed over her head.

"This is the pain of life," said her aunt, the midwife.

Jemel smiled tartly. Birth was painful, death was painful. Life? Life was joy, if you had the strength to tear it out and eat it. That was the way the Moon Woman saw things.

P-a-a-a-i-i-n-n!

She reached up for the poles, lifted her body up a hand span, and pushed. This was the old way of birthing. The midwife wanted it and so did she. But now everything was kicked out of her mind but pain.

When it eased and coiled back on itself, she let herself drop down and rest. Why so much pain? She wished she could take a whip and scourge it.

"Think of the child coming to you," said the midwife.

She couldn't, not now, and certainly not when the pain swamped her.

"I'm excited to see if its left fingers are webbed," said the midwife.

Jemel choked on a laugh. That was the last thing she cared about.

Pain came roaring back, and she inched herself off the ground. Torture.

❖

Zeya stripped off his clothes. Ninyu set down two small pots of paint, one red and one white, which only members of the Paint Clan could make.

Zeya waded into the water, shivering from the night air and the cold liquid. Then he dipped himself all the way into the river.

On the bank Ninyu drank the tea. Until the baby was born he would search for omens to guide the child's life.

Soon, where a slice of clouds lay against the ridges to the east, Zeya saw the day's first appearance of the sun living in the day—the clouds were turning red.

"A good sign," he murmured. He sang:

Draw near and hear me, sun living in the day
You have come from the east to paint me red
The color of power and success
And white, the color of happiness.

He got the paint pots from the bank and carefully covered his face with the red paint on one side, white on the other.

> *My name is Ulo-Zeya, born to the Tusca people*
> *My wife is Jemel, born to the Soco people*
> *Sun living in the day*
> *You have come from the east*
> *to cover us in the red clothing of success*
> *and the white clothing of happiness.*

He painted his neck and arms.

> *Sun living in the day*
> *You come from the east*
> *You are bringing us a child*
> *I will paint our child in red and white clothing.*

He painted his torso.

> *Sun living in the day*
> *Grant our child a life painted red.*

He heard shouts from the house. He was a father.

> *Sun living in the day*
> *Cloak our child in the white clothing of joy.*

A shout of triumph came from the house. As he waded to the shore, Jemel came out.

Hurrying, he stepped onto the bank naked.

Jemel was beaming, and she carried a small human being.

Zeya ran and got there first. He had never felt so happy. It was time for him to paint their daughter.

AUTHOR'S NOTE

I set out in this novel to write a fantasy about the predecessors of the Cherokee people, my own ancestors, well before their world had been altered by contact with Europeans. I wanted the freedom to explore a culture filled with mysticism and magic, which theirs was. At the same time, I wanted to make my picture of them as accurate, as historical, as possible.

In practice, the job turned out to be to learn all I could about Cherokee in the historical period (after contact with the Spanish in the mid-sixteenth century) and imagine it backward. Anyone who wants to study historic Cherokees is obliged to start with James Mooney's monumental *History, Myths, and Sacred Formulas of the Cherokees* (my own copy is now down at heels). Then I read what little is known about their culture in prehistoric times—and created the rest.

The result, I hope, is a story with some solid foundation but freely imagined.

What here is historical or reasonably extrapolated from history? Their physical culture—their agriculture and hunting, their utensils and weapons, their houses. Also their customs, their tribal organization, their family relations, and so on. I've used a lot of their language, ceremonies, and songs. *Su-Li*, for instance, is the Cherokee word for buzzard, and *tsola* the Cherokee word for tobacco. The songs Zeya and Jemel sing in their wedding ceremony are based on real Cherokee songs. Many, many other details are authentic in that way. At the same time, I felt obliged to remember that cultures change, and that the ways of the Cherokees (or their ancestors) two millennia ago would have been different from those of two centuries ago, and especially more mystical, more alien from modern ways.

In finding out what is known about the early culture, I got a great stroke of luck. Vincent Wilcox became my neighbor and close friend. Vince had recently retired as curator of Native American Artifacts at the Smithsonian Institution. A super-knowledgeable anthropologist almost next door!

"Vince, when did they get corn?"

"No one knows. You can give it to them or not."

"Did they have bows and arrows?"

"Not until about 700 A.D."

"What weapons did they have? What were these things called banner stones?" Etc, etc.

For a project like this, no writer could be luckier than to get the knowledge and wisdom of Vince Wilcox.

In the end, I emphasize, this book is a fantasy, an imaginative reconstruction of a mystical culture in a little-known past. It is created with respect and love.